RESOLUTION

RESOLUTION

IRVINE WELSH

JONATHAN CAPE
LONDON

1 3 5 7 9 10 8 6 4 2

Jonathan Cape, an imprint of Vintage, is part of the Penguin Random House group
of companies whose addresses can be found at global.penguinrandomhouse.com

First published by Jonathan Cape in 2024

Illustration on p. 346 by Graham Roumieu @ Dutch Uncle

penguin.co.uk/vintage

Typeset in 13/16pt Fairfield LT Std by Jouve (UK), Milton Keynes
Printed and bound in Great Britain by Clays Ltd, Elcograf S.p.A.

The authorised representative in the EEA is Penguin Random House Ireland,
Morrison Chambers, 32 Nassau Street, Dublin D02 YH68

A CIP catalogue record for this book is available from the British Library

HB ISBN 9781787334755
TPB ISBN 9781787334762

Penguin Random House is committed to a sustainable future
for our business, our readers and our planet. This book is made
from Forest Stewardship Council® certified paper.

For Emma,
with all the love on this green Earth and beyond.
You shine in the light and glow in the dark.

The past is never dead. It's not even past.
William Faulkner

Day One

1

TUNNEL DREAMS

You cannot move.

*Holding you, those men are: those monsters. One of them –
man or big boy – this demon, has gripped your hair in its fist,
grinding your burning face into the gravel. A pain so intense,
you're certain your scalp will be ripped off your head and held
triumphantly aloft by this ogre. Its thick, rancid smell of stale
alcohol and cigarettes in your nostrils and throat chokes you.
Your heart is thrashing. The blood is rime in your veins . . .*

*. . . the impotent snarling threats of your friend, also seized by
the monsters, give way to desperate, defeated pleas for mercy,
then high-pitched, disbelieving screams of torment. The head-
light on your blue Raleigh bike, on its side, provides the only
illumination in the dark tunnel.*

— Noice boike!

*The battery will soon run down. But you've ceased fretting
that it will be stolen, stopped worrying about your parents' wrath.
The eleven-year-old you is already aware that something devastating and profoundly life-changing is happening to you both,
and that things might never be good again.*

— Open yawr fookin mouth . . .

2

SLEEPING TOGETHER

— *Open yawr fookin mouth or I'll carve yawr fookin face up . . .*

. . . the searing voice recedes into silence as the pain deep in the core of him retreats through his flesh, scuttling into the air. Its departure is so swift and emphatic that Ray Lennox can't detect its source, as he blinks awake into columns of glittering dust trapped in the beams of light shooting between the blinds. Where did this winter sunlight come from? His large bedroom slowly pulls into focus. The archway leading to the en suite bathroom he is inordinately proud of. The sliding wardrobes: functional, but perhaps a bit too modern for the high-ceilinged Regency building.

He feels the heat, then its source: the form next to him. Leans over into the mop of collar-length brown-blonde hair, filling his nostrils with her scent. Nuzzling into Carmel Devereaux, he enjoys her waking murmurs as the erection he becomes aware of rakes up her spine. Hears a giggle, feels her hand going around her back. Patting his cock in appreciation. — Good morning . . . a low, throaty purr exacerbated by the cigarettes she smokes.

Listening to her is sexier than kissing her.

Guilt at that thought.

— Morning to you too. Can I do anything for you?

Carmel rolls around and arches a solitary brow. — Very tempting. She pulls back the duvet, her gaze sweeping Lennox. — God, you look good . . .

It is balm to the ego to be furnished with such information

4

by a lover almost fifteen years younger, and Ray Lennox lets it seep appreciatively into him, on this Friday morning, on the cusp of a weekend awash with possibility. He is in more than decent shape. The south coast has been good to him. His obsessive-compulsive mindset facilitated a determined switch from harmful fixations like alcohol and cocaine to the beneficial ones offered by a fitness regime. He works out most mornings at a local gym he accesses after a run along the beachfront from his elegant flat in Kemptown's Sussex Square. Has graduated from kickboxing classes to expensive but rewarding one-on-one sparring with Tom Tracy, a former marine and British champion. Drinking is now enjoyably controlled: he and Carmel have taken to splitting a bottle of wine over dinner maybe once a week, with a solitary glass and Netflix at either his or hers at the weekend. Also, the odd couple of pints of Stella with his business partner, George Marsden, over some pub grub. It will only get out of hand again if it's not controlled.

Lennox hopefully reaches out, but Carmel pushes him firmly in the chest. — You can make me a cup of tea. I don't have time for anything elsc. We have to do our run. Then I've a seminar to teach on the production of phenethylamine in the human body.

— Is that some kind of sex chemical?

— Nice try, Ray, but kindly fuck off and get me some tea please, Carmel cheerfully instructs, throwing the duvet from her, doubling it over him, as she springs off the bed towards the bathroom.

Lennox lets cheerful defeat mould his features. Besides, he likes to run, and he has a morning inspection in Eastbourne with George. Carmel finishes teaching early afternoon at the university on a Friday.

Perhaps later . . . or maybe you're pushing too hard.

Last night was only the fifth time they'd slept together. They have entered that zone of exalted bliss, the dopamine smash isolating them from the myriad problems he knew they'd soon encounter; age difference, conflicting career demands, potential lifestyle clashes, those melodrama-prone family members and friends who always had a stake – but never a big enough one for their liking – in new relationships. They would also learn that they were both a little more complicated, baggage-laden and *real* on the inside than what was chirpily emblazoned on the tin.

Let that shit slide for now. Don't borrow trouble.

He gets out of bed, walking through to the large open-plan kitchen-lounge conversion to switch on the electric kettle. Peers out those big windows on the north side of the square that look across the gardens to the English Channel; it's a squally morning, and the sea is turbulent. In the reflection, his eyes seem baggier, the laughter lines deeper than he recalls. His hair receding at the front, but combed-back buzz cut in *don't give a fuck* style. Looks through his image to the circling gulls, their squawking muted by the replacement windows, which fairly seal in the heat. From the bedroom, Carmel sings as she changes into the running clothes she brought over yesterday.

The flat also has a smaller boudoir, and a long hallway. Too much of Lennox's income goes on the mortgage and all of his assets are tied up in it, but it is luxurious, and he has long believed that living well is the best revenge. He looks over his black leather couch and chairs, which Carmel describes as 'too nineties man', and runs his finger over the top of his stylish vintage 1960s cocktail cabinet. It needs dusting and polishing.

It's the second time he and Carmel have gone on a run together. The first was more competitive than either acknowledged. He was dissonantly torn between chivalrously hanging back and taking no prisoners. Both seemed inept responses: one patronising, the other bullying, enjoying the advantage of a more powerful physiology. While he hesitated, she went for it. Lennox is a non-smoker but Carmel has youth on her side, and it will be a close-fought affair.

After a sparkling water and cup of tea, they set off, stepping out into the vanilla of the ornately pillared Regency square, to be swatted by a gelid, bracing winter gale. Carmel sets the pace, but Lennox feels he has her measure. Then, as they pass the tunnel at the bottom of the square, all the energy drains from his legs and he stumbles to a halt.

Aware of him seizing up, Carmel stops and turns to find him gaping at the black mouth of the underpass. — Ray?

His skin seems to be slithering away from him and he shudders to try and stop it. — Where does that go?

— It used to go under the road to the beach, and she wraps her arms around herself, jumping on the spot. — It's a tunnel, long blocked up. Lewis Carroll was inspired by it to write *Alice in Wonderland*. C'mon! It's fucking freezing!

She tears off, and Lennox follows, his pursuit compelled by the need to run off a deeper cold than the one from the air that prickles his skin.

The one that shivers his marrow.

3

EASTBOURNE

If the traffic is kind, Eastbourne is just under a fifty-minute drive away from Ray Lennox's flat. Underdressed for winter's bite in bomber jacket, jeans and T-shirt, he shivers, the Scot in him unable to comprehend that the south of England can get cold too. But the Alfa Romeo's heating satisfyingly kicks in, and his body relaxes as he lets his eyes flicker lazily in the weak but welcome December sun.

Then he's jolted: an angry toot from a BMW tearing past him. He lowers his sun visor, and in the absence of the chewing gum he likes to keep in supply, sucks on his bottom lip.

The seaside resort retains a crusty air of decline. Unlike Bournemouth or Hastings, it's yet to be injected with new life by an influx of the artists priced out of Brighton. But the town's traditional old retirees are his bread and butter. Lennox has keyed the address into the GPS, and he turns into town past the golden-domed pier, gleaming in defiance as it sucks shards of radiance from a murky sky. Heading north, he halts at a set of lights.

A crowd of children mill around outside an old theatre with their parents. Lennox notices a board advertising Santa's grotto. The waving Santa lumbers through a cheering crowd, a fat reality TV star, calibrated for disposable fame. Probably some nonce, Lennox scorns.

Fucking nonce bloaters everywhere; yo ho ho, yo ho ho . . . ah'll yo ho ho ye, ya fucking paedo cunt.

Another blaring horn makes Lennox start before he pulls off, as a bus driver behind him shakes his head.

The centre beckons, a chalky, sprawling, low-rise structure, and he pulls into the sparsely filled car park in front of it. Lennox clocks George's motor, as its driver exits. A six-foot-four mass of square-jawed, baton-backed imposition, his partner, sixty-two years young, full head of wavy grey hair, rugby-player build only reluctantly going to seed, is sensibly but stylishly clad in a long black cashmere coat, woollen scarf and leather gloves. The vehicle is a BMW and it crosses Lennox's mind that it might have been George that tooted him.

Though an unlikely duo in many ways, representing the archetypal sensibilities of two men fashioned from English boarding school and Scottish housing scheme, the friendship and partnership nonetheless worked. George was another maverick ex-cop, driven by something other than salary cheque and a diffuse notion of service. In his world, things had to be done absolutely right. He exhibited little patience for a warped criminal justice and legal system that served up fudge, corruption and compromise, protecting wealth and power, dressed in shabby, bad-faith realpolitik clothing. In his world if you were guilty, you were guilty. It was as straightforward as that.

The two men regard the white pebbled-dashed building, replete with incongruous mock-Tudor sign:

ROSE GARDEN RETIREMENT COMMUNITY

Bordering a yard of paved flagstones is a strip of compacted earth, from which trellises run up the wall. They are entwined with dry, cracking twigs, presumably resurrecting in the summer to bloom roses. Ray Lennox doesn't care where he dies, but knows he will never want to live one day of his allotted life span in such a place.

— Let's get this done, George barks, as if endorsing his sentiment. — Leave the manager to me. Polly Ives. I saw her at the security trade conference. Dishy, he says, and Lennox has never heard anyone use that phrase outside of old Ealing comedies. — Have my beady eye on her. He rolls a brow.

A slight unease grips Lennox, as he recalls an intervention he was required to make, after relocating from Edinburgh to join up in business with George. His partner was having an affair with Millicent Freeson, one of their first clients. He opts to let it slide as they enter a musty reception hall, its central heating like the blast of a furnace. It feels like walking into a sauna, the mugginess extending into a lounge area bedecked with tables and chairs. Lennox waves his hand across his face in acknowledgement of the humidity, as the pungent trace of old sweat and piss permeates the air.

He suspects the staff and inmates (a veteran associate of closed institutions, he can't stop thinking of the residents like that) will now be oblivious to this odour. A wheezing man on a walking frame stumbles by them, bellicose eyes bulging implausibly. A withering plant sits in a pot. At a table by a window, three old boys sit playing cards. One, as much due to his pompous, bombastic manner as his glasses and chubby frame, Lennox thinks of as Captain Mainwaring from *Dad's Army*. He loudly pontificates about foreigners of some designation or another. — We got to get 'em out. We can't even look after our own! Right, Brian?

Mainwaring has turned to an outsized but frail and buckled pyjama-clad man crushed into a wheelchair, the last of the flesh on his gargantuan shoulder bones wasting away as his feet steep in a basin of warm water. Something about his eyes deeply troubles Lennox, who decides it must be the utter defeat and hopelessness in them. The other card player, a skeletal man with a liver-spotted scalp, studies his hand intently.

— Look at the poor old bastards, Lennox spins to George as they wait for somebody to appear at the reception desk. — It's all fear. Foreigners who want to take their jobs, even now they're long past their working lives, socialists who want to give the homeless their money, even though they're skint . . . what a fucking way to live.

— Of course, you do know their fear is our friend, Raymond, George observes. — Without it, we aren't in business!

— Does it ever bother you? Lennox asks, noting the panting Zimmer Frame Man being joined by a toilet-emerging cohort on a similar contraption.

— Not at all. Compared to police work it's a positively noble trade, George advances. — This is the south of England, Raymond. There are council estate dwellers here who would literally part with their life savings for the honour of having their offspring buggered by an Old Etonian, while wishing to set fire to a Pakistani who sat too close to one of them on public transport, he cheerfully observes, looking back over to the card-playing men, obliging Lennox to do the same.

Captain Mainwaring is on a roll. — They shouldn't be allowed to wear those bloody veils. Let them go back to their own country if they want to dress like that, and he rubs at his reddening neck. Mainwaring looks close to seizure, but the big man disturbs Lennox more; to have carried the strength that frame suggests, and now manifest as little more than a vegetable . . . But perhaps the alternatives are worse. He trembles, fleetingly thinking of his mother in her slow but inexorable decline in his sister's spare room in Edinburgh.

— Besides, George elaborates, — those tight, hoarding old bastards are my people. We need to be separated from our money: just give the lot to the banks so it becomes meaningless and we're finally liberated!

Lennox's head swivels, concerned that George's booming

11

tones have carried. — Fuck sake, you're buoyant today. How did you get on last night?

— Left leg first, Raymond, George takes the hint, lowering his voice and winking, — Viagra is the best thing that's happened to me. I'm praying it sufficiently weakens the heart in order that I can die on the job. To think I'd resigned myself to only having a couple of women on the go. Now I can manage a handful once again! Happy days!

Lennox is about to interject, but George's urging eyes tell him that the centre manager has appeared. Polly Ives looks the epitome of stress. A nervous aspect and dowdiness cling to her, embodied in the shapeless pullover she wears, drawing attention from her fine features and cheekbones. Her half-shut eyes jump around, and a slight but visible tremor shakes her body. She ushers them to sit at one of the vacant tables in the lounge, close to the card school. — I'm afraid the office is being redecorated. They made rather a mess with the break-in.

While failing to see the Venusian attraction George insinuated, Lennox is grateful for Polly's potential business. It was she who had called in Horsham Security Solutions after a second burglary inside a month had spooked the residents. — We believe it's a gang from Brighton, or maybe even . . . she whispers the word as if it was Hades, — *London*.

As the two men with the Zimmers move past them, the wheezer man now upping his pace in the competition, Lennox tries to place her on his social matrix: a leftist social worker type or right-wing Christian do-gooder? Polly seems to straddle both camps. He can somehow picture her at both church and radical feminist group meetings.

— This used to be such a nice place, she ruefully muses.

It's a fucking death camp, Lennox thinks, as Mainwaring, having run out of steam, lets his head slump into his chest. He surmises that Polly's penchant for cheap fake nostalgia fixes probably places her on the right. Despite now being in this business over eighteen months, Lennox elects to remain silent, knowing to let George do the talking in such situations. His partner carries the air of empathetic authority that plays well with the old and, more importantly, their carers. A truculent joviality that stops short of buffoonery and pomp, George delivers his lines in refined public-school vowels given clipped urgency by employ in the Special Boat Service, the naval equivalent of the SAS, and the police force. — Alas, changing times, he nods, looking around in a sweep, before making strong eye contact with Polly. — It's obviously of paramount importance that your residents, and his eyes flash across to the card school, then back to Polly, — *and their relatives* feel safe and secure.

Polly's bug-eyed nod of affirmation indicates that George has hit the spot. The families are the paymasters and two break-ins constitute a terrible end to the year and not good for business. Confidence needs restoring immediately. — Yes, we're all very concerned.

George casts his eye back over to the front door and the windows. — Well, I've only partaken in a cursory glance, but already I can see that this place is a soft touch for burglars. Of course, you do know this, right?

As Lennox looks around to watch the Zimmer combatants strike out across the hall for the corridor, Polly's hand reflexively goes to the chest of her knitted sweater. — What are you suggesting?

— Well, *Ms* Ives . . . may I call you Polly?

— Yes . . . yes, please do, she responds.

George falls silent but raises a prompting eyebrow as if to say: *are you quite sure?*

Lennox breaks his enthralment of the old shagger's performance to enjoy the two Zimmer frames taking the corner and vanishing from sight. He feels cheer glowing through him at their surprisingly formidable burst.

— Then Polly, George lets his tone slide back into business gravitas, — let me ask: do you plan to finance the installation of any new security system as a one-off from an existing fund, or will you be levying some sort of additional charge from the residents in order to pay for it?

— Well, that all depends. Polly looks nervously to the card school. An orderly has arrived and is carefully drying the big man's feet. Mainwaring is animated again, trying to draw the young carer into the conversation. He's resisting with diplomacy, staying cheerful as the captain derides him as a remoaner. Polly seems to be making a quick calculation of their offsprings' means and commitment levels. — What kind of money are we talking about here?

Two elderly women come into the hall and sit at a nearby table. One has bat-wing flesh wobbling off the upper arms, illustrated by a sleeveless dress, which, far from implausible, seems practical in this cranked-up heat. It's as if she's sucked all the life from her pale, anaemic, stick-thin friend, who huddles up in a cardigan, with a coat draped over her shoulders. They start knitting. As Lennox looks them over, one waves at the card men.

Wonder if there's shagging going on in these gaffs . . . dirty old bastards cowping, it fucks everything up. The old girl . . . fucking rampant auld hoor . . .

. . . yes, you certainly mind when you were a kid and you got up in the night for a piss and heard noises coming from the bedroom. You pushed the door gently and looked through the crack between the edge of it and the frame. He was on top of her, fucking her.

Was it your dad?

Was it that cunt of a mate? Were they at it when your father was on backshift?

14

No. It doesn't fit the time frame. You are imagining things.
The cold air.
The shining moonlight.

— Well, let me say firstly that any system we install won't be a one-size-fits-all effort, simply pulled off the shelf, George declares to an all-ears Polly. — Those are absolutely useless, and I guarantee if you go cheap, no burglars worth their salt will be deterred. He whips to Lennox. — Ray?

— Indeed, George. Lennox is happy to be pulled back into the room. — In fact, I'd go further; some of those systems are so inadequate that they serve as a marker, a sign that says to the real pros: *please break in.*

Polly's brows knot, her expression crumbling into undisguised gloom.

— Quite. And this is the crux of the problem, George nods. — With many of them you really are literally better off with no security at all. They may deter kids, but will be a magnet for the seasoned players from . . . he hesitates slightly, — *London,* whom you believe may have targeted you.

— Oh gosh, Polly murmurs under her breath.

Lennox is tuning out again, as George says something reassuring.

Mainwaring in a threesome with those two old girls . . . maybe the poor old bastard in the wheelchair getting his numb cock sucked . . . fuck me, what a place . . .

. . . the wheel on your bicycle, the way it stuck when you pushed it into the garden shed. You had just got it that Christmas. What a goofy, innocent kid you were, still practically believing in Santa Claus, or maybe just wanting to, right up to your eleventh birthday. But after the tunnel, you knew there was no Santa Claus. There was none of that fucking crap.

He hears the briefcase snap open to see his partner sliding brochures across the table to Polly, followed by George

15

scooting his chair round alongside her, letting her get the scent of his aftershave and pheromones. His voice lowers to a warm background buzz. Lennox doesn't know about Polly Ives but it is certainly having a soothing effect on him.

You tried to tell your mum what happened in the tunnel, but she didn't listen. Why the fuck didn't she pay attention? It was down to that cunt she was shagging. Sex stupefies us all.

Then George rises, urging Polly to escort him round the centre. Lennox makes to follow, but his partner waves him down. And he sees it: that light touch on the woman's arm, as George points to a skylight, his other hand waving his iPad, the one with the digital forms on it. His eyes follow them outside, then lazily scan the room. Mainwaring is back in his pomp at card school, holding court. The orderly wheels the huge, stooped-shouldered gent away, as the two women move across to join the other men. Lennox tunes into the lulling hum of the strip lights.

Mainwaring has pulled, the cunt . . . now that big wheels has fucked off . . . your wheels, the bike you grabbed and frantically rode out of that dark tunnel, leaving Les behind . . . you somehow got away . . . how did you do that? Then you came back home, but there was something that made you go right outside again. Back out to wander those cruel streets of monsters, away from the refuge of your house, before you returned late for your tea . . .

Again, the click of George's briefcase fractures Lennox from his line of thought, marking the onset of a low rattle in his chest that disconcerts him. Polly holds a copy of the printed-out contract, lowering it to the desk and signing it, handing it to George. Lennox had barely even noticed them returning. *Always get the perishers to sign the bloody contract,* George would say, *life is too fucking short.*

As they say their goodbyes and walk out the centre, George

rubs his hands together. Out in the cold, he chuckles, — That's twelve grand's worth of kit sold, Raymond. Right from the catalogue! Money for old rope!

— Nice work, Lennox concedes, looking at the hard ground and wondering whether the rose garden will bloom again. The strange rasp in his chest seems to have subsided.

— And I've a dinner date into the bargain. What do you think of pretty Polly, Raymond?

— Looked a bit starchy to me. Like, a wee bit of a cold fish.

— All the more satisfying, George bellows, with an almost imperceptible sashay of the hips. — Of course, you do know that she will go off like a fucking alarm clock when touched in the right spots, Raymond. You really are terrible at reading women, and he shakes his head in mock disdain. — How is your new squeeze, by the by? The scientist, right?

— We're squeezing, Ray Lennox purrs in anticipation of this afternoon's rendezvous with Carmel Devereaux.

— Good form. George bleeps open the doors on his BMW. He thrusts the hard copies of the contract and specifications at Lennox. — Will you drop this bumpf off to Ria in the office?

Lennox nods, takes the papers and unlocks the Alfa Romeo, saying goodbye to George. Gets in and blows on his hands, keying the ignition and switching on the heater. Thinks about investing in a beanie hat, scarf and gloves. It was hard to sanction George's behaviour around women, though he hadn't detected this Lothario tendency when they first met, over twenty years ago, at a forensics workshop in Harrogate. But what was quickly evident was the connection between the two men.

Penny, his then girlfriend, was a Buddhist, and had told Lennox that sometimes you get a strong sense that you know someone *before* you know them, perhaps, she'd ventured, from a past life. That had been too much of a stretch for Lennox, but when he'd extended his hand to George and said 'I'm Ray Lennox' the response of 'Indeed you are' seemed particularly knowing. And then George had been Lennox's guardian angel, convincing him he had the wrong person arrested in the case of the child murderer known as Mr Confectioner. Finally, he had taken the broken, burnt-out Lennox from Edinburgh, and the force, to this new life in Brighton. Fortunately, for Ray Lennox's material world view, his straight-backed partner was just as cynical as he about any spiritual dimension to life.

He heads back to the offices of Horsham Security Solutions in Seven Dials, an area taking its name from the road intersection at its epicentre. The company moniker indicates its origins in the town where George was a short-lived resident, evacuating after the woman he was living with caught him canoodling with her sister. George moved to Eastbourne briefly, 'no, no, just no . . .', and Brighton followed. After teaming up with Lennox he resisted changing the company name to something more apposite, dubiously contending that the existing moniker had 'premium-brand cache' in the local security industry.

Lennox swerves past a group of oval-mouthed carol singers who have gathered on the busy street outside his office. As they chant in slightly distressed tones, replete with the crestfallen wide-eyed stares that Lennox associates with nonce victimhood, he climbs several steps from pavement level to access the ground floor of the Victorian building.

In a reception area, her back to the big support pillar that divides the room in two, assisted by bookcases and filing cabinets, Ria Thomson sits at her desk, battering a computer keyboard. — Hi, Ray, she says breezily. Still a teenager, she has only been at Horsham Security Solutions a few months. Lennox has warmed to this efficient, conscientious and buoyant young woman. Feels he should talk to her more; find out what makes her tick. A few weeks back he wouldn't have even thought about this, but his liaison with Carmel has made him feel youthful to the extent he now almost sees Ria as a peer. Lennox hands her the paperwork, then examines the clock on his phone. He has to be somewhere else. Doesn't even stop to go into his own small office, situated next to George's identical space.

While the high ceilings and big windows made his Sussex Square summers such a blessing, at this time of the year it could feel fridge-like if you tended to be overly careful with the central heating, as he did. Fighting his inner Calvinist, Lennox cranks it up hoping the temperature will rise to clothes-shedding levels by the time Carmel arrives. When she appears and he makes that point to her, Carmel replies, — I'm horned up to the max, so it could be fucking arctic in here for all I care, and she jostles him towards the bedroom, pulling off her garments as she goes, commandingly barking, — Get them off, Lennox!

He complies and they tumble onto the bed. Carmel's eyes blaze as she mounts Lennox with an athletic smoothness, lowering herself slowly onto him, letting him fill her. His big hands go to her waist, shocking him at the way his fingertips almost touch at its thinnest point. The fuck is slow and intense, Carmel controlling the pace, him going with it. The vehemence builds and he's happy to let her climax in a low growl before her light bones seem to dissolve and she collapses onto him. Lennox tries to get her off him, keen to shag her in a different position. His preference is for a woman to have several orgasms before he blows his load, as that generally means game over for him, at least for a few hours. But she insists, — No, I want you to come, and he does, as in unity she jerks and thrashes herself into a second climax.

Afterwards they reflect how the *good in bed* construct for

experienced adults is largely about chemistry and communication. As a research chemist and university lecturer on the subject, Carmel knows about both. She believes that love and life is simply about chemicals: dopamine, oxytocin and serotonin. High on them all, she talks about how their sex life may develop, sharing views on the things she wants to explore with him: bondage, spanking, anal, threesomes and swinging. It's a salty conversation, yet one that gives Lennox the disconcerting feeling he's the *older guy project*. Is glad to receive a distracting call from his friend and former colleague Ally Notman in Edinburgh. — Got to take this, he apologises.

Carmel's *I see you* look.

Hits the green button and coughs, — Ally.

The returning voice seems to have to fight through crackles and hisses before it reaches him. — Raymondo! Notman sounds half cut already. — So ye up for Doogie Gillman's retirement do the morn?

Gillman? Not a fucking chance. Nothing in the world could induce me to come to that cunt's send-off. — Couldnae get the time off, Lennox winks at Carmel. Her hand slides under the covers towards his cock. He feels a piece of cord become an iron rod. Circumstances alter cases. — Listen, Ally, something's come up . . . have to get back to you.

— Ray, I –

— Later, Ally, and Lennox switches off the phone and chucks it across the bed.

4

A CHATTERING CLASS

Expensively fitted and swish of decor, the wine bar, its walls bedecked with the efforts of local artists, is noisy and boisterous. Clustered groups cluck contentedly over Greg Lake's hopeful declaration 'I Believe in Father Christmas', as Ray Lennox, walking in with Carmel Devereaux, senses that after the Rose Garden home, he is now firmly in 'remain' territory. He watches Carmel, dressed in Friday-evening casual elegance in a tight-ribbed purple jumper and long checked skirt, nimbly flutter through ensembles of her university colleagues, some of whom he has met previously. He wonders if those academic types scorn him as an ex-cop, now working in security, exploiting the fears of scared retirees? Looks at the sleeve of his black leather Hugo Boss jacket, the tailor of the Nazis and also his off-the-peg choice. Glances up, unable to see Angela, whom he had chatted to extensively on the night he and Carmel met in that Hove pub.

Only stopping in for a quick beer after his kickboxing training, he had struck up an easy conversation with his new girlfriend and her workmates at the bar. The mutual attraction had been evident from the off, and both Lennox and Carmel immediately understood that they would pursue it. It led slowly but inexorably from coffee to dinner to bed, all within the context of regular dates.

Carmel introduces him to Gilbert Mason, a tall, fine-featured man with an exotic quiff and camp mannerisms. Soon they are talking shop and Lennox is bamboozled. — The major technological issue for the setting of the geopolymer, Carmel declares, — is facilitating it in volume through the polycondensation of potassium oligo or sialate-siloxo into the cross-linked potassium poly or sialate-siloxo network . . . Oh, sorry, Ray, I'm being incredibly dull!

Gilbert smiles tightly at Lennox and excuses himself.

— You've even blinded your fellow scientists with science, Lennox laughs, watching him depart. — Layperson's terms please? I was shit at chemistry at school.

— Oh, okay, I'll stop being a science dick. But this is more construction technology, which should be up your street, Lennox; the Scots were great contributors to civil engineering.

— The ones I came into contact with specialised more in uncivil disobedience. So how is this newfangled cement better than the old-school stuff?

— Geopolymer concrete versus Portland cement? Oh, more durable, quicker setting, takes between ten minutes and an hour, as opposed to half an hour and five hours; and environmentally better, uses less water, energy and CO_2 emissions per tonnage. See her, she points to a woman in a light blue business suit, — she was a builder's daughter.

— Yes?

— Cement a lot to him.

Lennox draws in a breath. — Oh, Jesus Christ . . .

She pulls him to her. — Kiss me. Then excuse me for roughly five minutes.

Lennox dutifully complies then watches her glide off.

Now she is talking to a man, whom even with his back to him, Lennox is cheered to see is older, with a bland south of England accent that dips into a pleasantly performative ersatz cockney. The man wears flannels, a corduroy jacket and cravat. His greying blond locks curl around a bald spot on his slightly egg-shaped head. His hands move in a robust, confident manner, as he jabs a finger in the air, while shrugging with wide, powerful shoulders. Their conversation seems intense and animated, and Carmel appears excited and highly engaged. Then she spies Lennox and waves. And as the man turns round displaying caterpillar brows and a lopsided grin, Ray Lennox feels the blood ice up in his veins as his head spins dementedly.

What the fuck . . .

He has to look away, and collapses to the floor on one knee, fiddling at a non-existent loose shoelace. Heart thrashing as he fights to get breath into his lungs, Lennox's first reaction, through the blood swelling and pounding in his head: *it can't be.*

Carmel is over by his side. Her hand is on his shoulder. — Are you okay, Ray?

— Aye, Lennox coughs out. He is staying down, like a boxer taking the full eight count, giving himself time to recover from the devastating blow. For as long as it takes to get in control and process what is happening, he will remain on the floor. — Something in my shoe . . .

5

TUNNEL VISION

You had taken your bikes, you and your best friend, Les Brodie, down the Water of Leith walkway, like you did most Saturday mornings. That ritual you had: getting up before the dog walkers. The sun was already climbing and it was really hot. You could feel it on your legs, especially your shins. You both wore khaki shorts and you had a white T-shirt with a maroon heart on it, while Les had one that was reverbing brown and green stripes, which made you feel sick to look at when you'd drunk too much juice. You were glad of the shade from the overhead trees as you walked on, now pushing the bicycles, as the path was too uneven to cycle. In any case, Les had gotten a flat tyre earlier from a puncture, and you had debated about turning back but decided against it because some big lads were meant to have put a barry Tarzan swing up on the other side of the railway tunnel on that disused single-track line from the defunct Caledonian station to Currie. The trail was practically deserted as you got to the dank Victorian passageway, with its towering, foreboding brick face covered in a rash of ivy.

That impenetrable darkness ahead.

Les and you did what you always did: gave each other a wee look to show you werenae feart, then edged the bikes and yourselves into the gloaming. You couldn't see much, especially as you got further in. You'd look above, at those weak, orangey-yellow overhead lights, which showed up the wet gravel under your feet. Then, at the middle of the tunnel, that dreaded blind spot, where no light at either end was visible.

The voices . . . and then . . .

And then his face . . . that hair . . . those snidey feeble, manipulative, cruel eyes . . . cunt was thaire . . . cunt was thaire . . . then what, then what the fuck . . .

Nothing.

Why can't you see?

You were running; no, you were on your Raleigh, cycling. He was coming after you . . . Les was still in there with the other two.

He was trying to pull you back in . . .

But after the tunnel . . .

What happened after the tunnel, when you got help from those walkers and went back with them? As you got there, you saw the broken ghost of Les emerge into the light, pushing his bike.

Nae polis.

That was what he commanded through his pain.

Nae polis.

You went hame.

Where you saw your ma.

Your ma and Uncle Jock.

You came in with your precious blue Raleigh, ready to tell her that something had happened. Something bad. But then, coming downstairs: the family friend, Jock Allardyce. The fucker looked at you and said something like: — Aye, pal.

Your mum was in the kitchen. She had been cutting vegetables on a chopping board, and started washing up. — Jock's toilet is broken; he's just been using ours, she told you, as she looked around anxiously from you to him. You thought she was looking at you as if you had done something wrong. But it was her who had done something wrong. — What's wrong, son, you okay?

— Nowt, you mumbled, heading back outside. Home was now different. It had changed in an imperceptible way. The light in the kitchen seemed blinding. The sound of the dishes

clattering together as your mum washed them, like duelling swords. There was no refuge here.

You went down to the shops. Wondered if you could get a bus. Somewhere. Anywhere. You walked around until it got dark and you became scared, worrying you would somehow run into those monsters from the tunnel again. Maybe they would try to get you into a car. You backed away from every motor that slowly passed you on that main road, terrified if there was a group of men in one.

When you finally got back home again, your mum, dad, baby brother Stuart and big sister Jackie were eating at the table. — Late for yir tea again, Raymond, your dad was laughing. — These gannets have got most ay the tatties. C'mon, son, fill yir boots!

You didn't know it then, and you would only find out after your dad's death years later, that your mother had been filling her boots with Jock Allardyce.

You left. Went up to your room. You never went to bed early but this time you did. Kept the light on in case the monsters came back.

And now the monster is back . . .

6

THE MONSTER

Get up off the floor. You're making a cunt of yourself. You can rise. You can stand. Do it. You are a man. Not a wee boy. You don't know it's him. It was forty fucking years ago! Get a grip. Your memory is playing tricks on you: too much nonce hunting. This guy is no old lag . . . that fucking beasts' register . . . first on paper, then on the screen. All those faces: a sea of perverts, some confused, others knowing, all fucking deviants.

Ray Lennox has no awareness of his legs, just the giddiness in his head and nausea in his abdomen, but he is suddenly standing. The big smile he forces at Carmel feels like nothing less than pathetic, idiotic resistance. Yet he sucks in air and enquires as to what she's drinking. But no response; her head whiplashes away following a distracting shoulder tap from someone in her group of colleagues.

And a shaky-legged Lennox walks past the man, *the monster*. He can only force stolen glimpses at it, each one slapping more dizziness into his head, making the sickness soar through him, hammering his teeth together.

Get a fucking grip.

It is chatting to somebody else now.

He tugs in a breath, and tags Carmel's arm gently. — Hey you.

— Oh, Ray . . . so you're back in our line of sight!

— Damn laces, Lennox looks at his shoes, — always working loose. Going to hit the bar, what are you for?

— Red wine, you select, but not Merlot, Carmel says. He

27

smiles in forced lightness, then a chilling blast: sabotaging, rending, as he nods at *the monster*. It is impossible to avoid each other's eyes. The brief acknowledgement is reciprocated by a cold, tight grin but not one of recognition. Yet the full fat lips have registered something in Lennox.

But I was just a boy. Why would he identify that young kid as me?

Lennox permits himself another glance at *the monster* in passing. It has turned back to Carmel.

It has the puffed-frog under-chin that many men develop with age. Its eyes dart in a startled way that hints at timidity, before blazing into a rapaciousness that intimidates. Lennox knows that one of them is an act, a pose. In a successful businessman, it could be either.

There's nae mistaking that reptilian profile. A small tongue, playing on those tight lips. The beady eye, with those thick brows. Tunnel tunnel tunnel . . .

Carmel leaves her company and follows Lennox over to the bar, just as he's caught the pressured barmaid's attention. As he orders two glasses of Shiraz, he feels perspiration on his collar and down his back. Picks one glass up. Hand shakes so badly, has to lower it to the marble bar top without taking a sip in case she notices.

— This mine? Carmel's crimson nails click around the glass, like a fairground arcade claw grabbing a trinket, raising it from the polished surface.

— Aye.

— Be honest: you're not too bored?

— No . . . not at all. Funny though, and I didn't want to make a thing of it in front of your mates, but I came over a bit queasy there: like I'd eaten something that didn't agree with me, and his ticklish cough is not contrived. It came back at times like these.

— Oh, how horrible. You okay now?

— Yes, the worst of it seems to have passed, Lennox sings, fighting a low asthmatic croak as he looks back towards *the monster.*

Why here? Who the fuck is he?

Another Geiger counter surge in Lennox's heartbeat, as a choking rage wells up in his chest. He heaves in some air. Now he feels compromised; a fraud. All those years in Serious Crimes, trying to interview people who would be in a similar state as he is at this moment: undermined by a visceral fear and rage. Nothing prepared you for it. It was crazy. It was a drug. A poison. — Who . . . who is that guy you were talking to?

— Mathew Cardingworth; a very big patron of the university and of my department in particular. He's funding our new chemical research facility, and a big project I'm heading up, Carmel purrs in appreciation.

Lennox nods. Recalls that Carmel had driven him past the new laboratories' development site, en route to the university, near the Brighton & Hove Albion Football Club stadium.

— Very well known in these parts. He's a local business-man. Owns this place, also has an auction room and a share in several nightclubs. But his real wealth comes from property development. He's absolutely minted, she contends in dis-cernible respect, even awe.

Lennox darts his tongue across his lips, buoyed by this knowledge. *The monster* has a name: Mathew Cardingworth.

It is real. It can be hurt. It can feel pain. And now it will feel all the fucking pain of the world. You will see to that.

Lennox looks over at Cardingworth again. Feels his body in revolt against himself: the sweating, the increased heartbeat and, most of all, the jaw spasms. Fights it down.

Fear is no longer an option: you arenae the wee laddie in the tunnel now. This is a pathetic old has-been. You have him; he's yours now. Stalk him. Hunt him down slowly. Savour every fuck-ing second of this forthcoming revenge – you've waited long enough! Now he's here!

Suddenly, Ray Lennox has never felt so excited or alive. Bells ring in his head. Chemicals surge through his body. This is stronger than new love. This is his quest. His hunger. His destiny. And it has finally fallen into his lap. His gaze beams on Mathew Cardingworth.

Will people not notice? Stay cool.

Cardingworth heads off in the direction of the toilets.

— Are you sure you're okay, Ray? Carmel asks.

— Yes, just going to take a leak.

Carmel nods as Lennox follows Mathew Cardingworth's retreating figure to the back of the room and into the toilets. He stands two latrines away. Looks ahead. How easy to smash Cardingworth now, the element of surprise over an out-of-shape man, probably in his early sixties.

His shoulders are big and broad but his gut hangs over those scabby nonce genitals he now huds in his hand . . .

A crimson mist leaks from the back of Lennox's brain into his vision. Obliterating this monster is essential. But it is also insufficient. *This beast has to hurt. Like the one in Miami. This is my chance. It has to feel so much pain that it will welcome the respite of death.*

But this is self-indulgent psycho shit. Stay calm. Breathe. You must think this through.

Lennox knows his reaction means a hugely significant *something*, but he still has to ascertain *what*. Those blurred faces in the tunnel. Three men in that long, stone passageway of torture. Which one was Cardingworth?

He hears the businessman expel the last of his urine. Peripherally watches him shake out his penis . . . *was that the cock that I was made to* . . . Hears *the monster* zip up. As it moves behind him, the hairs on his neck rise. He feels dizzy. It is too much. His overheated brain peppered with the brutal impulse to destroy. He has to explode with violence or he will pass out, suffer a seizure . . . His mouth cloying with thin metallic gunge. He remembers Miami . . . the similar scenario when such a creature was at his mercy, one he didn't pass up. Then the Lollipop Man with Ginger Rogers . . . *nonce justice . . . smash him, smash the cunt . . . no, it's too soon . . .* He heaves in a long breath.

No. Fight this. Think!

It can't be Cardingworth. There's a strong resemblance between him and one of the men in the tunnel, but it was forty years ago!

You were no more than a bairn, so he would have been a young guy . . .

This man, this strutting, foppish, old coxcomb who drips wealth and success, he surely isn't one of those semi-destitute jailbirds who stank of cheap drink and old cigarettes. But why this dark, consecrating, visceral reaction? *Why?*

There was a younger one! What did he do?

Cardingworth *the Monster* Cardingworth *the Monster* washes his, *its* hands. *Its dirty hands.* Hot compressed air hisses from a machine. Its rasp persists as the toilet door squeaks shut. Lennox lets go of the breath he didn't know he was holding on to. The piss. First trickling, then gratefully exploding, from his strained bladder.

When he's done, Lennox heads back to the bar. Stands in a quiet corner. Observes Carmel once again in deep conversation with some friends. Colleagues. They have an air about them: slightly smug, yet unsatisfied. Knowing features tight, well-honed gym-and-diet bodies comfortable, though less than relaxed. But where is Cardingworth? He spies *the monster* just as he gets out his phone to dial George. At ease,

Mathew Cardingworth works the room, gabby and loose with the patrons. They all seem to be *his* people. He is popular. Influential. — Raymond . . . George's voice is tinged with impatience.

— You busy?

— You could say that.

— I'll keep it short.

— Please do.

— What do you know about Mathew Cardingworth?

— Hold on . . . and he senses that George is moving out of somebody's earshot. — He's very wealthy, a bit of a local success story.

— Is he bent in any way?

— Other than the usual way of the rich and successful? Haven't heard anything but I'll check.

— Thanks, George.

There is a brief pause on the line. — What the suffering fuck is all this about, Raymond Lennox?

— Something or nothing. Hopefully nothing.

— I'm really not liking the sound of it.

— Try the sound of this then: lunch at the Ivy on me tomorrow. You killed it in Eastbourne this morning.

— Hmmpf. Twelve thirty for cocktails at the bar, table for 1 p.m., George snorts, before hanging up, but Lennox feels his business partner's satisfaction radiate through the airwaves.

As he slips his iPhone into his pocket, Carmel approaches. — Angela called: she's running late. Shall I get us another drink?

Lennox looks blankly at her then glances over at *the monster*. Once more the energy had discernibly changed. Cardingworth is again an other-worldly force. The reptilian head takes in everything, the bearing that of an untouchable emperor. But then . . . it *isn't* like that. Cardingworth seems to be completely engaged with everyone he converses with. A shiver runs up Lennox's backbone, seeming to dissolve verte-brae on its journey north, as that scared wee boy from the tunnel claws his way to the vanguard of his psyche. This part of him will always jostle to the fore, *until he exterminates that beast.* Ray Lennox nurses his wrath, burying his fear deep inside him, as a blistering rage wells up to the surface.

— Ray, are you sure you're okay? You're acting a little pecu-liar. Has the intrinsic emotion and raw sexuality of the occasion, she looks around the room of scientists, — just overwhelmed you? Carmel's voice pulls him back into the present.

He needs to get out of here.

Later. You know who he is. Take it easy. He's going nowhere.

Looking pointedly at her, he nuzzles, whispering, into her ear. — The truth is that you are turning me on so much. Just watching you flit around, so cool and sexy, it makes me want to take you home right now and shag your brains out.

Carmel's harsh, evaluating look makes him fear chronic misjudgement. Then she delves into the purse in her bag, pro-ducing a ticket and handing it to him. Her throaty voice drops an octave. — Get the coats. I'll join you outside in a minute; I just have a few quick goodbyes to say.

Happy to leave the bar and Cardingworth, Lennox retrieves the garments and orders the Uber. In the lobby, his lungs start operating normally. Carmel appears moments later.

The ride back has their mouths fastened on to each other.

You will be a man, not a boy, you will fuck her, you will fuck your younger girlfriend to your mutual satisfaction. The pair of you will walk the streets, dripping your smug, smooth sexuality. Men will envy you, think of you as a stud, as a player . . . like Cardingworth . . .

No!

You are nothing like that fucking monster! That perverted rapist of young children! How many more? How many more

33

frightened kids fell prey to that vile creature . . . to those monsters?

But is Cardingworth really the guy in the tunnel? Plenty people have that lopsided grin, that oval-shaped head, those brows . . .

Those much-studied mugshots of sex offenders; all of them flashing now in Lennox's mind, imprints blurred to the point of meaninglessness . . .

You need to look at those bastards again! If Cardingworth isn't the tunnel man, he is somebody . . .

They come up for air. Carmel curves a brow. — You really do deserve a good seeing-to, after putting up with all that shop talk.

— No worries, it was interesting, and he fishes, — It looks like things are getting pretty busy at your work.

— It's crunch time for the research facility.

— This seems a big deal. What's it all about?

— My research involves using synthetic complements-slash-substitutes for fly ash, which we get from coal. I'm developing these to make construction tech more energy-efficient and green, but we're way behind China. That's why Mat Cardingworth's land deal for the custom-built research facility into the new tech materials is vital.

When they arrive at Sussex Square, in spite of his big declaration, Lennox is now uncertain as to whether, in his preoccupied state, he can fuck anybody's brains out but his own. Then Carmel's hand is on his cock and it's thickening and hardening. They quickly conjoin and their activity goes from gentle to frenetic. He hears sounds, high torturous bleats that he thinks manufactured by her, but to the alarm of them both, they are coming from him.

The subject is broached in the climactic aftermath, as they lie in each other's arms. — Ray, you okay?

— Better than that, he gasps. — Pretty much blew me away.

And it was no lie. This thirty-eight-year-old woman was a powerhouse in bed. The force of hormones and personality dictated that this would go on for some time. That was a delicious and intimidating thought.

Surely George's Viagra supply will need raiding soon. But behave: you've only known the woman a few weeks!

Right now, though, Ray Lennox's main impediment to real romance is, as always, what is going inside his own head.

Cardingworth. The monster is here. And you will slay it. And the others.

Bim.

Get him, Bim! Who the fuck is that? I –

— Ray! Have you thought about what we were discussing earlier? About stuff to do in the bedroom? Carmel asks, index finger tracing circles on his chest suddenly becoming an urgent stab of a nail.

— Like what specifically? We were talking about *everything*.

— Like the swinging.

— Yes, I'm game. Depending on who it's with, obviously.

— Angela is into it. Do you fancy her?

— I fancy you.

— That's the obviously correct, highly politic answer and I unreservedly applaud it, she sings cheerfully, pushing her hair out of her eyes, pinning him with her gaze. — But you wouldn't say no?

— Well, I said I was in, Lennox grins. — Happy to take one, eh, give one, for the team!

— Her new boyfriend might take a bit of coaxing though. It's just as well that I don't mind older men!

Lennox's blood runs cold. — Who is he?

— That guy I was talking to. Mat. The businessman you were asking about, Mathew Cardingworth.

All Ray Lennox can hear is a muffled sound in his ears, as if he is underwater.

— Ray? Ray? Carmel's voice, like it's coming from a long way away. Persistent. Insinuating.

— What . . . ?

— I said should I get on to them and we can set something up for tomorrow or Sunday?

Lennox hauls in a slow extended breath through his nose. Looks at her. — I can't this weekend, it's that retirement do back in Edinburgh tomorrow.

She looks at him, nonplussed. — But you didn't seem too keen to go.

— I know, and I'm not at all, but I worked in the Serious Crimes Unit with this guy like, forever. Going to have to jump on a stand-by. I just don't think I can miss it . . .

— Of course, Carmel breezes. — We can sort something out when you get back. It'll give Angela time to get Mat onside!

Ray Lennox can think of nothing to say. A stupefied, pre-occupied mood settles on him, continuing right through to the next day. It even renders him oblivious to the cocktail and wine bill he has to foot at the Ivy, with George in extravagant mode. And that teatime he is relieved to vacate Brighton and fly to Edinburgh.

Day Two

7

I WALK WITH YOU IN DREAMS

. . . I cannot for the life of me recall how many there were . . . those I snuffed out and others I just hurt so badly that the pain and terror would subsequently define their miserable existences . . . problem is they blur between the physical world and the dream state I now mainly occupy . . . but this dreaming business . . . well, I was initially wary of course, I recall my gran's fancy man, Mr Baxter: 'dream but don't let dreams be your master,' he would say . . . still shudder at that and not a lot makes me do that . . . but dreaming, of course I wish I could be here all the time, life is easier, you can come up against as little or as much opposition as you want . . . and it's as real as reality . . . as a rule, I tend to play out all the old adventures and create new ones . . . I can kill them and bring them back to hurt them more, sketching new levels of pain and terror into them, like now . . . as my hands are on her throat and she's laughing and thinks it's a game but I've had her do this so many times, so I make her a young man with a foppish lick of greasy hair, big gleaming white teeth and a mischevi- ous arrogance in his eyes which I shall strangle into terror . . . and I'm at the point where he looks very uncomfortable . . . that moment where he knows it's no game no game no game and there's the rapture, the point of transition between cockiness and terror and you think *I did that* . . . thirteen of them . . . that's the number that rings a bell, the ones I took the life from and, of course, the countless more I damaged . . . but we've all had to put up with that and what goes around comes around as my grandmother and Mr Baxter used to say . . . now that was an education . . .

 . . . can't say fairer that that . . .

Hurt – hurt – hurt –

8

SHY AND RETIRING

Sometimes the loss of an old nemesis can affect you more deeply than the demise of a valued friend. This is particularly the case with cops and gangsters, who tend to allow rivalries, rather than loves, to define them.

This thought further subdues the already listless Lennox, feeling that dull fug of alcohol in his head, mouth drying and gut full, as the jet engines roar and the plane rises, pinning him back in his seat. A melancholy ache has foisted itself into his core. This is the spirit in which he heads on a late Saturday afternoon flight to Edinburgh and DS Douglas Gillman's retirement party. As the seat belt signs ping off and he views an approaching flight attendant, he thinks of his current psychotherapist, the impermeable Elaine Rodman. How long it's been since he visited her.

If you can stand being beside Gillman it might desensitise you for meeting Cardingworth. But going to a fucking orgy with THE MONSTER, your clathes off . . . no fucking way . . . it might just be a little triggering . . .

He laughs loudly and manically at that notion, his shoulders shaking. Only realises when an air hostess jiggles his arm. — Sir: are you alright?

— Yes, sorry, got a little preoccupied there, he smiles tautly at her, with a nod to the anxious passengers in his proximity. To his astonishment there is a plastic miniature red wine bottle with a beaker on his fold-down table. His head fuzzy

40

from the boozy lunch with George, he can't recall ordering it but pays with his credit card, grinding the seal open and pouring, raising it to his mouth. He takes a solitary sip, which foreshadows how it will further weaken his flesh and shake his hornet's nest mind. Lowers it to the table and decides to leave it. Gets a coffee instead.

Almost as soon as he steps off the plane, stopping at the duty free to make a solitary purchase, which he sticks in his holdall, Lennox feels his home city whispering its tepid, bitter resignation. It seems a theatre of cowardice, its sullen populace hunched against the cold and wind, thus a perfect incubator of his personal hesitancy and confusion. The tram gliding him smoothly into town summing up Edinburgh's failure to embrace its destiny as a European capital. Citizens begrudged the scraps of their own money they were reluctantly permitted by the moribund imperial concern down south to spend. Yet they fell silent while the multitude of their tax pounds were squandered on infrastructure projects like HS2, Crossrail and the Essex–Kent tunnel, with absolutely no benefit to them. Now they've been dragged against their political will from a twenty-eight-nation multicultural and trading entity into a reactionary, provincial backwater. Lennox steps off the vehicle at St Andrew's Square, feeling the haar settle into his lungs.

It's like breathing vapour.

His gut bubbles and burns, the acrid coffee blistering his stomach lining. *I'd have been healthier on the fucking wine.* On that short walk up the Bridges, his sports bag slung over his shoulder, and in spite of his hefty old overcoat and a new hat, scarf and gloves, he experiences the reactivation of childhood respiratory diseases believed long gone. That cough that had come right after the tunnel incident, the one they said was psychosomatic. He'd broken into that spluttering wheeze

41

when he'd tried to speak to his mother, who had been joined in the kitchen by 'Uncle' Jock Allardyce. It always came back in times of stress. It was here again. The buzz of a crowd: close, but still unseen. Wisps of fairground music swirling sickly in his ears. Then a sledgehammer gale assaults him, almost forcing his breath back into scratchy lungs, focusing a determination to never complain about a south coast winter again.

He slouches through the narrow Gothic passages of the Old Town. As his feet pad the cobblestones, from one of the winding alleys floats the high, whimsy burst of a nursery rhyme of ruined ghost children. Relieved to get to the Royal Mile and the sounds of traffic and raucous drunks, he heads for his destination, the bar that Serious Crimes officers habitually refer to as the Repair Shop. On entering the abstemiously furnished cop-infested pub, he'd expected animus, and indeed would have felt short-changed had he not gotten it. He just didn't think it would arrive so quickly. Almost immediately Dougie Gillman pounces on him. Now a portlier specimen, the angry silver-backed gorilla nonetheless retains both trademark crew cut and eyes burning from the dark slits they are screwed into. — Lenny boy! So, you're locksmithing for auld English wankers doon in arse-bandit country!

— I love you too, Douglas, Lennox states, poker-faced. There's more to it than that, he thinks, before conceding: *maybe not that much more.* And the best way to disarm Gillman is to agree with him. — But aye, that's about it.

— Right, Gillman stretches his five ten frame into six foot. It takes effort; his neck has vanished into a bulging sack, pus even more concertina-gnarled than Ray Lennox remembers. The mole on his chin has grown and changed colour and shape. Lennox can't help but notice those huge crushing hands that hang loose at his sides like a gunfighter's pistols:

they remain formidable instruments of hurt. — So, happy in your work, likes?

— Ecstatic. Can you no see it written all over my face? Lennox hears snide tones of old reinsinuate in his voice, presumed checked out at Hadrian's Wall. — And what about your own retirement plans? Golf? The Algarve?

Hesitancy flickers in Gillman's blazing orbs. Despite habitually scorning police work, his horizon had never evidenced any plan B. Gillman will be lost without the job. He will corrode. The thought gives Lennox a surge of pleasure, before making him despondent at just how intense this feels.

Another Serious Crimes ex-colleague, Ally Notman, sidles over as Gillman manages: — Fuck knows. Daein fuck all and only that when I feel like it!

It's lame and paltry defiance; Lennox knows he's drawn blood, but decides not to follow up. He's in civvy street, with Gillman not far behind, and the habitual jousting of old no longer holds appeal. He contents himself with a man-hug from Notman, also chunkier than a year ago, and glassier-eyed. Silver wings have sprouted on the side of his trademark jet-black number two cut, like time-served decorations. — Ally!

— Raymie! Great tae see you, buddy, Notman sings in drunken animation.

— Get a room, youse pair ay buftie boys, Gillman leers, executing the *laugh* and *sneer* that word implies in perfect combo, and with customary aplomb.

The evening wears on in this mode. No longer self-styling as a heavy drinker, Lennox nurses a solitary bottle of beer, savouring the reformed pisshead's disdain for his old cronies' activities. But it soon grows unbearable: the camera phones come out, snapping pictures of a sloshed Gillman cavorting with a strippergram girl. Cop etiquette means that such images will be spared Facebook and Instagram exhibition, but a wide sharing within the police community is their destiny. The activity jolts Lennox back to the Infamous Thailand Beano. He'd hated it from the off.

The Gary Glitter-faced obese white men, swaggering around in nonce entitlement with young Asian women, made him almost physically heave. Worse still, the snidely complicit expressions on some of his colleagues' faces, often men he'd respected. They'd run into some Australians who'd recommended the Scottish cops should try the notorious street known as the Diamond. Then . . .

. . . Gillman catches him nervously fingering his nose, which psychologically draws his rival to the same event. It precipitates an edgy glance between the two men, before Lennox turns away in the face of his nemesis's expression: hard and knowing with a smattering of triumph.

If you can't even look Gillman in the eye, how the fuck can you go to an orgy with Cardingworth?

Watch that monster fuck your girlfriend?

Maybe even more . . . fuck naw . . .

Then Notman practically stumbles into him. Lennox has always thought of his ex-partner as one of 'the young team', but now he looks the soiled way Scotsmen in their thirties can get when they have to decide whether to try to stay in their late twenties or fast-forward to their mid-forties. Bucking the trend is Scott McCorkel, whom he glances at over Notman's shoulder, as he helps his old charge stabilise. The pint-sized technology wizard must be near his thirties now, but still looks about twelve. In wolfish contempt Notman blearily focuses on Gillman, who has taken off down the bar to carouse with newcomers. — Cunt's finished. He'll be daein fuck all except . . . he makes a noose gesture and choking sound, — checking oot!

It's not just his concern at how alcohol is debasing his formerly fresh-faced colleague that surprises Lennox, but the undermining compassion he feels for Gillman. He focuses on his own pressing concerns. — Ally, I need a wee favour.

— Anything for you, Notman booms.

Lennox looks around, tugs Notman a few feet down the bar, pointedly lowering his voice. — On the QT likes, mate.

— Of course, Notman says, literally pulling himself together, standing up straight, forcing in a deep breath, which makes his eyes bulge.

— Going to email you a photae ay this guy. Can you get into the beasts' register and check him out?

Notman nods slowly. — Cost ye a large voddy n tonic . . . He looks at his empty glass.

— Done. Lennox shouts up another drink.

The subverting reservoir of empathy he has tapped into for Gillman continues to unease Lennox. Under the snarling, combative faux bonhomie, his old enemy seems lost. Quite probably he always was. And Lennox feels he's not the only one.

You are all over the place.

This sense of affinity lasts until Chief Superintendent Amanda Drummond arrives at the party. Drummond's presence occasions a silence: her tight 'as you were' stare can only enable, rather than prevent, the zeal being instantly ripped out of the proceedings. She is now even thinner than before, Lennox considers, making her eyes look bigger and more haunted. He reads Drummond's movements as stiffer and more authoritative, as Gillman suddenly rasps in his ear, — Did ye ride her, Lenny, back in the day, aye?

Lennox hears himself drip more overt contempt than he knows is wise when addressing Dougie Gillman. — What would it prove, one way or the other? Who's really that bothered?

— Well, ye never rode the hoor well enough, Gillman slurs, looking to an assembled snickering gallery of middle-aged

45

male cops for affirmation. — He probably pit her oaf men forever! N whae suffers? Gillman points to his chest, then at Notman. — The monkeys whae huv tae listen tae aw her shite. Man-hatin feminists . . . needed a proper fuckin slammin, Lenny boy. Came up short, son. Lit the team doon!

Lennox feels his teeth grinding together. This is a tough shift. He's forgotten the extent of the slagging culture north of the border, and the unremitting relish of the more embittered strain of Scot, who, hiding in plain sight, amps it up to the maximum. — I deliberately refused to bring her to orgasm, knowing how much pain would be transferred onto you, Douglas. Anything else ah kin dae tae fuck up your existence in a roundabout way?

As the others laugh, Gillman scoffs. He's angry at being slapped down, yet delighted that he's forced Lennox into the game, with the promise of more sport ahead. Deflecting his rage to Scott McCorkel, who has done nothing but twitch uncomfortably during this exchange, he sneers, — And you can shut it, laptop boy. Website wire-pullin cunts, he craws generally at the several younger cops present, hanging back behind the veterans. McCorkel retreats, ears burning red, to the rear of them all.

But they all suddenly disperse like school-gate-loitering nonces on seeing an approaching police car. This flight is occasioned by the appearance of the thin, angular woman at Lennox's shoulder. — So, Ray, Amanda Drummond enquires, — how is your . . . he can see the word *retirement* playing on her lips, before she settles for, — career change working out?

— It's not wildly exciting, but it pays the bills while I paint, learn Italian and do my kickboxing, he smiles. Lennox didn't dabble in art, but knew it was a hobby of Drummond's, one she often used to complain she never had time to pursue. She'd have even less now. If his barb's hit home she's hidden

46

it well, showing no overt sign of regret. He carries on. — Brighton's a lovely town, pretty lively, and London's less than an hour away for museums, shows, et cetera, and he catches her evaluating eye slide to his torso, before heading north again. — So, it couldn't be better really. I suppose I've stopped looking for self-actualisation from a job of work.

— Nice, she coolly retorts, and Lennox can tell that she finds him inconsequential. This is new. He'd sensed himself as exasperating and challenging to her before, but never irrelevant and trivial. Then a sudden brief glance of pathos burns between them, the sharing of a fleeting human acknowledgement of how things could have played out had circumstances been different. It's quickly snuffed: both are ultimately pragmatists, regarding nostalgic sentiment as a cloying, sickly indulgence. — Look after yourself, Ray.

— You too, he says and Drummond nods, turning and ghosting across the room to the senior staff corner. This is a detested turn of duty for them: they would leave en masse after one drink.

The only part of Lennox's past now haunting him, however, is not here in his native city of Edinburgh, but down south in his adopted one of Brighton.

Cardingworth . . . how the fuck are you going to do this?

But the clues might still be contained here, and he has to find the answers quickly.

Let's see how the dirty cunt swings behind bars on the beasts' wing.

But would that really be enough? Would it be sufficient to have Cardingworth brought to justice? He wanted to hurt this man and his cohorts. Hurt them badly. But isn't this merely his personal pathology playing out? Wasn't that visceral roar for vengeance simply an indication of Cardingworth's ultimate victory? Brutal experience had taught Ray Lennox that plenty of survivors of far more extreme abuse than he'd suffered had dispensed with these internal and external psychodramas. They'd moved past it and got on with their lives.

Why can't you?

On Drummond's departure, Gillman teeters back over into his orbit, flanked by Notman. — So, how's arse-bandit country? Brighton? Poofsville? You'll be at hame there, Lennox!

— Give a little action to get a little action, Dougie, Lennox says in tired affection. Gillman's obnoxiousness, in an environment rendered immediately censorious by Drummond's presence, far from offering offence to him, now seems weirdly quaint.

But his response is not designed to give the drunken Gillman solace. — Aye . . . you'll ken, he says threateningly.

— Dougie, it's great to see you as well, brother, and Lennox dips into his sports bag and produces a bottle of Macallan eighteen-year-old malt. — All the best for your retirement, buddy, and he pushes it into Gillman's big hands. — And now, gentlemen, I must bid youse a fond goodnight, and Ray Lennox turns to Ally Notman. — I'll email those details to you. Speak the morn.

— Sound. Notman high-fives him sloppily and slumps back against the bar.

Gillman cradles the offering like it's his first-born, looking at the departing Lennox as if the love of his life has just run out on him. Lennox hears the faint, melancholy tones, — Aye . . . let bygone be bygones . . .

Day Three

9

THE SPRINTER

Puddles splash under rubber Adidas soles, as warm breath steams out in front of him. It may be cold but Ray Lennox no longer is, moving at a steady, even pace down the Water of Leith walkway. From that old single-track railway line, the river crashes below him where it hits a small waterfall. It isn't more than an eight-foot drop, but as kids they had called it Niagara Falls.

The tunnel looms ahead. Lennox has been back here several times as a man, hoping in fervid irrationality his assailants would return to the scene of their crime, to be confronted with this version of him. How he still voraciously hungers for that conversation, all the time knowing that it's wishful thinking. Or at least it had been, until now. But why is he not acting on his instincts, or his memory, and challenging Cardingworth?

Why are you so unsure?

He entertains the prospect that he might be scared of Cardingworth. Not on a personal, physical level, but in the way that so many of his class were of those who had wealth and power, aware of the connections and influence that could destroy them. No longer a cop, his relationship with the state is now different.

Enraged, he sprints into the tunnel, decelerating abruptly to halt right in the middle: that black spot of only several feet where the bend obscures both points of entry and exit and you experience nothing but absolute darkness. In this muffling void he hears only the agitated whacks of his own heartbeat. Shuts his eyes tight. He wants to envision Cardingworth's face, or that of the other men.

Bim.

What?

His regular pilgrimage back to this place of terror and torment; a blind faith that the force of his will could somehow drag them back here from their shadows, into this tunnel to face him.

Get him, Bim . . .

But, as always, there is nothing other than the pulse and burn of the muscles in his heavy legs. Lennox opens his eyes into the same darkness, detailing no perceptible change. He's still alone. Then he hears a loud scream echoing out from the tunnel.

Face me, you shiteing nonce cunts, come on and fucking face me.

Knows that he's the one making that long howl of anguish; that it's wrenching from some bleak chamber within him he's never been able to fully excavate. It lies buried in there, that malignant force, stress bursting it to the fore. Every time it returns, he curses his naive conceit that he could ever have believed it was gone.

Then he's taking a step forward, breaking into a trot as nausea tugs at the contents of his stomach – then Ray Lennox thunders out the tunnel, almost knocking over two Sunday-morning dog-walking men who hurriedly pull their alarmed animals into the side. One shouts after him in reprimand, but although his lungs throb like embers, Lennox sprints onwards, lost in the liberation of his own power and velocity.

Exhausted by the time he reaches his sister's home, he

enjoys the pervasive, juddering ache and burn in his chest. Though desperate to slump onto the settee, the driveway's gravel is crunching truculently on his heels, informing him that Jackie is returning in her 4x4, which she has taken down to the shop to buy bakery goods and milk. — Wait, Ray, she shouts as he prepares to step inside the house.

He turns and places his hands on his knees, hauling in the cold morning air as she steps out the vehicle. — Jack, he says, looking up.

— You look knackered, his sister observes. Jackie mainly lives at home with her family, but is having a long-term affair with a fellow lawyer, Moira Gulliver, who is always on at her to divorce her husband Angus and move in with her. The sister of a deceased adversary of Lennox's and once an embarrassingly unrequited object of his attentions, Moira had grown disconcerted when Jackie had moved first her mother, Avril, then her brother, Stuart, into her home.

Looking toned with her formidable gym and diet ministrations, Jackie runs a manicured hand through highlighted hair. Lennox reckons that her pleated cashmere skirt would have cost as much as he spent on his latest leather Hugo Boss jacket. He pulls himself upright. — I hammered it a wee bitty more than I intended.

Jackie flicks an uninterested nod, dropping her voice in the way of lawyers, — I need a quick word, about his lordship in there. She points to the house. — Little Hamlet.

— What . . . about him? Lennox forces more damp air into his lungs.

Jackie explains how she and Angus staged an intervention and got their baby (perennially, Lennox thinks) brother Stuart into rehab for alcohol dependency treatment. He is now apparently working the AA programme, which is positive, but there's a downside. — He won't move out, Ray. Jackie shakes

53

her head. — He shows absolutely zero ambition to get a place of his own. Maybe you could speak to him?

— Like he would ever listen to me?

— Both addicts, and you do the NA thing . . .

— Maybe not a good idea, Jack. Stuart and I, well, I do love him, but cops and thespians . . .

His sister hauls in a sharp breath, regarding Lennox in the challenging, authoritative way he remembers as a boy. He knows what follows will not be advantageous to him. — Look, Ray, Angus and I were thinking: it's not really fair us being lumbered with Mum *and* Stuart, while you've swanned off down south with zero family responsibilities. I mean, and she cocks her head to the side as she warms to her theme, — it's all very *Ray*, isn't it?

— Well, I – Lennox begins, while thinking: *you've been away from home licking someone's fanny. Don't hit me with this family shit.*

But Jackie is on a roll. — The comfort blanket of an *important case* in *Serious Crimes*, well, that's all gone now, Ray. Busy at work in the twilight pastures of selling alarm systems to old people . . . well, it just doesn't quite cut it in the same way, does it?

Lennox purses his lips. Manages to cough out, — If you need me to send up some money to help out –

— No, Ray. Jackie's nose crinkles like somebody has expelled an odious fart under it. — It's not financial assistance we need. That certainly isn't the case, and to underscore the point she waves at the grand house in its generous gardens. — It's *practical help* that's required. It's about sharing the psychological and social burden.

— What dae ye mean?

— What about having Stuart stay with you for a bit? London is close to Brighton and it'll be easier for him to get to auditions for acting jobs.

— Well, the thing is, Jack . . .

As Lennox fatally hesitates, Jackie ploughs on, — He really needs to work, Ray. That's what's hampering his recovery, all this sitting around. He's been at a loose end since they cancelled his terrible TV show, that *Typical Glasgow*.

Every fabric in his being says *no fucking way*, but Lennox has zero emotional stamina for a family row at the moment. He can only retort, — I'll give it some thought . . . maybe have a wee word with him. And *Typical Glasgow* wisnae *that* bad . . .

Jackie can't help a smile mould her face, as she opens the front door. — It was awful, she declares, handing the small plastic bag of groceries to her brother, singing in triumph, — Take those through, I'm going back up to bed to have phone sex with Moira for an hour!

Ray Lennox shuffles through the lounge into the kitchen, putting the bag onto the worktop. Then he gratefully slumps on the settee, close to his nephews, Fraser and Murdo, a year apart, and both at university, technically living away, but always around the house. Apart from this couched trio, the entire Lennox clan is now domiciled at the large villa owned by Jackie and her husband. His mother, Avril, resides in a spare room, while Stuart ironically lives in the *granny flat* at the bottom of the garden. Lennox has only been in Avril's room once. Has no inclination to go back again. Because he saw it there, when he'd helped move his mother's possessions from her old house. That big oak-wooden chest; among other things, it contained his paintings. She'd kept three of them from his schooldays, one a young 'Mummy and Daddy and Jackie' effort, the other an older but still pre-Stuart offering, of his father driving a train, hanging out the window and waving, as he and Jackie and Avril waved him off. But that third painting, of the three men standing outside the tunnel, was spectacularly out of kilter for a mother's choice of keepsake from her child. It had startled him to look at it: he'd broken out in a trembling sweat, slamming the chest shut. Why had she kept that? There were details in that painting he couldn't recall. Was it still there, in that chest upstairs?

— Seen this, Uncle Ray? Fraser watches the television, a Netflix show.

— No. It isn't one he has heard of. These days he tended to get recommendations from people who had the combination of taste and time on their hands. There seemed to be less of that breed every day.

He regards Murdo, sitting in a lotus position on the settee, reading a law textbook. Lennox can't quite understand these kids; both are at university, one living in halls, the other in a flat, yet seemingly unable to cut the mental umbilical cord. They were so mature and erudite in some ways, but incongruently chronically infantilised in others. Fraser, with his long, tumbling black hair, slender build and honed cheekbones, starts talking to Lennox about transgender politics, which continues an ongoing discussion between them. His nephew personally identifies as something that makes no substantive sense to him. Lennox is unsure of his current personal pronouns, and resists the temptation to ask Fraser who he could actually have sex with, as doing so would sound sleazy, and the boys already have to contend with one deviant uncle in the form of Stuart.

His brother comes in through the kitchen back patio doors from his outbuilding and starts preparing some granola, fruit and yogurt. He glances into the lounge. — Raymondo! No hangover for you either, he sings. — Still off the piss?

— Not strictly, but pretty much in reality, Lennox says, wondering how long this will last. Now that his anxiety levels are up again, fully-fledged alcohol abuse has been sending out daily party invites, growing increasingly impatient for an RSVP. Lennox hauls in a breath and tries to bolster himself against a pervading, bleak defeatism. — How long has it been for you?

— One hundred and seventy-six of the most boring fucking days I've ever had the misfortune to spend on this cunt of a planet!

This draws a giggle from Murdo, who drops his book and stretches out across the settee. Jackie and her husband Angus, despite separate bedrooms, maintained a business marriage etiquette. They generally didn't tolerate swearing in the house but Stuart, as the baby of the family and an *artist*, seemed to have sole licence. This grates on Lennox, although the boys love their transgressive younger uncle. — He looks well though, doesn't he, Uncle Ray? Murdo offers.

Lennox contemplates his brother, now filling up the coffee maker. He rises and moves into the kitchen area to experience closer scrutiny. Enjoys the genetic confusion: how he is the slimmer, wiry one, while Stuart's supposedly poetic soul haunts the chunky physique of a club doorman. They share the restless eyes of their mother; busy, suspicious and a little troubled.

He thinks of that spare room upstairs. Would the painting still be in the chest? Might it perhaps reveal more detail of the men in the tunnel or trigger further memories? He turns back to Stuart, who, clear-eyed, with shining brown hair cut short and sporting a well-trimmed goatee, did in fact look hale and hearty. He was one of those people who recovered quickly from spells of debauchery. A burgeoning paunch has been shed, and his tensile skin has snapped back in a tight wrap around his skull. Of course, this won't always be the case. He will blob out one time too many and gravity would ensure he'd fail to resurrect in the way of old. But, so far, his actor's vanity is his saving grace, giving him enough of a sense of despair in front of the mirror to compel him to suffer the odd bout of detox and rehab.

— Leading man good, Stu, Lennox smiles, patting his brother's burly shoulder and making for the coffee pot. Another acid burn in his gut would be silly but he needs the cogent caffeine hit. — Where's Mum?

— In bed, Stuart thumbs in the direction of the ceiling. — Sleeps all day, Raymie, wanders around at night like a ghost.

— Hmmpf. Lennox rubs at a long-shaved-off moustache. He thought he'd heard a noise coming from the spare room when he'd got in last night.

— How goes work?

— Resting so prolifically, Stuart miserably groans, — that I'm cryogenically frozen in a draughty vessel heading through deep space. Since those TV cunts cancelled *Typical Glasgow* – exclamation mark – screen work has been as dry as a nun's chuff, and as for Dame Theatre, well, she has simply refused to raise her skirts in this direction, despite being ostentatiously free with her favours elsewhere!

Lennox is reminded how much he actually likes the sober version of his brother, his pretention deployed as an amusing affectation rather than acerbic weapon.

— And, Stuart coyly looks at him, flipping his bottom lip over his top one, — I'm struggling financially to make those auditions in the Smoke. That's where the real work is.

— Got to be in it to win it, Lennox quips, checking his phone, smelling the set-up, desperate to swerve it.

— And I'm decidedly not, *mein Bruder*, Stuart raises his brows hopefully, — so I might have to avail myself of that spare chamber of yours in the fair Regency town of Brighton.

Whether Stuart still possessed (or ever did) leading-man

looks was debatable, but time had not weakened his delivery and obvious penchant for rehearsal. And he suspects that Jackie has shared screenwriting duties. He can almost hear her celebratory telephone orgasm with Moira ringing in his ears from upstairs. Now the middle sibling is floundering. — Eh . . . maybe we're jumping the gun a bit . . . Ray Lennox is mercifully interrupted by a call flashing in from Notman. — Got to take this, he says to Stuart's goldfish stare, and makes for the garden via the patio doors, lowering his voice. — Ally . . . how goes, mate?

A desiccated sound abrades down the line as the cold prickles him. — Fuck, Raymie, some night last night, ay?

Lennox is tempted to declare: *for you, aye, but I wasn't pished and I've been up for hours and gone on a fucking run*, but fighting the impulse, he manages, — Aye. But it had to be a mad one to send Doogie G doon the road. He's a cunt awright, but he's our cunt.

A series of incidents flood his consciousness to overload, like spinning plates crashing to a floor.

Thailand.

The boys' trip, where some of them had availed themselves of local prostitutes. Lennox hadn't partaken, but didn't judge the others, bar Gillman, whose companion looked way too young. They had argued about it and he had taken a sore one: a broken nose courtesy of the forehead of his Serious Crimes colleague. As his blood ran through his fingers and his head spun, Lennox's watery eyes contemplated both the devastatingly deft motion of his rival, and his impressively arrogant pirouetting walkaway.

His appraisal of Gillman now seems way too generous.

On rising, before embarking on his run, Lennox had emailed Notman a picture of Mathew Cardingworth he had downloaded from the *Brighton Argus* website. *The monster* had given a young entrepreneur award to a member of the junior chamber of commerce.

— He is that, Notman concedes. — Listen, Raymie, can we meet up, maybe a wee hair ay the dug?

Lennox shivers in the chilled air, pulling up the hood of his top. The cold freezes the sigh that bursts from him. — Okay.

— City Cafe, half an hour?

— I'll be an hour. I need to jump in the shower.

Notman mumbles something in grudging concession. As Lennox hangs up and comes back in, his mother trundles slowly into the room, seemingly legless in a long, billowing dressing gown, a minor stoop around her shoulders. Her eyes screw up. — Raymond . . . is that you?

—Aye, Lennox announces, pecking her on an arid cheek. — Got tae nash but ay, and he heads to the door, watching her turning to him in slow, creaking confusion, — catch ye later.

By the time he arrives at the bar, Notman has emptied half of a pint of lager, and his sloppy demeanour and uneven shave indicate this isn't his first of the day. It is barely noon and the City Cafe is almost empty. Lennox gets a soda water and lime and sits down beside his grubby-looking ex-colleague.

— Did I make a cunt of myself last night? Notman forlornly requests, his eyes hooding and reddened.

— A bit, Lennox concedes, deducing that Notman would place zero credence in any strenuous denial of this proposition. — I appreciate you checking out that picture for me.

— Aye, Notman says miserably, — dae ma best likes.

This response gives Lennox scant encouragement; last night's enthusiasm was alcohol-fuelled and his friend has done nothing. He only wanted a drinking partner. Moreover, with his fretful, bulging eyes and his halting breaths and tense posture, he seems bursting to dump dramas of his own on Lennox, who, within five minutes is thinking about Brighton. And every time he contemplates his beautiful younger girlfriend, any penile twinges are ruthlessly stomped out by the image of a persecuting young man in a dark tunnel: a beast aged into a Sussex businessman.

And one he must now confront. He makes his excuses and leaves Notman floundering in his own weakness.

10

REMINISCENCE AND RECALL 1

— Aye, those were the days, right enough: simpler times, in a lot ay weys. I worked on the railways for a bit. In some ways I wish I never had that spell. Because I was always a maritime man. Life at sea was the best. My own father was a seaman, on the whaling. As a boy it was all I had ever wanted tae dae. Get the fuck away. (Pause.) Pardon my French.

— Adventure on the high seas!

— I went to Leith Nautical College and did my papers there. Aye, I loved life at sea. God, the stories I could tell you about those days!

(Laughter.)

— Of course, there were no boats sailing oot ay Leith by then. But we would get a ship from anywhere, and no just England and Europe: we'd fly aw the wey tae Rio, or Monty or Miami tae pick up a boat . . .

— Monty?

— Montevideo.

— Uruguay?

— Aye! Monty!

Fuck this shite . . . I click the old cassette player off. Those two minging C45s, never seen the likes in years, which means a solid hour and a half of this slavering old tramp, and the poncey cunt trying to interrupt him. I'll pass, thank you! What the fuck is this pish, and why does she want me tae listen tae it? You'll see, she said. It was obviously important to her. I asked her why they were recorded on shitey old cassettes. Apparently, that's what keeps them engaged in that group; an artefact of the analogue era, she goes. Well, it's no keeping me fucking well engaged.

But good on her, and working in that care centre has helped her sort herself out. We certainly can't go through all that daft nonsense again. For one thing she's too old for that now. As for the tape itself, fucking underwhelming: some ancient cunt slavering shite to a therapist about his days on the merchant fleet. They reckon that letting old bastards chew the shit stops them from going nuts and helps them orientate themselves. Reminisce and recall therapy or whatever they call it. Fuck that. Had tae listen tae that pish growing up every fucking day of the week from my old man, always telling me how things were better back then and how spoiled I was, and how lucky I was to be alive. How his dad belted him every day and how I was fortunate that he just battered me occasionally. Well, thanks for fuck all.

Anyway, I'm done with it. I'll tell her later. There are easier ways to entertain yourself. That bottle of whisky is not going to finish itself!

Days Four and Five

11

MY BROTHER'S KEEPER

Lennox heads south on the Sunday afternoon flight, a black cloud of depression draped over his shoulders, a twinge of anxiety nipping his spine. He hadn't had the opportunity to look in the chest in his mother's room: his painting of the three men outside the tunnel. He was eleven years old when he found himself doodling in the art class. Miss Hamilton, the teacher, had commented positively on it, though disconcerted at the black sun, which she'd asked him to explain. He'd shrugged and remained silent. As cooperative back then as Ally Notman is now.

Even more galling, he's allowed himself to be browbeaten by Jackie into taking Stuart on the Gatwick flight with him. His brother had claimed to have a possible audition with a theatre company, not even in London, but Brighton itself. This seemed bullshit, but Lennox is also thinking that his presence might help buy him some time with Carmel, and put off talk of the orgy.

Actually, it's not the first time that Mat and I have been involved in a multiple sex scenario, is it, Mat? Although I certainly didn't consent back then, and in any case was too young to do so. You do remember that time in the tunnel, Mat buddy?

Stuart, crushed into the seat next to him, breaks his concentration, handing him a small package wrapped neatly in Christmas paper. — This is yours. This is mine, and he waves an identical parcel. — They weren't sure that we'd be up for Christmas.

Lennox opens his to reveal a Hearts FC snow globe. It features a reindeer in a maroon strip against the background of a grandstand with a Hanna-Barbera-type sign indicating TYNECASTLE PARK. He gives it an obligatory shake.

— Well, if you've opened yours, Stuart says, seeming slightly put out as he unwraps an identical offering but in the green and white of Hibs, with EASTER ROAD STADIUM on the signage. — Ah, bless, Stuart muses. His brother had broken family tradition, deciding to support Hibs rather than Hearts. It was a rebellion thing, which he specialised in.

This heralds a long silence.

Both siblings are jonesing for a drink, nervously trying to conceal this from each other. Stuart's constant drumming of his chunky fingers on the armrest is getting under the skin of Lennox, who now laments that he never had time to catch up with his old mate Les Brodie. Les hated to talk about the tunnel, but this was before Cardingworth re-emerged.

While apprehension leaks from the older Lennox brother, he gives thanks that Stuart is too caught up in his own dramas to notice. — I'm wondering why I chose this life, Raymie, this *actor's life*, with all its precarious nonsense and constant rejection. His eyeballs roll under trembling lids. — But you don't choose it, that's a myth: it chooses you, and his head suddenly lashes round to Lennox. — Of course, you like to cling to the illusion that you're somehow in control, but what is control, Ray? his brother asks, without waiting for an answer. — Control's an illusion in itself; but let's not even go there right now. Stuart waves a dismissive hand in the air. — They all say though, you're fucked at forty, they just don't know how to cast you, but you come back into your own at fifty. You suddenly slip into the frame again. Yet whether this is substantive or just more delusional nonsense we in the profession tell ourselves simply to get out of bed, I don't know . . .

As he goes on, Lennox reads Carmel's texts again:

> Angela is so game! I think she's totally hot for you!

> I'm going to eat Angela's pussy, make you watch, get you to dominate us and do what you want. Sound good?

Lennox feels a tremor in his trousers.

> You and Mat, watching Angela and me get it on! Of course, you two can also get it on if you like!

The palpitation is gone.

You will let that bastard get naked with his fucking overhanging gut. Then you'll expose him; really expose him, in front of them all. THIS CUNT IS A FUCKING MONSTER. YOU, MAT CARDINGWORTH, ARE A SHORT-EYES NONCING BEAST. TELL THEM, YOU CUNT! TELL THEM ABOUT THE FUCKING TUNNEL!

His hands, white, gripping the armrests.

— . . . was only natural that I believed I was the best person for that part: course I did! But did I bear Gerry Butler any animosity? Of course not! For fuck sake, it happens. Get on with it. But my big bugbear is the directors who somehow think . . .

Lennox would be the last to shed his clothes. He'll wait till Cardingworth did, so they could all see the beast, naked, suddenly vulnerable, the way he'd made Ray Lennox and Les Brodie all those years ago in that dark, spectral tunnel. He would point at Cardingworth in derision . . .

That's the fucking noncey cock that abused a young boy. That's what you dim, useless fuckers are about to take inside of you. SO ON YOUSE GO: SUCK ON THAT DISEASED THING! JUST AS I WAS FORCED TO DO AS AN ELEVEN-YEAR-OLD KID!

— . . . because I feel I've devoted my life to a craft that has increasingly turned its back on me!

— Aye . . .

— You can't even begin to imagine what that feels like, Raymie. Nobody who isn't in this game can grasp the debilitating nature of the constant rejection, and yes, how it does, granted, make you stronger in some ways, but ultimately just how fucking corrosive to the soul it becomes . . .

You will crush his nonce balls, watch them flatten under your stomping heel. See you in court, you will tell the fucker. You'll watch his friends look at him, a pathetic wretch on the floor, then at you, in disbelieving horror. HE WILL LIE BROKEN IN PIECES, WHINING HIS HALF-HEARTED NONCE PLEAS THAT IT'S ALL BEEN A TERRIBLE MISTAKE, BUT YOU'LL LOOK INTO THOSE FURTIVE, PANICKING STOAT EYES AND YOU WILL KNOW!

Suddenly Stuart closes in on his face and is ranting at him. — You're not even listening to what I'm saying, are you, Raymie? I mean active listening, as in *attending*. I'm floundering here; I'm in pain and I'm bearing my *very essence* to my own *brother* and –

— You were talking about rejection, Stuart, and how it's the actor's lot.

— Yes, yes, yes, *well done*, but also how corrosive to the soul it is!

Ray Lennox swivels in his seat, grabs his brother's head in both his hands. Looks in his eyes with maniacal focus. — You're strong, Stu, stronger than you think. And I love you. Mind that. I might no say it but I do. My baby bro, and he kisses his forehead, before catching a perturbed monitoring stewardess, and lowering his hands to smile leanly at her.

— Well, thanks . . . I love you too, Stuart responds in edgy conviction, seeing his brother for the first time. — Is everything okay with you?

— It couldn't be better, Lennox almost snarls in a low voice, frenziedly defiant. He wraps his knuckles on the aircraft's perspex window covering. — I've got my wee brar coming down to stay, and I've a girlfriend setting up something sexually adventurous!

— Great . . . well, whatever it is, it fair looks like it's got you excited!

— Oh, it certainly has!

THE NONCE FUCKING DIES!

The privatised rail transit system in the south-east of England seemingly exists to suck any zest for life out of its inhabitants. Lennox's adrenaline store is already dissipating, but the Gatwick Express train to Brighton is late due to engineering works. By the time it rolls into town an exhausted ennui has beset him. This has infected Stuart, who, at the station, does not complain as Lennox opts to flag down a taxi, although he'd informed his brother that Sussex Square is only an enjoyable, brisk twenty-five-minute walk away, and Stuart is relatively unencumbered with a small roller case. But there are too many pubs en route and he fears his brother will probably find them all soon enough.

On reaching their destination, Stuart gets quickly acclimatised. — Nice gaff, Raim, he moves to the window, looking beyond the gardens to the sea, — the bourgeois Regency pomp of Sussex Square is just the setting for a jaded artist to replenish. Already feeling like this is a good move!

You are in a gang of one.

As Stuart dumps his case in the spare room, Lennox notes he hasn't taken off his jacket. Nor does he intend to. — Right, later, Raymie, he says re-emerging into the lounge, one thumb pointed upwards.

— Where are you going?

— Two types of cat you take home from the rescue pound, my brother-keeper; one is the contented bastard you set down in the nice basket by the fireplace and listen to him purr, he contends, thoughtfully rubbing his chin, before taking up a karate stance. — I'm more the curious type, the abrasive tom who wants to mark his new territory, he declares, and Lennox can only shrug as Stuart sets off to vanish into Brighton's streets.

His brother will be back on the piss, in search of the bar where like minds hung out; those underemployed actors, writers, musicians and painters who'd started out as young guns, possibly had some minor success, perhaps not. Now they spend their time alternately dropping their associations with household names, or bitterly lamenting, within their own compelling narratives, why those supposed lesser talents had usurped their place in the natural order.

For his part, Ray Lennox is happy to be watching *Narcos* on Netflix, working his way slowly through a Chinese takeaway. Then another text from Carmel pings into his phone:

> You back in town? We need to start tying down potential play dates with the others . . .

Play dates?

You were on a real fucking play date when you first met that cunt.

Ray Lennox does not remember opening the bottle of white wine, does not really see it until half of it is gone. It sits on the coffee table, almost bashful, one side in darkness, the other dancing in the shifting light from the television, like an inexperienced but aroused lover caught half naked. In panic, he pushes the cork back into its slender neck and roughly escorts it to the fridge, slamming the door shut like a harsh jailer.

Still sweating in bewilderment, Lennox tenses as the key turns in the lock. It heralds nothing more sinister than the confirmation of the success of Stuart's quest. His younger brother makes a semi-drunk, stumbling entrance with a woman in tow. Stuart Lennox has gone through a few 'sexual orientation readjustments' as he refers to them. From straight to bi to gay, then back to bi. Currently 'reassessing and defining my sexuality in favour of women while still identifying strongly as LGBTQ', he now seems to have returned to his point of origin.

The woman, with her inky hair and razor-sharp features, clings to vestiges of vamp. Stuart hastily introduces her as Juliet before they stagger off to the spare room. Lennox postulates that she's probably an actress. Sitting on his couch, his depression mounts as sex noises emanate from the other side of the wall. They escalate and ebb intermittently in a series of crescendos, punctuated only by what appears to be Shakespearean recitations.

Lennox stumbles through to his bedroom and has a broken sleep, waiting for cruel Monday morning to do its damage.

The next morning he's bleary, feeling the wine, and absent-mindedly walking naked into his front room, his luxurious stretch immediately becoming horrific recoil as he sees his brother standing boxer-short-clad in the bay window looking across the square, towards the English Channel. Two steaming mugs of coffee sit on the top of the folded-down cocktail cabinet. — Fuck sake – Lennox charges back to his room.

Stuart's voice rings out after him: — You didn't tell me it was *that* sort of household, Raymie!

When he re-emerges, fully clothed, Stuart retrieves the mugs he'd left on the cabinet, Lennox irked by noting the hot drinks were not placed on coasters. — Sorry about that, Stu, forgot you were here, he says, inspecting his prized furniture, relieved it seems unmarked.

— Easy to do. I'm very quiet.

— Well, Romeo, the same can't be said about fair Juliet. Where is she?

Stuart nods to the spare room. — Just taking some coffee back to bed, he winks.

Lennox makes tea and prepares some toast with banana and honey. During his ministrations, last night's soundtrack starts up again. He quickly grabs the breakfast, cursing as a couple of banana slices fall on the floor. *Fuck.* He scoops them up into the pedal bin.

As he steps across the room the phone goes and it's Carmel, following up on her previous theme. — My friends Theresa and Mike are part of a group. It's all very safe; professional people, no weirdos.

— If it's what you want to do, I'm game, he restates.

— Can we meet Angela and Mat tonight, and have a chat about how all this is going to go down? There are some issues to resolve . . .

Some fucking issues will be getting resolved awright . . .

— Aye, sure.

74

— Come over to mine after work and I'll roast a chicken for us all. About seven?

— Okay, see you then.

The noises from next door grow louder and more intense. Juliet shouts out a request to be fucked harder. It sounds to his ears like a drunk at a karaoke.

— What's going on there? Carmel asks, intrigue in her tones.

— It's my brother, Stuart, who came down with me. It seems he has a woman with him next door.

— He doesn't waste any time!

— Aye, well, certainly no in that department. So, I should probably get moving too. See you later!

Outside, Lennox finds that the temperature has lifted with the clearing of the morning mist. The sky is a blue you rarely see in Edinburgh in the summer. There's a heat in the sun and it feels almost springlike. The Alfa Romeo is parked behind a window cleaner's van, and the two operatives are wearing army shorts.

When he gets to the office in Seven Dials, Lennox almost collides with a body hastily exiting the building. Both men swivel in time at the front door, the younger man's head jerking as they fleetingly check each other out. He has a surly, contemptuous set to his mouth, and belligerent square-go eyes. The confrontation enrages Lennox, but more so because he realises he is holding a full bottle of wine. Recalls going into the grocer's for some chewing gum. How did this offensively cheap bottle of plonk get in the mix? In flashback he sees himself take it from the shelf and part with five pounds ninety-nine pence. Another entity, a ghostly past self, flitting through Edinburgh's cobbled Old Town streets en route to addiction, has briefly reassumed control of his body and mind.

Sucking down some breath he opts to let the business with the young man slide. Swaggering off, the other party is obviously buoyed at his perceived victory.

Heading into the office, Lennox puts the flask of gut-rot into the big pocket of his overcoat. Greets Ria, checking emails on her computer. — George has gone straight to the Rose Garden for that assessment, she informs him without looking up. — He'll be back at lunchtime.

— Thanks, Lennox says, wondering just what George is assessing, as he heads into his small, dull office. The familiar musty smell assails him; it rises from the damp-ruined carpet tiles caused by an old leak in the roof above, where a disconcertingly light brown stain swells from a corner of the bellied-out ceiling. This seems to have dried out but requires repair work both partners are disinclined to undertake. Lennox kicks a loose tile back into position and places the bottle of wine on a shabby chipboard-and-veneer desk, on which sits an Apple Mac. He falls into a castor-propelled office chair, which seems designed to facilitate back problems. The other embellishments include a grey filing cabinet, inherited from the last tenants, and two discoloured yellow padded seats. The only vibrant splash is provided by a framed 2007 Hearts Scottish Cup poster. Between desk and wall stands a baseball bat.

Switching on his computer, Lennox starts searching local land deals. One theme emerging over the last ten years is Cardingworth has bought a lot of it: he seems to be aiming to become Sussex's very own Duke of Westminster.

Lennox's attention wanders. He thinks about being with Carmel. They will meet after work today. Excitement grips him, before he remembers they will be with Angela and *Cardingworth* and he is crushed. But this deflation doesn't last. He feels his fists clench until he is certain they will crack, as a different brand of euphoria surges through him. Vengeance's hunger dances in his taste buds, itches in his throat. He is going to end this soon. Allows his hands to relax, enjoying the slow throb in them. Jumps to his feet, assuming a boxing stance. Fires out the sharp combinations he knows will sink a bug-eyed, open-mouthed Cardingworth to the floor with an economy of effort. Looks to the wine, wrapped up in green crêpe paper on the desk.

It is telling him there is somewhere he needs to be before he addresses the issue of Cardingworth.

12

I TALK WITH YOU IN DREAMS

Perhaps you believe you're here by accident . . . well, I don't think that, not for one second, oh you'll get a shock alright, I should imagine, you see, it's a funny old set of circumstances that's led us to where we are and I never thought we'd end up this close again, this . . . I think 'proximate' might be the best way to describe it . . . not when I was, say, back in prison with dirty old Wang . . . ain't told that story, have I? . . . yeah, I met Wang in prison, in Shanghai, after trouble with a woman in a bar, she was a whore who brought in her pimp, who I subsequently had to deal with . . . but the cops came and that was that . . . yours truly banged up in that hovel . . . but no regrets as I would never have met Wang and been liberated . . . he was the only one of those bastards worth talking to . . . because he showed me how it was done, what he called the lucid dreaming . . . well, it took me ages to get it, but then I had ages . . . I was going nowhere . . .

. . . I felt myself leaning into the warmth of a body alongside mine as the vehicle turned off the Hunan Road into a slum . . . I could feel the Chinese man next to me . . . crushed by my bulk against the chassis of the van, gasping for breath each time it sharply turned a corner . . . I didn't care, my mouth was dry and my head pounded but you always have to prove master to your immediate needs in such situations . . . acknowledging weakness only saps strength . . . I felt my erection stir . . . I could hear the sly PSB men chattering in Chinese . . . could have been the local Wu or Mandarin or Cantonese or even bloody Greek for all I knew . . . at one stage a truncheon cracked my knee . . . I didn't even open me eyes, but tugged gently on me wrists, to feel the tight

78

metal cuffs that held them together . . . after a while, from under my half-shut lids, I studied me snared hands . . . they were covered in a blood which I knew wasn't mine . . . events rolled back into my mind; a mouth, a sneer, a challenge, my fists and feet flying, pulverising a skull . . . a scene played out countless times . . .

. . . then shoved through the arsehole of a gargantuan concrete building and along underground corridors lined by dank interrogation cells . . . passing prisoners slumped in metal chairs visible through the gaps in doors . . . I was pushed by one guard who was so puny, he couldn't even make me step backwards when I was face-on and he was shoving . . . I laughed and took a kick in the shins for me trouble . . .

. . . I had to remove my jacket, shirt, linen trousers and nice shoes . . . all this attire was covered in dried blood . . . another man's, obviously . . . I tried to estimate the level of damage I had done to him; nose-smashing jab, jaw-breaking right, broken bottle smashed on head that would gush blood everywhere, my hands choking the living shit out of him . . .

. . . photographed against a nicotine-yellow wall, front and profile . . . in the cell block, they made me strip and examined me everywhere . . . I prised me arse cheeks apart and let rip with a fart of rotting stench from the cheap beer and putrid street food I had consumed . . . they threw me some cotton shoes half my size and a rancid washed-out pinky-red vest with a 'V' torn into its neck, and 'Shanghai Detention Centre' stamped on its back . . .

. . . for the interrogations I was shackled to an iron chair inside a steel cage facing a podium where two PSB men questioned me. Why was I in that bar? In Shanghai? Did I know the man I assaulted? I told them he was a thief, that he had stolen my wallet . . . (I never had a wallet, just a roll of notes . . . I gave some of them to the man in exchange for opium and a whore . . .) I had a feeling he wouldn't return so I followed him down the street to another bar, where I saw him boastfully buying drinks for his cronies . . . of course I demanded the money back . . .

. . . he sealed his own fate with his dismissive attitude and laughter . . . his head cracked off the bar . . . then I went to work . . . the

PSB men told me he was dead . . . I felt no emotion other than the obvious mounting concern for my personal liberty . . .

. . . after ten months without trial in the detention centre, I finally went to court, where I was charged with the murder of a Chinese citizen . . . took them twenty-six minutes on the shabby digital timer in the ugly courthouse to find me guilty . . . well, I knew that going out drinking could lead to all sorts, but well, we do, don't we? There you are . . .

. . . at Qingpu Prison a shaven-headed Vietnamese lifer met me at the gate and assisted in the carrying of my prison bags . . . this impressed me . . . he looked a sad specimen but claimed he was cell block 8's 'king rat' . . . I just called him Rat . . .

. . . the nick itself was a dozen concrete blocks with barred windows, an office, a kitchen, a boiler house and a factory, and some nice things too, like a theatre, tended gardens, camphor trees, a football pitch and a parade ground . . . a gleaming, razor-wire-topped perimeter wall patrolled by armed guards . . . Cell block 8 was for foreign men, the adjacent block for the locals . . .

. . . they issued me the fetching summer attire of blue-and-white-striped shorts and a white short-sleeved shirt with blue tabs, and a number, 57829, before taking me to my cell . . . a skinny feller but with a massively distended stomach over tartan boxer shorts opened the door . . . the smell of farts and body odour, the racket of snores and mumbles from the dozen inhabitants of iron bunks with wooden planks and a foam mattress, less than two inches thick, covered with a rough striped sheet . . . 'sleep there', never seen the likes, me, and I'd done nicks all over, I had . . .

. . . Tartan Shorts dumped a filthy quilt on a tight spot between a disgusting toilet and a snoring bald man . . . how could I sleep? I lay with me eyes closed trying to tune out the teeming vermin around me . . . it was moving into autumn and getting so cold . . . and the snores of this old hairless coot . . . then suddenly it was light outside too . . . it must have crept up as slowly as I finally dozed off, but morning came as a shock, announced by a low-pitched horn it was . . . bodies sprang up . . . warders on the corridor banging on the bars, 'Qilai, qilai' . . . you knew what that meant . . .

. . . my teeth banging together as I regarded the bald old Chinaman next to me, for some reason domiciled in our foreigners' block . . . still in deep slumber, seemingly oblivious to the chaos around him . . . then his eyes snap open and he's wide awake, refreshed, a cheesy grin on his face . . . I dislike him less than the other inmates . . .

. . . Oscar, a wiry young Nigerian drug smuggler, serving a life sentence . . . his big eyes constantly scanning me, then whipping away when I met them . . . like a comedy routine . . . he sensed my racism straight away, I make little attempt to hide this . . . I've always regarded the white man as superior to the black man and the yellow man . . . I offer only the evidence of history . . . Oscar was one of the main men in the cell . . . the others were two Chinese-born inmates who held foreign citizenship . . . Zhang from Germany was doing a long-term stretch for people trafficking; Chin, based in Singapore, was here for corporate fraud and embezzlement . . . this trio spoke English . . . they were an obvious cut above the others in brainpower . . .

. . . then I met Wai for the first time . . . the head warden on the block, they all feared him . . . his crew cut with the big ears sticking out and slightly protruding upper teeth giving him a somewhat comical look . . . the meanness in his eyes . . . well, I know damage when I see damage . . . how could I not with my old nan and Baxter . . . dubious sorts . . . but there they were . . . looking at me . . . the humiliation of him blinking first . . . oh I knew he would take a special interest after that, you see . . . it came in the form of some warm powdered milk we were issued in the canteen in a battered aluminium cup, him telling the Vietnamese orderly to piss in it . . . Rat took out his dick, a long, thin toothpick, and urinated into my cup with a big smile . . . handed it to me . . .

'Drink,' Wai commanded. 'All of it . . .'

. . . I took a mouthful, as hot and acrid as expected . . . then I opened my flies, withdrawing my own penis from those rough, chafing linen shorts . . . told him this piss was too weak . . . blasted my waste into the overflowing tankard . . . glugged it back . . . 'This is a man's urine,' I declared . . . watched the Vietnamese Rat crumble dramatically, buckling as if he'd been shot, but from Wai, nothing other than a trace of a cold smile . . . I grinned back in much the same way . . .

. . . we both knew this would get interesting . . .

. . . Wai was notorious for instigating conflicts that led to prisoners getting a beating before being dragged off screaming to solitary, which everyone feared . . . not really a cheerful sort . . . he summoned me several times a week for a 'talk' even though he barely spoke English, in fact 'cocksucker' (which he seemed to find funny) and 'spy' (considerably less so) were the main words he directed at me . . . he got right in my face, attempting to provoke my anger, ordering me to undertake piffling tasks, threatening me with an extended sentence or solitary if I refused . . . instigating all manner of petty humiliations . . . but Wai meant nothing to me . . .

. . . however, I did grow fascinated with bald old Wang, how he took every opportunity to sleep . . . constantly out for the count . . . I had never seen anyone slumber so long and deeply . . . would wake only for food and to shit and piss . . . only sparingly used the stingy, precious recreation time to walk around the yard and stretch out . . . and his face when he slept: so many expressions pulled . . . I realised that in some way I couldn't quite understand, this was a man who was free . . .

I obviously sought his counsel . . . lucid dreaming was his skill . . . I was a keen pupil . . . it quickly became apparent to me that I had to sleep through my sentence . . . I'd always been prone to vivid dreams and found the ones in waking hours particularly wet in their nature, delivering erotic release . . .

. . . I invested more, indeed everything, into the lucid dreaming . . . after all, it became abundantly clear that my own government had little interest in me, just a common citizen in trouble . . . a journalist was sniffing around but evidently my backstory wasn't regarded as conducive enough for public sympathy back in Blighty . . . I was entitled to consular visits, but nobody came . . . I was hung out to dry . . . so I pressed on with my lucid dreaming studies and practice . . . I would even wake old Wang up, he wasn't keen on that!

Furthermore, I'd threaten to keep tearing him from his constructed utopia unless he gave me more instruction . . . but he recognised my serious intent, seemed glad he had a disciple . . . well, they can take their virtual reality and stick it where the sun don't shine . . . techno peasants . . .

. . . the ceiling light was kept on all night . . . at first it was a horrendous distraction, but old Wang taught me how to master it . . . the more distractions I could train myself to sleep through, the stronger my powers would become . . . but we had the harsh wake-up of the alarm and the obnoxious rattling wardens every morning at six . . .

. . . I resented this wake-up call more than anything as my skills at sleep and lucid dreaming progressed . . . I was always more in command of my material in the light sleep and REM sleep hours of morning . . . but Wang insisted food was paramount . . . you could literally die in your sleep believing you were satiated by the huge banquets you had consumed in the lucid dream state . . . and not always luxury stuff, sometimes a nice cheese cob did the trick . . . but they triggered the muscle memory in empty guts that lay heavy with phantom food, while furnishing me with zero nutrients . . . so it was essential to rise for a breakfast of plain rice congee or a steamed bun with salt pickles . . . every Sunday we were offered a boiled egg, regarded by the others as a luxury, but an irrelevance to me . . .

. . . before breakfast, in an open-air yard half the size of a football pitch, there was half an hour of exercise . . . again, I was assured that this had to be undergone to prevent muscles atrophying . . . I punished myself dementedly with push-ups and squats until the guard blew his whistle to tell us the time was up . . . then I walked straight back to the cell, the thin foam mattress and pillow . . .

. . . in my waking moments I was taking instruction from Wang, or we were comparing what we had done in our dream states . . . I asked him who he made love to (Can we call it love? Can we? I think we can!) and he smiled and told me all the things he had done with those beautiful women who would never look at him in the conscious world . . . when I asked him how he hurt them, his eyes would fill with fear and a strange despair . . . but it's all about getting inside their minds, you see, and now that you're intruding in my business . . . I will get inside your mind, if it's all the same to you, and even if it isn't, young Raymond Lennox . . .

13

PSYCHO THERAPY 1

Elaine Rodman's clinic is in Bedford Square, traditionally one of Hove's finest Regency addresses. It's now a mixture of permanent and transient wealth; residents enjoying the grand, high-ceilinged, sea-view dwellings vie with workers in converted office space and student flats and tourists in Airbnb accommodation. A Christmas wreath decorates the front door. Elaine Rodman lives in the ground-floor flat, but Lennox heads to the basement one which is her workplace. He rings the bell at 13.57, observing in satisfaction he's three minutes early for his scheduled appointment.

The room has dark rose walls and a black marble fireplace. A small Christmas tree, tastefully lit, sits in the corner by the bay window as another grudged concession to the season. Lennox feels his feet sink into a lush, burgundy-patterned Axminster carpet. The room is furnished with two large brown leather chairs and a long couch, which Lennox always lies on as it relaxes him. But this time he opts to sit in one of the chairs. He takes position opposite Elaine Rodman, under the huge print of what he thinks looks like a Picasso, but he isn't sure. Wonders if Carmel would know.

Elaine Rodman wears a white buttoned-up blouse and a long black pencil skirt, her legs crossed inside it. Her dark brown hair is cut shorter than he recalls, in a neat fringe, her face rounder and less gaunt. She often wore red-framed glasses, but she evidently has her contacts in, as the specs sit in a case on the table beside her. What has been preserved is the demeanour of contained intensity, as if the psychotherapist is about to burst out of her skin and the act of not doing so requires robust concentration. She regards Lennox, her brows rising a little as if to urge him to speak.

Lennox expresses his gratitude that she can see him at such short notice.

— You're fortunate that I had a cancellation, she says.

He wonders if that will prove to be the case.

Realises she can hear him thinking this, as she scoots forward in the chair. — It's been a while since you've been here.

Lennox blankly nods in agreement at this observation.

— What has occasioned this visit? Rodman asks, clasping her hands together on her lap.

— Well, unsurprisingly, it's to do with the tunnel incident.

— Right . . . She raises her eyebrows again. — How so? she gently asks.

— Well, I'm still confused as to what I saw, or what I remember. Sometimes I feel that I just don't know any more.

— O-kay . . . Rodman's smile is tight and wry. — Let me elaborate: memories aren't perfect reproductions of the past. Recalling a past event is a coalescence of processes, the blending of a profusion of separate details, before making inferences to fill in the gaps in order to create a coherent whole. Such processes generally serve us well, allowing us to make fast, accurate decisions about what we've seen and done. However, a system based on inferences can never be completely true.

Lennox crosses his own legs as he experiences this spiel as a stinging personal critique. He did the same as a police officer: hid behind cop speak. *You told yourself it was about setting boundaries. That putting up barriers was what other people did.* He realises how much he hates professional people.

The psychotherapist continues. — This inferential process, of creating what we remember, is fundamentally distorted by our current urges, biases, stereotypes and expectations. While we tend to permit that our more mundane memories sustain this kind of warping, most of us cling to the idea that traumatic events are different, somehow protected from this sort of remembrance distortion.

The faces in the tunnel: three men. But why can you only see Cardingworth now? They all have his face. He can't have been all three of those men. But which one, and who were the other two? Their voices . . . only two you can remember . . . one was Scottish, but maybe not . . . and not Edinburgh . . . not Glasgow . . . the other . . . English?

Open yawr mouth or I'll carve yawr fookin face up.

His thoughts compete in rattling internal cacophony with the therapist's observations to the extent Lennox has to work hard to focus on her, and tune out his own roaring imperative. — If we can't remember important stuff, what chance have we got!

— Well, current evidence does suggest that in traumatic experiences, a single event like a sexual assault is as vulnerable to memory distortion as a recurrent stressful experience that might involve multiple traumas, like war, Rodman contends. — But that doesn't mean we disregard memory.

— Right.

— Because . . . Rodman rubs her skirt at the knee, perhaps brushing something off, — traumatic memory distortion often follows a particular pattern, where people can remember experiencing even more trauma than they actually did. This can translate into more severe PTSD symptoms over time, as the remembered trauma *grows*.

— So, I'm making too much of this, that's what you're saying?

87

— No, not at all. It's the idea that we have control over this process, that's what's erroneous.

Lennox feels cast adrift. Remembers why he stopped coming to these sessions. They furnish the short-term illusion that you were closing in on healing, before reinforcing the reality that it was drifting away from you. All the while embedding a sense of dependency in the process. — The usual pish. Succumb to the fact that you know fuck all, he exhales in exasperation. — Well, what the fuck can I do about it?

Apart, perhaps, from a slightly raised eyebrow on the second, more emphatic 'fuck', Rodman remains unflappable. — You've been doing it. You work in security systems rather than serious crimes. You've cut out alcohol and cocaine. Right?

Lennox is suddenly aware his head is down and his eyes are tracing the patterns on the Axminster. He thinks of the chintzy wine he left on his desk. It was spooky. Looks up. — If I say 'not exactly', please respond with 'you fucking wanker' rather than this spirit-crushing professional detachment.

— Why do you need that?

— Well, I'm your client. If I've been, as you say, 'doing so well', I'm not now. You've invested time, yes, which you've been paid for, but if I'm bringing my authentic self to the table, I'd like to see some of yours, he looks searchingly at her. — To that end, you must be disappointed in me.

— *For* you, Ray, not *in* you. And you shouldn't be too upset with yourself. I normally struggle to make my clients more self-aware. With you, it's the opposite. You are so incredibly self-critical, in the broadest sense, Rodman asserts, making him feel both virtuous *and* a neurotic loser. — So how are you experiencing your latest reversion to intoxication?

— Shite. I feel I've let myself down. I haven't even properly hit the pish yet, but there seems a certain inevitability about it.

Rodman hesitates and Lennox reads it as her seeming ready to give a lecture on free will and choice. Instead she pulls back and asks, — How so?

— Today I walked into an off-licence to get some chewing gum and walked out with a crap bottle of wine I can't even remember buying. It was the same on a plane the other day, and with a takeaway, he says ruefully, wincing as he recalls the colourful cocktails at the Ivy with George. He was planning on just one. He had several.

— This is a reaction to stress. You are operating on learned alcoholic behaviour.

— You don't say!

— What triggered this stress?

Cardingworth. — New relationship, perhaps. I like the woman, don't want to blow it.

— Good for you, Rodman says. — So, what are you going to do about it?

— Probably get pished, he says. — But this time as a conscious decision.

And he's aware that she's speaking again but he can't really hear much of her response.

14

HOVE ACTUALITIES

Arriving at Carmel's place in Hove, a neat terraced house down a side street off the Brighton Road, Lennox, carrying a bottle of more expensive white wine purchased from an upmarket local store, can't believe his eyes.

FUCK.

Cardingworth, sporting a forest-green jacket, and fawn trousers, sits there on the couch with Angela. She is a slender woman with luminous eyes, long fingers and red-painted nails. Blonde hair spills from under a pink beanie hat, which she removes, to shake her locks out. They have obviously just arrived; she's yet to remove her ankle-length coat, which she does, to reveal a tight black dress and dark velvet boots. She drapes the coat over a chair as Carmel cranks up the central heating thermostat. Their presence blindsides him: he was hoping to settle into the space, psyching himself up.

He's fucking here . . .

Cardingworth holds a bottle of red wine, Angela reading the label while brandishing a corkscrew. No start-of-the-week reticence from either of them. There is something in their movements, the way they stare at each other, which renders them freakish to his eye: images of Francisco Goya's more grotesque paintings, once viewed with an ex-girlfriend at a Barcelona exhibition, smash through his pyrexial mind.

As she takes the bottle of red wine from Cardingworth and opens it, Angela smiles at him. — Hey, Ray! How goes?

All Lennox can do is force an inane grin at her as Cardingworth steps towards him, extending his hand. — Hi, Ray, I'm Mat, we didn't get a chance to be introduced the other night, and *the monster* raises an eyebrow at Carmel, who is rattling some pots in the kitchen area, — you guys scarpered pretty quickly!

Lennox, fighting with every fibre in his body not to be overwhelmed, forces himself to extend his hand.

With his eye contact strong but relaxed, Cardingworth's shake is firm, without conveying any pitiful sense of macho gamesmanship. Nonetheless, a shiver up his spine forces Lennox to confront his own wavering hesitancy in face of this man's ease. — Sorry, Mat, for a minute there I thought we'd met somewhere before, then he quickly adds, — You haven't been involved in the security industry round here by any chance?

— Probably one of the few I haven't had any direct association with. I could do with some advice for my new place, though. He raises his brows hopefully. — Ange tells me that you've moved down here to help keep our good citizens safe?

Yes, I have, you short-eyes cunt. But I won't be keeping you safe.

— Trying my best, Lennox says, waving the bottle of white wine at them. — I should stick this in the fridge.

— Nice Chablis, Cardingworth says approvingly, as Lennox nods and moves gratefully over to Carmel, — though I'm an unbearable red snob, he declares. — But I really would appreciate the eye of a pro regarding my home security, Ray. I tend to be a little lax on that front.

— He is, Angela confirms.

— It's a miracle the place hasn't been turned over!

— Right . . . I can swing by and take a look, Lennox says, almost not believing the conversation he's having, as he smiles at Carmel, noting the tight woollen blue dress that highlights her curves.

— Hi, you. Carmel kisses her confused beau. — Busy day?

— The usual. Lennox slips an arm round her waist, presses his lips to her cheek, then turns to watch Cardingworth slump back onto the couch. He chats with Angela, just out of their earshot. Carmel peels away to deposit the white wine in the fridge then beckons Lennox over to the lounge. He follows, her ushering him into one of the chairs opposite the couch, while perching on the arm. As she talks to Angela, Carmel plays absent-mindedly with Lennox's hand. This gesture almost solicits a cry of anguish to break from his chest, her so unselfconsciously showing *the man* human affection, when *that thing* on the couch desecrated *the boy*.

He looks at the corkscrew Angela still holds.

How easy to tear it from her grasp. To ram it into Cardingworth's eye.

No . . . stay fucking cool. Serve this dish cold.

Mat Cardingworth looks from Angela to Carmel, and then, in a heart-stopping, air-constricting moment, at Ray Lennox. — I'm going to cut to the chase here, *aaand . . .*

Lennox feels his grip tighten around the glass.

15

TRIGGERED

The pregnant pause into which the whole universe capsizes. You can't tear the monster apart, without seeing it in action first. You stand up, your hand going to Carmel's hair, which you take in a strong but teasing grip, as you announce to an edgy Cardingworth and excited Angela, — Let's get fucking started.

You unbutton your trousers with the help of a slash-mouthed, wild-eyed Carmel, letting them slide to the floor, assisted by the weight of your belt buckle. Into this game, without a second's hesitation, she has your cock out and her tongue deftly flicks its head. This is arousing, but you're impatient: you want to fuck her face. Most of all, you crave Cardingworth's reaction, but he's looking away. — Guys . . . he protests meekly, but titillation husks his tone, as Angela reaches behind, unzipping her dress. The way it falls to the floor from her glistening body, skin grey in the light, reminds you of meat being slithered from a kebab in a takeaway.

As Carmel pleasures you with her mouth, Angela falls to the couch, pulling Cardingworth onto her. He's now aroused. You can see that fat noncey cock under his gut pushing against her, his bony gold-ringed fingers tugging her panties down. Angela looks at Carmel in shocked arousal, eyes in excited augmentation, as Cardingworth mounts and enters her . . .

But then you tighten your grip on Carmel's head, not to demand more, but to yank her away, and you're over to Cardingworth. Grab his thinning hair and announce, — It's you and me

93

now, and he's stupefied in shock. A bland response, — This isn't the way it's meant to go down, and you say, — The tunnel, you cunt, as you thrust your groin into his face, but his mouth is shut . . . Angela is screaming, — What's going on here?

Carmel gasps in confusion, — Ray?

But you push your cock against Cardingworth's face, ripping hair out of his scalp. He still won't open his mouth, so you pick up the wine bottle and smash it across the coffee table to howls from Angela and Carmel. Hold the jagged glass against his terrified face. Watch the red wine roll down his cheek like blood. The tears spilling from his eyes. You demand, — TELL THUM, YA CUNT! TELL THUM ABOOT THE FUCKIN TUNNEL . . .

He hesitates, eyes opalescent in the light, yet witless with fear, then says . . .

16

THAT SWINGING BUSINESS

— . . . at the risk of sounding like the old fogey I probably am, this swinging business is *sooo* not my thing. Mathew Cardingworth's declaration pulls Ray Lennox back into the room. An erection he was aware of collapses in his pants as he feels his grip loosen on the glass. Sliding out of his hand, it smashes on the hardwood floor: a mess of wine and splintered glass.

— Ray . . . Carmel chides.

— Sorry, my hand went numb. Lennox rises to fetch a cloth and brush with dustpan. Notes Angela's disappointed frown, even as she snuggles closer to *the monster*. Cardingworth's tight frame tells Lennox that his nonchalance is performance: anxiety rips out of him.

What?

Cardingworth's evident discomfit has forged a defiant set to Lennox's jaw. He looks at Carmel. — Well, it is against my better judgement, but I'm game.

— Maybe it's me, Cardingworth addresses Lennox directly, his face visibly pained, — but don't you find it a little bit sleazy?

It's talking to you. This thing, this monster, is talking to you. About fuckin sleaze!

Lennox hears himself emit a low sound, the significance of which he can't decode.

— I mean, each to his own, Mat Cardingworth declares,

almost apologetically bashful, — but I'm pretty much a one-woman man.

Now Lennox can't reconcile *the monster* with the words coming from the mouth of this man.

Where is the fucking rampant beast of the tunnel? Cardingworth talking aboot being fucking sleazy . . . that fucking monster . . .

— Well, Ange and I were hoping we could all get involved as a foursome. It's just a bit of harmless fun, Carmel protests.

— It's not though, Cardingworth argues. — It goes to the heart of this narcissistic culture of ours. We're constantly urged to expose ourselves. It's like this is the way we as a species cope on an existential level, with this threat to our continuance. Trying to somehow self-actualise in this very inhospitable terrain of the cheap, visceral thrill.

Lennox is mesmerised at the way Cardingworth's voice grows more working class at the same time as his pontifications up their conceptual content. Then Carmel arches a brow in a way that sets up the horn in him. It short-circuits Cardingworth's pompous reason, as her throaty, plummy voice declares, — You might just be overthinking this a little, Mat.

Looking up at Carmel, Lennox marvels at her slender neck, the way her straight back tapers into her buttocks. *Does she really want to fuck this old nonce?*

— I'm not a cautious person by nature, Carmel, Cardingworth declares. — But this just doesn't fly with me.

— I know you have to be careful with your profile, Carmel looks first to him and then down at Lennox, — and that there's plenty mischief-makers on the scene, but Theresa and Mike insist that Gary and Linda's group are all discreet professional career people.

— They're carefully selected, Angela barks in accord, — with very strict rules on phones and recording, and obviously posting on social media.

Cardingworth looks unimpressed and Lennox is finding himself in a bizarre anti-sex alliance with this man. *This monster?* — I'm far from convinced this is all just benign play. What do you think, Ray?

The Serious Crimes cop in Lennox rises to the fore. — I worry about the extreme sexualisation ay our culture, he says, conscious he's mimicking Cardingworth's weighty tones, talking smart while heightening his own proletarian accent to convey a hard-won gravitas. — When ah worked at Vice, ah saw people become desensitised by pornography, and Lennox grabs the handset, flicking on the TV sports round-up.

— Yes, Carmel says, her eyes peering down on him, — but what were they like before? I reckon that we're all well-adjusted individuals here.

Speak the fuck for yourself, honey.

— The best sex I've ever had, Lennox changes track, — and this a bit Mills and Boon, his eyes flick up to Carmel, — has always taken place within the context of an affectionate monogamous relationship. The other stuff is fun, but it's just chasing a high and it becomes inherently unsatisfying. People get into it because they believe it adds spice tae their relationship. Usually, and this is only my experience, it signals the beginning of the end ay it.

— Couldn't agree more, mate, Cardingworth says. — I don't want to come over as a tired old mansplaining dinosaur here, but I suppose we've been around the block more than you girls!

Around the block and through the fucking tunnel, ya noncing cunt.

— Oh, I see, Carmel says, challenging tone incongruent with her smile, — because you've done it all before, we can't?

Angela nods in support of her friend.

— I haven't done it all before, that's the point, and I didn't say you couldn't do it, Cardingworth replies, then adds with finality, — just don't count me in, I'm afraid.

This cunt is a fuckin Boy Scout. He's nae nonce. He cannae be the monster. *Surely. There were three of them in that tunnel. But I see him. Holding Les. Grabbing me by the shoulders. I see the cunt!*

Cardingworth catches Lennox's eyes flitting to the football results appearing on the TV screen. — Not to obviously change the subject, but are you a footie man, Ray?

— The fitba? Aye, he says as Angela and Carmel groan.

— Edinburgh, Angela said you're from, and Cardingworth takes a good-natured elbow in the ribs from her. — Hibs or Hearts?

It impresses Lennox that Cardingworth knows about Edinburgh's two senior clubs, as most English people's view of Scottish football went no further than the Victorian freak show of the Glasgow derby. He is less elevated that Hibs merited the first mention.

— Hearts, Lennox nods. — Not doing badly this season. Brighton's been going well, since they moved to that new stadium. It looks a cracker.

— Oh God, I'm going to check on the chicken. Carmel rises and heads to the kitchen, nodding at Angela to follow her.

— It's been great for the club and the town, Cardingworth purrs, watching Angela depart. — Have you been along?

— No, will definitely try to get tickets for a game at some point though.

— No need, I've a box, join me there any time you like.

— Aye?

— Of course. Cardingworth places his phone on the coffee

98

table in front of Lennox. — Punch in your digits; let's get on each other's radar.

A flabbergasted Lennox can only oblige. A couple of seconds after handing the device back he receives a text, experiencing an undermining surge of gratitude. — Thanks.

Fuck sake . . . this cunt cannae be that good at bullshitting! He really doesnae know me from Adam. He wants tae be fucking mates . . . he couldnae have been one of the guys in the fucking tunnel . . .

— Call me any time, give us a couple of days' notice and I'll sort you out two hospitality box slots for any game; great views, private bar, the lot.

It strikes Lennox that Cardingworth is not only charming, he is possibly the most engaged, *present* person he has met.

The cunt seems plausible, but you wouldn't have reacted like you did, if he's this fuckin saint he makes himself out to be . . .

Angela looks back from the kitchen area. — Well, it looks like we've moved on from boring old sex to riveting football, she says in only partly affected grimness.

Carmel is more direct. — I can't believe that two *men*, both considerably older than us, are trying to talk us out of swinging. She looks at Lennox and Cardingworth in disdain. — It's not exactly nourishment to the ego . . .

It is fucking weird. I can't believe it myself. What's Cardingworth's game?

— How do you find Brighton after Edinburgh, Ray? Cardingworth asks him, pointedly ignoring the women's concerns. Far from taking offence, Carmel steps back, looking from one man to the other, as if she has overstepped the mark. This concerns Lennox, as she never seems unduly deferential in male company. — Such a beautiful city you came down from, Mathew Cardingworth adds.

Lennox takes his chance. — Have you been?

— Yes . . . quite some time ago now. I was at the Edinburgh Festival one year. Got involved in financing a show some college friends were involved in. Back in '84, I think.

Time scrambles through Lennox's head. *That summer of '81, you cunt . . .*

They don't match the tunnel. But Cardingworth could be lying. He has to be sure. How can he be sure?

As Angela tops up the grateful Cardingworth's drink, Lennox gets on his phone to check the Hearts score. Then he notes they have a Wednesday-night fixture at Livingston.

Days Six and Seven

17

LIVINGSTON 5, HEART OF MIDLOTHIAN 0

— JESUS. FUCKING. CUNTYBAWS. CHRIST . . . a mouth opens wide in a salt-and-pepper buzz cut granite skull, fastened on broad shoulders by thick, corded cables of neck. Others in the soulless, sparsely populated, new-build Lego-style stadium glance to the barrel-chested, bow-legged man; chronically underdressed in a black Harrington. Probably thinking, like the recipient of Les Brodie's anguished moan, Ray Lennox, still benumbed in overcoat and scarf, that you could punch that head all night long, only pulping your own knuckles. In the freezing cold at this Livingston arena, name-changed so many times that nobody cares what it's called, if they ever did in the first place, within a fleeting fifteen-minute meltdown for the away side, the home team's fifth goal has gone in, further deadening the visiting Hearts fans. A sending-off had changed the game, but this bizarre capitulation is something else for a club universally known as short on foot-balling skill but seldom lacking in application. — Makin they cunts look like fuckin Real Madrid!

Lennox sees that Les's status as a leading member of the old Hearts mob means his aggressive utterances can still occasion ripples of anxiety among his own support. Two anoraks recoil, while a father with his young son smiles tightly in nervous indulgence. Of course, Les's fighting days are long gone, and a few sneering curses aside, he is a man at peace with himself.

103

Even as cooling grease from his fatty pie congeals on his fingers, lips, chin and cheeks, Lennox draws a perverse delight from proceedings. It feels *great* not to be a cop, freed from the burden of judging petty misdemeanours. Inhabiting a normal world of engagement and friendship with *civilians*. Always circumspect about his police background, Lennox is aware that in working-class Scotland 'ex-cop' often sounds like 'ex-paedophile'. The subtext: *these cunts never change*. His rebonding with Les, however, is about more than his altered employment status.

Both men were resistant to discourse on the trauma of their childhood. Les had let it be known that he had moved on from the tunnel, and that his wife and family had long supplanted it as the defining force in his life. Lennox had taken a more protracted journey to get to that vantage point where he could trust himself around his boyhood friend, to retain the vow of silence on this matter. Leaving the force has been good for him. The remorseless hunting of sex offenders, abetted by copious alcohol and cocaine usage, had a hugely depolarising effect on his brain. Since then, Ray Lennox has been healing. Everything about him was getting better.

Now this truce with himself and the world at large has been shattered by the presence of *the monster*.

But it can't be Cardingworth.

He considers his recent discussion with Elaine Rodman. Has his memory, always tenuous and distorted through poring over thousands of Sex Offenders Register mugshots down the years, now become a tool rendered useless? Were its filters so hopelessly eroded that continued indulgence of this fixation would only propel him into madness? His track record of intoxicant-fuelled obsession leading to mental breakdown is well established. He can't go there again.

But he still has to be sure.

Les has to know.

A twinge insinuates itself in his knee, his long leg pressing against the seat in front of him. Plenty of space in the stadium, but Les had opted to go to a zone stuffed with bodies. Lennox wishes he'd sat by a gangway instead of penned in like this. Such confinement oppresses him. The cold air seems to thicken and gather mass, stiffening his lungs. He turns to Les: — How do you fancy a trip to Brighton? They've got Liverpool at home this weekend.

— I'd love tae, mate, Les shivers in his thin jacket, — but wi this redundancy pish ah'm a self-employed contractor these days. The shekels are gaunny be tight till ah get some work oan the books.

— Ah ken how that yin feels, Lennox nods in support. — But ah'm daein okay now. Let me treat ye tae an easyJet cheapo down tae Gatwick. Stay at mine and I'll get the match tickets buckshee fae a ma— he hesitates, — a gadge ah know. All you'll need is beer money. You'd spend that up here in Luckies anyway!

— That's true enough, Les concedes. — Looks like you've just made ays an offer ah cannae refuse. Thanks, Raymie, lookin forward tae it. Les's smile changes him from grizzly to teddy bear, and he sings a few appreciative bars of 'I Do Like to Be Beside the Seaside'.

They head back into Edinburgh in Les's rusty old van, which grates and wheezes at every gear change. Dropping Lennox outside his sister Jackie's house, his friend asks, — Everything okay wi you, mate?

— Sound. Ray Lennox forces a smile. He's just thinking of Carmel when she rings. He nods to Les with a shrug and hits the green.

— Ray, I owe you an apology. Ange and I got a little *folie à deux* about this swinging nonsense.

— Sound . . . Can't really talk as I'm with my mate Les, up in Edinburgh. He's coming down next weekend.

— Excellent . . . be nice to meet him. We should all have dinner. No talk of swinging, honestly!

— That's a relief . . . sounds good.

— Yes, you helped me dodge a bullet. On level-headed reflection it would have been massively inappropriate to get involved in that sort of thing with someone I'm in a business relationship with. Mathew, she stresses, as if there was doubt. — Incredibly compromising for us both. Ange and I got very childish. Anyway, I appreciate your experienced head on this matter.

— No worries.

— Like I want your experienced head on other matters, she says in her low yawn of a voice. — Get back south, bold Lennox!

— Will do, and he looks at Les. Fancies that if he hadn't been in the van he might have said: *I love you*. What a mistake that would have been, with everything that's going on. — See you soon.

— Look forward to it, honey, she says, and rings off.

He turns to Les, a little coy. — Got a new bird down there. I'm sure you'll meet her.

— Ride?

Lennox feels his lips tighten. — Fit as a butcher's dug, he gleefully concedes.

— Young thing?

— Younger than us: that's for sure. But a professional woman, and he slides open the vehicle's door.

— What, a hooker?

— Fuck off, there's other professions women find themselves in!

— No the yins ah meet for some reason, Les laughs.

Lennox grins, shakes his head and steps out into the cold

air. — I'll be in touch aboot the weekend, and he slams the van door shut, watching Les silently mouth *sound*.

Getting indoors to the welcome blast of central heating, he finds Jackie and Avril sitting up, enjoying a glass of wine. Refusing his sister's offer of a drink, Lennox contemplates his mother, instantly swamped by a familiar, bitter sense of betrayal. How she never comforted him, that time he came back, wheeling his bike, his knees and cheek scraped from being impacted into that dirt in the tunnel.

Because your mother was distracted by the neighbour she was fucking.

The thought seems to intrude, as if placed there by someone else. He raises his hand to brush a pulse in his cheek. Just a nervous tic. How it wounded him to learn of the long-standing infidelity. Quiet and introverted John Lennox, tall and handsome, matching the lovely Avril Pettigrew in looks, but never her outgoing and vivacious temperament. Emasculated by his heart condition: the blood-thinning pills that kept him alive.

Catching her son's gaze, Avril glimpses the judging appraisal that's haunted her for years. Ray Lennox, in turn, tries to fathom his stinging antipathy to his mother.

You don't hate her. She just disappointed you. She knows what she's done.

To his scathing glance, his mother's militant lack of concession to the ravages of age has rendered her grotesque; red warpaint adorns cat's-arsehole lips, mascara highlights baggy eyes riven with tension at the rapidly changing world unfolding in front of them, thick foundation makes a crumpled skin look blistered like cheap paint on a park bench, and a tight dress highlights a body long sagged into shapelessness. — You'll have a wee drink wi your auld mother, Avril requests in snide, manipulative plea.

— No, I'm fine, thanks. Early flight the morn for work.

Avril seems to frame then discard a sentence in favour of, — So, how's my wee Stuart getting on down there?

He's shagging some dipstick.

— Seems to be okay.

— It'll be a good move for him, Jackie declares, as Lennox crumbles internally. All parties now seem to assume that Stuart's current residential status is to be a permanent arrangement.

He's shagging some dipstick and he's back on the pish.

— He's no drinking again, is he, Raymond? Avril asks. — You've got to keep him in check.

Fuck you. You're his mother, not me.

— He's a big boy. He can do what he wants.

Jackie nods in agreement. — It doesn't work that way, Mum. Stuart has to take responsibility for his own recovery. *Is he drinking again, Ray?*

— Fuck knows, Lennox snaps irritably, as Jackie recoils, while Avril bristles in a strange vindication. — Look, he comes and goes. I have a life of my own, and he shakes his head emphatically. — I'm not babysitting him. He does seem to have a girlfriend already.

— Who's this then? Hope it's no some slut, Avril scorns. It seems as if she knows nothing of Stuart's homosexual past, or at least doesn't care to acknowledge it.

That's your way. Denial. And YOU are the fucking slut! You were banging that cunt Jock Allardyce for years when your husband was sick and dying!

— Seems a nice person, Lennox says. — Right, ladies, I'm going to hit the hay, and he rises and pecks both women on the cheek.

Avril suddenly stands up and wraps her thin arms around him. She is surprisingly strong. — C'mere till ah git a hug oot ay ma laddie . . .

This was what you wanted when you came back from the tunnel. How could she not have been like that back then?

She holds him for a full eight seconds before relinquishing her grip. Only the last four are mortifying.

And he still can't bring himself to ask her about the picture.

Day Eight

18

SEVEN DIALS

Ray Lennox returns to Brighton via the early flight and the now normally functioning Gatwick Express. Instead of going directly to his Horsham Security Solutions offices in Seven Dials, Lennox opts to take a circuitous route, meandering to better acquaint himself with a part of town he's only sparse experience of. Hastily cutting through the rickety maze of bland construction at the back end of the station, he descends a set of steps, enjoying the blue sky and a defiant sun's lick on his face through the gelid air.

The giant railway bridge looms ahead. Passes under it. Immediately bereft of illumination and heat. Plunged into dark, wet gloom. Surrounded by damp, weeping stone. Filthy rubbish and teeming vermin. A familiar pressure insinuates on his chest. His breathing ragged.

Lennox pushes his lungs open, focuses on the light ahead, mouths a silent *fuck you* as he steps once more into radiance. Pressing on up the hill, he lets the small triumph invigorate him. On arriving at his workplace, he jauntily mounts the steps from street level, using his key to open the heavy front door.

From the hallway, he notes the ceiling light bulb is missing; it dims things somewhat, though he sees the entrance to the company offices is ajar. This is not the usual practice.

He stops, listens for sounds.

Nothing.

He doesn't touch the door, but steps tentatively inside.

There's no sign of Ria in the reception area, but he immediately senses another presence.

The soft screech of a metal filing cabinet sliding shut.

From behind the support pillar, a shadow spills out across the carpet tiles.

Lennox feels his fists ball as he shouts, — Hello!

A young man, the one he saw outside before, steps out and issues a surly nod. Lennox fights every instinct to ask: *who the fuck are you and what the fuck are you doing in here?* Instead, settles for an official, — Can I help you?

On closer scrutiny the man is older than he first thought, perhaps pushing thirty. Piercing cobalt-blue eyes and dark good looks support his cocky assurance. Something in his face offers Lennox recognition: not in the obvious way of Cardingworth, but still inciting a disconcerting burn. The intruder is about to find his voice when Ria comes in, following him, nervously pushing her hair back, face flushed in embarrassment. — Oh, Ray, this is Chris. He just came round to drop something off for me.

— Hi, Lennox manages to cough out.

— Alright, Chris nods, evaluating him with a gap-toothed grin. — I'd uhm . . . best be going, and as he slowly walks out the door, he trains a glare on Ria. It's tyrannous enough to make her turn away, rapidly blinking.

Lennox senses that she wants to say something, but has registered his anger at the presence of the young man in their workplace. Aware his patience is depleted by his own dramas swimming through his head, he's disinclined to lose his temper at her for admitting this guy. Sucks down his disquiet. Heads into his office, pulling the door shut behind him.

Switching on his computer, Lennox checks his emails. Nothing yet from Notman, so he fires up a search engine and types in 'Mathew Cardingworth'.

A forest of links immediately manifests on the screen. On

opening them, it's the photographs, particularly one, which skewer him. The young Cardingworth looks out at him, hair slicked back, a piercing stare and smug, full lips, as he sits in a chair, chin resting on his fist.

Ray Lennox still can't breathe for a full five seconds.

It's him. He was there.

His fingers exert pressure on the mouse in his hand. He hears it start to crack.

Which one was he?

Takes a snatched gulp of air.

Stares at the picture, the gleaming hair, the self-satisfied, arrogant stare. Feels his neck burn red. Thinks of the killers he's studied down the years, men guilty of far more heinous crimes than Cardingworth. Permits the cop in him to surface. Detaching. Abstracting. His hand relaxing on the mouse as it squeaks in gratitude.

He's just a man. Down you must take them; then you can break them.

As Lennox diligently works through the magazine profiles and articles from trade journals, a composite of Cardingworth slowly emerges. The early days yield scant internet information; he needs to rely on sycophantic business depictions, where Cardingworth, like many of that ilk, presents as a self-aggrandising unreliable narrator.

'I suppose I was always different, perhaps marked out by this burning desire to succeed,' says Mathew Cardingworth. He may be a council estate lad, but projecting an endearing serenity, Cardingworth is no bustling barrow boy on the make. But in this underlying air of calm, one senses something of the swan about him, gliding imperiously on the surface, but paddling frantically just out of sight. 'As they say, you have to keep on keeping on.'

The story unfolds of a bright

scholarship boy from a working-class home on Brighton's notorious Whitehawk estate, who broke from the feral pack of his street peers to head up to London and study chemical engineering. A tough transition for many: but not so Mathew Cardingworth, dynamic and entrepreneurial from the start. Injured in a Tube train derailment, which resulted in a double fracture of his wrist, the Imperial College undergraduate successfully turned setback into opportunity, pursuing a compensation claim with London Transport. With the £3,000 he was awarded, Cardingworth made a deposit on a flat in Camden Town.

'I shouldn't have qualified for a mortgage as a student on a full grant and scholarship, but I told a little white lie about my employment status and claimed that my part-time job as a bookmaker's claim settler was in fact full-time and permanent. So, stick me in the naughty corner, but it was the best fib I ever told. I was off,' Mathew Cardingworth beams, though appearing rather scandalised at his own transgression.

He went on to sell the flat eighteen months later, turning a handsome profit. Cardingworth, though, was never interested in the quick buck. Investing in bars and nightclubs, he rebranded tired establishments into the stylish emporiums that enabled him to slip comfortably into the Blairite Cool Britannia zeitgeist. The land and property development deals increased in scale, but in an era littered with casualties who kept gambling till they lost, Cardingworth, restrained, intelligent and strategic in his investments, seems to have written a neoliberal-era playbook for social mobility and sustained success.

The first thing Lennox notices in those profiles, apart from the fact that he detests their authors, is that Cardingworth, as effusive as he is about everything else, ensures that relationships and romance are a closed book.

'The whole purpose of having
a private life is to have a
private life.'

The second big takeaway, as the clock runs down and Ria
enters with a mug of tea and a sandwich, placing them gingerly
beside him before vanishing, is that absolutely nothing ties
Cardingworth to the tunnel in Colinton Dell in the summer of
1981. What would an undergraduate chemical engineering
student from Imperial College be doing there, with those two
shadowy, older men? *Were* they older? Some sense of them,
opaque, ethereal, flitting in and out of his consciousness, tells
him that it's so. If this is the case, Cardingworth's connection
with them makes absolutely no sense.

The business portfolio outliers catch Lennox's attention.
An investment in Carmel's research establishment is under-
standable, given Cardingworth's own science background: a
way of keeping a toehold in a world he seemed destined for
before his moneymaking drive took over.

One of the branch companies of Cardingworth's group,
Sussex International Developments or SID, is attempting to
buy an old hospital from the NHS trust, to convert into flats.
It's mainline Cardingworth, but it's the campaign against this
project that interests Lennox: the first real sign of local discord and opposition.

'The likes of Mat Cardingworth
and SID are never what they
appear to be,' said Ralph Trench,
of the Saving Health in Brighton
(SHIB) campaign. 'They promise
the world, but will put personal

117

profit before community gain
every single time.'

While this strikes Lennox as a *no-shit-Sherlock* moment,
the use of the informal 'Mat' draws his attention, possibly
hinting at some familiarity. However, three years on from that
article, it seems that Trench has changed his tune:

> 'All we're looking for in this deal
> is that the proposed development
> will have some element that
> encompasses affordable housing
> for families who've been priced
> out of the area. Fortunately, Mat
> Cardingworth, a local man who
> always strives to keep the com-
> munity's best interests at heart,
> has been able to offer such
> assurances.'

Cardingworth wasted no time in backing this up, in what
Lennox is coming to see as a signature move:

> 'I'm a local lad myself, an ordin-
> ary working-class guy who grew
> up very close to here. To me
> this balance between business
> opportunity and meeting the
> economic and social needs
> of the community is basically
> the whole Sussex International
> Developments ethos.'

Lennox looks up the Saving Health in Brighton website. As good fortune would have it, their bimonthly meeting is tonight. He wonders whether Ralph Trench will be there. He'll attend, find out.

But the biggest anomaly is the purchase by another subsidiary, Sussex Conglomerated Industries (SCI), of an old cement works outside of town. Closed for years, such an enterprise seems a bit old-school industrial for Cardingworth. Yet, he acquired it back in 1993, and Lennox is curious as to what he wants such a site for.

The imposing Shoreham Cement Works, the stark remnant of a bygone industrial era, finally closed its doors in 1991, laying off 125 workers. The site, situated by the Beeding Chalk Pit, had been in operation since the Beeding Portland Cement Company began cement production there in 1883, with a weekly output of 144 tonnes. The location was picked due to the proximity of the River Adur, which facilitated transportation of raw materials (clay, coal, sand and gypsum) to the site by barge.

In 1902, a large-scale expansion consisting of several large kilns and chalk wash mills saw production increase to 800 tonnes per week. Railway links and further infrastructure development took place at the site up to the Second World War, when the works temporarily closed. In order to accommodate the rising demand for cement after the war, a total rebuild took place, completed in 1952, with the plant being renamed the 'Shoreham Cement Works'.

Production finally ceased in 1991, mainly because of the limitations of the old technology in comparison to newer facilities in the area. Additionally, concerns were raised that the dust expelled by the plant across the surrounding area constituted both environmental and anthropological health risks. Following the end of cement making, the site was used for various functions, including commercial and industrial storage. In 1993, it was acquired by Sussex Conglomerated Industries. Since then, it has not been used for commercial purposes and has lain derelict.

Lennox's attention is caught by the postings of some intrepid urban explorers. The group's activity involves breaking into old buildings in order to photograph them. Stark pictures and racy text confirm the dangerous nature of the site; indeed, this is the principal attraction for the self-confessed adrenaline junkies. Their website spins tales of avoiding guards, traversing wrecked gangways, scaling the insides of the plant up to its roof.

The need for security is obvious for health and safety reasons, given the perilous condition of the decaying building, and possibility of hazardous materials stored there. Lennox taps his pen on the screen. Wonders if there might be other reasons to keep people out.

His tea has gone cold, but he gulps it down anyway. Takes a bite out of the unappetising cheese sweating between two slices of disintegrating bread described as 'granary'. It proves one more mouthful than he needs; chucks it in the bin and rises, looking out into the reception area. Ria is scanning hard contracts onto a digital file. Lennox does not want her to think his distaste for the inedible sandwich she furnished is related to his disapproval of her boyfriend. Chris managed to incur his loathing without culinary assistance. As the device shines its info-grabbing beam across the documents Ria lifts on and off the glass surface, it strikes him how little he knows about his young work colleague, other than that she lives at home with her parents in Hove.

As he sits back at his desk, brushing some sandwich

crumbs onto the floor, a text pops into his phone. It's from Cardingworth:

> A bit of a sore one for your boys the other night!

Fuck sake . . .

In his mind's eye: a young Les emerging in a broken hobble from the tunnel. *A bit of a sore one* . . . He sucks down air. Finds himself typing back into the iPhone:

> No comment. Still okay for 2 tickets for tomorrow?

> No problem. They'll be at the stadium reception under your name.

> Any chance of arranging that home security visit sometime soon?

> Of course.

Brief rhythmic thrashing at the door. George bustles into his office. — Let's move, Raymond! We're off to inspect the fitting at the Rose Garden!

Lennox breaks out a weary grin. — I ain't forgotten.

— Regarding the contractors, they can be a little snarky. So –

— Let you do the talking. Lennox kicks his legs out,

putting his arms behind his head as both men laugh at the unrehearsed double act. — So . . . how's it going with Polly?

— When a woman opens herself up to you, George says wistfully, leaning on the door, rocking slowly against it, — it truly is the loveliest thing in the world, Raymond, and his eyes expand in awe. — Remember that feeling when you were a small child and you came downstairs to all those presents stacked under the Christmas tree? That wonderment? That's how it feels: *every single time.*

Carmel's smile, fierce, enigmatic, burns in his head and Lennox finds it hard to dispute George's contention. The appearance of Stuart on the scene will be a fly in that ointment, and inhibition may now taint her visits to Sussex Square. Then another romance, less savoury, springs into his consciousness. — What's going on with Ria and that guy who's hanging around? He was here earlier.

— Yes . . . George's features crease, — a distinctly unpalatable flavour to that fellow, but young love and all, so let's cut them some slack.

— Fair dos. I'm just not sensing a lot of love in the mix.

— Good point, let's keep a beady on the situation. Right, see you in Eastbourne!

— Aren't we going together?

— Ah . . . I'll need the car, as in, without you in it, as I won't be coming straight back. Well, of course, you do know it is the weekend. George salutes and marches out the door.

Lennox smiles, and shakes his head. Succumbs to a rumble in his gut. Elects to nip out for something hot to supplement the literal bite of cheese sandwich, before setting off for Eastbourne.

At the cafe, Lennox is issued his requested sausage roll. Then Cardingworth's initials MC, which he thinks of as

MONSTROUS CUNT, flash up on his phone. He looks at them, sucks up some air. Stiffly presses green. — Hello?

— Hi, Ray, it's Mat. All good about the box seats; done and dusted . . . Actually, I'm really calling to thank you for your support in that very awkward moment with the girls the other night!

— Aye . . . no worries, Lennox squares up. Flips open the cafe door, steps into the street.

The following silence seems as awkward as that evening's sexual discourse. Heading to the Alfa Romeo, Lennox grinds his teeth and waits for Cardingworth to break the impasse. — Anyway, much appreciated. It was a bit stormy with Angela after, as I think she and Carmel have a real bee in their bonnets about this swinging stuff, but we've sorted it out.

— Tell me about it. Lennox opens his car door and slips inside, surprised at the sabotaging surge of jovial empathy suddenly springing from him.

— Ha ha, more later. See you at the stadium, Ray. C'mon you seagulls!

— Thanks, Mat, see you there.

As the line snaps dead, Lennox feels a warm glow inside him. Then the image of the younger Cardingworth, from the magazine article, pops into consciousness. His throat constricts. He's rocked by the perversity of his see-sawing emotions.

He draws in a long breath and starts up the car.

19

PSYCHO THERAPY 2

A curious scene greets Ray Lennox as he walks into the lounge-reception area of the Rose Garden Retirement Community. Somewhat precariously balanced at the top of a tall aluminium ladder, a technician tries to fit a ball-like multi-camera device to mountings on the ceiling. To Lennox this contraption resembles the decapitated head of a pedal-bin-like robot in one of the dreary science-fiction franchises he detests. A second operative below, looking nervously around, keeps a white-knuckle grasp on the steps. The problem is that the residents have refused to move from their knitting, cards and sudoku activities, clustering militantly on the furniture in the middle of the lounge. Compelled to work around them, the engineers struggle to fit the surveillance and alarm equipment.

Lennox can see no sign of George or Polly, but a care worker, a tall, bearded young man in white overalls, introduces himself as Gary, shaking him firmly by the hand. — Polly and your friend went for a coffee, he reveals, just about managing to keep the grin off his face. Lennox looks over at the inmates, as they play *one more hand* in an endless game of cards. Mainwaring is again prominent, first noticeable by his booming tones, then the light bouncing off the top of his shiny pate. In spite of his bombast, two men close by lie in comatose sleep. One snores loudly, the other discharges a gentle wheeze through a contented smile. The latter is the big pyjama-clad man in the wheelchair, and he has a visible erection. The other man, the skeletal wreckage, looks enraged even in deep slumber, his mouth ripping open with each snore, as if attempting to bite passers-by. One of the Zimmer frame men circles the scene, his goat-like eyes never leaving the technicians. A woman whom Lennox saw the last time, the fat one, lowers her knitting to follow his disbelieving line of vision to wheelchair man's tent-pole crotch. — Wish he didn't just sleep all the time, she cackles, harpooning a meaty, life-threatening elbow into the side of her bony friend.

— Bloody hell, Brian, Mainwaring shouts, tossing his cardigan over the big man's groin, instantly dismayed that this only seems to accentuate the effect.

Gary nods over to another approaching orderly, a slim woman, who wheels the erect man away.

— Long time since I saw one of those, the fat woman chuckles in playful reprimand, looking to an affronted, then resigned, Mainwaring.

Lennox is gleefully anticipating the captain's response, but then a text pings into his phone informing him that he's missed his psychotherapy appointment. This reminder is swiftly followed by a second note advising him of the two hundred pounds cancellation fee. — Fuck, he snaps, shaking his head as he approaches the technician at the bottom of the ladder. — Ray Lennox, from Horsham Security Solutions. How's it all going?

— Mike Farningham, the bath-brush-haired operative nods, keeping his hand on the metal. — This is Fritz, he points up to the engineer above, who winks down at Lennox. — We're getting there, Farningham declares. — Most of the alarms and cameras are in. This multi-angle HD-TVI-AD8 is a big job, mainly because of the mountings, and well . . . he scans the gloomy residents, before correcting a wobble on the ladder, as Fritz, cordless drill in hand, tries to insert another screw to secure the unit onto its mounting, — it isn't ideal. But we'll persevere. Well worth it, because they're great machines and the DNR produces a fabulous image quality by removing graininess, especially useful in black-and-white mode when the IR LEDs are active. It also –

— Great stuff . . . Excuse me, Lennox says briskly, turning away to text George:

> Where are you?

Not far. Is everything in hand?
Got a little bit involved on stuff.
Can come back if you need us.
Bit of a Friday vibe on though . . .

> It's all okay, you're good.
> Will see how long the boys
> are going to take to do a
> test then get back to you.

Lennox gets a rough estimate from the technicians, relieved that he won't be here more than an hour. Nods to Gary, then scrolls onto his phone, opening another link on Cardingworth.

— FUCKING WHORES OF BABYLON! A rasping screech in the air, like somebody being strangled. Lennox watches the skeletal man dramatically pop to his feet, like a puppet suddenly tugged into life.

Gary is moving over to try and calm him, but before he gets there, the skin-and-bone man pushes Mike, the ladder-holding operative, square in the chest. Off balance, the engineer topples over a chair. Mike contorts to avoid crushing the thin woman, but his minimal contact still results in her spilling her

126

scalding hot tea over the bare legs of her fat friend. The obese woman screams out in banshee violation, — YOU FAHH-HKING DOZY CAAAH!!

The skeletal man grabs the ladder with both hands and, his body rigid, shakes it with demented violence. — YOU'RE FUCKING ANIMALS! THE LOT OF YOU!

On his perch, Fritz desperately attempts to keep his balance as the ladder wobbles and swings. Gary is trying to steady it, while prising the old boy's hands away, but it's as if the hook-like fingers are welded onto the metal. — Connor, come on, mate . . .

Fritz jumps off the toppling ladder, leaping towards an empty couch. He manages to land on it, but as the metal steps fall, they smash the Zimmer frame man's shoulder, knocking him to the polished tiled floor. He drops like he's been shot in the head by a sniper. Checking his neck, Lennox finds a faint pulse. More orderlies, including the woman from before, are on the scene, trying to sort out the chaos. Lennox is happy to cede his place to Gary and get back on his feet, while two care staff members escort the shouting, cadaverous Connor away. Then urging cries to look up fill the air, as the dome camera springs free from its precarious set of mountings, hitting the floor in a mini explosion, which sees it miss Mainwaring by six inches. — Never a dull moment, the captain says passionlessly. There's a couple of seconds, which feels to Lennox like sleep, before something ignites Mainwaring into litigatious threat. — Lawyers . . . I'm getting in touch with my bloody lawyers . . . He attempts to make fierce eye contact with Lennox, who at that point whips out his phone and texts George:

> Looks like I spoke too soon.
> Wee bit of an incident here.
> You may want to return.

> Copy that. On our way.

George and Polly arrive fifteen minutes later. Lennox notices her hair is wet but it isn't raining outside. She immediately ushers Gary, who looks like a man preparing for his own execution, into her office. As she steps inside, she kicks off her shoes with angry purpose, slamming the door behind them. George raises his brows in deadbeat solicitude and confers with Fritz, who has hurt his arm in the fall. Then he turns to Lennox, dropping his voice, — Not a problem, Ray, it's all covered by their insurance.

The early reprieve is gratefully snatched at. — Enjoy your weekend, he sings to George.

— And you. Any plans?

— A bit of football the morn and a few beers with an old mate. Then we'll get dinner later with Carmel.

— Good show, George salutes him with two fingers above the eye, Benny Hill style, as a pugnacious-looking Polly and hangdog Gary emerge bickering from the office. Lennox now sees a more formidable side of the centre manager.

The early-afternoon winter sun is blindingly strong as Lennox drives back to Brighton. He decides it might be time to do that personal security check on Cardingworth's house. The cop in him opts not to phone in advance: always better an old-school 'cold call' if you want to catch someone doing something they shouldn't.

Western Esplanade, lazily dubbed 'millionaires' row' locally, is regarded as Brighton's most expensive residential street. As the luxury sea-fronted dwellings spin by, Lennox considers you would need more than a few million to live here.

He's a nonce. Or is he? You need to find out and quickly, before it drives you insane.

Circling around the Cardingworth residence, he's struck by how much its generic design evokes Hollywood rather than Sussex. From the road it's a white pillbox walled-and-gated LA cokepad. The beachside balconied rear, with its floor-to-ceiling windows, looks out over the sands and the English Channel, revealing nothing inside. The modernity is almost a disappointment: Lennox had pegged the vintage red wine-swilling Cardingworth as a resident of a traditional country pile. Of course, it's probable that he'll have both.

Slipping into pro mode, Lennox rounds the dwelling one more time. Breaking in here will not constitute an insurmount-able problem for seasoned burglars. The infrared IP security camera fails to display the small red light beneath its lens, and he reads it as deactivated. Knows most pros will see it that way too. Disappointment insinuates again: this laxness seems to further distance Cardingworth from the criminality Lennox is desperate to attach to him. Then the echo of staccato clanking as an electronic garage shutter door slowly opens up.

Lennox reverses back to the street corner. Watches Card-ingworth drive out in a gold E-Type Jaguar.

His first instinct is to sound the horn, but as Cardingworth drives past him, Lennox opts to track the car up Basin Road, past the seafood wholesale outlet towards Kingsway. He assumes that his quarry will be heading back into town, where the offices of SID are located. But Cardingworth turns left, making for Portslade.

Then the Jag sharply takes a corner off the coast road, tear-ing up a steep hill at a velocity so blistering Lennox feels his target must have not only detected him but also determined his intentions. He floors the accelerator, heading up a winding lane in pursuit, but it seems as if Cardingworth has disap-peared. Then, through a set of bushes and trees, a monstrous industrial building looms before him. Lennox casts his eyes on two conjoined austere brown-grey blocks, which he assumes are concrete storage silos. This is the disused Shoreham works that Cardingworth bought years ago.

The slip road ahead is deserted, so Lennox pulls up in a lay-by. Getting out the car, he crosses the road, and catches the golden, metallic gleam of Cardingworth's Jaguar, still eminent through the darkened shadow cast over it by the huge monolithic structure and the perennial foliage resistant to winter's bite. It's apparent the periphery of this formidable edifice has been landscaped for all-year-round concealment from the road.

The massive building has blotted out the sun, and Lennox, bitten by the cold, crouches behind a jumble of shrub to get a better view. Two voices come into earshot. One is Cardingworth's. His tones, replete with swaggering gesticulation, are earthier than the haughty fare he habitually serves up. The man he talks with stands at a makeshift checkpoint, wearing a security guard uniform.

Surveying as much as the shrunken bracken permits, Lennox notes that the Jaguar is the only vehicle around. The guard, and the tall barbed-wire fence rising from behind the mass of withered and sooty branches, means they are serious about deterring people from entering these abandoned works.

The men's conversation fades. Cardingworth climbs back in the Jag, tearing out the complex, presumably returning to Brighton. Rather than give pursuit, Lennox elects to take a further look at the plant. His gut screams that Cardingworth has secrets. Fancies some might be contained in this concrete castle. The guard looks to have vanished into the Portakabin. Opening the camera on his phone, Lennox starts filming the massive gunmetal building, taking care not to walk through the huge gates over the property line.

Suddenly the watchman egresses the cabin, rushing towards him with outstretched hands. — Stop!

Lennox switches off the phone, but stands his ground. The man continues to advance. Gets to within ten yards from the gate, slowing down to a rolling stride.

— Hello, Lennox smiles cheerfully.

Wheezy and overweight, the guard bears a startling resemblance to the Uncle Monty character played by Richard Griffiths in the film *Withnail and I*. — You have to delete that video, he commands, fractured words gurgling from his throat.

— Stunning example of Victorian industrial architecture . . .

The guard's setback eyes expand under his thick spectacle frames, as he squeals: — I said you need to delete that video!

— Really? Lennox stays relaxed. Allows a hint of cop to slide into his tones. — I'm not trespassing, glancing at his confirming feet, still on the right side of the line. — On whose behalf? Who is requesting this?

— I am!

— Who do you represent? He ramps up the polis voice. — Who owns this building?

It puts the guard on the back foot. — I'm not at liberty to discuss that –

— Then I'm not at liberty to delete my video.

The guard's nostrils flare, as he regards Lennox in a twisted pout, as if he's cheated at some game everyone should know the rules of. — This is private property!

The game is the English class system and traditional deference. — Whose private property?

— None of your business! I'm going to call the police, the guard screeches. His violated stare gets to Lennox. The modern working-class Englishman: the radicalism of yesteryear evaporated, this serf would defend to his death the right

131

of his taxation-avoiding billionaire master to pay him a pittance.

— I'll save you the bother; I *am* the police, Lennox lies. — And I'm returning with a search warrant.

The guard is almost hyperventilating, sucking in heavy breaths. Manages to clamp his jaw and cough through his teeth, — Good, please do that!

Lennox freezes on *I will*; breaks instead into siphoning laughter. *I'm being dragged into Little Englander last-word pomposity.* Waves nonchalantly at the guard in departure. Jumps into his car.

By the time he reaches Brighton, darkness has weaved in. The retreating sun has taken any warmth in the air with it. People are wrapped up in bobble hats, scarves, gloves, long coats and boots. Festive cheer, defiant, optimistic, hangs in the air. It induces an alcohol craving and Lennox still has an hour to kill before the commencement of the SHIB meeting. Parking up the Alfa Romeo, he opts to hit Nando's for some chicken and sweet potato wedges. Carmel calls and tells him that she's working late. He senses a detachment about her. Quickly puts it down to his own paranoia. A dinner is arranged for after the game on Saturday night, when she will meet Les.

With its fusty smell and oak panelling, the hall reminds Lennox of a hundred buildings of this era he's set foot in. Unlike many of them, it's perversely overheated. Sweating in a sparse crowd of about twenty people, he immediately removes some layers. Hangs his overcoat and hooded top on one of the hard, metallic green folding chairs at the back of the hall. On the stage, five people, three of them men. Lennox tries to determine which is Ralph Trench. But then they are joined by a chubby, ruddy-faced man. Flustered and out of breath, he mumbles apologies at the others present. Lennox realises that all along he was seeking the security guard he just left at the concrete plant.

So Cardingworth has given fat boy a security job to get him onside. I wonder what else he's put his way?

The meeting commences and Lennox quickly succumbs to boredom. Local politics in Britain was generally dull; the preserve of on-the-spectrum pedants, whether left, right or centre. Those procedurally obsessed committee nuts could suck the funk out off any occasion. Ralph Trench is silent, but the way people look to him makes Lennox deduce this is not his usual modus operandi.

Mercifully, the meeting wraps up in under an hour. As the participants disperse, Trench chats briefly to a small group before leaving the hall alone. Lennox, hanging back in shadow, follows him outside.

In the stinging cold air that has rolled in from the sea, the others head across the car park to the pub it was mentioned they would adjourn to at the end of the meeting. Lennox hopes that this will also be Trench's destination. Feels annoyance when the portly security guard-cum-campaigner heads off in the other direction. Thinks Trench is going to a car and prepares to confront him for another, more extensive chat. However, his quick-stepping quarry steals off, exiting at what his pursuer sees as a badly lit street of industrial units.

Taking care to hang back, Lennox follows the chubby man up a winding road. Hood up and head down, he looks at the wet pavement, avoiding puddles. The footsteps ahead suddenly stop slapping in their hollow, echoing sound. Raises his gaze to find that Trench has mysteriously vanished. He couldn't have already turned the blind corner up ahead, nor had any vehicle passed to offer him carriage. Trench had to have gone into the adjacent graveyard, through the narrow space at the half-open gate Lennox now approaches. Hesitates for only a second before stepping through it.

It's almost pitch-black inside the burial ground, to the

extent he struggles to discern the gravel path from the grass verges. Then it seems to flash into Gothic art-school photography life. A blinking moon, intermittently forcing its way through smoky clouds, provides the illumination. The boneyard seems deserted and he can't distinguish Trench's figure, even when he hears a mumbling noise softly insinuate through the still night. Thinks it might be a prayer.

Lennox creeps closer to the source of the sound.

Dry, frosted leaves crackle under his feet.

Then Lennox feels his shoes sink into soft, damp turf and he crouches down low behind a tombstone. Hands gripping the cold marble to assist his balance, he peeks out. Sees Trench in profile, kneeling in front of a grave, grey flannel trousers partly blackened by the sodden turf. Lennox hears him mutter, — Sorry I've been negligent, Gavin, but we're so close . . .

Then the voice becomes more muted. Struggling to hear, Lennox pushes himself to a standing position and slowly approaches. — Ralph Trench?

— What the hell? Trench squeals, turning and rising unsteadily to his feet, backing away.

— Ralph, I just want a word, mate. Lennox takes a further couple of steps towards him, and glimpses the grave Trench was talking at.

— Who the hell are you? You're not a cop!

— Look, I need to –

— Keep away from me, Trench shrieks, opening his coat. There's a glister, as he pulls out what looks like a large blade from an inside pocket. — I'm warning you!

— Whoa . . . Halting his advance, Lennox flips up his palms. Trench's nervous shaking indicates that the security guard is not used to carrying weapons of this sort. But Lennox is also aware that the most dangerous men are often the most desperate ones, and with his bulging eyes and man-boobs rising dramatically with hyperventilation, Trench fits the bill. — I'm not looking for trouble, Lennox insists. — I'm not who you think I am –

— You don't have a fucking clue what I think, Trench snarls, backing into the shadows.

— Ralph, wait –

— FUCKING LEAVE ME ALONE! Ralph Trench suddenly storms forward, waving the huge knife above his head. Lennox freezes only for a second before running behind the gravestone, determined to keep it between him and Trench's blade. Trench looks from him to the inscription on the tombstone. Something flashes in his eyes; guilt, remorse, Lennox can't read the look. Then he backs away, retreating into the darkness, leaving Lennox aware of the accelerated thrashing of his own heart in his chest.

Disinclined to follow Ralph Trench through the gloomy rows of stones, he instead steps out warily, and turns to the grave:

GAVIN KEITH CARTER

Born 1969
Died 1984

We will never forget.

Love from Aunt Lily and Uncle Tommy

What the fuck is this?

Trying to take a picture of the gravestone, Lennox realises that he needs to operate his flash function. His phone quivers so much in his hand it requires three goes before he gets a suitable image.

Just as he's satisfied, a more human and personal text, from Elaine Rodman:

> Ray, please call me. I want to talk to you about a treatment called EMDR. Eye movement desensitisation reprocessing.

This is not what he wants to hear right now:

> Aye? How much will that cost me? Another 200 quid for fuck all?

His cold, trembling paws shake as he slips the phone back into his pocket. Teeth hammer. Eyes struggle to adjust to the shifting light. Thinks of what could have happened with that blade, here in this lonely graveyard. Hears another text pop in. Ignores it, tugs his collar tight, and gingerly retraces his steps back out onto the poorly lit street.

Day Nine

20

EXECUTIVE BOX

Like the last match Ray Lennox and Les Brodie had attended, Brighton versus Liverpool takes place in a new-build stadium, but this one illustrates the television money disparities in the football industries north and south of the border. Lennox is ill at ease, though: he retains a fondness for the crumbling terraced death traps of his youth.

The box is actually a substantial room with a private bar running along one side. Banquet tables offer a bounteous buffet spread. An edgy, crusty-eyed Lennox scans warily for Cardingworth, peeping out through the glass doors that lead to the seated area overlooking the pitch. No sign yet. It's even more reassuring that Ralph Trench and his sword are absent; it's not beyond the possibility that the demented security guard will show up today. Taking position at the bar with Les, Lennox downs one pint, then another. It's the fizzy, cheap British lager he tries to avoid, but there is no pleasantly wrecking strong continental brand. The tension of the situation and the disinhibiting proximity of his friend are impacting on the pacing of his drinks.

He'd not slept last night, and stifles a tearing yawn. Online until the small hours, he'd tried to learn about Gavin Carter's death, focusing on the camera image of that tombstone. While inscribed with only the base details of a young life, it was clearly one that meant a lot to Trench. What happened to

Gavin back in 1984? Lennox shudders again. Could this be a boy who never made it out of the tunnel?

We're almost there.

Last night's researches had served up disturbing information. The perfunctory notices from the archives on the *Brighton Argus* website, the only press pieces he could find, were straightforward enough. The first one related to the boy's disappearance, with a picture of a Julie Wilkins, who looked in her late twenties, under the caption: WORRIED SICK: A MOTHER'S FEARS FOR HER FOSTER CHILD.

In the picture Julie, wearing a short-sleeved dress and a stagy mournful expression, sits on a settee smoking a cigarette. On her arm is a tattoo of what looks like a winged angel. But the grainy image exemplifies the photographic technology and bad newspaper reproduction values of the time, further compromised by sloppy digital transfer. Despite this, she evidences a fierce, hawk-like beauty in her sharp jawline and cheekbones.

But the strange thing was the absence of an accompanying article. Then the numbering sequence showed Lennox that two pages had been removed, or not put online. He could find no details of Gavin's vanishing, nothing about his Aunt Lily or Uncle Tommy.

His unease swelling, Lennox had moved from Gavin Carter's vanishing to his death. Engrossed at his computer, he barely heard Stuart stagger in, accompanied by the giggles of Juliet or some other woman. The *Argus* used the same photo of Julie Wilkins, but had blown it up and cropped it to a headshot, smudging the scant detail further. But once again, two pages in the newspaper archives were missing, and the only reference to Gavin was a short article:

FOSTERED RUNAWAY IN DROWING TRAGEDY

The body washed up on the beach at Hove on Wednesday evening has been identified as Gavin Keith Carter (14) who was reported as a runaway four months ago by his foster mum, Julie Wilkins. 'We are heartbroken. Gavin was a lovely boy. Yes, he had his problems, but he was fighting through them.'

Gavin had been in foster care with Mrs Wilkins (28) of 15 Rodgers Court, Preston Park, and her family for eight months. Unfortunately, during his spell with them, Mrs Wilkins became estranged from her husband, Clive, who then left the family home. 'I think this turmoil upset Gavin, as they were very close.'

Sussex Police had put Gavin on their missing persons register, and are now awaiting the coroner's report.

Gavin was the kid who never made it out of the darkness.

Now Lennox is here with Les, who did. After staying up all night, he'd met his old mate off the Gatwick Express at Brighton station. Les had obviously enjoyed a couple of drinks at the airport and on the plane. After some more, they took a taxi to the stadium, ensconcing on bar stools in the suite. Lack of sleep grits Ray Lennox's eyes, his stomach is tight, his mind fast and his tongue loose. — Do you ever hear from Curtis, the wee Hibby cunt?

The recollection of a childhood friend makes Les's face expand in a smile. — Was he no living down in Kent with some bird, last I heard? Thanet? Is that far?

— No too far, Lennox says, realising he doesn't know. How long would it take to get there from here? He toys with googling it, but is distracted by a tug on his bladder. Stretches, trying to expel his anxiety, heads to the toilet. En route he calls Mike Regis, a senior journalist on the *Argus*, asking him if they kept print copies of the old newspapers at the office. He's informed that the paper donated them to the Sussex local archive at the library, in return for presenting them with a set of the digital copies they made, subsequently put online via the *Argus* website.

In the toilet his evicted piss drills the steel latrine as Lennox's head spins with alcohol taken way too quick. Blood pounds in his brain and his heart thumps. Thinks back to that incident in Miami. As a beast washed its hands after urinating, he'd pounced, smashing the creature's head repeatedly against the sink. That thick, black-red blood on the porcelain, splashing onto the mirror and tiled floor. His vengeful triumph and elation; how it was swiftly followed by the evaporation of adrenaline, and the huge emotional downcurrent pulling him into blackness.

It's going to happen now . . . it has to . . . something has to happen now . . .

It's as if he willed it. As he returns from the toilet, the calamity unfolds right in front of him, in slow motion. Les Brodie staring, wild-eyed, at Mat Cardingworth, who chats easily with another man. A frozen Ray Lennox watches his friend's expression change in one heartbeat from shocked prey into focused predator. That beat chills the room, drawing the oxygen from it, immobilising everyone, as Brodie, in insect focus, swiftly advances across the floor.

Fuck . . .

Lennox hears a gasp of air leave his own body as his friend picks a beer glass from the bar, smashes then corkscrews it into Mathew Cardingworth's face in one viciously controlled movement.

Under the total paralysis of horror, Lennox can only observe.

Now I'm sure. But fuck sake . . .

In the chaos that follows, the shocked punters are further debased by Les Brodie's guttural roar, — YA FUCKIN NONCEY CUNT!

Brodie stands over Cardingworth, who has fallen to his knees, trying to hold his face together. Claret drips through his hands, cascading onto the beige carpeting. Brodie's animal certainty brokers no resistance from the box attendees. His own hand cut and spilling blood, Les heads bulging-eyed and trembling in rage to Ray Lennox. Pointing to Cardingworth, still on the floor, the shocked patrons surrounding him, his scarlet face declares, — It's him, Raymie! That's the fuckin beast right thaire! CUNT FAE THE TUNNEL!

It dawns on Lennox that in his state of immobilisation he and Les are once again those two young kids, frozen by the abomination of circumstance and the mounting hostility around them. Tightly grips Les's arm, holding it like he would the leash of a dog. Blood splatters from his friend's hand onto his sleeve. From the floor Cardingworth murmurs a lament of breathless injustice as his jolted cronies attend to him. Lennox no longer senses the wretched figure as a paedophile rapist. Wonders if Les feels the same. Then questions how fleeting this again rebooted perception will be. In a disconcerting haste, both security and police are on hand. Accusing fingers jab at Les, still too shocked to respond. He stands rigid, like an ornamental Spanish bull on its hind legs. Lennox can no longer see Cardingworth through the shouting, threatening forest of bodies edging forward. Mob-brave, the way men so often were in demythologised reality; now that the police were around Les, carting him away, coaxing and harassing him into animation.

Lennox looks at a squat youngish copper who has the main grip on his friend's forearm and bicep, and feels moved to declare, — There's things going on here that you know nothing about!

143

The cop shakes his head, turns to a now doe-eyed Les, still diminished into bewildered boyhood by events. — I know that he needs to go down the station!

Lennox can't disagree. Takes a step back, as the policemen remove Les. Feels a sudden push in his chest, and looks to see a sturdy man, silver hair slicked back, bolstered at his side by several others. — Fucking animals!

— Your friend is going to jail for a long time, another man, athletic build, thinning hair, stabs the air in front of Lennox's face.

Pivoting sideways into boxer stance, so the shoving adversary knows he is not for being moved, Lennox snaps, — Youse ken fuck all. You have no business to lay your hands on me, he barks in cop-like authority at the stocky hustler. — Do so again and you will lose your teeth. Am I making myself clear?

The would-be combatant is silent but his eyes flicker and his hands drop to his side.

— Your friend had no business attacking Mat! the finger pointer declaims.

Without taking his eyes from them, Lennox nods behind him, where Les and the arresting officers are vanishing through swing doors. — No, and he's being removed by the police for that. I've attacked *nobody*, he declares, looking at the assembled eyes, the unspoken *yet* hanging in the air. And he realises that he craves one or more of those men to come forward. Senses his growing power over them, wishes to unleash some of it.

This is fucked up.

Forces air into his lungs and turns, leaving the pack. Follows Les and the huckling uniformed cops. In the corridor, he runs to catch up with them. — Les, he shouts. His next sentence freezes in his mouth: *which one from the tunnel was he?*

144

— Let me handle this, Raymie, Les barks, half turning in the policemen's grip, yet offering no resistance. — Let Cathy ken and get a lawyer!

— Done, Lennox shouts, scrolling through his phone as he pursues them towards the stairs.

21

CLIENTS AND PAYMASTERS

After calling George, who puts him onto a lawyer acquaintance, Lennox lunges into the car park, jumps in the Alfa Romeo. Follows the police vehicle, bound for the local nick in John Street. Gets close enough to see the back of Les's shaven, thick-necked head. Wishes his friend looked like a hipster, rather than central casting's archetypal ageing thug.

The tall, stick-thin bespectacled solicitor is certainly quick off the mark. He's already waiting, thrusting out a hand, as Lennox enters the building of soft indigo and aquamarine walls, yet somehow rendered all the more institutional for this. — Perry van der Meer, the brief announces in a South African accent.

— Ray Lennox . . . That was quick.

— Was already here with another client. Van der Meer looks over to a group of cops by the reception desk, two of whom Lennox recognises as the ones who lifted Les. — Mr Brodie has already been taken down for questioning. I'm going in to see him now.

Lennox nods, watching van der Meer vanish with the coppers into the labyrinth of the station. Prepared for a long wait, he's surprised when the gaunt Afrikaner returns not more than fifteen minutes later. — I've advised Mr Brodie to say nothing. Mathew Cardingworth's lawyers have already been in touch. It's by no means certain that charges will be pressed.

— What? Lennox frowns in disbelief. — Les ripped his fuckin coupon apart!

146

— Well, Mr Cardingworth is being treated at the hospital now. It seems he believes that he was attacked due to mistaken identity, the lawyer explains, his eyes blinking. Lennox reads him as rattled, fighting to maintain a veneer of impassivity. Continues his burning glare in order to force expansion, and Perry van der Meer accordingly lets his voice sink into a more confessional mode. — The negative publicity seems to be of concern to his people. He has several big and very public development deals coming up and, you know, well, scandal tends to attach.

Lennox instantly thinks of Carmel, and the university. Sucks in a breath. — It's not Cardingworth's decision as to whether or not charges are pressed. That's down to the Crown Prosecution Service.

— Quite so, agrees van der Meer, — but the process is that the police investigate the crime and then decide whether they believe there's enough evidence to bring a charge to the CPS.

This was the kind of lawyer's bullshit that irritated him as a cop, but back then he was forced to bite his tongue. — Les attacked him in broad daylight and in front of several witnesses. His face will be badly scarred, Ray Lennox says, widening his eyes. — How much evidence do you imagine they would fucking well need?

Van der Meer remains unruffled. — Well, if the police do bring it to the CPS, then they will analyse the evidence provided and decide whether or not to pursue charges.

— The CPS would have to –

— And it's by no means certain they would decide to do so.

Ray Lennox raises his eyes to ceiling. — I don't believe this, he gasps, instantly recognising the nonsense in this pronouncement. In fact, he believes it only too readily. — Cardingworth! He's getting to them all; cops, witnesses, the lot, because he's determined his noncing past willnae come out in court!

Van der Meer literally looks down his nose over his spec frames at Lennox. — My priority is to get my client, your friend, Mr Leslie Brodie, out of jail. If those charges can be dropped, well, that's not to be sneezed at. Brodie could do serious prison time for a vicious assault of this kind, and he pushes his glasses back onto the bridge of his nose. — You don't want that, do you?

— Of course not!

Who is this cunt, and what is he to George?

— In the meantime, Mr Brodie is being taken to Lewes Prison where he'll be remanded. You can make an appointment to see him there tomorrow. It would obviously be unwise of you to mention the possibility of Mr Cardingworth not pressing charges, as this arrangement is far from cut and dried yet. Van der Meer removes his specs and rubs at the angry indentations they leave on the side of his nose, before replacing them. — Does no good to raise expectations.

— But you're Les's lawyer and you're talking like this is Cardingworth's decision, Lennox protests in exasperation. — As it's up to the police initially, they would decide based on other witnesses and any physical evidence such as CCTV, the injuries and any markings on the assailant, et cetera.

The lawyer shifts his weight onto another foot, glances at the manila folder in his hand. — Many potential witnesses are apparently reluctant to give evidence to the effect that they saw this assault take place, van der Meer says, looking challengingly at Lennox. — Do *you* want to testify and send your friend to prison?

— No . . . but for different reasons to them!

— The reasons are irrelevant. The fact is that nobody is coming forward. Presuming, however, that the prosecution is pretty reliant on the victim's standalone evidence, I think it is highly unlikely the police will take this to the CPS. As the standard is *beyond reasonable doubt*, they would at least want to have Mathew Cardingworth onside.

— Yes, and that fucking nonce won't want to be up in the dock!

Perry van der Meer pulls a fraught expression. His lower lip wobbles slightly. — I understand that you are a former police officer.

— Correct.

— Well, as you know, given human nature, the police may believe that some form of natural justice has been served by Brodie's actions. They could be reluctant to prosecute someone who has allegedly been abused by a potential paedophile, and a trace of a satisfied smile twists onto van der Meer's lips. — So I think this incident also brings into question what is going on inside the head of the investigating officer.

— So, Les won't get his day in court.

— If he did it could mean serving a heavy prison sentence. And I really don't think your friend *wants* his day in court. Whatever happened in the past between him, Cardingworth . . . and van der Meer looks searchingly at Lennox, brows rising over the top of his lenses, — and any other parties, the fact remains that he committed a very brutal and public assault.

— This is such bullshit . . . Lennox thinks of past arguments with his sister Jackie. Feels himself regress to a frustrated teen under the lawyer's cold logic.

Van der Meer presses home the advantage. His brows fly further north as his forehead accordions. — If you want me to summon you as a witness, I can put in a court order to do so. Of course, you could decide to go to the police to have Cardingworth charged with retrospective sexual abuse. Then the assailant, Mr Brodie, could potentially be called as a witness, albeit possibly a reluctant one. You would have to detail the crime and disclose the offence Mathew Cardingworth allegedly committed. I can set those wheels in motion if you like, and the lawyer cocks his head quizzically.

Bile rises in Lennox's stomach, stinging his gullet. As his pulse quickens, he inhales deeply, watery eyes avoiding the lawyer's busy scan. Fluorescent strip lights sear his brain. A chubby cop ambles past, holding a metal bucket and whistling the tune of 'No Woman, No Cry'. — No, Ray Lennox concedes, intoning in miserable defeat, — I need to speak to Les.

Sensing he isn't even important enough to be a pawn in this game, he leaves Perry van der Meer, who is already busying himself in the contents of his manila file. Walks out the station into the groaning, desolate streets.

In the fading light the cold hacksaws his bones. Lennox walks for a while until his hands feel so numb he can barely open his fists. But there's a furtive sense of mission about him as he slips into a London Road pub. Even the seasoned drinkers at this rapidly gentrifying but still earthier end of town perceive his edge, parting to allow him to take up a stance at the bar. Orders a pint of Stella and a double Macallan, as fragments of past conversations with NA sponsors, lovers, previous psychotherapists, Elaine Rodman and, most of all, former selves whisper like ghosts in his febrile mind. Ahead of him and above the gantry, a big plasma screen blares the highlights of the game he never saw.

He is avoiding all calls, but in the face of Carmel's volumetrically impressive texts and the loosening effect of the alcohol as he watches the football, Lennox discloses his location. Twenty minutes later, she strides into the bar, imperiously scanning for him. Lennox feels himself swallow; he now fully realises what a formidable force she is.

On seeing him, Carmel steals over. — Well, for an ex-cop you certainly seem to do a good line in thugs as friends!

The other drinkers at the bar look away, some exchanging gleeful glances, as if in anticipation of an entertaining domestic dispute.

— Maybe it's you who needs to think about who you're calling *your* friends, Lennox retorts, then tries to explain, — Look –

— I am, she cuts him off with an arctic stare. Turns away, storming out the door as emphatically as she had entered.

— It looks like dinner is cancelled, Ray Lennox says to nobody, then turns to the bar and shouts up more drinks.

22

AN EVENING NEWS

CITY THUG IN HORROR ATTACK

One of Scotland's most notorious football hooligans, Leslie Adam Brodie (53), was arrested yesterday in Brighton after the vicious maiming of a local businessman, Mathew Lindon Cardingworth (61). The brutal assault took place in the hospitality suite at the Brighton & Hove Albion FC stadium, during Saturday's home match against Liverpool. Shocked onlookers in the swanky executive boxes gasped in horror as Brodie, in an unprovoked attack, assaulted Cardingworth with a broken beer glass to his severe disfigurement. Father of three Brodie, said to be visiting the coastal resort with a friend from Edinburgh, refused to make a statement. The Hearts thug, who has several convictions for football-related violence, was fined £500 in 1998 for using abusive language at a game at Parkhead, Glasgow. He is believed to be one of the ringleaders of the infamous Casual Soccer Firm gang.

The motive for the assault remains unclear. An onlooker said: 'We're all deeply shocked by this. Mat is a great guy and a popular member of the local community. He's a respectable businessman who is liked by everybody. It's scary that this sort of thing can happen. The guy was a maniac; he just went for Mat. They hadn't exchanged a single glance, far less any hostile words.'

Brodie is being held in custody pending an investigation.

23

REMINISCENCE AND RECALL 2

She came round last night. Of course, we had another row. Yes, about my drinking. Started saying it was out of control again. I did what I usually do around her and bit my tongue, all the time thinking *pot-kettle*. Conveniently forgets what she put us *both* through on that score with her own mental health issues. Well, it *seems* like she's finally got her own house in order, but how much do people really change? Fair play to her though. She's stuck at this. That's my influence, I always said to her: you've got to stick at things.

We smoothed it all over. The evening was going well. I heated up one of these supermarket lasagnes they say serves two. *Does it fuck* serve two. Would not feed two fucking sparrows. We had to fill up on bread. I opened a bottle of red wine, expecting her ladyship's disapproval, but she joined me in one glass. After that I made a point of corking it and putting it away. She said nothing but I saw her clocking this. Was I desperate for another? Well, yes.

Then she asked me about the tapes. They had obviously made an impression on her. I thought it was because the old boy in the recall group narrating them had snuffed it recently, and that maybe she'd gotten attached to him. They encourage them to dredge up memories. Sometimes they forget that not all memories are pleasant, and might be buried for a reason. Well, honesty is the best policy so I admitted that I found them boring and couldn't listen to them.

She told me that I had to stick with them. That it was really important.

— How so? I asked her.

— Just listen to them!

Well, I said that I would, because I didn't want to set her off, and it did seem to be urgent to her. Of course, I was worried about indulging her craziness, and there was that strange look in her eye again. It put the shits up me: this was how it all started the last time. She would develop strange fixations on mundane things, amplifying them in their importance, before looking for selective data to back them up.

I waited till she left, poured another glass of red, and put the tapes back on. Same old shite: a pathetic coffin-dodging clown about to cash in his chips spraffing nonsense about being at sea. But I wind through more pish and then, well, it gets interesting . . .

— . . . but that's life at sea. You get used to living that way and it's hard to adjust to all the civvy stuff. The railways were fine, and when I was a young married man with a kid on the way they served their purpose, but once Teresa had passed with the cancer and Melanie had gone off to Australia, I was done with them. Always rootless, looking for another boat. But the real reason I went back was that I couldn't face my friend and work-mate, John Lennox. I couldn't look him in the eye, as I was having an affair with his wife, Avril.

— Are you sure you, uh, want to talk about this?

Let him speak, it's just getting interesting for fuck sakes!

— Aye. I cannae be bothered with lies any mare. Lies and sneaking around. That's all shore life ever was tae me.

154

— Well, carry on, please, if everybody else is comfortable. Those old seaman tales can get a little risqué!

— Aye, well, when you were on the same ship as Eddie Reece and Arthur McParland, that was always pretty much guaranteed. Leith never produced two bigger hoormaisters!

(Laughter.)

— But I missed the life at sea. A woman in every port, and in Eddie's case no just women. But I never met one like Avril Lennox. We met on a railway staff night out. She was with John. We just clicked. What's it they call it, chemistry? We just wanted each other. And I wished the situation was less complicated: the Lennoxes were a nice family. John was one of my best friends. Their daughter Jackie was my Melanie's pal, and a right wee brainbox; she became a lawyer. Then there was Raymond, who would join the police. Stuart wasnae there yet.

What the fuck . . .

— John Lennox worked as a driver, like me, but he had a bad heart and was on these blood-thinning pills. They moved him to the office. The medication meant he couldnae get it up, couldn't get erect. Like doonstairs. Of course, Avril was still a young woman. No even forty . . .

(Muffled comment.)

— . . . well, whether it was right or wrong, ah wis in there. We made love whenever we could.

Jesus Christ . . . click that fucking switch off. What the fuck is going on here?

Day Ten

24

LEWES TIN PAIL

With its walls of grey stone, barred arched windows and imposing brownish-maroon gates, Lewes Prison looks like a medieval fortress. If they built a new, customised jail in the fire festival town, a dry-mouthed, nebulous-headed Ray Lennox, glugging on a Volvic bottle, tormented by the Sunday church bells ringing out, knows this one's destiny would be reconstitution as flats or a luxury hotel.

Early for his visit, and knowing he'll have to surrender his phone, Lennox elects to sit in the car googling Cardingworth and his associates. Last night's drinking had been an error. His temples throb as his sweating hands smudge the screen. But that was the nature of intoxication, he muses, trying to encourage himself, it was always a mistake, but only retrospectively. His body and mind are unimpressed with this logic; an image of Trench's manic face and gleaming blade smashes into his consciousness. His chest tightens. Misses a breath. Coughs wildly. Steeling himself, he presses on with his research.

Cardingworth's schizoid morality seems indicated by the two main deals on his horizon, crazy Ralph's hospital site and Carmel's university research development. On the one hand he's razing to the ground a popular local health facility in order to build private luxury flats, while the other displays an altruistic desire to do something positive and progressive.

Might such a man not effortlessly steer between predatory nonce and respectable businessman?

159

His eyes water as Lennox sifts through the data on Cardingworth's core and associated businesses. He examines past deals, profits, turnover, subsidiary companies, partners, other parties involved in the proposed developments; who will gain, who will lose, and who wants to stop them. He checks out the public bodies, like the health authority, all with his hungover brain struggling to sift the perils from the pig shit.

A missed call from George, followed by a text:

> This women plate spinning is eating into my drinking time. If I don't see you this weekend, have a decent one.

> You too. Don't do anything I wouldn't – plenty scope lol

George's philandering dislodges the name Millicent Freeson into Ray Lennox's consciousness. He recalls his partner's affair with the very married senior social work department officer. Millicent had moved from Kent to take up a position at West Sussex Council, and Horsham Security Solutions had fitted out her new home. She fell for George's easy, confident charm. Distressed and drunk, she later confided to Lennox that she didn't know whether to leave her husband or simply end the affair.

Lennox had advised the latter course of action. He liked Millicent and George had form for promising married women the world, before riding off into the proverbial sunset. At the time, this guidance had been accepted with reluctance, but several months later, she'd called him, having embraced it wholeheartedly. Millicent admitted to being foolish; things with her husband were now better than ever. She let Lennox know that taking his advice had saved everyone from a world of pain. And if there was anything she could ever do for him . . .

Now Ray Lennox is calling in that favour. He bangs off an email from his iPhone.

A further search on Gavin Carter's case fails to yield anything of import. He discounts asking George, at best wary of burdening his business partner with his extra-curricular obsessions, at worst distrustful of his reaction to this.

Instead he elects to return Elaine Rodman's call. — I'm sorry I missed the last appointment. And I apologise for being rude. The EMDR sounds interesting, I'd like to give it a shot –

— I cannot see you as a client, she informs him, in a clipped and cutting tone, very different from her text. — I can put you in touch with an EMDR practitioner.

Lennox scents Cardingworth's ubiquitous hand in this. He knows few psychotherapists in Brighton are in a position to drop clients. Unlike Edinburgh there was no referral system from local doctors here, so patrons were at a premium. — Why?

— I don't have to give you reasons.

— Perhaps not technically, but I'd appreciate the courtesy of you doing so. I'm usually on time for our sessions and I never miss a payment.

— I'm sorry, Ray, Rodman impassively replies, and hangs up.

— What the fuck . . . Lennox holds out his phone and addresses it. — Are you for real, ya –

But a text reminder on the screen flashes up, informing him that it's visiting time.

On entry, the external aesthetics boasted by HMP Lewes quickly cede to conventional institutional mundanity. People sit with such dread fatalism in the harshly lit waiting room it seems almost inevitable they'll soon suffer the same incarceration as those they visit. Patted down by a jumpy, intense guard, Lennox surrenders his phone, keys and wallet, placed in a box in exchange for a numbered plastic token. The overtly edgy searches, he considers, are probably due to recent media publicity about relatives smuggling in the drug spice. Walking through a set of metal detectors he emerges into a bleak anteroom. Visitors sit on red plastic chairs, or stand around talking in whispers. He picks up a discarded *Metro* and leans against the wall under a barred window. Despite the room's NO SMOKING signs, a scent hinting at old tobacco tickles Lennox's nostrils. It's as if it has permeated some of the bodies present to the extent that they now expel it as naturally as carbon dioxide.

One man is particularly guilty. Stepping close to Lennox, he commences a monologue in a soft but insistent Scottish accent.

Did I get this cunt banged up once? Spare me . . .

The man's determination to talk is exceeded only by his intended target's resolve not to get drawn into conversation. Even though the Scottish obvious smoker had immediately indicated he was from Aberdeen, Lennox feels it's important for him to know he is being studiously ignored.

Suddenly the Aberdonian jars into silence, cowering back. Lennox looks to his source of discountenance. It's Cathy Brodie, in a black coat and red sweater, heavier and rounder than he recalls, but with the same highlighted blonde on brown hair and intimidating glower. Jutting her jaw out cash register tray style, she declares, — You set Les up! You kent he'd kick off when he saw that bastard!

— No way, Lennox protests, placing the rolled-up *Metro* on a window ledge, fervently wishing he could join the retreating Aberdonian. — How could I have known Les would have done that?

But what else would he have done? You used Les as bait cause you had to be sure.

Cathy is about to respond but a voice booms out over a speaker, announcing the commencement of visitation for remand prisoners. — On you go, Lennox urges.

— I'll be ootside in half an hour. Then you can go in, Cathy says, turning away.

— Thanks. Appreciate it.

She whips round, malevolence scoring her face. — Wisnae ma idea! *He* wants tae see ye!

Lennox sucks it up. Watches Cathy head off in a throng of visitors, ushered by two screws through a set of buzzed-open barred doors. Sits and waits, jonesing badly for his phone. Several chairs are now vacant. Takes one, folds his arms and closes his eyes. Tries to tune out those background sounds of hushed despair punctuated by the odd defiant chuckle.

Kids from foster homes, running away, or supposedly running away. What the fuck is going on here? You need to find those fostering parents . . . this Julie woman, this missing husband . . .

Maybe you can make it up with Carmel. She's such a beautiful woman. You landed on your feet again. But why, Ray Lennox, can you never seem to make romance work? Never convert that easy charm and likeability into anything lasting?

But perhaps this time is different. Maybe you can finally slay those monsters! You see her running alongside you, 'never above you, never below you, always beside you' as your old man used to say in toast, hair blowing in the wind, fringe swept back, the concentration on her face as she catches you glimpse at her in profile and you both share a laugh, before pressing on . . . Are you in love?

Yes, I think you might be, Ray Lennox. Can you earn that love?

He is aware of someone standing over him. Opening his

eyes, he sees Cathy has returned. She looks down, meaty arms folded across pendulous breasts. — On ye go.

Lennox flicks his fingers through his hair. That voice in his head: his, but yet not his. Growing more insistent, more disconcerting all the time. Becoming increasingly prominent in his waking hours. — When are you going back? he asks Cathy. — Are you sorted for somewhere to stay?

— Ah want fuck all fae you, Ray Lennox, n ah wish tae God Les felt the same, she hisses, malign coals burning through lids she tries to narrow over them. — You know what the sad thing is? He fuckin idolises you. He doesnae believe you set him up!

— I didn't, like ah sais, I only –

— Just go in and see him, she grimaces to the extent Lennox believes her chin could touch her forehead, before pivoting to exit.

He rises. Follows Cathy to the door. She halts, looking back over her shoulder at him. Lennox grasps the opportunity. — I really am going to get him out!

— Aye, right, she hisses, before growling, — Fuck you, Lennox!

As Cathy departs, all eyes fall on him. The other visitors and guards seem united in unvoiced malefic loathing. Shaken, Lennox takes a hesitant half-step forward, stumbling a little before following a group through to the visiting room, where he sits down at the table opposite Les Brodie.

Experience on the force has taught Lennox that people respond to arrest and incarceration in unpredictable and uneven ways. Les's features already seem sharper, and belligerence gives his jaw an extra half-inch in prominence. Lennox realises his friend has slipped comfortably into the persona of prison hard man. — I've nae fuckin regrets, Raymie, he says tightly. — I dinnae like being in here, aye, but ah'd dae it again. His eyes ignite. — It was him, Raymond! He was one ay they noncey cunts in that tunnel! You ken that!

— Ah dunno, Les. Lennox, clocking the severe face on a steroid-munching cord-necked guard, squirms at the putrid defensiveness in his own voice. — Ah got a vibe. Ah wanted tae see if you felt the same. I didnae think ye'd dae that though, bud. I thought we'd sort it out thegither.

Les stares at him, his face folding grimly. — No worries, I'm fucking glad, and Lennox can tell he's still enraged. His right fist clenches tightly. — It was him, Raymie, he repeats.

— Which one, though, Les? There were three. Which one of them . . . you know . . . ?

Les Brodie suddenly buckles, shoulders sagging. His skin instantly goes from an angry red to a sickly, fibrous grey. Silence hangs between them. Then Les looks up and says softly, — He was there, Raymie.

But which one . . . the words again form on Lennox's lips, but he can't bring himself to say them. *Who was it, Les? Which one of them skewered your eleven-year-old arsehole? Cardingworth? Or did he just hold you down so that the others could?* All he can manage is another, — I'm going to get you the fuck oot ay here, Les, and he looks around the cavernous hall before refocusing on his friend, — That South African lawyer boy is on the case, he declares, grappling internally to stop himself from mentioning that Cardingworth may not even press charges.

— I ken ye will, bud. Les's voice is suddenly hesitant and plaintive.

Then his incarcerated friend flinches at the screeching bell signalling the end of the visiting hour. The essence now flickering in his eyes is watery and diminished. Under the bluster, Les is scared. And with good reason, Lennox considers: glassing a rich businessman was a different gig from

165

punching another wideo at the football. And when all the hyperbole was removed, that had been the extent of Les Brodie's criminal career to date. Worse, he ponders, Les retains a troubling faith in the man who, along with Cardingworth's voice in their heads, has helped put him in prison.

He takes his leave of Les and Lewes Prison. Watches people waiting at a bus stop in the car park. Climbing gratefully into the Alfa Romeo, he lets the air from its heater warm him.

He checks his emails; one from Millicent Freeson, which announces he has a document from an encrypted server. He's impressed by her speed, and her sense of security. It cannot be downloaded and it will be erased in an hour, and he's already forty-seven minutes into that. — Fuck, Lennox scrambles, first opening, then screenshooting the document.

It's one page and it contains the following information:

Gavin Carter (14)	Julie and Clive Wilkins	(17 Aug 1984)
Thomas Millington (12)	Marsha and Kenneth Wade	(25 Dec 1986)
Ross Prior (9)	Julie Knowles	(13 Feb 1989)
Marshall Delaney (13)	Petra and Alan Crosby	(20 Mar 1997)
Jason McCabe (11)	Carly Reynolds	(4 Sept 2005)

These, he assumes, as requested, are children reported missing from care in Brighton and West Sussex from 1980 onwards, and their foster parents. They stop at 2005. Lennox realises that this is probably the last one that Millicent can issue without incriminating any present colleagues.

Notes that Ross Prior was fostered by a woman also named Julie, in this case Knowles rather than Wilkins, wonders about coincidences and connections, as his mind drifts to a news report on Mexican children in American detention camps, playing in the background on the TV the previous night, as he researched . . . it didn't even merit his conscious attention . . . *this is how these things happened* . . . then, in the corner of his eye, a red-and-black figure, and he looks up to see that Cathy is one of the people getting on the bus. He hadn't noticed her and she must have been waiting in the cold for over half an hour. After coming down from Edinburgh she had split her husband's visiting time with him, and Lennox didn't think to offer her a lift back to town, or to the airport.

You self-absorbed wanker . . .

Their eyes meet as Ray Lennox belatedly points to the passenger seat next to him. But Cathy Brodie trenchantly twists away. Vanishes into the guts of the big vehicle.

25

PRESTON PARK

Preston Park is a desirable neighbourhood of solid Victorian properties. Centred round the parkland of the same name, it plays host to Brighton's huge Pride Festival. Ray Lennox does not expect to find Julie Wilkins at this address after all those years, and he's not disappointed. A FOR SALE sign announces her old residence, which, set in an out-of-kilter run-down street, is empty and the windows boarded up. It seems to exemplify the dreary defeatism of the English Sunday.

As he navigates the overgrown weed garden at the front of the house to ascertain if any gaps through which to peer inside present themselves, a neighbour emerges from next door, cigarette in hand. She's a willowy, fine-boned woman with short white hair. In her fifties, she introduces herself as Joanne Rowling. His spirit soars: Joanne might have lived here some time. She tells him that the house has been empty for months: the previous owner drank himself to death. Not a happy residence.

He eagerly asks her about Julie Wilkins.

— Jeez, Joanne shakes her shoulders and gives a hollow laugh, — she left here like, years ago.

— Any idea where she went?

— No, but she went with *him*, after her and Clive split up. Such a bloody stupid move. Joanne shivers, taking a deep drag on her cigarette. — Clive was a lovely bloke, a proper grafter, before the drink got him. Took care of her. That other one . . .

she lowers her voice, — he hurt that kid, and Joanne takes another warping suck on her smoke, — everybody knows it.

Joanne is a gossip and such people are worth their weight in gold to cops. But Lennox is no longer one. His befuddled head buzzes, trying to piece together this information. — This kid was Gavin Carter, right?

— Nah . . . that was the older one that ran away, and her cheeks buckle again as she takes another deep inhalation on her fag.

— What was his name, this other guy, the one who hurt the kid? he asks, aware that something has changed in Joanne. Her gaze has developed a severity and suspicious scrutiny Lennox knows of old. — Who was he? Who was the kid? Was it Ross Prior?

Lennox's sense that he's overreached is confirmed by Joanne's terrifying realisation that she's said enough. It seems to bludgeon her as she throws down her cigarette butt and crushes it under her heel. — I dunno. I have to go now, and she steps back from the boundary fence, moving to her front door.

— What was he like, this other guy?

Joanne turns and looks him up and down. A petrified tint defiles her gaze. She informs Ray Lennox, — He was like you!

Lennox is sledgehammered. — In what way –

But she steps inside and slams the door shut.

— WHAT DO YOU MEAN BY THAT? Lennox shouts in bewildered panic, but Joanne has gone and nothing seeps through his fog of confusion to provide a satisfactory answer to his own question. He heads off, sensing the rippling effect of net curtains twitching in the street.

On getting back into town, Lennox parks in Sussex Square. There's no Stuart when he returns to his flat. He's sad and glad at the same time. Fires up his computer, intent on looking up the case of Ross Prior. Instead decides to follow the sequence of Millicent's list. Starts with Thomas Millington, nine when he vanished on Christmas Day in 1986.

The fact that there is nothing on the *Argus* site, with the same two missing pages, fills Lennox with a broken sadness he knows will flower destructively into rage. Unlike poor Gavin, the other foster children were not found, had no marked grave nor burial ceremony.

They weren't just erased: their pasts were too.

He trembles as he types in the name: Ross Prior.

Thinking of Julie, the alluring but pitiless-faced smoker, Lennox is besieged by one thought: *dodgy cunts always change their names.* You learn on the force that a name alteration in a man is highly indicative of a *wrong un*, as George calls them, usually a fraudster. This tendency exempts women as marriage still commonly accounts for such a change. The ones that are exceptions are generally on the run from dodgy men. Are the two fostering Julies the same person? Joanne wouldn't confirm Ross was the kid hurt by the partner who replaced Clive. Was he?

But with the exception of a few photographs, there is nothing on these cases on the *Argus* site. He again looks at Julie Wilkins in the pictures relating to Gavin's case.

Fast-forward five years and the other Julie (Knowles) has different hair, short and blonde to the longer darker mane of Wilkins. She also seems heavier, but people changed their coiffure and put on weight. The shape of the face is altered by the gain in poundage, but the nose, eyes and lips bear similarities. Yet despite Joanne's contention, the grainy images are inconclusive and give Lennox no confidence. The title of the incomplete article is: CONCERNED FOSTER MUM FEARS FOR RUNAWAY ROSS.

The remnants of the piece contain nothing of import on Ross, but state that Julie's husband was working away. It is the first mention of him, but no details are provided. Not even his name.

He calls Mike Regis, asking him who the reporter covering the story was. He learns that Gillian Nicolson was the crime features writer on the first three, but she died around ten years ago after a long battle with MS. Mike himself reported on the Jason McCabe vanishing. — Like I do everything now, with the help of a couple of interns and a few work experience kids from the local schools who still think there's a career in journalism, he mopes. — Why the interest in runaway kids, Ray?

Lennox has socialised with Mike, largely through George. — Just an old cop hobby of mine, missing persons, Lennox says. — What about the photographs? he asks. Those are all credited to a Derek Shabala. Lennox wonders if he's still around, and if, like many photographers, he's archived his own work. If so he may have a clearer print of Julie.

— Derek Shabala was our staff photographer then, Mike confirms. — Retired a long time ago. He's still with us, though not in great shape.

Lennox decides not to press further to avoid arousing the journalist's suspicions. But he'll find Shabala, and the image will either prove or disprove that Julie Wilkins and Julie Knowles are the same person.

There's absolutely nothing on Marshall Delaney; like Thomas it's as if he never existed. Lennox needs to know more. He fights back his reticence and calls Millicent. — I appreciate what you sent me. But I need to know if there are any more cases. Also: who the social work practitioner and management-level staff were during these periods.

— No, Ray, and Millicent's voice is detached and professional, lacking the warmth he associates with her. — I've repaid our little favour. I can't help you any more. I've compromised myself enough.

171

Lennox feels himself stalling on a cliché – *this could be really big/devastating/horrendous* – as he sees Cardingworth's face in wine-label reading mode: confident, self-satisfied. *He'll know Millicent Freeson. He'll know Mike Regis. He knows everybody.* — No worries, I appreciate what you've done already.

— What's going on here, Ray?

— Old cop habits dying hard, he says lightly. — Me being underemployed fitting alarms. An old case I've never quite been able to let go of.

Lennox doesn't know if that assuages her, but it's all he's got. They say goodbye. He returns to the case of Jason McCabe, the one Mike himself reported. The pages here are complete, but the article is *human interest* fluff, too perfunctory to be threatening to anybody. It states banal generalities about a kind, loving boy, studious but who also enjoyed sports, yet had a sense of mischief. There is nothing here that can help an investigation. Then he looks at the picture of Jason again. A smiling ginger-headed freckled kid. The caption: BRIGHT AND SCHOLARLY: RUNAWAY JASON.

Accompanying the clichéd story, another image, this time of his foster mum, Carly Reynolds, on the couch. A small-framed woman with short dark hair, her face is etched in concern as she dabs it with a hanky, presumably to remove tears. It's the cheesiest set-up possible from photographer Shabala and Lennox needs to find him. Carly has what looks like a white scarf round her neck with a pattern on it. His eyes sting, and he blinks rapidly. Drums his fingers on his desk. Feels a twinge in his back as he arches it.

Skittish, he rises and heads outside. It's gotten cold and a dark sky threatens to haemorrage its contents. Wanders through town. Drifts around the bustling Lanes, full of shoppers, homeless beggars and Christmas drunks who couldn't finish the weekend on Saturday night. Thinks of Stuart, already more at home in this town than himself.

As Sunday afternoon bleeds into the dreaded evening, the roast-lunch-eating families head home. Guts crammed with food and chests full of that uniquely English apprehension. For Lennox, this is when the pubs exert their pull. He's unable to discern whether he actually wants to get drunk or is being driven by that gently persistent tug that insinuates when he's under stress. Heads for an atmospheric old hostelry, a favourite of George's, and also frequented by Mike Regis.

The first Stella, its fizzy volume bubbling heavily in his gut, is a struggle. The second is easier. A brandy follows. Then the grand illusion returns: that alcohol and cocaine help him see things in focus. In reality, the most formidable part of his brain knows the reverse is true. That he is better in the gym, pulverising the bags, having Tom Tracy smash his abdomen with a medicine ball. To his horror, the realisation clobbers him: *You are pushing the 'fuck it' button. That means you are not right again.*

He is just into the troubling third pint, cocaine starting to gatecrash relentlessly into his thoughts, when George, sporting a checked jacket and flannels, coat over his arm and his hair positively bouffant, ambles into the pub. As he moves over to Lennox, his business partner signals for a large gin and tonic and a pint of Guinness. — Raymond, drink? Is that Stella . . . ? Oh fuck that, have a Guinness, and he orders up a second pint as Lennox shrugs in acquiescence. — Of course you do know that it's better for you, less calories, and George slaps his own gut.

— Sorry, mate . . . Lennox feels moved to apologise, — did you sort out the Rose Garden chaos? How were the security guys?

— Managed to smooth things over with the management,

he winks, picking up the dispensed drinks. — And our friends seem none the worse for wear! Cheers!

— *Slainte*, Lennox joins him in toast. — Did you ever run across Derek Shabala, a photographer on the *Argus*?

George looks at him in a wide-eyed combination of disbelief and dismay. — Very recently: as did you.

— Where?

— Rose Garden. He was the unfortunate chap walking around in circles with the Zimmer frame. Been there for five years, chronic dementia. His face rang a bell, but I would never have placed him. It was only when Polly addressed him as Derek, it all came together, George shakes his head sadly. — Sad tale, archetypal. Children grow up and leave home, splits from the missus, hits the drink. Responsible for a bad fire in his house, loses everything.

— Aye?

Loses everything . . .

George nods sombrely. — Yes. More alcohol: then dementia, rest home. Used to drink in here with Mike. He looks into the pub mirror in distaste, as if concerned that a similar fate might befall him. Then he bucks himself up, sitting rod-straight. — But I have some other news for you.

— Aye? What might that be?

In a low voice George declares, — Well, you might have to disclose a little first, Raymond. I'm happy to pull favours for you, but I don't like working blind. What's this thing with you and Mathew Cardingworth and your friend? I know a few box-seat holders at Brighton, Ray. Some of them coppers.

This explains to Lennox why the cops were on hand so quickly. — Fair dos. He nods over to some seats. They sit down in the secluded corner with their drinks. — Before I explain, Lennox says, — who is this Perry van der Meer guy?

— Run into him at the rugby club sometimes. Wouldn't

call us bosom buddies, but a decent sort for a Springbok. Pretty effective lawyer, by all accounts. But they're such a parasitic breed he's one of the few I retain on my contact list. George twists that brow, — Why? Didn't he shape up?

— Does he have any connections with Cardingworth?

— Not that I'm aware of, but Brighton isn't a big pond. So now it's time you spilled, Raymond. What in the name of the sacred vulva is going on here?

Lennox draws a breath, lets his teeth scrape over his bottom lip. Starts to tell George the story. Commencing at the tunnel, he ends, via Ralph Trench, at the fostered children, not mentioning the involvement of Millicent. His partner listens patiently, only interrupting a couple of times to get the detail right. Lennox can see how he was a good cop. He has the gift of not getting in the way when people need to talk.

At the end of the spiel, George deliberates between the fresh G&T and Guinness. Takes a long drink on the latter. Lowers it to the table. — I finally know why you did what you did for so many years, he tells Lennox, licking the froth off his top lip. — So, after a lifetime of hunting for those nonces, you run into one of them here, in Brighton.

— A coincidence.

— Most likely so, but strange all the same.

Lennox shrugs. — Chance or not, this shit is well fucked up. And my gut is saying that Cardingworth is involved in some terrible stuff.

— You can't even tie him to this tunnel business in Edinburgh, Ray, which was almost forty years ago, now you have him up to all sorts here in Sussex . . . Bit of a jump. George looks at his partner, who is breathing shallowly. — You okay, Raymond?

— Yeah, and he starts to tell George the story about the

cases of Thomas Millington and Marshall Delaney. — Those kids just don't exist. It's like they were never here, and he catches his breath, brushing his eye.

— Good God, Ray, I know it's distressing, but you've seen a lot worse.

— I know . . . just since leaving the cops, I've kind of opened up again, he said. The fate of Thomas and Marshall was wrong on every level. It struck deep into him. An eleven-year-old suffering the abuse that Les did was horrific enough, but the fate of those children, to vanish off the face of the earth, unlamented and unacknowledged; it lay on a different axis of existential cruelty. He thinks again of the recent news item he'd only half watched.

The Mexican children in those American camps, as a silver-spooned inherited wealth billionaire gloats. We now just turn away and shrug it off. Vote for, even celebrate, the vile specimens who perpetuate this bullshit. We are lost.

Thomas and Marshall never had a chance to become the men they could have been. But you are a man and you are going to take those fuckers down. You swear it to yourself and to the memory of those ruined children you never knew.

Those poor little mi—

George has suddenly thrust his phone into Lennox's hand. It shows a picture of a sun-kissed beach. — What's this?

— Tenerife. You need cheering up, Ray. Winter sun. Mate has a place out there. It's empty. Four-hour flight. You and thingamabob, me and a certain lady . . . His partner raises the G&T to his lips, as a text pops into the phone in Lennox's hand. It's from Polly:

Hi Mr Big Cock. I think it's time you were sucked.

176

He explodes in liberating laughter, handing George the phone. — Seems like those management meetings are going well.

— Oh dear, how embarrassing, George laughs, faux coy, slipping the phone into the inside pocket of his jacket.

Lennox mirthfully shakes his head, empowered by gravity's sudden ease on his vertebrae. George has certainly been able to activate a side of the manager of the Rose Garden retirement home that he never detected. He's long felt that his senior partner possesses a deep knowledge that eludes him. Now this appears to extend to women.

George takes another long sip of his G&T. — And what's all this *frightfully anglicised* 'seems like those management meetings are going well' nonsense? What the hell has happened to the signature guttural tones of my Caledonian chum? Has the soft south so corrupted you? *This shagging's working oot*, if you please!

— Looks like yir cowpin the erse oafay mare fanny, mate, ay, Lennox laughs, joyously reverting to a former self. — I suppose I got fed up of being misunderstood.

— We're all misunderstood, Ray. Of course, you do know it's one of the few assets we have left, and George raises his Guinness again, — our last zone of freedom. So how is your new lady? Do you think she'd be up for a quartet of winter sun in Tenners?

— I think I might just be flying solo, he says, as a poignant image of Carmel's easy smile fills his head, before he feels rancour rising in him. — Like most people in this fucking town, Carmel seems strangely moved to defend the paedophile rapist whose features my friend rearranged with a beer glass, and Lennox swivels to register the boisterous disturbance of a group of youths who march into the bar. — And I have to say that your man, van der Meer, as much as I appreciate the contact, seems tae be of a similar disposition.

— Come on, Ray, what do you expect? George sings. — Cardingworth has long been known locally as a good egg. Hauled himself up by his bootstraps, done some great things for the community, all that tosh.

— Yes, so he tells everybody. These fuckers are great at blowing their own trumpets, and they're rarely short of gushing sycophants to back them up.

— Even if a hero is tarnished, people still need them and they're never going to think well of the person who bursts their bubble, George contends, but his gaze flits across the young mob before he gives Lennox an eye-roll.

And following his line of vision Lennox sees that Ria's boyfriend, Chris, is present in the collective. The younger man looks over at them with even less deference than the last occasion they were in proximity. George is now off on one though, and Lennox wonders if his partner is actively trying to distract him from making eye contact with the young mob. — People are aware that we're fucked. Communities are gone and climate change is going to fry or drown us all. They know this at a deep, human existential level; they don't need educated liberals patronising the hell out of them. It's so much easier to maintain the sweet delusion that the Etonians have their best interests at heart. They need to believe in a notional merrie olde England they can get back to. They're bottom of the pile in this toff-shore paradise. And they swallow it, because although they know it's bullshit, it's simply all they have.

— If the king's shilling is the only one in town . . . Lennox agrees, scanning the bar. It had seemed a hostelry of well-heeled cosmopolitan types, but now appears to be stuffed with inbred yokels, scenting that hated émigré. He permits himself to succumb to a shudder.

Cardingworth . . . he's connected. I'm in the lair of the beast . . .

This doesn't go unnoticed by George. — The paranoia is fairly ripping out of you these days, Raymond!

— What do you mean *these days*? Lennox sourly laughs, drinking up and rising.

— Where are you going?

— Just to do a bit of nosing around.

— Well, I'm hoping that's not a euphemism, Raymond. I have my beady eye on you!

— Sadly, just some online research, Lennox grins in departure, all the while thinking: *you and me both.* As he passes Chris, his instinct tells him to blank the young man. However, he goes counter-intuitive and dispenses a wink. He gets only a glacial expression in return. However, it's not this adversary's look but his partner's words that deeply resonate: *I finally know why you did what you did for so many years.*

Not for the first time, Lennox wonders: *why did you do what you did for so many years?*

26

YOU'RE MINE IN DREAMS

... Wang had powers for sure and I learned most of the craft by prac-
tising his death in my conscious sleeping before enacting it in the real
world, because you need to tie up all loose ends as the saying goes . . .
and he was old and feeble . . . I envisaged his passing as a glorious
crossing into the next realm, where the senses control every
experience . . .

    . . . problematically, Wai knew that I just wanted to enjoy the tuition
of old Wang, then go to sleep, and he thus devised a decent torture for
me . . . put me to work, the little tinker did . . . the prison was a business,
you see, undertaking manufacturing jobs for some well-known brands,
whose shareholders benefitted greatly from having our slave labour as
part of their operation, has to be said . . . I needed the money for those
little luxuries, but I didn't have time to work, I wanted to do more lucid
dreaming, to have any woman or boy I wanted, in any way I saw fit . . .
I would get the prisoners to show me pictures of their sweethearts and
imprint them on my brain, enjoying a congress with them, their lover
and other objectifiers . . . is that even a word? . . . I don't know, self-
taught man, you see . . . but one day I saw Rat cleaning the toilet . . .
pushed his pointy head down the hole . . . as he retched, I told him, 'you
get me all the stuff I need . . .' he agreed . . . I was concerned that he
would try to cut my throat while I was asleep, and the afterlife lottery
might not turn out to be as good as the lucid dream state . . . but I was
never coming out of this place and I needed dreamtime . . . so it was
worth the calculated risk, and after that he treated me like a god . . . but
Wai was a cruel little bastard and I saw him, I knew the sport he loved,

and I wanted to crush him like I used to do with the others before they locked me away in here, so I ordered Rat, the Vietnamese weasel, who, for the purposes of this tale I shall now simply refer to as the Vietnamese Weasel if it's all the same to you and even if it isn't thank you very much . . . anyway, I ordered the Vietnamese Weasel to pick Wai's pocket, get the photo of his wife and two children, and every evening I would bring them to me and fuck them and destroy them and knew that I had made him witness this in some strange subconscious way, you could tell the way Wai looked at me, read my smile, saw what was in my eyes . . . in spite of the dictates of cold logic, he knew, he just knew because every day, with my training, I pulled them into focus until, when I woke up, I could smell them, her perfume, their blood, on my blanket and of course Wai could too . . . I have no proof of this but I believe he went home and interrogated his wife . . . asked her who her lover was . . . perhaps it was because my dreams had become so vivid to me, I felt the rest of humanity must also, in some way, be privy to their content . . .

. . . cut up rough, Wai did, with his associate Choy, a somewhat huge gentleman too . . . loved to josh with Wai, I did, see if I could morsel responses out of him for this evening's long head wank in dreamland . . .

. . . 'I'm betting you've got two, one of each would be my guess . . . lovely . . . well, your government's strict one-child policy certainly didn't do your own parents any favours . . . but I wouldn't let those ones get away with murder . . . could lead to all sorts . . . but I'm very much of a spare-the-rod spoil-the-child viewpoint . . . old school, you see . . . I'll wager your wife is shaggable, as your kind go, of course, but can't say I'm a fan, far too subservient those oriental ladies . . . I like a bit of a fight in 'em, better sport all round, see . . . you get that obviously . . . that's why you enjoy working with me . . . you have the power but I'm quite enjoying the victim role . . . the long savour, you see, when the tables are finally turned and you see how minuscule your petty tyranny is . . . you see only resistance rather than anticipation . . . I'm in your

181

head, and as your wife comes in with the bowl of noodles, as your children run to you . . . or do they now? . . . are they perhaps repelled by that troubling aspect you now project? . . . that's me they're seeing on your face, just poor little me finding refuge in your head . . . you see, that's what I always do, find lodgings in their head . . . that's how I win . . . but them babs of yours, cheeky little mites by the sound of 'em, I'll wager, I'd be sticking them in the naughty corner . . . how much they pick up you never quite know, do you . . .'

. . . of course, the detail went over Wai's head, but I'm sure he picked up the gist . . . you always pick up the gist, don't you, Ray? . . . you'll know that as an investigator . . .

. . . but you were always in my life, Raymond, you had never left it . . . I'd followed your career as closely as I could . . . at first out of curiosity . . . you always remember the ones that got away . . . it was early days and I was a novice . . . then, when I saw what you were doing for a living, I knew why you did what you did and I knew you'd be looking for us, you were dangerous . . . but I heard you had burned out, they put you right on the naughty step, PC Plod . . .

. . . oh yes, you had all but gone from my consciousness, except in my deep slumber where I replay events . . . fine-tuning them . . . they always culminated in the deliciously violent and totally merciless execution of you and your little friend . . . but while forever in my dreams, you had absented yourself from my physical life with me in that Shanghai prison . . .

. . . the same could not be said of my friend Wai, who was becoming more unhinged, threatening me with all sorts of punishment he was, Ray, and I realised that getting involved in such dramas was eating into my sleep and dream time . . . it was only when he said I would be going to solitary if I continued my rebellion that I intensified my efforts to undermine him . . . thankfully, he was as good as his word and he transferred me to a stinking hole where I was in heaven . . . I'll never forget his face on witnessing my grin as he closed the door behind me . . . with the darkness and the insects . . . it was like a man who believed that he was locking his wife and children in there with me . . . which, of course, he was . . . oh, it was bliss . . . I was disturbed only twice a day for food . . . a cold winter had dug in, but I learned to drift off, the beggarly blanket huddled around me, then I went wherever I chose, with whomever I fancied, doing whatever I wanted, with total impunity . . . gotcha this time, Ray, always as a poor little mite with your sad-eyed sidekick . . .

. . . I never had to wank once but the cell was fairly splattered with my cum . . .

. . . but then Wai found a certain weakness, you see, we all have 'em . . . I recall him sparking up a lighter, to light a cigarette . . . the flame . . . it came out too strong and I recoiled . . . no doubt he learned about me old mare and old Mr Baxter and their fire, me being locked in that blazing house . . . no, I don't like fire . . . the pain of my feet as they burned . . .

. . . but there were loose ends to tidy up . . . and as a naval man I was dedicated to the concept of keeping things shipshape . . . my old mentor, the frail Wang, he knew everything about me . . . my dreams . . . they were now so vivid they outstripped reality . . . what could he tell some witness, be it God or judge? . . .

. . . of course, it was easy . . . he and I, once I was out of solitary, always finished our exercise first and returned to the cell where we were briefly alone . . . rather than take my tuition, I bade my old friend to get straight to sleep, which he did with immense gratitude . . .

. . . and, mired in his deep slumber, he offered only puny resistance as I placed the pillow over his head, hands on either side of it, pushing down with all my weight . . . it was sublime to watch his thin arms flay in sad urgency as I encouraged him to let go and I wished my beautiful friend, this man who made me, who was my salvation, the most sweet- est and most lucid of dreams . . . as he struggled and as I mused in those waking hours as to how the trained practitioner can control image and narrative to a sharper degree than the misguided fools with their bogus virtual reality nonsense and their blunt instrument of technology . . .

. . . then he was gone . . . died peacefully in his sleep, they said . . . and I was alone . . . I was the dream master, and I needed no apprentice . . . just beautiful sleep . . .

. . . then suddenly, that terrible, jarring day, when I was ripped from my comforting womb with the heavy door creaking open and a torch-light shining in my face, ripping my retina apart . . . to my surprise, after anticipating I would be in there all my days, I only served sixteen months of a life sentence – God bless Her Majesty! . . . my company had gotten in touch with the embassy and some sort of arrangement was cobbled together . . . I was released from prison and met shivering at the gates by a government official in a long fur coat and hat who handed me let-ters of transit and two hundred pounds in yen, which I had to sign an IOU for . . . 'Get the hell out of here,' his thin, bloodless lips snapped at me . . .

'Fuck off, you little ponce,' I smiled back at him as I snatched the documents out of his weak grip and watched his scared, privileged eyes water . . . you know the sort . . . 'Now get out of my sight unless you want my heel in your scrawny neck . . . would you like that, my boot smashing down on your windpipe, crushing the very breath from those puny lungs?'

. . . of course, he made his farting, blinking hasty retreat to his car . . . you know what those people are like, Raymond, how they scuttle off like rats when the heat is on . . . like I thought you had . . . but no, you kept coming back for more . . . some would say an admirable trait, I prefer to keep my counsel on that . . .

. . . well, they took their time, but to be absolutely fair, I was genu-inely surprised they even bothered with the likes of me . . . no money, no education to speak of, other than the books I'd found discarded as I travelled around the world, indulging in my simple pleasures . . . so I located a cheap hotel and went back to sleep, then the following day I was off to Pudong Airport for deportation in the form of a flight to London, courtesy of the head of that particular global airline, a man I'd always found quite torture-able (is that a word?) in my dreams and had indulged in a couple of times . . .

. . . slept all the way home on the journey . . .

. . . when I awoke, the air stewards, as they served breakfast, looked at me, terrorised to their very souls . . . in some way they understood that I had unspeakably violated them all on that flight . . .

. . . but home I was, free to indulge in the world of lucid dreaming . . . but I would need to be careful; my frame was weakened drastically by my incarceration . . . I was skeletal, and could see all my ribs . . . I took a one-bedroom flat in a nondescript English town, filled it with gym equipment and a large fridge freezer, with minimal, but nutritious food . . . I was what one might describe as content . . . like an ideal weekend where Blues have emerged victorious while Villa slump to defeat . . . but with the added spice of dreamworld, which was my substantive existence . . . of course, I did have to dabble in the real world, to keep my hand in more than anything . . .

. . . the local children on the estate . . . most of them were well trained, the feral tykes, they tended to scarper, to be fair, but you could see the neglected ones, the look in their sad little eyes, desperate for any kind of affirmation . . . snatching was easy for an old hand . . . and of course I'd make all those cheeky little devils stand in the naughty corner . . . 'I don't want you to think about what you've done,' I'd tell 'em, 'that's in the past. Look to the future now, it's only just begun. I want you to think about what's going to happen to you . . .'

. . . can't say fairer . . .

. . . and then something happened, some funny stuff I don't quite understand . . . and now, Raymond Lennox . . . it's all happening, all of it!

Day Eleven

27

HOME SECURITY

Mathew Cardingworth's office is situated in a saturnine chrome-and-glass reinvention of the seventies. Close to the old hospital, in a street undergoing rapid redevelopment, it's only a ten-minute drive from Ray Lennox's flat. In the cheerless car park on a cold Monday morning, he looks out through the tinted glass of the Alfa Romeo, envious of the gold Jaguar in the dedicated parking space marked:

RESERVED: MC

A long yawn breaks from his marrow. Some sparse, jagged sleep had been taken last night. He'd picked up a Chinese takeaway. Eaten late, the indigestion resulting in fevered dreams. Had just attained peace when Stuart noisily rolled in.

Tunes self-flagellatingly into the grating voice of a Scottish compatriot presenter on the radio. Loud and bombastic, the host's line in dumb chauvinism is crafted to both patronise and bait his intended audience. Silences the gobshite, lets Mahler wipe their oral excrement out of his brain. Outside, a woman skips along with her three children, getting them into a car. Lennox is seized by a poignant image of a younger version of his own mother. Avril picking him up from Firhill School: a beaming smile on her face.

Sadness chokes him.

There were good times in that house after the tunnel

189

*incident. Your mother tried. But some dark little part of you knew
what was going on. And she knew that you knew. That ugly
truth: it hung between you, unspoken, slowly festering away.*

No good to let things fester, Ray.

Stop this.

He finds himself almost dozing off with fatigue, but about
twenty minutes later, Cardingworth emerges from a shabby
back door. One side of his face is swaddled in gauze bandages.
This look, on approaching his incongruously stylish vehicle,
replete with a furtive swivelling of his head, ripples a spasm of
laughter from Lennox's gut, echoing inside the Alfa Romeo.

Ridiculous fucking noncing cunt . . .

Yet the moments Cardingworth cuts a pathetic adversarial
figure are fleeting. His would-be quarry stops, looks around,
car keys in hand, his expression puzzled and hesitant. Punches
something in his phone before climbing into the vehicle. This
paused consideration of his nemesis thumps Lennox hard in
the chest. Hints at something deeper and more terrible than
anything he'd recalled from the tunnel. Feels a shiver down
his back. Cranks up the Alfa's heating. Then the Jaguar's
engine roars and Cardingworth again has become one of the
omnipotent bullies of that time and place, though something
else too. Now Lennox senses a darker power lurking behind
him, pulling the strings. Mathew Cardingworth is scared; but
disconcertingly, Lennox knows it's not of him.

Starts up his engine. Follows the retreating Jag into the
streets. It seems to glide rather than roll, and Lennox again
experiences the sensation of the Alfa Romeo struggling to
keep up; an enthusiastic gym rat in pursuit of an Olympic
sportsman.

Bypassing the town centre, heading towards Hove, Cardingworth then turns left towards the sea. Lennox follows his
target to the Western Esplanade dwelling, where Cardingworth

reverses the Jaguar inside. As the doors sluggishly close, Lennox elects to park in a driveway of another huge dwelling, situated round the corner. It has the whiff of deserted second home. Gambles the owners will be in their Florida or Canary Isles residence, not to resurface till spring. It provides a decent vantage view of two sides of Cardingworth's giant white pillbox.

But just as he starts to google more about Cardingworth's enterprises, the on-street garage doors of the best house on Western Esplanade swing open. A nondescript white van makes a truculent egress. Apart from the fact that in Britain the drivers of such vehicles statistically commit the most crimes, Lennox's heartbeat spikes. Cardingworth, whose face he catches in gauzed profile, drives past him. This seems ludicrously low-rent transport for the property developer. Why has he returned to switch to the less ostentatious jalopy?

Where are you going, ya noncing cunt?

The van turns the corner. Lennox, about to start up the Alfa Romeo in pursuit, realises how painstakingly slowly the metal garage doors are closing. Whips his head around, storms out the car. Slams it closed. Sprints towards the creaking shutters. In a desperate footballing tackle, he slides across smooth concrete. For an instant, fears decapitation; the door edge brushes his hair and shoulder as it closes firmly behind him. As the chink of light at the base recedes into blackness, his explosive euphoria at gaining entry quickly dissipates. Fear, stark and uncompromising, floods his body into paralysis. Forces in deep, conscious breaths. He stands up in total darkness. Waits for a visual adjustment that never fully comes.

The stillness . . . the incontrovertible inky black . . . you know about this . . . you can do this . . .

 . . . but it engulfed you, didn't it, completely absorbed you. It always engulfs you . . .

Heaves more oxygen into his lungs. Steps forward into a controlled explosion of pain in his shin, forcing him to stifle a yelp: the fender on Cardingworth's Jaguar. Sucks through pursed lips as he finger-traces along the bonnet to the rear of the car. The sharp jab recedes to an indignant throb. He can just about discern a door ahead. Thankfully, it's unlocked. Blinks as swarming light from the house floods his retina.

Makes his way from a utility room, and through a large, open-plan kitchen. The residence looks like an unlived-in show house, emphatically vended on a regular basis, as with most homes of the very rich, whether it's required or not. On the wall of the dining area, a series of framed pictures. One catches his eye: parents, with their children. The oldest one stands apart from the others. It's most certainly Cardingworth, the rest likely his younger siblings. The divergence of ages, looks and ethnicities indicates adoption or fostering. He's the only one smiling, and it's forced, clownish: tension tears from his face. Lennox's blood freezes for two full seconds. At the sight of the children, but it's more than that: he finds himself pegging Cardingworth as a pathetically solitary character and scarily identifying with this. Starts capturing the images on his camera phone. Notices that one of the children is a fat boy of curly hair and sulky pout. It more than suggests a young Ralph Trench.

Rummages through cupboards. Nothing remarkable bar a portrait picture of Cardingworth, decades younger, with a very beautiful woman. She has long, luxuriantly curling black hair. It's a strange and haunting photo; both in profile, looking at each other. They seem relaxed, but a tint of doomed, trepidatious sadness reflects in the eye of both. Lennox fancies they might be in love. Cardingworth has hidden this image from public view, from the gaze of future lovers like Angela. But he has never been able to get rid of it and it seems he needs it close by.

Who is she and what is she to Mathew Cardingworth?

Heading upstairs, he moves through the rooms, enters the master bedroom to the rear of the house. Looks through big glass doors, across a patio balcony. There's an open view out over the Channel. Turns back into the room, which is dominated by a huge bed. Succumbing to a moment of poignant jealousy, Lennox sees himself there with Carmel, making love. Them perhaps living there. A brutal thought spikes him: has she already been in this bed? Was the readjustment to the swinging setback perhaps resolved by a threesome with Cardingworth and Angela? Did they decide it was best to keep him out of *all* of their business?

It seems inevitable that she's been here. She'll do anything to get this facility funded; her work is everything to her.

Cardingworth has taken everything. What can you do? Take him down with you!

Stakes out a prodigious marble-tiled en suite bathroom. The toiletries are male only, the stock shaving foam, aftershave, shampoo, body wash and moisturiser. Heads back to the bedroom. Slides open the patio doors. Shivers as the cold air bites at him.

There's an immense outdoor kitchen beside a huge pool, into which he sticks his hand to discover that it's heated. He is tempted to take off his clothes and jump in, before laughing out loud at the stupidity of that notion. Close by is a jacuzzi and several loungers. Lennox then sets eyes on a large telescope. Looks through it to the dark and squally sea. No boats are anywhere to be seen, whether passenger, leisure or freight. Fancies he can make out the twinkling lights of France dancing on the distant horizon, as a yawn rips from him.

A vicious chill, breaking from across the Channel with sudden ferocity, forces him back into the bedroom. The relieving schlurp as the doors shut. Sits on the bed. There's a deep comfort in this mattress, one he hasn't experienced in any before. Looks at himself in the mirrored wardrobe doors. Rises, walks towards them. The snide malevolence on his own face unnerves him. Like he's watching someone nefarious on CCTV. Slides a wardrobe door open, fingers the expensive cashmere wool of an overcoat. Flicks at an array of designer suits and silk shirts. Ray Lennox suddenly feels all-powerful.

You are in the lair of the beast and the pathetic creature can do nothing to stop you.

He's aware that his bladder is full. Resolves that he will urinate over those clothes. They will be saturated in his DNA.

So what? Let the cunt have you arrested! You'll see him in court. He won't go there. Will he? Let's find out!

Unzips, points his penis at the cashmere coat and the suits. Watches as a thick jet of urine saturates and darkens the materials in front of him. A white shirt satisfyingly stains yellow. Piss like the corrosive blood of the creatures in the *Alien* movie franchise. When done, shakes out his cock to laughter, fastens himself up and slides the door shut.

Sits back down on the bed. So soft, yet firm. The duvet, pillows and decorative cushions like puffy, luxurious clouds. He's very warm, the thermostat set to a high temperature. Wonders if Cardingworth has thin blood and feels the cold severely. Lets his weary head sink back against the pillows. It is blissful. Shuts his eyes. Allows his thoughts to unspool.

There were good times . . . and you see your mother's face as a younger woman; beautiful, indulgent of you. You feel her taking you by the hand. Yet it's as if you're in control of this dream, willing the idyllic state, banishing all negativity from the simple domestic scenario unfolding in front of you . . .

You love your mum . . .

A door slams. Lennox springs up, groggy, head pounding, mouth dry. How long has he been asleep? A few minutes?

Maybe more? Then more noises: music blares out from downstairs, Michael Jackson singing 'Don't Stop 'Til You Get Enough'. Lennox tries to force himself into alertness, can't quite pull it off; as he gets off the bed, nausea rises in him. The sounds of feet as they thwack on the stairs. Adrenaline surges: he quickly makes his way out onto the balcony.

Cardingworth . . .

Is he alone or with somebody?

Looks over the parapet. A good fifteen-foot drop to the ground. On one side, a large green double dump bin, around five foot high.

A creak as someone turns the handle of the bedroom door.

Ray Lennox slips over the balustrade.

Jumps.

He lands feet first on the bin; wide-eyed in surprise he's not gone through the lid. But on contact it gives him the spring to kick off, and he falls the further five feet to the ground, rolling onto his back. A scrambling rise in winded pain, around the corner to the front of the house. As his returning breath slowly oozes strength back into his body, he can hear activity from inside the house. A figure starts to form behind the dimpled glass of the front door. Striding up and filling his lungs, Lennox rings the buzzer.

Mathew Cardingworth opens up, startled eyes, one curling over the facial bandages. — What the fuck do you want!

— I was going past, Lennox hauls in air, and I saw your security was poor. Thought I'd bring it to your attention, a sneering gaze at Cardingworth. — You did say to take a look, and he gives the thumbs up, suddenly grinning in expansively cartoonish mania.

— Are you stalking me? What the hell is going on with you and this . . . nutter? Mat Cardingworth touches the gauze on his face. — Look . . . whatever your friend thinks happened to him, I had nothing to do with it!

— It wasn't just him though, was it? Tell me aboot the tunnel in Edinburgh, Cardingworth, Lennox hears his voice go nasal and sly, — where you first met me and my wee pal, Les. Tell me who your fuckin mates were!

— Get the fuck away from here, Cardingworth snarls, leaning forward, as if trying to get into Lennox's face. — Speak to my lawyer if you –

— Way ahead of you –

The track playing changes. Stevie Wonder sings 'I Just Called to Say I Love You' as Cardingworth steps back, making to close the door. Lennox tries to stick a foot in, but the Brighton businessman is too quick, slamming it shut. One lock, then a second, clunk in noisy turn. Through the door comes a muffled threat: — You'd better make yourself scarce, Lennox!

— Okay, but I'll be back, ya noncing cunt. Lennox hammers his fist on the glass three times, but in a controlled manner. — I always come back for them, you know. I never let it go. Remember that, *Noncingworth*, he shouts, turning his chant out to the neighbourhood as he skips down the steps. — I'LL BE ON YOU EVERY FUCKIN DAY, YA PAEDO PRICK!

A burning silence, and he turns and heads off. As 'I Just Called to Say I Love You' is cut into silence from inside the house, Ray Lennox laughs until both his sides buckle in pain.

28

SOLE DESTROYING

It's barely noon when he arrives at the office in Seven Dials. Immediately, George enters his room with two coffees. — You've finally deigned to join us this fine Monday. He looks through the dirty windows out into the gloom of the street. — What happened? A little make-up romance with what's-her-face, Carmel?

Lennox sucks in one cheek. — I wish . . . So, what have you been up to?

— Checking with the Rose Garden management that the fitting was to her satisfaction. The alarm, of course. George raises an eyebrow, as Lennox smiles while groaning inside. — I've been sorting that out and uh, mending fences of the interpersonal nature. George sips at the coffee. His face screws up. — This instant is damn well undrinkable. You do realise that?

— It is, Lennox concedes. — We should get a coffee machine. Fancy a pint? Goodies?

— Oh, I've a lunch date with Polly. George shakes his head, checking his Rolex. — Catch you later, he smiles, departing.

Lennox goes back online at his PC. Hasn't eaten breakfast, so decides on an early lunch. Outside, a hiemal air stings, as he walks towards town, mood alternating between anxious and buoyant.

You fairly set Cardingworth on edge. Good.

He heads down the Lanes where the Christmas vibe is

heavy with the useless excitement and empty promise of cocaine. Yet the mere consideration of that drug has induced Lennox to step into a chemist and purchase some Kleenex paper tissues. Sighs heavily in recognition. The wet chill means he might need them anyway. Exits the shop and immediately sees Polly. She's wrapped up in a coat, hat and gloves, her breath freezing as she looks into a shop window. Lennox cranes his neck around the crowds to find George. No sign. Approaches her. — Hi, Polly.

Startled, she jumps back, touching her chest. — Oh, Ray, you gave me a proper fright there!

Lennox apologises, doubts George has seen her for lunch. *Where is he?* Decides to remain silent. A brief sense of panic fuses him, before he deduces his partner is probably with another woman.

The cunt might have said.

— How goes?

— Fine! It's my day off, so I'm shopping for Christmas presents. I've two younger sisters and a host of nieces and nephews, so it's a costly old affair, and she holds up two full bags. — I'm meeting George later on this afternoon.

— You guys having a late lunch together?

— No, I've eaten, and he called to say he had too. What are you up to?

— Just nipped out for a stroll and a bite myself, Lennox nods. — Better let you get on. See you later.

— Righto!

As they go their separate ways, he turns back to look at Polly, feeling sorry for her. Wonders how much she knows about George's philandering ways.

If you can deceive a lover so readily, would it be that difficult to do the same to a friend?

A sudden downpour: shoppers scatter for cover. Wet

needles prick Lennox's scalp and neck. Walks on through relentless, stinging rain. Soon the coat is sodden, hangs heavily on his frame. The dark, void sky ahead. A harsh laughter erupts from behind him, first urgent, then derisive. A tremble in his spine: between his shoulder blades.

Thinks of Chris and his friends in the pub the previous night. Is he being followed? His hands fist up inside his coat pockets. But he's disinclined to succumb to this insecurity; if no pursuit, self-outing as paranoid will do him no good. If he is being shadowed, the streets remain busy. Fear is an emotion best left unexpressed, and he pushes on.

Up ahead, two large glass rectangles: one cobalt blue, the other silver grey. The Jubilee Library. Decides to take refuge. The students are on their Christmas break, so in spite of the downpour it isn't too busy, but the bright and airy building fizzes with the magical efficacy generated by collective concentration. This is common to libraries, yet those operating at only one frequency won't register it. Lennox looks around the rows of tables and chairs. Goes to an issue desk and is assisted by a member of staff, wearing a badge indicating the moniker 'Norris'. With his stocky build and lumpy, pugilistic visage, he looks more like a nightclub bouncer than a librarian.

Requesting the *Argus* records from the dates of the disappearances of the foster care boys – Thomas Millington, Ross Prior, Marshall Delaney and Jason McCabe – Lennox is issued a piece of paper with a website link on it. The library digitalised the records for the newspaper, so, if the pages here are similarly doctored, this happened under their watch rather than that of the *Argus*.

Taking a seat at one of the computer-topped desks, Lennox begins his search. Very quickly realises that the key pages are missing from those copies too. In fact, even *more* seem to have vanished, including the grainy pictures of Julie Wilkins, or

199

Julie Knowles, if they are the same person. He rises, to speak to the library assistant.

— Why were those pages removed?

— They shouldn't have been. That's strange . . . Norris heads back behind the desk, goes into a cupboard, returning with rolls of film on a spool. — Let's try the microfiche. They were copied onto these first, then digitalised later.

They head over to some desks, each one with a large metal box sitting on it. The hulking machines seem ancient contraptions to Lennox. Norris loads a spool into one, switches on a huge backlit screen to reveal the newspapers. Starts scrolling to the relevant issues.

They too are missing the pages, which, he speculates, will be key ones.

— What could have happened to them? Were they ripped out?

— Might have been damage to the original documents, I suppose, Norris ventures.

Across twenty years?

— When were the hard copies of the newspapers put onto microfiche?

— Around '84, '85, then ongoing from there, till they were digitalised in 2006 from the microfiche. What was the story you were looking for?

Lennox can see Norris is enjoying playing detective. — Just some family stuff: births, marriages, anniversaries, that sort of nonsense, he lies. He now trusts nobody in Brighton, Edinburgh or the rest of the world. — What about the original documents, the print copies of the papers that the *Argus* donated? A lot of libraries bind and store them.

— We used to, but we had a librarian who didn't like having duplicate technology around. I suppose the purpose of new technology is to update and replace the old, Norris dolefully explains. — Anyway, this guy had our original papers shredded. As far as I know, the *Argus* moved all their archive here, so there's no hard copy at their offices.

— Who was the head librarian back in '84?

Norris rubs his chin, pondering this. — It would be Tom James.

— Is he still here?

— No, he retired three years ago. Died last summer.

— Anybody else I could speak to?

— From 1984? I very much doubt it.

— What about the librarian who insisted the hard copies had to be destroyed after they were put onto microfiche? Would they be still around?

— That would be big Ralphie Trench. He left the service a long time ago. Always wanted to make it as an actor. Did a bit in panto, once played an antique dealer in *The Bill*. Looks a lot like the guy from *Withnail and I*.

As the librarian explains this, the wooden plaque on the wall behind him catches Lennox's attention:

SUSSEX LOCAL HISTORY ARCHIVE
Made possible by a generous donation from
Mathew Cardingworth

— Thanks for your help, Lennox mumbles. Heads to the library coffee shop, befuddled and numbed.

The fucking nonce bought the archives, and had Trench doctor them before donating the bastards . . . you know it!

In the cafeteria, Lennox puts his wet coat on a seat close to a radiator. Orders a cherry scone, a cappuccino and bottle of Highland Spring mineral water. Decides to try and wait out the rain, watching it lash on the big glass windows.

Peristalsis kicks in as the coffee makes its presence felt,

demanding an extensive manoeuvre. Obtaining the lavatory code, he goes downstairs to an empty hallway. Keys in the issued number, pulls the door open, raising the lever to lock it behind him. In the large space, a latrine, sink and a toilet. This is enclosed in a booth of mahogany-effect wood and has a further lock, which Lennox closes but neglects to bolt. The door outside is already secured. Lowers himself onto the cold plastic toilet seat. Opens his bowels, lets his waste surge home.

He is enjoying the relief when he hears a faint click.

Does it indicate that somebody has come in?

But how? The main lavatory door locks from the inside.

Lennox feels his pulse kick up as he rises quickly, wiping his arse, tugging up his underpants and trousers. Pushes at the door.

It won't open.

There was no lock on the outside.

He pushes harder.

It doesn't give. He feels feeble and inadequate against whatever is behind the door. Hears his heart pound as the blood swooshes in his head. It seems important to say nothing. Then a mechanical voice, as if through a vocoder, blurts out: — **You've been warned. Leave it.**

A hissing sound. A fluidic substance seeps in under the door. Bleach-thick, its corrosive rasp urges his reticence as it creeps along the tiled floor towards him. On contact with the soles of his Doc Martens, sibilation and rising steam, and Lennox feels them stick him to the floor. Realises his shoes are *melting*: in panic, slides back onto the toilet seat, tugs the laces apart, pulls his feet out of them, raises his legs. Watches in disbelief as the base of his footwear dissolves further. Tension rips through his gut as he strives to keep his feet off the floor. Whips out his phone, calls George. — I need help! I'm trapped in the toilet of the Jubilee Library cafe. Get here as soon as you can, and call the library staff and fire brigade, ask them to get buckets of water and alkaline substances down here! I think some fucker has put down acid – tell them to be careful with their feet!

— Ray, what's going on?

— Just do it. And get me some shoes. Size eleven. Do it!

— Right! I'm on it!

Calls the library on its website number. Slips into clipped cop vowels to circumvent the effect on local ears of a Scottish accent that thickens dramatically when in panic mode. Asks for Norris, gives strict instructions. Soon the staff arrive with cleaning materials, followed by the fire brigade and then the police.

A chemical solution is put down, and the acid neutralised. All that is ruined of Lennox are the soles of his Doc Martens. As this footwear is touted as acid-resistant, he reasons it must have been a very strong and corrosive compound.

Carmel would know . . .

An owl-faced detective, introducing himself as Tony Robson, asks Lennox perfunctory questions, while the police check CCTV footage and interview staff to determine who went into the toilet. — They would have needed the passcode, which is issued at the food counter checkout and changed every day, Lennox suggests.

Robson and his colleagues all but ignore him, asking Norris and the canteen supervisor to get descriptions of the customers. The police don't seem to be too interested. But Lennox knows this MO: keep the public *experts* at bay until you need them. Is he just experiencing the frustration of being on the other side of this divide or *does Cardingworth have them in his pocket too?*

When George arrives, a stocking-soled Lennox is sat in the cafe, sipping a cappuccino. His partner shakes his head in confusion. — What the hell is going on, Ray?

— Where's they shoes?

— I asked Polly to pick up some brogues, and a text pops in to George's phone, and he raises his head to scan the canteen. On cue, Polly arrives, carrying an additional cumbersome item among her multiple Christmas bags. She dumps her cargo on the chairs round the table. One box she opens up, to reveal a pair of sensible black brogues. — George's idea, she says.

— Why am I not surprised . . . ?

— Am I a fashion consultant? George barks. — Shop for your own shoes, Raymond!

— I did try, Ray, Polly protests wearily to Lennox. Her attention wanders to two women seated at a table across the other side of the cafe. — If you gentlemen will excuse me, I've just spotted a couple of old friends.

Forcing a smile, Lennox tries the brogues on. They pinch. His face screws up.

— You do know they'll expand, George contends. — So, what the hell happened to your old ones, Ray?

Lennox bites his lip for a full two seconds. Then discloses everything about the acid attack. — It has to be Cardingworth's doing. I went to his house, he confesses, omitting to mention he entered uninvited. — We had a bit of an argument. He's obviously pissed off at me for Les's attack.

— Did he threaten you?

Lennox raises his brows. — It was a heated exchange, but there's a lot more going on, and he tells George about the missing news pages.

— So, somebody in 1984, George blows on his tea, — three years after your tunnel incident, during their transition to microfiche, removed the articles dealing with a missing foster kid.

— Yes, not just for 1984, but 1986, 1989 and 1997 as well. Even more sinister, he holds up his phone, — I can't find a

204

thing about any of those cases online in the national tabloid archives.

— Pre-millennial and therefore pre-internet crime though, Ray, they wouldn't necessarily cover the disappearance of four fostered orphans in Sussex over a period of twenty-odd years.

— Some newspaper archives are now digitalised from before the First World War. The nationals simply didn't report those cases. Surely such horrific events would be tabloid staple fare.

— Only if there was a connection, George advances, — and you're the only one making it. Otherwise each one is just the disappearance of a random, runaway foster kid, surely.

— Anybody at Sussex Police been investigating those disappearances down the years?

— Not to my knowledge.

Would you be able to find out? The sentence gets lost. Lennox pushes his gripped toes out against the unyielding leather of the shoes. — No police investigation, and no tabloid interest. Doesn't sound right. Unless . . .

— Well, Raymond, George raises the cup, and then lowers it again, — you do know how much I like a good conspiracy theory, but are you trying to say the establishment, the newspaper barons and national politicians, have Cardingworth's back?

— It all depends just who Cardingworth did favours for, and what he has on them.

George turns his head dismissively. — Massive overreach. He's a regional businessman. He's just not that big a player.

— It's not net worth that buys influence, Lennox sips some coffee that has grown tepid, — it's how much somebody is willing to shell out for it.

George's mouth is turned down. — So where are you going with all this? Cardingworth is in a paedophile ring that kidnaps, abuses and murders orphans who have supposedly run away from foster care? That's really your contention?

— Yes, Lennox realises it is. — And I think the concrete factory has something to do with it. Why does Cardingworth have it on his portfolio but done nothing with it, has no plans for it? He develops and flips, that's his modus operandi. What profit is there in a derelict and decrepit factory standing by old chalk pits, which was only ever good for making technologically obsolete Portland cement?

— How do you know this?

Lennox remains stone-faced.

— Trench told you . . . George makes the leap, — he's not exactly reliable, is he?

— No, Lennox concedes, — Trench was duck's-ringpiece taciturn. It's what he *didn't* tell me. Anyway, the factory isn't going anywhere. I want to check it out.

— Well, we can't go inside. George rolls his eyes. — For one thing, you are aware that it's private property and illegal. It will be dangerous from a health and safety point of view, and it has security –

— I wouldn't ask you to –

— Thank God for that –

— But if you drive me there, I can.

George gives out an oddly mechanical sigh of exasperation, as if burrs of phlegm generated by the ubiquitous flu bug have lodged in his chest. — This obsession, Ray, it's taken you from a disused railway tunnel in Edinburgh to an abandoned concrete factory in Sussex.

— So?

You've taken me here! You suggested moving down here and going into business with you.

— So, I'm just not seeing the connections that you are. The men who abused you and Les in that tunnel were opportunists, not serious kidnappers. Had they been, they'd have taken you somewhere remote and secure, not attempted rape in the tunnel of a public walkway!

— Maybe they were just starting out. Amateurs grow into pros if they learn quickly, Lennox contends, pulling his heels backwards, to spare his brogue-crushed toes. — I've no doubt that was a chance encounter, but there was a prior, acknowledged shared love of noncing, inevitably through prison. Nevertheless, my gut is telling me that there's something bent about that factory. So, are you going to drive me there and wait while I break in?

George Marsden looks across to where Polly Ives sits with her two friends. Nods tightly. — This, of course, stays between us.

— Of course, Lennox agrees.

29

THE FACTORY

Lennox sits in the passenger seat of George's BMW, a catalogue of sex crimes and criminals past flitting through his mind. 'Demented' Rab Dudgeon, the steroid-munching, body-building 'carpenter of lunacy'. Trawled Edinburgh's rougher bars, befriending isolated young men, plying them with drink, drugging them into a weakened haze before battering them unconscious. The same signature method was generally deployed: one blow smashed square on the forehead with a wooden mallet, which whipped the brain back against the skull, causing blackout. Then he'd blindfold the victims and beat them to a pulp before sodomising them. Three died, though he probably never set out to kill them. He generally released his prey, after telling them he knew everything about them. Most were too scared and ashamed to tell the authorities. But it only took a couple to rediscover their courage and he was finished. There was Lennox's own ex-psychotherapist Sally Hart and her cohort Rawat, the most unlikely killers and ones he had a worrying sympathy with. After all, they were like him, on a vengeful quest. But they all proved you could get caught. Lennox, however, wouldn't get caught.

Then, the most infamous of them all: the kidnapper, rapist and strangler of young girls, known as Mr Confectioner. The arrogant civil servant led Lennox to mental breakdown, and also, inadvertently, to his partnership with the man now driving him, who had been investigating the same multiple killer from his own patch in Hertfordshire.

By the time they drive out to the factory, the anaemic sun is falling behind the concrete towers. George parks up in the lay-by twenty metres from the building's perimeter fence. Pursing his lips tightly, he urges, — One more time, Raymond, do not do this. You do realise that you could be arrested, or worse. It's a derelict factory and probably very dangerous. Besides, it's bloody cold and there's a lovely country pub up this road, with a roaring fire . . .

Lennox looks at his partner. Thinks of Perry van der Meer, the lawyer George recommended, who obviously had some connection to Cardingworth. Considers the falsehood about Polly and lunch. George has always operated in mysterious ways. Now, for the first time in their friendship, Lennox feels driven to find out what those ways are. But there are more immediate matters of concern. — I'll be back within the hour. You don't need to wait if you don't want to.

George lets out a sharp exhalation of breath: — Of course I'll bloody wait. Call me if you run into trouble.

Nodding tightly, Lennox gets out the car. He's opted to shed his overcoat for mobility and the cold smarts through his dark hooded rain jacket. But George's brogues have been replaced, to great assuagement, by black Adidas trainers. He walks back up the deserted road towards the plant. In a low crouch, sheltered by bushes in front of the security point, he traverses round the peripheral fence. No sign of Mathew Cardingworth's Jaguar. Then, a security guard, lighting a cigarette, steps out from the large Portakabin offices. It's not Trench. This younger man, around thirty, hatchet-faced with busy eyes, wears a bulky parka over his uniform as he takes a deep drag on his smoke.

One security camera, then another, catches Lennox's eye. They seem to comprehensively cover the factory from the front. To the rear, the desolate chalk pits stretch out, making any encroachment and escape hazardous. The camera system is a make known to him; quite old, sloppy technology (Cardingworth really could do with a consultant in that department) and he calculates potential blind spots from the angle, sweep and direction of their stationary lenses. Skimming the fence, he darts along the right-hand side of the perimeter. If he goes over at this point, the Portakabin hides him from the guard. The last camera will catch him fleetingly, but the man still has a large part of the cigarette to smoke before going back inside to the security monitors. Pulls up his hood, scrambles up a section of the barbed-wire fencing – sees a gap that will only deter the obese, and he slides through effortlessly.

In the failing light he steals across the loading bay at the rear of the factory. No visible cameras here, nor any sign of patrolling guards with dogs. Corregated plastic canopies top the walls of the dock, under which are stacked bags of concrete. As production stopped years ago, Lennox wonders why this old stock is retained here. Several skips, he counts four through the murky darkness, are full of rubbish: mainly rubble and old machinery. Several heavily padlocked doors would afford access to the building, but it would take a lot of time and noise to breach them.

Then the obvious, but still daunting, point of entry manifests; a swinging crane, growing out of an extended steel joist, protrudes from a big square orifice raised about eight feet off the ground. A rusted rolling metal shutter, probably long jammed open, hangs above the potential gateway. The hoisting equipment looks as though it operates electrically, but Lennox pulls the chain into his shoulder. Starts moving towards the building, exhilarated as he looks up to watch the drum unit moving by his efforts, gliding along the purlin towards the dark entrance.

The tunnel . . .

Looks at the black gateway above him. Swallows hard through a throat so dry it's like gargling glass shards. Grips the chain in both hands, starts pulling himself up. It's an assiduous and painful process: his arms are strong, as is his core, but his legs flail wildly, struggling to get purchase on the slippery links. Fills his lungs and concentrates, locking his lower limbs. Adrenalised by the mastery, he struggles home and steps into the building, heart thrashing in his chest as euphoria swarms him.

Eyes fighting to adjust to another layer of darkness, Lennox withdraws the phone, activates the torch. As he advances, noises; like the sound of somebody spraying plants. He freezes.

It's the sleeves of the hooded rain jacket brushing against his sides. Breathes in deeply. Looks around, through his paltry torchlight.

This barren and cavernous level befits a storage and distribution centre. More bags of cement, piled high around perimeter walls. Heads towards an ancient goods lift, with a grated industrial double door. Wonders if it still works. Warily opts instead for some rusting metal steps: two sets are adjacent to either side of the antiquated elevator. Ascends, heading for the top floor of the building, concerned at the rickety nature of the stair as it creaks and wobbles in loose mountings under his feet.

The next level he passes with a cursory glance. It seems deserted and spooky. Realises that the three floors above ground level are only part of the factory; moving over towards broken parapet railings, he shines his torch into a dark void. Two giant metal tubes run in parallel with each other for the entire length of the building, huge silo pipes like the tunnels of the London Underground. The light cannot illuminate the bottom, only those enormous conduits. He turns and continues to head up the wobbly stairs.

As he steps onto the top floor, beamed moonlight spills in through holes above, lasering a barren concrete deck.

Then, a demonic rustle and squeaking: his heart skips two full beats.

A crowd of bats fly out through the damaged roof into the night. Unleashes a breath he was unaware he was holding.

There seems little up here; Lennox retraces his steps, heading for the lower level. The banister shakes. He loses his footing, but urgently tightens his grip and corrects himself.

A damp, nascent smell, seeping into the air. A metal *plink* of water dripping from somewhere. The plant literally disintegrating around him. Points the phone torch at his feet to help navigate the dangerous terrain.

Works his way back down, the increasing musty scent of wet concrete and *something else*, something malodorous, builds in his nostrils. These are fresh smells: they indicate some kind of recent activity. Something decomposing. The stairwell darkens further as he descends slowly. At every step the skimpy, murky light from above fades. His phone battery is low. It will die soon. Senses he may need to summon help, switches it off. In order to ensure his footing, kicks his heels back against the steps, creeping slowly down into the factory bowels.

A tawdry beam of light coming through a long window is cast over his trainers as he pushes on down to ground level, that space blocked off from potential intruders by heavy locks and doors. It's almost pitch-black.

He would be relieved to hit the bottom, if he didn't feel his left foot gripped by something sticky. Disconcertingly, he tries to free himself in a steady tug. The word *acid* fuses his brain, but this feels different. Adjusts his weight towards the right peg, thankfully still on terra firma, yanking the trapped one free. Through his trainer sole, he feels the join between his heel on the hard floor and where his toes probe into what feels like quicksand.

Steps back to place both feet fully on the solid deck.

Decides to reactivate his torch: it illuminates his trainer print on the edge of a soft rectangle of wet cement. Crouching down, Lennox touches it with his fingers. Then starts to scoop at it. The fresh-poured concrete hardens as he pushes further down into its thickening mass. Rises and looks around, eyes still struggling to gain focus in the meagre light from the phone. Needs to find a spade or some other implement to test how deep this recent pour goes. Sees a pneumatic drill propped up against one of the turbines.

As he searches the labyrinth, he discerns other patches of concrete, all solid, but where the old has evidently been dug out and replaced by the new. They are all approximately five foot by two.

A shiver chills him in the back of his thighs. Nausea in his gut.

The names of the lost orphans whispering in his ear: *Thomas, Ross, Marshall, Jason* . . .

A thin fissle from outside, as moonlight filters through the windows: it sets his heartbeat at a race. Then, a sharp barking sound ripping out from somewhere close. Lennox stands still in the almost vaporous encroaching dark. Inhales two breaths and looks at the torchlight shining on his feet.

Something has to be buried under there.

Sweeping the thin light over the desolate chamber, he sees a long, thin metal spike. It's a steel bar for the reinforcement of poured concrete. Picks it up. Moves over to the wet patch. Begins to dig. The damp cement starts to break up. Lennox works frantically, forcing the spike in, scooping congealing chunks out from the damp rectangle.

A twanging sound behind him, from the metal gangway. It's followed by a more emphatic, familiar jar and a crunch of footsteps. Lennox whips round. Dancing shapes flit across his vision in the near darkness, then an urgent pounding, like fists on the concrete floor.

— Who's fuckin there?

A disturbance in the air: a faint rustle of a garment and Lennox sees a dark figure running through the murkiness towards him. A swishing noise in the air above his head; instinct makes him duck down. Swings the steel bar; the connection he feels confirmed by a yelp and a clattering din of metal hitting concrete.

Again, that strange bark coming through the darkness, followed by scuttling sounds from the periphery of the space.

Sweeps his meagre phone light. Two bright keen eyes stare back at him. A high, almost birdlike shriek freezes his blood, before he realises it's an urban fox. Then, the glint of metal: a sword lying on the ground. He was so close to decapitation. An echoing thud: Lennox follows its source. From the bend by the lift shaft, he sees the guard, sitting on the metal steps. The man holds his face as blood pours from his nose. — What the fuck . . . he squeals, slowly getting to his feet.

Lennox knows this is not the swordsman. This is confirmed when the twisting mouth of a man in a balaclava and goggles appears right in front of him. It's there for a frozen second but one into which all time seems to collapse, before a fist crashes into his jaw. Lennox feels his neck muscles tear, unable to shock-absorb the terrible blow as his brain smacks the back of his skull and his legs melt. As he goes down, he can see the figure in silhouette, pummelling the bemused guard back to the ground with one blow.

A defiant internal voice roars at him to get on his feet. He rises immediately; unsteady, almost toppling again. The masked assailant, now five metres away, looks at him for a still second through the measly light, before stepping into the shadows and scuttling up the metal stairway. Lennox fights through his weakness, using adrenaline's blazing surge to give pursuit, chasing the retreating figure as they run alongside the giant parallel rotary kilns. His feet soak as he splashes through water, hurtling towards what seems an opening in the wall, murky light pouring in ahead. Can't see the man, but hears his feet slap, ringing against more metal steps in ascent.

Ploughs upwards on his attacker's trail, onto the mezzanine. The thick dark yields nothing to his sight. Suddenly, a creak at his side and his eyes adjust as he turns to see the balaclava man standing there, looking at him.

Lennox does not know what to do.

His head still swims from their last encounter and it seems pathetic to say something.

A strange numbing silence hangs between the two men.

Then before Lennox has time to move aside the man barges into him, the momentum carrying them along the flimsy gangway. As Lennox tries to force wind back into his sick frame, he hears a screeching and the popping of rivets from the crumpling metal under him, the platform wildly swaying. Feels the man in the mask being violently decoupled from him. Reaches out to grab a handrail but gravity tears it from his grasp, and he shrieks in a long, unbroken sound, jamming his fingers through a grate, to stop his slide into the oblivion of darkness as the platform tilts violently. A wrenching din scrapes his eardrums at cruelly resonating frequency followed by a hideous snap, the metal underneath him seeming to fly through the air like a surfboard for several moments, before crashing down to earth . . .

. . . the completion of the journey is not the slo-mo he had anticipated but a demented showreel-smashing biopic beats into his head, featuring a cameo cast of thousands, friends and foes, randomly spliced together . . .

. . . the breath is brutally hammered out his lungs as something pushes, in pitiless, skewering violence, up through his tailbone. His one thought: *I'm finished . . . it ends here . . .*

Then a white light and a muted, tranquil state, before he opens his eyes. All is still. Near silence but for the soft, defeated moan of buckled metal and the dripping of water. His solitary consideration is to get away from wherever he is, but this is not possible: he can't move . . .

It takes him several hazy moments to discern his location is the wet floor of the factory, surrounded by the mangled and torn metal of the collapsed staircase and gangway. A body is close by him: the goggle- and balaclava-clad man. His black top and trousers render him insectlike, like a super-villain darkly reinvented in some Gothic comic. A gold tooth gleams in his mouth. Astonishingly, to the tired eyes of the prostrate Ray Lennox, the man pushes himself up onto his feet, shaking out one leg like a peeing dog. Instinct makes Lennox shut his eyes just before the balaclava man glares down at him.

He stops and says something. Lennox, eyes still closed, pain filling up in him, can't be sure what it is but it sounds like: *what are you fucking doing?*

Waiting for several beats before he opens his eyes, Lennox witnesses the man limping off into the darkness. Then sees blood coming from his torso. Pats it with both hands. Realises that he's numb from his hips down: his legs won't move. Raises his head to see there's a gash on the right one, so deep that the bloodied white of what he presumes is his shin bone is grotesquely visible. Struggles out of his hooded waterproof and tourniquets above his knee with the sleeve. With the rest of his garment he tries to cover his shin. This is not good. His heart pumps frenetically as if trying to burst out of a tight corset.

Ray Lennox cannot move. He believes that his hip bones and spine have shattered. He knows it's important to stay awake, but he just can't.

Day Twelve

30

GRAFTING AT THE MARINA

The darkness.

The light.

Your frenzied pedal through the tunnel; heavy, burning legs pumping, hurtling towards the radiant freedom of the blue-and-green arch ahead. But the bad people are in crazed pursuit: pounding steps, tyrannical taunts . . . menacing voices distorting as they ricochet off the curving walls, dissolving into a cacophony of lunatics screeching in bedlam . . .

Naw naw, Raymie . . .

You fookin idiot, get after him . . .

. . . your legs now barely moving. As if you're wading through a glue, pulling on the leaden soles of your feet . . . a touch on your shoulder, calling you back . . .

— Raymond . . . yes, you're with us . . .

Lennox opens his eyes. A big mass of a man looks down on him. Fear and panic rise in him, and don't completely abate, even when George Marsden pulls into focus.

— Finally, his partner ticks. — You've been out cold right through the night. The Royal Sussex County Hospital, George's eyes widen as he consults his Rolex, — 11.17, Tuesday morning. He shakes his head. — Ending up here, in this state, George raises his voice to blast through a debilitating burr in his windpipe, — I told you that place was bloody dangerous!

Lennox's own throat, glass-gargling raw, has sealed up. Noting his distress, George takes a cup of water from the bedside locker. Presses it to his lips. Lennox sips gratefully. Ascertains he's in a room ranked in gradations of green: bottle, emerald, lime, mint. Plastic bags hang overhead, delivering two sets of tubes into him. Then his glance shifts down to where his legs would be. He croaks in urgent despondency, — What the fuck –

A cage tents out in front of him. The fearful raising of his bedsheets exposes a heavily bandaged right leg. On his opposite thigh, a dressing stained by spots of blood seeping through. If his limbs appear badly damaged, their very presence still occasions massive relief.

— You have thirty-two stitches, George gravely explains, as if to an unruly child. — Skin grafts from the inside of your other thigh. You're on antibiotics to prevent infection. Now we have to go, they need your bed.

On cue a nurse comes in and starts removing the drips from his arm, as Lennox expels a long breath. Looks at George in disbelief. — Like, this moment?

— Quite so. I shall leave you to get dressed, George curtly nods in departure.

The nurse looks at Lennox, raises her eyebrows, follows his angry partner outside.

Lennox struggles to get out of bed. It isn't the slashed leg; the graft on his other thigh burns with greater severity than that wound. The problem is his tailbone. The excruciating agony produced by every step taken that tells him it has to be fractured. He vocalises this to a doctor who enters, accompanied by a medical student. Under Lennox's interrogation, he insists that the X-rays show nothing other than bad bruising, before beating a hasty retreat.

Pushing on, Lennox moves slowly-sharply, as if on hot coals, to the bathroom. Through a mirror, under jangling light, he examines the extent of the damage visible to him. The whole of his groin and perineum area is inky black, purple and yellow.

Just putting on his clothes is an ordeal.

Outside, George is on hand to help him down the corridor. As they leave the building, crossing the car park, Lennox hears his tranquilliser-fevered brain send confused mutterings to his partner about the balaclava man; how he will find out who has done this. But they only underscore his impotence, sounding nugatory and performative to his own ears.

His face a series of horizontal slashes, Lennox hobbles towards the BMW. Every step in the biting cold is an excruciating dagger twist into his tailbone, his hips seizing up under each stiff, tentative movement. The leg wound itches. The donor skin on his thigh graft pulsates in petulant rage at the blowtorch sear of the cold air. It's as if it will tear itself off and creep away from the laceration it vexatiously covers.

In the car, he reactivates his phone; messages truculently tumble into it like drunks jostling to get to the bar at a sports event. The voicemails are all Stuart's, except one each from Cardingworth and Carmel.

Cardingworth: — Who the fuck are you? Your friend attacks and disfigures me, probably because of you! What do you want from me, you utter fucking psychopath?

Vengeance, ya noncing paedo!

Carmel: — I don't know what the hell is going on with you, Ray. If you want to leave it there that's fine with me.

He looks at George, who, after helping him into the passenger seat, has taken a call of his own. His pained face tells its own story. Finally, his partner gets in and starts up the BMW. — It was getting close to the hour mark and I hadn't heard from you, so I left the car and walked up to the factory. I heard these crazy sounds coming from there, like all hell was breaking loose. The guard came running outside, terrorised, badly beaten about the face. Said he'd only started last week and wasn't getting paid enough for all this bollocks.

Lennox thinks back to the guard. The poor bastard genuinely didn't have a clue.

— I went in, saw someone running away, well, sort of limping quickly, then you lying there completely poleaxed, almost wrapped up in this metal stairway, George adjusts the side mirror, pulling out the car park, — I really thought . . . well . . . when I saw you were still with us, I loaded you into my car and drove you straight here.

— Unlike you not to call the police, the accusing jab flies from Lennox.

No, it wasn't wise. George raises a hand. — I bloody well should have! And you'd have ended up in the bloody jail! Not a good place for an ex-cop, Ray. Note the *ex*. We're security men now!

George's rage demoralises Lennox. They have rarely had a cross word in their many years of friendship.

Perhaps you aren't thinking straight. Maybe it's you who is doing all this to yourself. Not George or anyone else.

Mistrustful of his own judgement again, Lennox decides to let some time elapse before calling Carmel back. Slips his phone into his pocket. Looks out at bustling streets full of Christmas shoppers.

It's evident that George finds the strained, silent discord between them equally galling. Suddenly pulling into the side of the road, he places an affectionate arm around Lennox's shoulders. Regards his friend with a searchlight gaze. This unnerves the recipient; neither man inclines towards the tactile with his own sex. — This is where you have to cool it on this moonlighting. We have a business, Ray. You do see that, yes?

— Aye, Lennox concedes. — It's way past that time.

— Dark stuff is going on here. You're getting close to something, George further softens. — Only a fool would dispute that after the acid attack, and now this. But you're not as close as they seem to think you are. All you have is circumstantial stuff and conjecture. So, either back off and take it to the cops, or let me help you. I can do more digging.

All Lennox can do is cough out, — Appreciated.

— I'll set up an off-the-record chat with Tony Robson. A decent sort . . . for a copper, George laughs, delivering a theatrical salute. — I think you met him earlier.

Aye, he couldn't give a fuck.

Easing back in the BMW's upholstered seat, Lennox attempts to negotiate a new status quo of misery. The pain remains pervasive but at least it's now steady. Dreads exiting the vehicle, grimly aware the horrendous assault at the base of his spine is on the cards to reappear with a vengeance. Checks his voicemails again. The ones from Stuart immediately tell him: *the self-indulgent cunt is back on the piss big time.*

— I have news! Called at your office, but no El Mondo. Had a long chat with the lovely Ria. A stunner, Raymie! Bet you appointed her . . . fucking sex case!

Lennox feels his blood crystallise in his veins as a deep, incalculable loathing for his brother rises inside him.

— Just decided I'm madly in love with your secretary or receptionist or admin assistant . . . or whatever designation you give the gorgeous Ria in your post-polis patriarchal pensioner protection project . . .

For fuck sake, ya alcoholic mess, there's nae time for this pish . . .

— . . . I'm going to pull her and there's not one single fucking thing you can do about it!

What about rearrange your fucking face?

— Cancel that. You're off the hook. She has a boyfriend. I

saw him round there, a right narky wee strop-bag. Where the fuck are you! I have news!

Lennox sucks in a breath. Goes to his texts. They are more Carmel's territory. He reads the last one first:

> We need to talk.

Responds:

> Come over?

> No, meet me at the Marina.
> Café Rouge.

The texts ruthlessly shred any testosterone-fuelled triumph of hope over experience; that niggling delusion make-up sex could possibly be on the agenda. In any case it's more than his crushed body could take.

He's vaguely aware that George, pulling out into heavy traffic, is in discussion on speakerphone with a woman he assumes to be the Sonia he's been seeing on and off: — We can't go there just now, sweet pea . . . you do know that my partner Raymond is sitting next to me in the car.

— How convenient . . . Sonia hisses.

George starts to cough, and hacks out some phlegm, spitting it into a hanky. — I think I've got this bloody flu coming on . . . later . . . He hangs up.

Lennox bursts with intent to inform Carmel that Cardingworth tried to kill him in an abandoned concrete factory. Knows this would only make him seem even more ludicrous

226

in her eyes. But he no longer trusts her, unsure of the extent of her relationship with Cardingworth and the university project.

George drops him off at his rendezvous point. Helps him out of the vehicle. When he puts his weight on either foot Lennox feels like he's being smashed in the coccyx with a hammer and chisel. — Are you okay, Raymond? George asks, now looking watery and baggy-eyed himself. — Listen, you're more than welcome to stay at my place while you recover.

— No, I'm fine, but I appreciate the offer, Lennox grimaces, almost reflexively adding, *besides I've got Stuart*, but reasons that's an excuse *not* to go home.

He watches the BMW depart. George seemed to sail through life, but as another maverick ex-cop, he doubtlessly had his own demons. Were they now starting to manifest? Could he have been the assailant? It was a rugby-style tackle that brought him down. George has two gold teeth. Was he limping? Lennox couldn't ascertain, blinded by his own pain . . . Cardingworth wasn't the perpetrator; too heavy, not athletic enough. Was it the same person who got at him with the acid? *You wouldn't let it go.* If it wasn't George, at either library or factory, where was he on both occasions? Why did he lie about being at lunch with Polly?

Semi-crippled from grasping that grated metal that collapsed around him and the cold, Lennox's stiff fingers work his phone from his pocket. The freezing wind says, *you don't really want to do this, do you?* but he perseveres, hobbling into the bizarre city state of bad shopping and cheap drinking that has grown up on the town's east side, around a complex originally planned for affluent high rollers. Its original design envisaged boats in a coastal inlet with brown stone cliffs towering above. It manifested differently, as a rash of crass, shabby developments seemingly designed to puncture the pretensions of the

227

yachtspersons who look up from their sleek, moored vessels into that sprawling, concrete farrago of fast-food chains and bars. If England's proletariat ever gained some measure of revenge on the bourgeoisie for thirty-five years of neoliberalism, then Brighton Marina is a monument to it. Lennox presses on in pain, through the strangulating rash of tired-looking outlets. This dripping of dirty money tinting the opaque pool of opulence dark; it seems to point to the inevitable appearance of Cardingworth.

He huddles in the doorway of a disused shop unit, aching hand once more checking phone messages. The silent treatment from Ally Notman continues. Lennox calls him again, but it goes straight to voicemail. The synthetically chipper tones on the other end of the line almost feel like those of a deceased man, a previous version of his now dishevelled friend. It's difficult to see Notman being any help with information on Cardingworth. Could George's police contacts assist? Are they really in Cardingworth's pocket, or is it seriously time to reveal all? *Not yet*, a voice comes back: the one that never provides solace. The one that confirms to him he was always just a vigilante in state clothing.

The Brighton businessman wasn't Balaclava Man, while George's story about the mask-wearer's egress was as lame as both Lennox himself and his limping assailant. But if the assailant was his partner, why not finish Lennox off instead of taking him to the hospital? Easy meat for an ex-SBS man. Lennox casts his mind back to the tunnel: if the other men were both older than Cardingworth, they'd now be in their late sixties. Lennox certainly didn't feel that way at the moment, but logic stated it would take an exceptionally strong and fit man of that age to overcome him. The money was on a hired gun; cash bought you muscle. The grim truth is that Cardingworth, over forty years on from the tunnel, is still wrecking his life. Lennox is broken, having fallen almost to his death. His friend languishes in prison, though he knows Cardingworth will get his way with dropping charges. He is estranged from his girlfriend, the first romance he'd had in a while that offered affection, laughter, vigorous sex and the hope of a lot more to come.

All this is happening because of your obsession with Cardingworth and that tunnel. Maybe just let it go, Ray.

No!

And . . . you had a decent pair of Doc Martens ruined . . .

That intermittent voice in his head: sly, not his own. How it annoys and torments him. He takes a slow, jarring walk up the steps in the whipping wind, to the upper deck of the complex, overlooking the harbour. Reaching the Café Rouge, Lennox immediately sees Carmel sitting at a window table. She pours Diet Pepsi from a bottle into a glass of ice and lemon. As she looks up, they swap stiff, civil nods. It's an acknowledgement of former work colleagues rather than lovers. It stings him perhaps more than it should, given the still-fledgling nature of their relationship. He orders a pint of Stella from an approaching waitress and joins her, sitting down slowly, visibly pained.

This does not escape Carmel. — You're limping . . . what's wrong?

— Industrial accidents, he says. It was originally a phrase Keith Richards would use in reference to yet another rock'n'roll casualty. They'd adopted it at Serious Crimes, which had a higher rate of suicide, alcoholism, drug addiction and divorce than any other division on the force. — But I'm okay.

— What sort of –

— Please listen, Carmel, he emphatically begs, — I need to say something to you.

Carmel seems to fight down her confusion, before raising her brows to declare: *yes, you do.*

He has no option but to go for it. Clearing his throat, Ray Lennox starts telling her the story he'd recently told George: about two boys with their bicycles, back in Edinburgh, many years ago. And the dark tunnel they vanished into, only to partially re-emerge from. He falters a few times; despite reliving the tale with depressing regularity, he is unused to performing it in front of others. To his own ears, he sounds like one of the many sex abuse victims he's interviewed down the years in his professional role; monotone voice indicative of the detached, fatalistic frame of mind they called *disassociation*.

Carmel listens mutedly, her initial impatience dissolving first into horror, then a head-shaking disbelief. As he concludes, her eyes are misty, but she refrains from reaching for his hand across the table, as he hoped she might. — It was forty years ago, Ray. Have you ever thought that you might just be mistaken?

— Both of us? Les hadn't clapped eyes on Cardingworth since then. He knew nothing about all this until that visit to the hospitality suite. Whatever you've heard about him, he isn't in the habit of glassing strangers.

— And you didn't mention this to him: about your suspicion of Mat?

— No, Lennox concedes, self-punishing by clenching his buttocks to induce a searing shot of pain from his tailbone through his nervous system, — and I'm fucking ashamed of myself. Obviously, if I thought there was a chance of him acting like that, I certainly would have.

Liar!

Carmel shakes her head. — I know Mat Cardingworth. He's done great things for this town, and for my university. This just isn't him, Ray.

Lennox feels *you know fuck all about him* freeze on his lips. Forces himself into the investigative mode. — Okay. So, tell me, what's *really* going on with this research?

— As I might have mentioned, Carmel says in accusatory tones as if to state *you never listen,* — it's about making stronger, cheaper, more durable, energy-efficient and green building materials.

The wind changes direction as buckshot rain lashes the pane of glass. It briefly warrants Lennox's strung-out attention. — Cardingworth owns an old concrete plant out on the road to Shoreham. What does he want with that if he's massively investing in new technology at Falmer?

— I don't know, Carmel says in exasperation, — Ask *him,* for fuck's sake! The only involvement I have with Mat relates to the purchase of the land and the development of the university facility!

— You getting a backhander?

— Fuck you, she says, deeply offended, getting ready to rise.

— You say it isn't him, this noncing, Lennox offers, in restrained rage. — Well, I think it is. So does Les. There was only the two of us in that tunnel. How many do you need to verify that the guy is a fucking short-eyes rapist?

Carmel picks at the skin around her dark nail extensions. Raises her head to meet his eyes. She's now a model of composure. — You said those guys were obvious jailbirds. Mat's never been in prison, she explains in mother-to-toddler patience. — He would have been at Imperial College then, doing his chemical engineering degree.

Lennox blows out compressed air. *Cardingworth has gotten to her. Has he mentioned the break-in, perhaps the pishing on his clothes?* But what she says is demonstrably true. Ray Lennox can find nothing to tie Mathew Cardingworth to that grim underpass in south-west suburban Edinburgh in 1981. — I know, I made enquiries. It was the college summer break: he claimed he was at home studying. But he was in that tunnel on that day. I know this. Les knows it.

231

— It's just not Mat, Carmel repeats, shaking her head. There is an acid finality about her bearing.

— What is he to you?

A turned-down sardonic smile greets him. She reframes statements as questions. — I've told you that he's the major sponsor of my project? Many times?

— Is that all it is?

— *All?* It's only something I've been working on my entire adult and professional life!

— Excuse me for trying to equate the importance of your career with the sexual abuse and possible murder of several children.

— What the fuck are you trying to say here? You've lost it, Ray. She stares at him in disbelief. — You really need to get help.

Do you see how diminished you've become in her eyes, nothing but a ranting fool? That's right, look across the bar, outside to the rain thrashing off the pavement. Look at it running down those gutterings, draining away, just like your useless life . . .

Fuck off, fuck you all . . .

The rage won't subside. Lennox clenches his left fist. — Everybody is so keen to keep this guy out of jail. He slams it on the table. — They don't seem to mind that the young boy his gang seized and brutally raped is now a man who's stuck in there!

If Carmel is jolted, it's only for a second, as a brief softness presents itself in her eyes. — If he's guilty, he should fucking well hang as far as it goes with me, she spits back at him with an impressive, controlled rage. — But I don't think he is. And if *you really believe this*, you need to prove it by taking him to court. You can't take the law into your own hands. You're an ex-cop, for God's sake!

At her words the energy inside him vanishes in a crashing shudder. His groin tingles, sending another pulse of pain to his core. Of course, she's right, just as van der Meer was. But Lennox is no cop, just a driven avenger who deployed the resources of the state to assist him in his personal war on sex offenders. And the last of the ones he was after, that final itch to scratch, has fallen into his lap. But Lennox has nothing on him except the emphatic endorsement of Les Brodie, a man who is now languishing in jail.

Only he isn't.

His friend's name flashes up on the screen of his phone. Ray Lennox slowly rises, feeling his flesh rending apart, angling his head in apology at Carmel, mouthing 'Les' as he pulls himself up and heads out to the terrace.

You move like you've shat your fucking pants.

Thankfully the rain has subsided to a drizzle, but frosty air bites at his wounds. A pale moon shivers above him in sympathy. Below the green yacht club building: the remnants of a swisher, minimal incarnation of the Marina. — What's up, Les?

— Raymie . . . they let ays oot. He's no pressing charges, that's aw they said. The lawyer boy, that South African cunt, he wouldnae tell ays nowt else. But he says there might be compo in it.

— You're having tae compensate him for the assault?

— Naw . . . the other wey.

— What has *he* got to compensate *you* for?

We both know the answer to that.

Les's cacophonous silence compels Lennox to reflexively look away from the phone, before glaring at it in accusation. Then he hears a tinny, distant voice and crams the device against the side of his face. — . . . if there's dosh tae be had fae that cunt then it's gaun in ma fuckin poakit . . .

Van der Meer wisnae bullshitting. And Cardingworth wisnae bluffing.

Lennox looks back inside at Carmel, who stares ahead,

locked in introspection as she calls somebody. Cardingworth's face flashes in his head. He asks Les in urgent panic, — Where are youse?

Paranoia. Stop it.

— At yours. Wi Cathy. We're just off hame. Stuart was here wi some woman, but they left just after we arrived. They were in a bit of a state, Raymie. He's right back on the bevvy. He started aw that Hibs–Herts shite.

Stuart. It's like we're wee laddies again.

— Fuck sake. The daft cunt, Lennox muses. — Anyway, Les, make yourself at home. I'll be back soon and we can talk about this.

— We have tae move tae get our flight back, Raymie.

— If I miss ye I'll come up tae Edinburgh tae see ye, he says, perhaps a little too urgently.

— Aye, okay, Les says reluctantly, and Lennox believes he can hear Cathy's dissenting voice cluck in the background.

— Whatever happens, I'll see ye later. Let's see what the brief says, and we'll have another talk.

— Right, Les concurs. — Raymie . . . ah ken ye pulled some strings tae get me oot. Thanks for that. Later, bro.

Les clicks off before he can respond. Ray Lennox is humbled at how his friend continually believes the best in him. He's done nothing. Is not in a position to pull strings. Or is that true? Has somebody pulled them on his behalf? Cardingworth? George? How things can change in a few days. What was hard and fast becomes a testimony to the fragility of the human mind.

He heads back inside. Just as he thinks the pain is settling down, one complacent, over-emphatic step skewers it to the core of his being. Water tears from his eyes. Forcing composure, he lowers himself back into the seat as Carmel ends her call. — Right, speak later, she says impatiently.

— Was that him?

Carmel doesn't respond. Temporarily blinded by his own stinging discomfort, he now realises she looks a little dishevelled herself. The horrible sensation that she's just left another man's bed besieges Lennox. Even more, just who that man might have been.

Those sheets and pillowcases in that place, you can see her sprawling over them, can't you?

He is all over the place. Surely Carmel can't be working with Cardingworth to set him up? But he's running off at the mouth. If he can't trust himself any more, how can he trust anyone else?

Reading his confusion, Carmel corroborates. — Look . . . for your information it was Angela. This is horrible publicity for Mat, she stresses, in case there was any doubt, — he just wants to drop it. He's not pressing charges and his lawyers have made Les an offer.

— I know. Lennox holds up his phone. — Fuck sake, he's admitted it! Some cunt glasses ye and you want to offer him compo in order to keep his mooth shut! How fucking guilty do you need to be, to behave like that?

— No, Carmel stands her ground. — As you know, there's a *multimillion-pound* development deal for the research facility, which is dependent on the acquisition of the land adjacent to our university buildings. Any bad publicity could scupper it. We've invested four years trying to make this happen! Mat's passionate about it and it means everything to him. He and Angela are obviously upset at the whole business!

— Not good enough, Lennox insists, riled by her snooty air. — Les and myself have been *very upset about it* for forty fucking years. And the land deal will be *scuppered* alright. I'll make sure of it, he cop-stares straight at her. For the first time she wilts visibly, and the fear in her eyes makes him feel like a

bully. Shamed by this, his tone becomes breathless and pro-
pitiatory. — This guy seems to have a hold on everybody. What
the fuck is going on here?

— I'm only telling you what I know, Carmel retorts, face
pinching in a meanness Lennox has never seen in it before. —
Tread carefully, Ray. Mat has powerful friends.

— Yes, I know. They fucking well tried to kill me yesterday.
He struggles to his feet, pulling his coat from the back of the
chair.

— What . . . ? Carmel's dish-like eyes sweep sheer dread
into him, as she discerns his vitality-sapping trauma. — What
happened? What are you talking about? Mat did this to you?
Mat Cardingworth?

Lennox doesn't know how to respond. Again, he has no
proof. Settles for a gruff, — I think we're done here.

— Ray, please sit down, she urges.

But Ray Lennox hobbles towards the exit, index finger jab-
bing the Uber app on his phone. Takes the agonising, jarring
steps down to the car park, not wanting to see the Café Rouge
or the Marina ever again.

31

MUESLI MOUNTAIN

Heading back into town under the dark late-afternoon sky, Lennox is as averse to bumping into Les and Cathy as they obviously are to seeing him. In no hurry to go home to explain his state to Stuart, in flight from resurgent rain, he finds himself laboriously exiting the cab at his Seven Dials office. A text from his brother:

> Pull last night then? Or is it back on with Ms Chemistry? Guess who was baw deep in a red-headed architect last night? Clue: a very handsome Scottish actor.

Crushes the phone into his pocket. Switches on the light. Allows his eyes to adjust. There is something different about his workplace. He and George were both OCD enough to stamp down the loose carpet tile. Had more or less inducted Ria into this practice through repeated example. But there it is, untethered, sprawled across two of its neighbours. Somebody has been in here. Lennox gets out his dusting equipment to check the cupboards and filing cabinets for prints. Nothing. But some black lint, caught between the edge and the clip of the foremost suspension file, indicates a possible new presence.

After checking nothing is missing, he fires up the computer. Locates an article on the university development. This has accompanying staged pictures of Carmel, first wearing a construction worker's helmet, as she stands looking over an empty field. Caption: UNIVERSITY CLOSE IN ON FALMER SITE. Then, in a white overall, carrying a clipboard, *a ludicrous prop in the day of the iPad*, as she leans over a glass-topped model of the new facility. Caption: CONCRETE EVIDENCE: UNIVERSITY BOSS AIMS TO GET THE CHEMISTRY RIGHT.

Local businessman Mathew Cardingworth is in negotiation to purchase a strip of council-owned land at Falmer. Close to the existing University of Sussex campus and the Brighton & Hove Albion stadium, he plans to offer it to the university as a research facility, specialising in advanced polymer technology. Dr Carmel Devereaux, head of the department, said: 'These are exciting plans. China is currently leading the way in developing this technology. In the West, we're a little behind them. Though we have been constantly innovating, our amenities are not up to scratch. But like the Brighton & Hove Albion stadium, this development would offer us Premiership facilities, and I couldn't be more excited.'

The chair is excruciatingly uncomfortable. Lennox knows that getting out of it will only induce further agony. Opts to go back to the missing boys, and the banal write-up on the 'bright and scholarly' Jason McCabe with his open-faced grin. Then, a closer scrutiny of the picture of foster mother Carly Reynolds, and suddenly his heart thumps in a heavier beat.

Because Ray Lennox is not looking at the image of Carly, handkerchief stuck to her face, but at what he thought was a

238

scarf. It's not. On closer examination it's the cut-off arm of another woman, draped around her shoulder. It's flabbier than in previous pictures, but the angel tattoo on it tells him that the consoling limb belongs to a seasoned foster mother called Julie Wilkins.

The night closes in on him and he barely notices, disinclined to check the odd purr on his phone indicating that messages are coming in. The ubiquitous traffic buzz, outside the window, recedes to the odd swoosh. It's his bladder that compels a crippling rise, and Lennox hauls himself onto his feet, actually screaming out in pain as he twists upright. After relieving himself in the small toilet, he leaves the office. The steps onto the darkened street feel like down payments on an excursion to hell: a torturous death by instalment as another series of painful detonations blast through his skeletal and nervous systems. The walk is slow and shaky. Avoiding the railway bridge, he cuts downhill towards London Road, through the charmless warren of flats behind the station. It's tough going and he craves anaesthetic. But he's getting somewhere. The streets ahead are almost dead, drizzling lamp-post lights reflecting off them. From a doorway, a solitary jakey, can in hand, mutters a threat at an invisible tormentor.

Then shouting.

Lennox looks down one of the backstreets leading to the common. Some kind of brawl or mugging is going on. Two younger men shake down an older guy, pushing him against the wall.

Lennox knows the victim.

It is Ralph Trench.

In no shape to intervene as a concerned citizen, Lennox walks down the alley towards the altercation, holding his phone up.

Under the street lamp, the first man comes into his view.

Around forty, straight-backed, wiry but broad-shouldered, with silver-grey hair scraped and tied in a ponytail. He grabs Ralph Trench by the neck, and in one rapid movement thrusts his petrified prey's head down while simultaneously driving his own knee upwards. The portly victim's spectacles fly off, hitting the paving stones, as blood sprays from his face. The ponytailed assailant takes a step back. Strokes his chin, hooded eyes studying his quarry like a gastronome considering which part of a buffet feast to attack first.

— ENOUGH! Lennox roars, as the second man, around thirty-five, turns to look at him. He wears a leather jacket over his brawny frame. In the harsh lamplight from above, Lennox can discern blue eyes dancing in a deeply tanned face. Over a crew-neck top a thick gold chain hangs on his chest. As he takes a couple of steps towards Lennox, advancing in a boxer's shuffling lateral motion, he breaches the overhead street lamp's zone of radiance, plunging into darkness before another sector of light reveals a nose covered in a fine network of blood vessels. As Ponytail puts the boot into Trench, who has col- lapsed to the paving stones, Boxer snaps, — You want some n all? Go on, fuck off!

Despite having issued the threat, the man halts his advance. The reason is that his accomplice has finished with Trench and shouts, — C'mon!

Boxer backs away, joining his ponytailed friend in retreat up the alley. Lennox is relieved; he's in no fit state for a street brawl, content to let their intimidating gazes screw him. Pony- tail, a glint of gold in his mouth, is slower to move away, as he gives Lennox a slightly exasperated shake of the head, then turns to vanish up the dark alley onto the main road with his shuffling colleague.

Lennox feels he's seen this man before, perhaps shared a crumpling metal stairway with him. This realisation makes him even more relieved that the two assailants opted to cash in their winnings at that point. Moves over to the slumped figure half kneeling on the paving stones, holding on to the wall with one hand and his face with the other. Mindful of his own wounds, Lennox struggles to help the bloodied and dazed Trench to his feet. — You okay?

— What's it to you? Ralph Trench clutches his glasses, pulling their warped frames onto his face. One lens is cracked.

— Could have done with your blade there. Lennox looks at him for a reaction. — Fall out with your friend Mat Cardingworth, did you?

— Fuck off, Trench snaps, holding his head back to try and stem the trickle of blood dribbling from his nose down his front. Lennox digs into his pockets, hands him some tissues, which Trench tears from his hand to wrap around his nose. A keening sound he utters might be gratitude, before he waddles off down the lane towards the common.

Looking back up the alley, Lennox thinks about the two assailants. Yes, the one who battered Trench might be the man who took him out, walking away from their fall while he was smashed onto the floor of the concrete works. Trench has to know more about them. Lennox follows him to the edge of the park known as the Level; fancies he is heading for Muesli Mountain, a district of old artisan homes, locally redesignated from Hanover Hill due to its gentrification. Even with Trench having suffered a fair beating, Lennox's pain-wracked body is still the stiffer and slower of the two. Once again there's no way he can catch the fat man. Frustration and cold gnaw at him. — RALPH, he shouts in desperation, — the people who want to hurt me seem to want to hurt you too!

Trench stops, turns slowly, gasping onerously, — Well, they've bloody well succeeded, haven't they? He looks Lennox up and down. — Who the hell are you, anyway?

— The daft cunt who stopped you from taking an even worse beating than you did.

— Well, thank you for that, but it still doesn't tell me much! Mister?

Lennox limps towards him. — My name's Lennox. Raymond Lennox. Maybe we should talk about this.

— Kindly fuck off, Mr Lennox, Trench says, and, as if he's summoning patience, dealing with a child, — You do not have a fucking clue what you're dealing with here.

— Everybody says that, Lennox observes. — And it always leads back to Cardingworth. What is he to you, Ralph?

Trench's stare is watery and diminished. — Cardingworth? Ha! He's the very least of your problems, he barks, moving away.

— What? Ralph, listen –

— KEEP THE FUCK AWAY FROM ME! Trench bellows, then suddenly starts throwing up over the scrub grass of the park. Lennox has never seen so much puke emanating from one person. It keeps coming. When it finally abates, Trench heaves for sweet air, his hands on his knees, eyes watering and nose bleeding heavily again. Lennox hands him the last of his tissues.

Trench gratefully accepts with a nod. Tries to clean up. Lennox risks a light touch on his shoulder. — Ralph, we're both in a fucking mess here, mate. And I'll wager the same people are responsible for this. Are they responsible for Gavin Carter?

Lennox feels Trench's shudder down his arm. It would be visible from space.

— Where do you live? I'm down in Kemptown, Lennox offers.

— Across the park . . . up Hanover Hill, Trench gasps in confirmation, before he starts convulsing again.

Lennox goes to his aid, the two exhausted men linking arms, literally carrying each other over the grass and up the hill. Three youths, camply swaggering past, eye them mischievously. — Looks like you pair of lovebirds didn't hold back on the naughty fun! Rough sex in a public park; sooo Generation X!

Lennox more feels than hears Trench growl something back, before both men share a cathartic laugh. It doesn't last: Ralph Trench's degenerates into a debilitating pant. He manages to galvanise and they plod the rest of the way up the steep hill in silence broken only by the soft wheezes that accordion from both men's damaged bodies. Eventually Trench says, — You'll have to take me as you find me.

It takes Lennox a lot of concentration on the cracked pavement in front of him not to break out in painful laughter again.

Trench's comment is contextualised by the condition of his home. The living room, like a giant refuse sack split open, reeks of the chaos that devastating loss and loneliness can bring. Clothes and takeaway cartons, cans and plastic bottles lie strewn over furniture and floor space. For the wealthy, cleaners will cover up the multitude of illness, sins and misfortunes. But for a person like Trench, any personal disaster was likely to be written over his home. Lennox's attention, though, focuses above the fireplace, where a collection of swords and long knives are mounted on the wall with symmetrical neatness: samurai, claymore, broadsword, rapier, cutlass and scimitar. It's not the fat one Trench was packing when they met in the graveyard that catches his eye. It's the one that isn't present, though it's outline on the dust between the two pegs is visible.

In his ears: a phantom swish.

— Nice collection. But looks like there's one missing, Lennox says.

— Burglary, Trench snaps.

Lennox believes the missing sword that came close to chopping off part of his head was carried by the balaclava man in the factory. *If he is Ponytail, why was he beating up Trench? Where is the sword? Did he retrieve it, or did George see it on the floor? George . . . Stop this!* — Did they take anything else of value?

Trench does not respond, instead points to an alcove, with a kitchen beyond it.

Lennox is ushered through in dread, but the contrast is stunning. Clean to the point of compulsion, each of its surfaces fronts a pristine gleam. A corkboard with pins and Post-it notes is kept meticulously neat, adorned with shopping lists, hospital appointments and campaign meeting dates. Swords display aside, it's impossible to believe that both rooms are part of the same house, far less used by the same person. Trench instantly acknowledges this as he bids Lennox to sit at a small oak table. — The living room is a tip. I generally eat and sleep there these days. I should sort it out . . . but you know how it is, he adds hopefully, raising one brow as he bustles to a cupboard.

Lennox allows himself a slow, taciturn nod. Descends creakingly into a chair. — You campaigned against Cardingworth. Then you changed your tune. Why?

Trench cannot meet his eye. Pours two brandies, into proper snifters. — For the shock, he offers, before taking a seat opposite Lennox and contending, — Mat can be persuasive.

Lennox points to Trench's swollen lip and his eye, which is now almost shut. — Was that his persuasion in action?

Trench remains silent, swilling the amber fluid around in the glass, but shoots Lennox a sulky, violated pout.

— Did he bribe or threaten? Lennox pushes, reckoning he knows the answer. It's evident he did both.

Trench sits, resting forearms on large stomach. Seems to Lennox to be staring at something on the floor. When he speaks, it's in a low lament. — Richard and May Cardingworth had their darling boy, Mathew. They condescended to let me into their family. Of course, I was laughing stock, the fat fostered kid, a figure-of-fun loser compared to their magnificent offspring. They kept me around longer than the others, probably for that purpose. His face creases in a bitter smile. — Golden Boy Mat did well in business. Made money. The Cardingworths were ever so proud, he mocks. — I got into acting. I had some success in theatre playing the bloated, pompous oaf. Comedy value, Trench says, still looking down at the same spot.

His chilling disassociation is reminiscent of victims of all types of abuse Lennox has interviewed in the past.

Maintains silence, lets steady eye contact encourage Ralph Trench to continue. — Then I had a breakdown and was homeless on those streets, and he gestures outside through the window.

Lennox raises a brow to urge Trench to carry on.

— Mat saw me begging, maybe he was just being helpful, or perhaps he thought it was embarrassing that his foster *brother*, Trench spits out the word like a bitter pill, — was a destitute tramp, but he got me some work. First the library, then the council, admin stuff, but holding down a job didn't come easy. Although when I started on the security, I saw something I shouldn't have. I thought it would give me leverage. I was wrong.

— What was that? What did you see?

Trench swivels and looks pointedly at him. Like many abused people, he seemed to oscillate between victim and bully at the drop of a hat. — I've said enough. It's not your business, Mr Lennox. My advice to you would be to keep out if it.

— You don't know what my fucking business is, and Lennox feels his lips rolling back over his teeth. He gestures to Trench's front room. — Some cunt tried tae take ma fucking heid off with one ay your swords.

Ralph Trench matches his wrath; bristling in the chair, he puffs himself up. — Well, *I* didn't, and you don't know what my business is either. Keep out of it or you'll seriously regret it.

— Are you threatening me? Lennox, instinctively glancing back into the front room at the swords on the wall, can't believe he just said that.

Trench's dark, hollow unnerving laugh. — Do I look in a position to threaten anyone? I'm strongly advising you. A cell of evil operates in this town. It will consume you if you try to stand against it, and he rises. — And Cardingworth is the very least of it. Now I bid you goodnight, sir.

— Tell me about this cell. Lennox places his knuckles on the table, rises shakily. — Did it capture Gavin? The others? I can bring them down, Ralph, I –

— Colour me doubtful, my friend. Trench, looking the broken Lennox up and down, shakes his head in pity. — They'll come for you quick enough. It seems like you're already on their radar. My advice: get the fuck out, and he points through the alcove to the lounge and front door.

— Just tell me about the concrete factory, Ralph! Tell me about Gavin and the fostering –

— I said *goodnight*, Mr Lennox! This is my home, Trench assertively declares, rising, lumbering through to the lounge. Opening the front door, he places hands on hips. — You are no longer welcome here!

— Cardingworth got you a job in the library first, didn't he? Lennox stalls. — Digitalising the hard copies of the *Argus*. But he didn't realise that in digitalising them, you'd be able to research the missing kids. Then what happened? Did he find out: have you expunge the records, yes? His wild eyes watch Trench bloat in apoplexy like a pufferfish. — Later on, he offered you the factory security job, drew you further into this –

— GO! Trench's pop-eyed hyperventilating commences, as he turns a reddened face to the swords.

As the cold air floods in, Lennox gets the message. — Okay, I'm going. But if you need to talk. He scribbles down a number on his notepad, tears out a page and sticks it on a small table by the front door. — I know you're a good man, Ralph. Work with me. They are not invincible.

— Yes? Well, neither are you, Mr Lennox. Good*night*, Trench jeers through his teeth. And as Lennox steps outside, he slams the door so hard it shakes the frame.

Heading downhill, bound for home, Lennox craves a drink. He has stuff to process. Wishes to do this with a huge malt whisky. Sitting in a warm place that isn't his Stuart-infested flat. Alongside that of Gavin, and probably Ross, he can now put Julie Wilkins at Jason's disappearance, due to her encroaching arm round the shoulder of Carly Reynolds. Heads back over the Level, electing to visit a Ditchling Road pub on its edge. It's one he's passed several times without venturing inside. The full moon hangs in the sky, shining down to illuminate the piles of vomit it has helped generate. Lennox fancies he can see Trench's contribution.

Outside the pub, a woman, a scarf covering her hair and the lower part of her face, stands holding a cigarette. On every drag she takes she turns away, her body almost recoiling with the effort of the suction. She wears a green jacket with blue jeans tucked into thin-heeled black boots. Trying to get a glimpse of her eyes, Lennox notices angry scarring spilling out from behind her mantilla.

Aware his limping doubtlessly labels him as drunken, he heads indoors. Is swiftly informed by the barman that the shout for last orders has passed. Back outside, his visage is decorated lost and forlorn.

The scarfed-and-scarred woman looks at him through one

eye. He sees that what he'd first taken to be shadow is a patch that covers the other one. — You've had it, mate, she cheerfully observes.

— Too bad. Could have done with a drink. Been one of those days, and he leans back against the wall of the pub, feeling the demented orchestra of aches clash in his body.

— I know those days, she says, taking a half-step towards him.

— Well, if you're having another one, Lennox says flatly, — I've plenty to drink at my place in Kempton.

Fuck Stuart, it's not his flat.

Out of her one eye, the woman, whom he can see is older than he'd previously thought, looks at him, evaluating and puzzled. — Do you like women?

— Yes.

— You ain't a weird sort?

Lennox responds deadpan, — Can't really plead *not guilty* to that charge.

The solitary eye blazes at him. — You can't be that freaky if you say you are. Weirdos normally aren't that self-aware.

— I could be bullshitting, Lennox says, texting Stuart to ascertain his location, then punching at his Uber app. — Anyway, the offer's there and will be for another . . . he looks at the display and holds it up to her to indicate that Marvin is heading towards them in a Toyota Corolla, — two minutes.

— Cool. I'll take my chances on your lack of weirdness.

They take the short hop to Kemptown and Sussex Square almost in silence, only commenting on their fortune in avoiding the rain suddenly teeming down again, leading to an evacuation of the streets.

Lennox struggles on the stairs to his flat. Senses her impatience behind him. They get inside and she sits down on the sofa, still in her green jacket. — I'm not on the game.

— Me neither, Lennox says, his lack of conviction failing to surprise him. Opens a bottle of Malbec from his cocktail cabinet and pours out two glasses. Wonders if she thinks it's classless that he keeps both beer and wine in such furniture. Checks again that there is no stain on the top. Feels relieved Stuart is not back. Must mention to him to avoid putting hot drinks there.

She regards his limp. — You look like you've been in the wars.

— Yes, an accident at work, just yesterday.

She is still strategically concealed in that red shawl to the extent he can barely see her, and the soft lighting of the table lamp behind doesn't help. — Looks like you've got a dangerous job!

— Not really. I suppose I'm just a little careless.

She puts her hand to the scarf in front of her mouth. He senses she is stifling a chuckle. — Is that why you asked me back? You recognise a fellow casualty?

— No. I invited you back for a drink and a chat, that's it, Lennox explains. — If you suspect ulterior movies, I can assure you that I don't have the desire to sleep with anyone right now. My leg is gashed, I've a skin graft on my thigh and my groin is black and blue, he explains, lest she takes offence the other way. — It would be nice to know your name though.

— I'm Mona, she says, taking his proffered glass.

— Ray. He lowers himself into the black leather armchair opposite her. — Pleased to meet you, Mona.

A solitary eye scans him with an intensity most pairs fail to match. The words still spill from behind that loose, mouth-concealing shawl. — Usually guys in pubs, generally mingers or perverts to a man, invite me back because they want to fuck me.

Lennox raises an eyebrow. — How do you tend to respond to such overtures?

249

— Well, I know that my disfigurement isn't a turn-on to *most* men, so you get a sense of yourself as pretty low down the food chain. But I have my needs too, and she turns away from him and sips the wine by tipping it slowly in one side of her mouth.

— What happened to you?

She lowers the glass to the coffee table. Hesitates for only a second. — A guy I was seeing was a bastard. He hurt me so I broke up with him. He didn't like that so he threw acid in my face. I was disfigured and lost the sight of one eye.

ACID . . .

Lennox can't conceal his horror, at both the attack, barbarous and cruelly medieval, and the offhand way she's recounted it. — Fuck me, I'm so sorry. What did they do to him?

— He did time, now he's back outside.

What is his name? The question burns him. But he forces composure. — Can I see your face?

— No. Mona shakes her head quickly. — When they said I was beautiful, they never saw the real me. Now that I'm hideous, they still don't. If we fuck, I stay covered where I want to stay covered.

— I told you, Lennox says, now disconcerted at her again sexualising their encounter, — I huvnae got a ride in me. It's no slight on you, he emphasises, a little too fast, over-mindful of her self-description, — I'm just in a lot of pain.

— I get that. I know pain.

Lennox raises the glass to his mouth. As he sips, sadness overcomes him, a pulping of something in the core of his chest. It's for her, but he knows it's also for him, so he doesn't trust it. — So . . . nobody saw the real you because you were beautiful, now they don't see the real you because you're disfigured? And he whispers softly, — Please let me see you.

— I'm a monster.

— NO! Lennox shouts so loudly that Mona recoils. — The monster was the one who did that to you. He thinks of his Doc Martens. They know him. Maybe they always have. Now he has to know them. He lowers his voice and makes the plea: — Who is he?

— You don't want to know. She shakes her head emphatically. — Brighton is a beautiful town, but like any other, it has a small proportion of damaged souls that need locking up.

— I do want to know. Lennox shuffles to the edge of his seat. — That's why I'm asking you.

— Well, I don't want to tell you, she insists. — Like I said, I don't want to think about him.

Lennox nods. Why ever would she? — Take the scarf off your face, he begs.

Mona looks at him. Then she does. She turns left to show the profile of a beautiful woman, with sharp cheekbone and glimmering eye.

Fuck . . .

But then she twists slowly to reveal the other side of her face. It is red and shrivelled with a lipless mouth almost melted away. The patch covers what she tells him is an eyeless socket. — And you really will have to take my word for that.

Lennox feels thin air entering his body, seemingly coming from a hole in his throat. Shaken, he waves the bottle of Malbec in paltry defence to cover up his shock. — Shall we take this to bed?

What has disturbed him is not the ruined side of her face, as shocking as it is, but the beautiful one. Because he's seen that profile before: in the drawer at Mathew Cardingworth's house.

Mona nods calmly and rises. She has to help him get off the couch and through to the bedroom and the shedding of his clothes. As she looks at his injured genital region, she observes, — That is some serious bruising!

He pulls the duvet over himself, not wanting to see his wounds. Lies back, propped up on pillows, and fills their glasses.

The wine soothes them, but their eyes grow heavy and he switches off the bedside lamp. Almost immediately Mona's hand goes to his groin, and he feels his cock instantly stiffen in her grasp. It's sore at first, but it's just her hand adjusting to the changing dimensions and feel of it. He turns on his side to face her in the darkness, experiencing the delicious charge of her deft touch, as it supplants his awful pain. He starts to stroke her thighs then gently finger her, working inside her, feeling her moisten, tracing up to a hard knot of clitoris. They pleasure each other, building a slow, mutual wave; he feels her buck and gasp in delight as his jizz explodes from his cock in a dizzying surge. His eyes roll back into his head as she lets out a whimpering sound that releases into a long groan as her body tenses then relaxes. It's safe to remove his fingers, and as he does, sleep takes him, but not before he feels her scoot up to rest her head on his chest.

Day Thirteen

32

IS THERE SOMETHING
I SHOULD KNOW?

In the morning, Lennox wakes up in a pain so ubiquitous, he feels like he's been crushed in a giant vice in a car breaker's yard. Mona has left the bed, but he hears singing coming from the en suite bathroom. It sounds like Duran Duran's 'Is There Something I Should Know?'. Lennox struggles to rise, propping himself up. Downs two more of the painkillers he left on the table by the side of his bed. The near-empty bottle of wine looks at him in accusation. Mona enters the bedroom, wrapped in a big towel. He fights the urge not to be startled at her striking wounds in the daylight, and this shames him. Feels it best to acknowledge his reaction. — I'm sad for what happened to you.

— You really are, aren't you? Don't be, she whispers, sitting on the bed. She rubs his forearm. — It was a very long time ago.

— Does that make such a big difference? I mean, how do you come back from that?

— You just do. It does take a while. And I like a drink, and more than I probably should. But I hold down a job, she says.

It's impossible for him not to notice that she is presenting her unspoiled side. He tries to comprehend the type of evil that would want to destroy such beauty. Can't. It's beyond him completely.

— You're different, she contends.

— Different from what? Lennox says, thinking of Carding-worth.

— Most men I meet.

Lennox does not take this as a compliment. One thing he has learned in his life and work, and through his counselling, is that overly sensitive men can be as problematic to women as the more gruff, distant breed. Especially if this reactivity is rooted in the self-obsession they share with their stoical brothers.

Mona gets dressed, but Lennox can only manage to clad himself in a short towelling gown. They head through to the lounge. To his astonishment, he learns she's two years his senior. — I always looked young, she muses, — not that it matters now.

He thinks: *it still matters*, but can't bring himself to say it, as it will entrap them in the agenda of her disfigurement. This is the real Tophet the monstrous attacker visited upon her: to make it almost impossible to talk of anything else. Drinking coffee and fizzy water, they look out over Sussex Square, across the private gardens and towards the sea. — See that tunnel? Lennox points at the entrance to it, thinks, with a leaden heart, of Carmel and their morning runs. This newfangled hell has made last week seem like a lifetime ago.

— It's the one that inspired *Alice in Wonderland*, Mona anticipates, with a smile on the beautiful, unsullied side of her face. — I should head, she says. — Thanks for the hospitality, and she prepares to decamp, pulling on her coat.

Lennox does not know what to say, caught between want-ing her to stay for eternity, and wishing she would vanish and he'd never set eyes on her again. And every conceivable option between those two polarities flashes through his mind. Then it's displaced by something more imperative. — I'm sorry, but I really need to ask you for the name of the guy who did that to you. I need this because I think the same person could be responsible for my injuries.

— Are you a cop?

— No.

— What are you mixed up in?

— That's what I'm trying to work out.

— Darren, she says softly. — Darren Knowles. If he's after you, leave town.

Knowles.

Leave town. Again. Trench.

— Yet you're still here.

— What else can he take?

The burning word *Cardingworth* is on his lips, he has to ask her about him, when a laboured twist of metal in the lock makes him jump to his feet, tensing under the pain of his wounds as he does. Mona flinches too, but then a voice sings loudly from the hallway, — Ray-mondo! Guess who's got that aud-i-tion?

It heralds the entrance of a bleary-eyed Stuart, and Lennox lets assuagement rustle from his chest.

— Your wee broth— The actor sees Mona, who quickly tugs her scarf up to cover the bottom of her face. Although Stuart has discerned everything, he betrays no emotion as Lennox introduces them. Mona nods in tense embarrassment and promptly departs.

— Wait, Lennox pleads, following after her.

In the hallway, she turns and raises her hand, forcing him to stop. — No, last night was a mistake. We won't see each other again, and she exits with haste. — Take care of yourself.

Making a half-attempt to pursue, Lennox feels his brother's strong arm grab his shoulder. His depleted frame and enfeebled mind cannot resist. — Leave her, Raymie, Stuart says, his face pulled tight, as the outside door slams shut. — Buyer's regret. Classic case. Such a stud, he laughs. — But I suppose I should applaud you, in your condition. He looks him over, oddly impressed. — Well now . . .

— What that fuck are you going to say?

— Just that you've suddenly become a whole lot more interesting to me, brother . . . He looks at the bandage on his thigh spilling out with the bruising from the bottom of his short gown. — What the fuck, Ray?

33

REMINISCENCE AND RECALL 3

— Stuart was my bairn: that was pretty much an open secret, though John never talked of it and Avril refused to broach it with him. Or maybe she did, but she wouldn't speak of it in front of me.

Then finally another big heart attack took John away. I suppose I felt mixed emotions. There was a guilty elation, but also a great deal of loss. John was a decent man. He had been a valued friend from the railways, then a detested enemy, through no fault of his own. All this tormented me.

It should have been us together after that: me and Avril . . . Stuart was all grown up by then of course.

But Raymond found out about me and Avril and badly sher-ricked us at his dad's funeral. He was barmy, of course, no right in the head. He'd had some kind of a breakdown, and was taking aw that cocaine, and bevvying away. I mean real bevvy-ing; I ken about all that, and he never had the head for it, and it's no surprising, the poor wee bugger . . .

Aye, that was my fault n all . . . I did something far worse to him than I did to his dad . . .

— You really don't need to continue.

— Oh, but I do.

— This has gone way beyond the remit of this group. This is reminiscence and recall therapy, not confession. –

— I ken what it is. It's confidential, right?

— Of course. How do the others feel about this?

(Some sounds of affirmation.)

— Well, yes, it is confidential. So please respect this. Would people like Jock to continue? Can we respect that confidentiality?

(A series of affirmative noises.)

— Carry on, Jock.

These fucking tapes. This is a . . . what is it those trendy liberal cunts in the media say? . . . a *clusterfuck*. I'm switching this shite off and hitting the fucking boozer. She's left about half a dozen messages on the phone asking whether I listened to those tapes and what do I think? Well, what I think is that I've had enough of this pish for one evening. This is worse than paid poliswork.

Off out on the lash. That's the only way I'll make any sense of this fucking nonsense.

Day Fourteen

34

OXGANGS MOONLIGHT

A shave, a shower and change of clothes are Stuart's only prep-
aration for his audition. He sports a quilted red-and-black
jacket, which looks like it's being worn inside out, and baggy
checked trousers. Nonetheless, it seems that his brother is
blaming Lennox, rather than staying out all night on cocaine
and alcohol, for his mounting anxiety. — I'm a nervous bloody
wreck here, Ray, and thank you for your support, he says face-
tiously, heading off.

Ray Lennox is too fuzzy-headed and preoccupied from the
dealings with Mona to react. A text comes in, reminding him
of his appointment at the Royal Sussex County Hospital.
Thankfully, it is close by.

They change the dressings and take more X-rays. After an
examination, he gets some mixed news. The skin grafts appear
to have taken, but his bruised groin area resembles a swamp
of putrefying fruit. Even after gut-wrecking amounts of paracetamol, the tailbone pain remains acute. Lennox still finds it
difficult to accept that nothing has cracked.

A thought has parked in his brain: *get the fuck out of
Brighton for a bit. I need to vanish. Confuse them. George knows
my every move. As long as I'm around him, I'm not safe.* He calls
his partner. There's no midweek Hearts game to use the season
ticket he still renewed out of loyalty, so he needs another
excuse. — My old mum had a bit of a fall. I'm heading up to

see her, he says, hitting the easyJet app on his phone, looking for a standby. — Back tomorrow.

— Oh God, I'm sorry to hear that, Ray. Is she okay?

— I think so, but I'll feel better when I've seen her. He feels the power of that lie scorch him. He went out of his way to avoid his mother. It shouldn't be like that.

— Of course. Good on you, George encourages, and asks, — How are you doing?

Lennox is wrong-footed by his concern. It seems genuine, but then so did a lot of things about George. — Not so bad. The hospital tests confirm nothing's broken, so a wee bit of a morale booster.

— Excellent! Well, look after yourself up there and take your time.

A mad dash north follows, although the Gatwick–Edinburgh flight has become routine to the point he's now on casual chatting terms with staff at both airports. Such places had seemed incubators of stress, mainly based on his Heathrow experiences. Yet here were two of the nicest groups of people one could encounter in the UK. With his restricted mobility and discomfort, Lennox is glad of this, as they cheerfully endeavour to make his transit easier.

On the aircraft, a canvas duffel bag he had no real reason to take, apart from it containing two Christmas presents for the nephews, sits annoyingly at his feet. He downs two more paracetamol. In order to distract his mind from the morass of pain that is his body, he slumps back into his seat, forcing his eyes shut. This brings no peace; he perversely tortures himself by thinking about Cardingworth, Mona and Carmel. And also: Balaclava Man. Almost certainly the same one who, in addition to causing his own awful injuries, beat Trench senseless. And now there was the name: Darren Knowles.

And he remembers where he is going: back to where it all started.

Ah cannae go hame, Raymie, a tearful, shocked Les Brodie kept saying, as he pushed his shabbier bike alongside yours. Neither of you could look back, not even to thank those middle-class strollers, two men, a woman and a dog, whom you had stopped and got to help. When Les emerged from the tunnel declaring: no cops, they had looked uneasily at you both as you hurried away.

You walked home pushing those bicycles, a subversive thought nagging at you: THERE'S NOWT WRONG WITH HIM. Unlike you, Les had no blemishes on his face, though his legs were marked and bruised, and his knees skinned. Then you saw that the blood vessels in your friend's eyelids were haemorrhaged. You later learned, as a rookie cop, dealing with domestic violence and sex offence cases, that this indicated asphyxiation. Only then did the inky-finger discolorations visible on Les's neck take on more sinister prominence in your consciousness.

And Les walked strangely, as if every step was agony.

— Did they batter ye? you asked.

— Aye, but ah didnae let them get the bike, Raymie.

— Is that aw they done? Cause ah thought –

You were going to ask: 'did they pit something up your hole?' but your friend knew this and screamed at you, fists balling, face contorted and wretched, — THEY BATTERED AYS! THEY BATTERED AYS, RIGHT, AND YOU BETTER NO SAY NOWT TAE NAE CUNT ABOOT THIS, RAYMIE!

You nodded and fell fearfully silent. Watched Les Brodie totter forward, shoving his ramshackle bike, every step as if anticipating a landmine under his feet.

But who were those other two faces in the tunnel? Why can you still only see just one?

Disembarking in Edinburgh, he takes a taxi to his friend's Oxgangs home. On approaching the old scheme, it strikes him that the devastating tunnel incident that had so marked both men happened just under a mile away on the Water of Leith walkway. Yet, after a family relocation to Clermiston, Les had moved back to the area. Unable to stay away.

Lennox pushes the buzzer on the front door.

You were almost smashed to pieces after falling through the darkness onto that concrete . . . your hand trying to stay fastened onto the metal that was tearing from its mountings. Yet here you are, still more devastated, more deeply marked by some silly thing in a tunnel that happened more than forty years ago!

It's not fucking silly . . .

You make no sense.

The doorstep appearance of Cathy, mouth an arch of hostility, disturbs Lennox from his troubled thoughts. — What you wantin? she asks, before her eyes soften a notch on noting his discomfort.

Les quickly appears behind her. She is about the only person he ever defers to, though not often, and certainly not now. — Sokay, Cath.

— But, Les, he –

— Ah sais *sokay*, His tone gives no room for further dissent. Signals Lennox into a 1950s council-built house, shunted into the fag end of the private sector under Thatcher's Right to Buy legislation. They head through the lounge, entering a small, well-heated conservatory. At first Lennox considers it a ridiculous affectation, but quickly sees that holding such a view is the real lunacy. Bright and cosy, it showcases a magnesium glinting moon in a darkly dramatic sky. Why would you *not* want one? He slowly sits down in a wicker chair. Les disappears briefly, before coming through with two identical Hearts FC mugs full of tea. He seems not to have noticed Lennox's limp or discomfort.

Disinclined to preamble, as Les was never one for small talk, Lennox asks, — So how much did he offer you?

— Enough, Les barks, sitting down in an identical chair opposite him.

Lennox is confounded by this response, unable to tell whether Les is shutting down the conversation, or means the compensation was sufficient.

His friend reads his confusion. — You dinnae get it, Raymie: I'm fucking skint! A year away fae finishing ma mortgage payments and the cunt's fuckin well pey ays oaf!

— So, he took care ay that?

— Aye, and some, says Les, knitting his brows. — And ye ken what? Ah looked intae his scared wee noncey eyes and his ripped-up coupon, and ah thoat: job done. He scowls in a manner that smacks of pub hard-man performance. Les has evidently doubled down on this persona. — Ah've got aw the compo ah need!

Lennox raises his mug to his lips. Watches dark clouds bruise the sky. Thinks of his groin, then the cold, twisted metal, snapping all around him. Yet, in spite of everything, he got out of that factory. Perhaps others weren't so lucky. — Mibbe it's no just aboot you.

Les slides back in the chair, without breaking eye contact. His body remains tense and brittle. — What, you're hittin ays that 'ah suffered n aw' routine, wi the daft wee gam that cunt made ye gie him?

Which cunt which cunt which cunt . . . there was three of the cunts . . .

— Well, it's no aw aboot *you* either. Les glowers in the face of his judging silence. — You've had your wee crusade aw your life. Ah'd moved on till you set me up with that fucker, and his stare now possesses the vicious belligerence Lennox has seen trained on others, but has rarely been recipient of. — Now I'm done wi *ma* revenge. Ah've been compensated!

— Okay. Lennox raises his hands in a surrender gesture, before letting them fall into his lap. — I meant it's no just aboot you *or* me. I'm convinced there were others.

Both men ice in the gaze of the other.

Get him, Bim.

Bim.

Who was it? This Darren Knowles? Him or this Bim?

Who is Bim?

Les seems to actively consider Lennox's contention. Then his face freezes. — Well, let thaime sort it oot thair way! That cunt's coupon is never gaunny be the same again. Les leans forward. — Let thaime take thair revenge thair wey, n you take yours your wey if ye want! Ah'm done! Ah signed the agreement, ah took thair poppy!

— That agreement won't stand up in a court of law. It's not America. I can get a lawyer and we –

— I'm done wi it!

Lennox presses his lips tightly together. Knows this is about more than money. Les's sense of self is still on the line, even after all those years. Although he was just a kid, the way he sees it is that he constituted weak prey. This shames him, undermines the self-image of the omnipotent hard man he's spent years constructing. Les would be shattered to imagine football mob rivals reading the paper in city pubs, perhaps outwardly sympathetic to the noncing at first, but once the drinks flowed, making ugly, snickering comments. He could never have the world seeing him as that scared, vulnerable young boy in the tunnel, totally in the power of others. His quest in displaced violence – to become so notorious that nobody would (literally) fuck with him again – had been as thorough and all-consuming as Lennox's own vengeful nonce hunting.

Are you not just the same?

But he *would* go to court, though it would be pointless without his friend. — You really think that's enough, Les? That some rich fucker in his sixties is going to be worried about his pretty face being ruined? He thinks of Angela. — You think he pulls gorgeous younger women on the basis of his looks? Anyway, some plastic surgery wanker on Harley Street will make that intae nowt mare than a cool duelling scar. Aw it'll be is a conversation piece for him tae concoct another bullshit tale aroond!

Half shutting his eyes, Les points to the door. His big chest goes in and out. — Just get the fuck oot ay here, Raymie.

Lennox nods, tries to rise, but is burned by a sharp, knifing pain, emanating from his core. Grimaces. — You might have to gie us a hand there, mate.

Recognising his friend's incapacity for the first time, Les springs up. — What the fuck's gaun oan here? he demands, offering a strong, tattooed forearm.

Ray Lennox takes it, slowly hauling himself onto his feet. — An accident at work.

— Fuck sake, Raymie . . . are ye awright?

— Getting there. He pushes off towards the front door. As he passes her to exit, the compassion Lennox sees in the hovering Cathy's eyes emboldens him to turn sharply back to Les: — One thing. Which one of the three was he? Rapist? Enabler?

Les glares at him, and his eyes spark in a fear Lennox hasn't seen in them since the tunnel. Wants it to go, as it's unbearable to witness. Then embarrassment kicks in. Les tries to fight it down as his face reddens and his eyes water. Clenches his fists and grinds his teeth together, abruptly turning his back to Lennox, hands still balled menacingly by his side.

Lennox feels Cathy's firm tug on his elbow. — Just go, she urges.

He embarks on the trammelled walk outside; down a path

lustred by a flaring moon and along the stale street onto the main road. Never once looking back. Instead of heading to Jackie's, he flags down a passing cab. The driver cagily chats about last week's Hibs and Hearts results, trying to ascertain his allegiance in order to talk himself into, rather than out of, a tip. Lennox grunts back in monosyllables, too distressed and distracted to partake in a game he normally enjoys. Climbs out in a Southside backstreet. Enters the Repair Shop, where he suspects Notman will be drinking. Stepping inside, Lennox almost hopes he'll be wrong but he isn't; his ex-colleague is the first person he registers, propping up the bar, reading the sports pages of the *Evening News*.

— Hey, Notty.

— Raymie . . . Notman's eyes expand in panicked guilt.

— What's the story? You're no picking up. Something wrong? This is a rhetorical question: Notman looks awful. Worse than the last time and the last time was bad.

Lennox suspects that he is appearing much the same, but reckons his friend is too messed up to even notice. — Listen, Raymie, Ally Notman moans, bleary-eyed, — I feel like a cunt for saying this, but I cannae help ye, mate.

— Right . . . Lennox nods, keeping strong eye contact. Facial pores he's never seen on Notman before excrete toxic sweat. The sweat of the guilty.

Notman shifts uncomfortably under his gaze, trying to straighten himself up against the bar. — It's no like when you were there, his voice rises in biscuit-ersed appeal. — Drummond has us keying in our case numbers tae get intae the beasts' register. It's her wey ay monitoring our ooirs on each job. His old friend is practically beseeching. — It looks shan on my sheet if I'm daein a homer and tapping it into an existing case. Totally fucks my numbers and makes me look like a right useless cunt. Changed days, Raymie. ·

Lennox feels a crushing disappointment deep in his core. It sears like the pain in his groin. Yet all he can do is indulge in the mock-formal pantomime James Bond used as the default setting for so many white Western males to mask their emotions. — An efficient officer like you should have plenty spare capacity, Notman, the way you get through cases!

— I'm on a second written warning, Raymie. Notman, not playing the game, ruefully shakes his head. — It's the Christopher Reeve. He raises the glass of lager, looking at it in accusation. — They're talking aboot a transfer tae fuckin Traffic wi the uniformed spastics there! Only reason I'm still in Serious Crimes is the recruitment freeze and the shortage ay experienced detectives . . . the joab's fucked, Raymie.

— Okay, Ally, I get the message, a downcast Lennox sighs. Briefly thinks about asking Drummond for a favour for old times' sake, but she is already the most by-the-book person he's ever known. Her promotion will only have intensified that. There's simply nobody left there to help him.

— Sorry, Raymie. Notman's wretched tones tell Lennox his old charge is in pieces. Just as he feels he's looking at a younger self, the more chilling thought insinuates: *or maybe a future or even a present one.* Realises this conflict with Cardingworth is more likely his perdition rather than salvation. Catches his own slumped figure in the pub mirror, acknowledging the broken round-shouldered slope that has replaced the straight-backed confidence of old.

It's breaking you up right now.

It's not a case and you're not a cop. What the fuck are you doing?

Silly Ray.

What?

On the TV up above the bar, an appointed government

spin doctor arrogantly announces: — The truth is what we say the truth is.

What?

As his febrile mind toys with the concept that there are few ways things can get worse, so the reality of Dougie Gillman manifests. He enters the bar with a younger woman of unplaceable familiarity, who looks pale and drawn. They settle at a corner table. Lennox nods over. Gets a confounded look back, followed by a curt incline of that quadrilateral head. This time Gillman says nothing, preoccupied with his company.

— Why is he still here? Lennox asks Notman.

— He's got a couple of weeks left on the job.

Lennox looks over at Gillman, more tightly wound than ever, sprinting towards seizure. The sinew in his neck bristles as he talks to this woman. But the bar mirror reflection, in the form of himself and Ally Notman, evidences a comparable mess.

Who would be a copper? Or even an ex-copper?

Ray Lennox leaves his former Serious Crimes charge to his dialogue with the half-full or -empty glass of beer. As he slowly stumbles off, he nods again at Dougie Gillman. But the veteran cop, deep in conversation, either doesn't see him or pretends not to.

And as he walks down the haunted Royal Mile, a call comes in.

— This is no longer salvageable, Ray, as I think you've probably now realised. You've unleashed something that is not within my power to stop.

And Mathew Cardingworth hangs up before he can respond.

Lennox calls back immediately, but the phone is switched off. The fear crawls up his skin. Cardingworth's voice: Lennox experiences it as that of another dead man.

When he gets back to Jackie's, he heads in stealth mode

towards his mother's room. Through the open door, he sees Avril, in pink nightdress, sat on the bed. Eyes distracted and far away, she brushes her long silver hair in even strokes. She has something of his, and he wants it back. Lennox lifts his hand, goes to knuckle the door. Can't do it. Can't bring himself to ask, could not bear the terrible discussion that would arise.

Turns and heads for the spare room and bed.

35

REMINISCENCE AND RECALL 4

— Most of them really were the salt of the earth. But, of course, there was the odd bad apple. The sea always attracted people on the run: sometimes fae the law, or fae others, or more often than not, as the auld saying goes, fae themselves. And aye, one or two of them were evil bastards. The worst of them was Bim, as we called him.

He was a monster of a man, a huge felly, with hands like shovels. Big, slack, laughing mouth and eyes full of mirth that could just suddenly glaze over. You didn't want to be around then. That's when he would create havoc, but in such a cold, cruel way. Always plausible until that gaze switched. I swear he became something not of this world.

You didnae ask questions about what you aw got up tae when we were at sea. You did what you did and stuck together, pulling each other out of scrapes. The secrets rarely made the shore. Aye, it all stayed at sea.

Then everything changed that one morning . . .

We had docked in Porto and Eddie Reece had taken us tae some party. Hooked us up wi some lassies. That was Eddie. There was a lot of drinking and it aw got out ay hand, as it tended to do. But we were at sea, right? It was different at sea. Different rules. You did what you did.

(Hacking noises, heavy breathing.)

— You don't need to do this to yourself.

— But I do! I do, I do! Because . . . because when I woke up, the lassie next to me in the bed . . . she was gone. Stone-cold dead! On everything I hold sacred, I don't know how. We'd drunk a lot, done a load of dexies; like pills, Dexedrine. I think they call it speed now. I mind telling her tae take it easy, but she widnae stop. Just popped one after the other.

I rode her that night, but there was nothing weird went on. Nowt kinky. Anyway, in the morning this lassie was gone. Like cauld.

Deid.

I panicked, as you would. The way I saw it my life was over.

— I can switch off the tape. I should switch off the tape.

— Keep it the fuck on!

— Okay . . . but this is a crime that's been committed, and I feel –

— KEEP IT THE FUCK OAN!

— Okay, okay . . . calm down. If you need to do this . . .

(Indecipherable sounds.)

— Basically, Bim, well, he took charge. He removed the lassie's body. Came in with a big sack and put her in it. Slung her over his big back like a sack of coal. I couldn't believe she, this woman whose name I shamefully never even knew . . . I never knew the lassie's name!

(A choking sounds.)

— Stop . . . we have to stop . . .

— Then he got rid of her. Never said where.

— Enough –

— SHUT UP! I need tae say this . . . Later on Bim told me: 'All you need to know is that it's done, Jock. These things happen. It was an accident. One life wrecked: fucking your one up isn't going to bring that little mite back. We look after each other.'

That was what he said.

He was right. Or so I thought. At sea you learn tae compartmentalise. It's a different world.

So, I went back home.

— Jesus Christ . . .

It's her voice. I switch off the tape. I put my hand out in front of me. It's shaking. I don't know if it's the peeve or this shite. Or the sense that it's all closing in on me. It's all closing in on everybody.

I'm going to hear this through. I go to the kitchen and open that bottle of malt. Pour myself a glass. It looks great the way it twists into that Edinburgh crystal tumbler. I pick it up, enjoying the satisfying weight of it. I take a couple of sips and savour the burning trail it weaves through this tired body. Then I hit play. The voice of the ponce starts:

— I'm leaving the room, and the others are doing the same. You can talk into the tape if you like.

— I like: go!

I stop the tape to get a top-up. The old guy's voice is loud, commanding. You hear the others get up and leave. I'm not sure if she stayed in the room, but she certainly heard the tape all the way through, before she gave it to me. And apparently it was with his blessing. Play.

— Avril. Our affair didn't resume; it never stopped. Not really. I wanted to be with her. It was many years later that she fell pregnant, with Stuart. Jackie was still at secondary school, but she would be off to university soon, a very independent lassie. I wanted Avril to leave John, that grumbling eunuch of a man, and come with me and take Stuart. I wanted for us to have a family life. I was done with the sea, and people like Bim . . . oh God . . .

I . . . I . . . she would have done it, but it was Raymond.

It's no exaggeration to say the kid haunted me. His eyes followed you everywhere. We went on holiday to Lloret de Mar once, me, a girlfriend called Jeanette, with Avril and John. They brought young Raymond along. He would be nine or ten. Avril was expecting Stuart. She hadn't told John yet. He was actually quite jovial, but I think Jeanette knew something was up. It was a strained break.

Raymond . . .

. . . the way that kid looked at you, like he saw right through you. Piercing eyes, but old man's eyes, adult eyes in a boy. Silent. Just looking. Like he knew everything about you. I suppose it was the guilt about the Portuguese woman, about John even . . . although I'd grown to hate him it was still there . . . I wanted to run away with Avril and our baby. But she wouldn't hear of it, wouldn't leave the boy in particular.

I was finished with the sea, but those associations werenae finished with me. It happens that way with relationships. You get to say when you're done with them, but you rarely get tae state when they are finished wi you.

So Bim got in touch. I knew what his tastes were. We met at a pub in Edinburgh, the big one at the East End called the Café Royal. The sun spilled in through the large stained-glass windows. We stayed far away from the dock taverns of Leith where our faces were known. He was there with two friends. A guy, Mat, younger than Bim, who seemed out of his depth, and then another one, who was a sort of gangster type. He was an evil-looking bastard, sharp, piercing nasty eyes, sallow skin. I forget his name. Bim said they were looking for some action. As I said, I knew what his tastes were.

So, help me my God, I steered him towards those bairns. I served those young boys up tae these fucking monsters on a plate. Raymond and his wee pal: a kid who was just in the wrong place at the wrong time. I knew they rode their bicycles through that tunnel every Saturday morning. I thought Bim would just scare them, that there would be too many people around for him to hurt them. But I wanted the little bastard to suffer: wanted him to pay for me not being with Avril and Stuart . . .

. . . but he was just a wee laddie . . .

(Choking, sobbing noises.)

36

DREAM, BUT NOT LET DREAMS BE YOUR MASTER

. . . this burning of the feet business was highly distressing, Ray, no two ways about it . . . his fault of course . . . my grandmother was no angel, wont to put my little hands on the ring of the cooker, she was; but her lover, Mr Baxter, always occasions a slight chuckle to think of 'em at it, he was altogether more creative, I'd say, burning the soles of my feet . . . can't begin to tell you the pain involved, Ray, not that I'm looking for sympathy, not really . . . very much inspired by the Romans, was Mr Baxter, they would press red-hot iron plates on their victims' soles . . . then, of course, the Spanish Inquisition . . . very naughty they were . . . secured the bare-footed prisoner in stocks, basting the soles with either lard or oil, then it was barbecue time, nice and slowly over a burning coal brazier . . . not exactly endearing behaviour, but only if you're on the receiving end of it, otherwise it would be a bloody good laugh and let's not kid ourselves . . . but, well, a life lesson taught . . . tears shed till they stopped only to be replaced by blind rage . . . his big mistake of course . . . you have to finish 'em off or some of them, not all, but some, they come back . . . like you, Raymond . . .

. . . you see, Ray, you can't hate those people who do those things to you, educators they are . . . you can hate yourself for not being strong enough to stand up to them . . . then make sure that you get stronger . . . then you can destroy them because you've replaced them with a better version of them, you see . . . their time is over . . . but you don't hate them . . . your destruction of them is like a salute to them . . . showing them what they achieved . . .

. . . it's different with you though, Ray . . . I had hopes for you . . . but you've taken the wrong path, the path of the weak and self-righteous . . . I'll have to take care of you, sunshine, like I did Wai . . .

. . . you see, Wai was very smart, had an intuitive scent for weakness . . . had me working in the boiler house by the furnace, stoking it, just cause he saw my unease around fire . . . started to torture me that way . . . of course, he then slipped up, went round the back of the boiler to see me . . . I was distressed by the fire but not as much as I made out, or as much as he thought, with me writhing on that stone floor, crying like a baby as I crawled towards him, then suddenly sprang to my feet . . . 'you're bloody good,' I told him as I grabbed his head and snapped his neck, though I confess I was disappointed he fell for that one . . . oldest trick in the book and whatnot . . .

. . . and hurled his crumbling sack of a body from me with an actual flourish, which, well, I appreciated, if nobody else did . . . slung him right in the bloody furnace, I did, but a guard saw him roasting away in there and they pulled his charred body out . . . oh, those spoilsports, those inscrutable little orientals . . .

. . . oh, they did go all funny in the investigation, Ray . . . 'do you have any idea who could have done this?' the usual bollocks, Ray, you're a former investigator, you know how it goes . . . of course, I had the retort to hand: 'it is my considered opinion that there is a strong criminal element within these four walls . . . with that in mind, could be anyone . . .' well, what can you say? I glanced at the interpreter and wondered how he responded because the commissioner looked sternly at me and nodded slowly, like he bade me to continue, which I was happy to do . . . 'family man, or so I hear' I found myself moved to state, 'a couple of little mites minus one daddy; no longer coming home to them, don't get much more sad and tragic, I'm sure . . . if the mother's a looker I daresay she'll be in the arms of another before long . . . people are more adaptable than they think, there's gonna be a little toing and froing, I suspect, but life goes on . . .'

. . . and it does, dunnit, Ray? . . . maybe not for everyone though, maybe not for you, but let's face it, it'll be a mercy killing . . . already a physical wreck with more damage to come . . . but while the ending will be merciful, I can't make that promise about the process . . . you know how I roll, Ray, you've tried to blank me out of your frightened little boy's head for ages now, haven't you? . . . when I've been sort of hiding in plain sight for years . . .

. . . cause you see, Ray, we were meant to be together, right from the off . . . you were never supposed to leave that tunnel, that's a wrong I have to RIGHT!

Day Fifteen

37

NOTHING INHERENTLY
GOOD OR BAD

. . . it is not happening . . .

Early Thursday morning Gatwick flight: Ray Lennox, crumpled into a small seat, perspires in the overcoat he's too sore to attempt to remove. He sits bitch, obese priest on one side, stick-thin goth girl on the other. It's as if the cleric is some kind of matchmaker, intent on pushing them together. This moves Lennox to raise an eyebrow in apology at the sable-apparelled woman. *Papes*, he finds himself vindictively thinking, before chuckling in bitter, self-harming shakes at the almost quaint lunacy of Scottish sectarianism; how it effortlessly supplants every other racism as that country's go-to bigotry.

This chamber of plastic, Perspex and cloth he is sealed in, makes him feel more *animal* than ever. The canvas duffel at his feet under the seat in front smiles *fuck you* at his attempt to shift his ravaged lower limbs. In his trembling hands he fans out the crisp new twenties the cashpoint dispensed earlier. Purchases two small bottles of red wine, to top up the chalky painkillers that scour his gut.

The fat priest, chin now embedded in chest, snores next to him. It isn't unpleasant; the sound of a soft Velcro strip tearing, perversely rhythmic with his own shallow breathing and the pulsing pain in his body. He succumbs to a welcome delirium, lying immobile the rest of the journey.

They are trying to kill you. Or at least cripple you. But the good news is that you're still here. Maybe it can all work out. Maybe you'll get past all this. Find those bastards. Put them all away. Square it with Les. Take off with Carmel. Perhaps to a little place in the sun . . . Tenerife . . . somewhere the heat just drains you, but in a good way. Where you never have to shiver again . . .

I'm sure you will . . .

Yanked into verisimilitude by a text popping into his phone on the descent, he is cheered. His recent X-rays are all clear of breakages. This news instantly seems to herald a reduction of the pain. Then, the unnerving scrunch and sear of aircraft wheels on tarmac tears up through the fuselage and his ruptured body. Lennox almost cries in relief as it smoothens itself out.

Hobbling off and down the gangway, to the aggravation of fellow passengers and the strained pity of the airline staff, he phones Tom Tracy, who doesn't pick up. Leaves a voice message explaining that it will be a while before he can go back to the kickboxing. In the arrivals lounge, an airport employee swerves an implausible chain of conjoined baggage trolleys through stupefied winter holiday crowds, filling Lennox with dread as he negotiates past it. Shuffling to the toilet, he struggles through his pain to defecate. Wiping his arse is almost as dire an undertaking. He looks at the floor and the tile pattern. The lines vibrate and blur.

Mona. Julie Knowles. Darren Knowles.

You are the clever one.

But how can you face them, Ray? You can't even face your own mother!

FUCK OFF.

Yet Ray Lennox is first in at Horsham Security Solutions, heedfully placing his coat on the flimsy stand, hoping not to topple it, then sitting tentatively in a chair he has been obsessing in dread about all the way back on the Gatwick Express. Almost reassured that it's more uncomfortable than ever, he grimaces and fires up the desk computer.

A sudden shout from outside: it provokes his jangling nerves, drawing him to the window. It's just a red-faced deliveryman ushering his colleague's vehicle into a tight parking space.

The murky streets are busy with traffic and bodies battling against the cold on their way to work and school. Most places in Britain aren't shy about letting you know it is winter: a seaside town always screams the point.

Lennox sits down, gets online, tries to ease into a bout of intensive research. The Falmer development seems littered with nothing more unsavoury than Cardingworth's bland platitudes. Nonetheless, immersed in his screen, he's only vaguely aware that Ria has come into the front office. This is followed by some hushed but urgent voices, more demanding of his attention. By the time he's prised his stiffened body out the chair and crossed the room to investigate, they have stopped.

When he opens his office door he finds Ria alone. Her furrowed focus as she waters the plants indicates forcible immersion in the mundane in order to shut out bigger, nagging issues. The steaming kettle clicks off on the worktop by his side. Lennox considers saying something, but instead heads back into his room, just as he hears a whistling of Depeche Mode's 'Just Can't Get Enough', informing him George has arrived. Sure enough, he enters Lennox's office, closing the door behind him. Flashes a pearly smile, despite wiping his nose with a handkerchief. — How's Mumsie?

— Seems okay, just a bit of a fright.

— Excellent, George says. — Terrible thing, old age. We see our future in those poor blighters and it ain't pretty. Damned if I know how Polly can do what she does.

287

— You okay? Lennox asks.

— Just this damn flu bug, bashing it with Lemsip!

Ria comes in with two steaming mugs, setting them down on coasters. They are ones George had made last year:

STAY SAFE!
THERE IS SHAM SECURITY
AND THERE ARE
HORSHAM SECURITY SOLUTIONS

Usually joining them for coffee, Ria's frown indicates an air of preoccupation and she promptly exits.

George tracks her departure. Picks up the Hearts snow globe on Lennox's desk. He gives it a perplexed once-over, before laying it back down, muttering a confirming, — Curious . . . and shaking his head.

Unnerved at his hovering, Lennox clicks off the windows on his screen. As George is about to speak, he cuts in and says in a low voice, — Maybe you could have a wee word with Ria about this boyfriend who always seems to be hanging around here.

— You do it. You understand that generation better than I do. George's mouth puckers in distaste. — You have nephews.

— But you've got *daughters*, George, Lennox responds, anxious to bring in some levity. — They must have been Ria's age once!

— I rest my case, George says morosely. — Besides, I have to go; a damage limitation exercise to undertake. Sonia saw some pictures Polly posted on Instagram. Honestly, some women believe that just because you sleep with them regularly and pledge undying love and absolute fidelity, that they somehow have the right to pass comments on your every single sexual transgression.

288

It's not the words, but their deadpan delivery that makes Lennox convulse, despite both his ambivalence to George and how it is sore on his body. — Ah, the dating game. Well, you will have multiple romances.

— Damn social media, why the hell do people over fifteen even bother? George snorts. — Anyway, fences to mend and all that, so see you later, he takes a sip on the coffee and screws his face up. — We *definitely* need a coffee machine. Lemsip is infinitely better than this crud. Long lost its charm, Raymond.

Lennox nods in the affirmative. — Speaking of which, is Sonia out the picture then?

— Don't ask silly questions, George pivots in departure, stamping down the unsecured carpet tile as he goes.

Easing himself slowly forward into the chair, Lennox returns to the screen. Looks to the window, catching George skipping down the front steps in swift egress, with straight-rod back and purposeful stride. Any limp he might have had is gone. Not even a hint of surrender to the flu's ravages. Thinks about Cardingworth; the clobbered tone of his voicemail indicates that the monster has been wounded, but he suspects not principally from his or even Les's activities. And nowhere near Lennox's own extent.

It still has to be taken down.

Who is key? Trench? Mona? Worse, who is behind him: foster mum Julie, or Darren, the acid monster?

Knowles.

Darren and Julie: husband and wife? Brother and sister? He needs to find them.

Then, from outside, a male voice again, creeping into his ear: insistent, badgering.

Ria.

That wee cunt.

His pulse explodes as he forces extrication from his seat.

Grabs the baseball bat, shuffles painfully across the carpet tiles. Despite George's efforts, he slides on the persistently loose one and almost falls. Staggering forward to keep his footing, he sucks back the pain, resisting the urge to scream out as his eyes water.

When he hobbles back into the front office, Lennox hears the term *drama college* deployed in haughty tones. It's not Chris who is chatting to Ria. — Raymondo! His brother Stuart spins round in an office chair, barely registering Lennox slip the bat into the umbrella stand.

It's instantly evident that despite the early hour Stuart has been drinking: — This lassie is a *light*, he extravagantly gesticulates, — a beacon to guide us all through this increasingly dark and inhospitable terrain!

Ria's face flushes deep scarlet.

— Stu, please stop harassing my colleagues and get out of my place of work.

— Hey, Stuart spreads his arms, — I got the part! The audition for that play: *The Harlot's Revenge*, by G. L. McGinnis! At the Theatre Royal!

— Drury Lane, the West End! Lennox says excitedly. — That's a big deal, Stu –

— No, not the one in that dreary metropolis, the Theatre Royal right here in beautiful Brighton, he bellows, as Lennox's spirits sink to rock bottom.

You're never getting shot of this little cunt . . .

Who is bigger than you . . .

— So . . . I naturally thought I'd come round and take my injured big bro out to lunch to celebrate! To thank him for putting me up and facilitating my *career* recovery, Stuart's mouth turns down in hammy violation, — Was I so wrong to think in this way? As the Bard said, love all, trust a few, do wrong to none . . . He whips back to Ria: — *All's Well That Ends Well.*

Lennox reasons that his complaisance will at least get Stuart out of the office. Grabs his heavy coat from the stand, gestures to his brother to help him into it. — Sound, he mumbles, nodding at Ria in half-apology.

Outside the cold is biting. The treacherous, slippery frost, crystallised on parts of the pavement, makes the stiff Lennox even more tentative in his movements.

You are going to slip on this fucking ice and shatter like a glass vase.

Stuart is too preoccupied to take this in. — That Ria, mmmm-hmmm! A wee honey for sure. But that boyfriend ay hers is no good, Ray. As Shakespeare said in *The Tempest*, hell is empty and all the devils are here! That girl deserves better!

And you're better? Lennox wonders, then suddenly snaps: — He was here again?

— Oh aye, Stuart puffs himself up. — Fair took off quick enough when he saw me come in. He's a bad yin, El Mondo; mark my words.

— Fair dos, but you keep away fae her as well. She's a young lassie.

— C'mon, Ray, lighten up! Ah'm only flirting wi her to tease you. Some of us do prefer our sexual partners tae be a roughly proximate age tae within a decade or two . . . but then, I may rethink if and when I attain your advanced years, Stuart sings, holding back to watch his brother slowly navigate round a patch of ice. — For fuck sake, you move like one Jambo central defender collie-buckying another, bro. What was the *wee accident at work*, fitting alarms for old cunts? Fall off a ladder?

He thinks of the steps of the collapsing gangway, holding on to that grille, before crashing into the void. The terrible smash onto concrete, the metal all around him. — Something like that.

— Shit, Raim, watch yourself. I mind on set in Romania

291

once; was playing a dodgy geezer in *Bad Shit 3: Unleashed in the East*, Stuart recalls. — Long story short: I was doing a complicated stunt and I fell off a rig. Thought I was finished. Would have been but for the safety net. I was swinging fifty feet up on the side of a skyscraper till they got me down, almost an hour later. Of course, the weather changed, and it started to snow heavily. Thought I was a goner a second time, with hypothermia! I had my phone in my pocket, so I switched it on to try and distract myself till they rescued me. Immediately a text pops in, from that cunt Geoff Moriarty, telling me Hartley had just scored again in the Hampden semi. A dark time, Raymie, Stuart muses sadly. — The film was decent, but it went straight to DVD.

Lennox can only produce an instantly dwindling smile, as they enter a hostelry suggested by Stuart. Immediately he sees why he's never set foot in it: the assembly, including Juliet, could have been cloned from Stuart's friends back in his Edinburgh haunts. His brother immediately orders a magnum of Krug, the crowd gathering round as Stuart ceremonially pops it open, pouring it into several glasses, handing one to Lennox. — This is my big brother Raymond, whom I adore more than anything in the known universe . . . he booms, before raising a provocative eyebrow, — with the possible exception of decent champagne!

Lennox exchanges greetings, watching Stuart apparently having the time of his life, regaling the company with a story of a spell in panto with the Krankies. Judging by the way they hang on his every word he seems to be shagging the entire party. Far from unlikely, this is inevitable to Lennox, knowing their Edinburgh equivalents; how they jadedly passed each other around for years, to the point that even this most world-weary of souls would constitute fresh meat for them.

The early lunch dissolves into the afternoon, Lennox

drinking more champagne ordered by Stuart and then feeling obligated to buy a bottle himself. The alcoholic fizz and buzz swaddles him in its solacing blanket, facilitating a smooth, deceptive omnipotence. Above all, it makes him less aware of the pain. This state of mild euphoria will be augmented by the line of cocaine Stuart has racked out for him on the cistern of the toilet. — The choice is yours, *mein Bruder*, choose wisely. Remember, there is nothing inherently good or bad, but thinking makes it so, he quips, helpfully adding, — *Hamlet*.

— Cunt, Lennox snaps, hesitating for one second before traversing to the dingy toilet to smash the line up his nostril. Instantly his bones throb as he feels his wounds pulse and radiate. But the remaining pain is rendered an almost delicious sharpening of his sense of self; the hunched shoulders straighten, the corded muscles in his legs tighten as the android life is pumped into him.

When he strides back into the bar, his brother starts bending his ear about Ria's boyfriend. — These snide, ferrety eyes . . .

. . . a blinding flash blitzes Lennox; he suddenly sees it to the point he has to place a white-knuckled grip on the bar.

Chris . . . Ria's boyfriend . . . he was one of the men from the tunnel. It can't be, but it's true. He was there!

It makes no sense.

Then, suddenly, it makes complete sense.

— You okay, El Mondo?

Lennox's eyes ignite in manic blaze. — I don't fucking believe it!

— That coke is pretty good: *all hands on deck*, Stuart trumpets. — You need another drink!

— No, I've got to go, but the coke is excellent, so thank you and well done. When I say I love you, Stewpot, I mean it more than ever, and he turns to Stuart's new friends and bellows, — Look after my baby bro! This big little cunt is fucking precious to me!

And Lennox steals towards the exit, already sensing a Shakespearean quote sliding from his brother's lit-up brain to his excited lips.

Stepping outside, he calls George. Feels the drug hauteur in his own mouth. — Are you successfully mending those fences?

— Trying to, George rasps. — You sound pissed, or worse; harbouring a flu somewhat different from mine. Go home, Raymond.

— That little cunt hanging around the office, Ria's boyfriend, his first name's Chris, what's his surname?

— I don't know. Go to bed, Raymond.

— Okay, Lennox says. He hangs up and calls the office. But Ria, as expected, has long gone home. Her mobile number will be in her file there. George would surely know it, but he doesn't trust him. Still feels his partner might just be the source of all his problems.

38

FOREVER IN DREAMS

. . . all those faces in my life and one of those struggling, begging, ter-rorised expressions that never leave you, always nourish your appetite for more destruction . . .

. . . one has re-emerged through the sea of them, and I see him in the domain of sleep coming out of the tunnel, escaping our grasp and in my sweet mind's eye I am leaving this other boy, this feisty little tyke I am about to smash in order to pursue young Raymond and I catch him this time and force him to the ground, tearing into him, while strangling him as I should have the other but didn't, in fear that Raymond would raise the alarm . . . but I hear his voice and see him again, him now a middle-aged man but still haunted and I have to stop him in the con-scious world with all the difficulties and risks this entails . . . but you must impose your reality . . . enforce your power . . .

. . . but later . . . first dreams . . . dreams . . . dreams . . .

. . . tell me what to do and talk like you always do, little lovely, and I'll do what I did in my mind to Wai's bitch . . . fuck her from behind, feel her tears and her reluctant tortured orgasm cause I'd never stop pump-ing her stiff hole until she moved and her tears and wails and pleads just make me harder and pump more and as she spasms I'm at her neck with my blade and I feel my cold steel rip the life out of her, tearing open her throat, as we witness her bound children's searing screams as their mummy's blood splashes across their faces, all of them knowing they're next, the poor little mites, ha ha ha ha . . . they always had it coming to them because we all had to put up with that, you see . . . a long way from Dudley Zoo this place is I can tell you, MISTER RAYMOND LENNOX . . .

. . . but me waking up in this prison, their joking voices all around me all beside the point, maybe chuckling quietly at my erection poking into what they see as nothingness, all insignificant cause all I need is one image through my fuzzy eyes one smile one frown one whiff of perfume and you and him and her are as real to me as you are to each other and I possess you totally and irredeemably . . .

. . . I let him struggle last night before my blade severed his penis and my burning torch cauterised the wound . . . as his eyes popped I set him to work watching what I was doing to you, Lennox, ordering him to scrub your fresh blood off the floor and the feast, oh I must contain the feasting as my muscles and juices activate and I'll never stop, never wake up, and as I gorge my body will rot away under the oppressive captivity . . .

. . . God bless Wang, sleep is the empire, forget your virtual reality, the woke moments are nothing, they are lies, lies you have constructed to prevent all men reaching their natural states and becoming emperors in the realm of their senses . . . but . . .

. . . but . . .

. . . but at some point they came for me . . . those jailers . . . could have been days, weeks, months or even years later . . . I could hear their faint cries, but this time I could do nothing . . . they truly could have been up to all sorts and I wouldn't even have noticed . . . loaded me into a van on a stretcher and I heard the tearing of sirens . . . somebody had done damage to someone . . . I wondered what had happened . . . had my division between dreamtime and wakened time blurred? . . . was I sleepwalking and committing heinous acts? . . . it was impossible to make sense of, but I was comfortable and safe . . . all those voices around me were intrusive at first, but I soon learned to tune them out and I spent most of the time lucid dreaming . . . madness and sanity, the idea of the division was strange enough where I was in that prison, in my life at sea, but here where I was king, there was no need to observe those false norms and segregation the small minds in straight-street imposed on us all . . . or tried to . . .

. . . then one voice compelled my rise to the surface, demanded my attention . . . it was from years ago . . . more than the first one, young Les . . . you remember the one that got away . . . Raymond Lennox . . . wasn't best pleased, not going to lie . . . I have to get you, and in the real world too . . . can you hear me, young Raymond? . . . can you feel me coming for you?

39

PSYCHO THERAPY 3

A shaky Ray Lennox walks off the drugs along the blisteringly windy seafront. Turns into Montpelier Road, heads uphill into town. Despite suspicions of his partner's chicanery, he intends to take George Marsden's advice and go home. Aspires to enjoy the respite cocaine and alcohol provide from the pain, while ignoring their nagging advocacy.

But something gets in his way.

Nose already both streaming *and* bunged up, he goes into a chemist to buy another small pack of Kleenex. Immediately assaults one grouted nostril. Exits the shop to see a familiar figure on the other side of the street.

Wearing a striking vermilion coat, matching her ruby-framed glasses steamed with condensation, Elaine Rodman is at the ticket machine by the Waitrose car park. Immediately recognising her neatly parked Audi, Lennox crosses the road. It's the same car as Carmel's, but blue to her red. When Rodman returns to the vehicle, she finds him there, sitting on the bonnet, arms folded, affecting a nonchalance he does not feel.

Though visibly stiffening at his confrontational bearing, she nonetheless remains cool. — Ray.

— Why did you drop me as a client? Elaine?

Elaine Rodman takes another step forward, but halts at that distance, seeing that Lennox is in no hurry to remove himself from her vehicle. — Please get off my car.

— Please answer the question.

— We've come to the end of our practitioner–client relationship. There's no more to be gained from this.

Lennox shakes his head, but retains his gaze. — Shite.

— Like I said earlier, Rodman snaps, — I don't need to give you a reason. Sit on my car all fucking night if you like, and she opens the Audi door, fastening the ticket inside the window. Slams it shut, and turns, making her way across the car park towards the town centre. Lennox, sliding off the bonnet to a jarring impact with the ground, lets her boot heels click half a dozen times on the concrete, before he follows.

Rodman heads to the Lanes, which bustle with Christmas shoppers. Although weaving deftly through the human traffic, she's highly visible in her red coat. But even with the drugs anaesthetising his pain, Lennox struggles to keep up. Bristles in violation as a backpack smashes into him. A bearded man is attached, blinking nervously as Lennox feels himself baring his teeth.

— Sorry . . . the man's Adam's apple bobs.

In his brief distraction, Rodman has vanished into one of the shops. No sign of her in the clothing boutique or the record store: it has to be the vegan restaurant. As he enters, the heat from the premises instantly activates a cascading gush of mucous slime from his nose. Wipes it and sees Rodman sat at a table. Opposite her, a blandly handsome man of about forty, curly dark hair, greying at the temples, wearing a wine-coloured jacket.

But Lennox isn't looking at him. — How long has Cardingworth been your client?

— What's this? Elaine Rodman's companion tautens in his seat.

— Excuse us for a second please, Will. Rodman regards her dining partner, then rises as an investigating waitress looks on.

— Is everything okay? Will contemplates Lennox, who again shuns eye contact with him, focusing on Rodman.

— Yes, back in a minute, she smiles wanly.

They walk over to the exit, standing in the vestibule area. Lennox has one eye on the shoppers milling by outside, as Rodman hisses at him: — You've got a bloody nerve. I told you –

— How long has Cardingworth been your client? he repeats. — And please dispense with the shrink's poker face. I was a detective for years.

Rodman seems to weigh up the possibilities of fabrication and circumspection. Lennox guesses she might reason he'd have followed Cardingworth to her office. He controls her level of uncertainty. She opts for: — Longer than you, now please go away.

Suspicion confirmed. Savours the small victory. — What did he say to you?

Not a nerve twitches in Rodman's porcelain face. — You know how this works, right? It's called client confidentiality. You signed a contract when we started this. Well, so did I. It involved disclosure of conflict of interest.

Lennox thinks of his relationship with his previous therapist, the murderer Sally Hart. Is unimpressed. — How did you know that Cardingworth and I were connected? he nips. — He fucking told you everything, didn't he? Over her shoulder, spies through a gap in the velvet drapes, Will, the dining partner, looking protectively across.

— It's more mundane than that. Rodman's head shakes in exasperation. — I read about the assault on the *Argus* website and joined the dots. Her jaw tightens. — Now go!

— What does he tell you in those sessions? That he's a beasting paedophile? Does he mention the tunnel? Raymond Lennox's eyes blaze, and Elaine Rodman is shocked, even more so when he seizes her by the throat. — Don't fucking hold out on me, he demands in a low, sibilant whisper, looking shiftily out through the gap in the curtains.

Can this Will guy, now studying the menu, tell what is going on? No.

Maybe he can, maybe you need to hurt him . . . maybe hurt them all . . . you'd be perfectly entitled, Ray, within your rights, really . . .

Then he's aware of her hands clasping round his wrist, tugging desperately, her voice croaking, — Let . . . me . . . go . . .

That's it, Ray. Teach 'em!

What the fuck . . .

His senses crash into him as Lennox releases his grasp. Looks at her, then his own hands, in mortification. He has assaulted a woman, and one who, in her own way, has been trying to help him. *What the fuck is going on with you?* — I'm so sorry, Elaine. That was out of order, he appeals, in shock, — I've never done anything like that before . . .

— My God. Elaine Rodman hauls in a breath, rubbing at her neck, looking at him in disbelief. — You really need to be on medication!

— I am, and he opens his arms, — look at the state of me. He feels a sob break from him. — Cardingworth did this. It was attempted murder. Tried to bust me up, and he thinks of the man in the balaclava who first felled him with a single blow, then charged at him as they both tumbled down a floor into darkness, — I can hardly walk. I'm desperate.

Rodman is even more rocked as she ponders his words. — Mat Cardingworth . . . what . . . do you really think I would tell Mat Cardingworth anything about *you*?

— Has he asked?

— Enough, Ray! You know the rules before you take part in the game, she insists. — I play by them. Always!

301

— Okay . . . it's just that everyone else in this town seems to be in his pocket.

— Well, he hasn't got me in it!

— Did he say anything . . . ? Lennox's face opens up. — Please . . . give me something!

— He said nothing about any tunnel, Rodman declares in stark finality. — You allege that he is one of those paedophile sex abusers. He has said and done absolutely nothing to give me that impression, and I've worked extensively with perpetrators and victims of this kind of abuse for years! If he disclosed any criminal acts I'd be duty-bound to inform the authorities!

— Thanks, Lennox says in timid misery, unsure whether he believes everything, or not a single word. How that's the way he's felt from the start. But the acid attack in the library toilet was real. The terrible injuries he carries from the assault at the concrete factory sting with every step and breath. — Enjoy your dinner.

Rodman's shake of the head and rolled eyes say *are you fucking joking?* — I can't help you, Ray, but you do need to get some. You have an extreme delusional empathy, you put yourself in the shoes of the most despicable characters to find them –

— What's that got to do with –

— I'm telling you for your own good: you do that too much, and you become them. I've a colleague who –

Lennox turns his head in slow, emphatic deliberation. — No, and he opens the door, slipping back out into the numbing cold.

Under a squally sky of smoky clouds, he hobbles and sneezes back to the white uplit Regency buildings of Sussex Square. The cocaine, and the illusion of power it confers, has started to fade. His aches searing acutely, Lennox is glad to get up the stairs.

What the fuck is happening to you?

You assaulted a woman. You've spent your whole life locking up pricks that assault women. You've become what you hate . . .

What does that make you?

It makes you you, Ray. Don't fight it. You know how this virus transmits!

Fucking shite.

Firing on the TV from the remote, he hopes the mundane drivel will drown out the squabbling voices in his head. Just as he settles on the settee, his phone rings. A nameless number appears.

Lennox pauses five full seconds, then hits the green button. — Hello? Who's this? Then he feels himself winding up tightly in the face of an equally long silence on the line.

Suddenly, a gravel-gargling working-class Edinburgh accent barks: — Doogie. Doogie Gillman.

Lennox's first impulse is to hang up, but intrigue gains dominion of his discrepant senses. He then mentally scrambles to shut down his second reaction, which is to ask: *what the fuck do you want?* Instead he utilises the camaraderie-inducing remnants of the declining intoxicants in his system. — Hey, Doogie, what's up, bud?

— I found some stuff, Lenny, Gillman's death-sentence-pronouncement voice, — stuff you should ken aboot . . .

Why the fuck would you . . . ?

Lennox is flabbergasted. Then something fearful eats at him. *Why is Gillman getting involved? Did Notman ask him? What the fuck is he looking for?* — Thanks, Dougie . . . I thought you were gone . . . he corrects himself, — like had left? Notman told him this wasn't the case, but it's the only small talk he can make.

— Still workin a month's notice, Gillman slurs, late-night cop drunk, where a sober part of the brain can still strong-arm a concept through a fog of nonsense. — You think I was gaunny roll over and go quietly for that wee pump-up-the-drawers Drummond?

Gillman's sloppy regression to old grievances makes Lennox aware of his own enervation. His bones feel like lead, held in place by muscles and tendons straining at their tensile limits. The skin grafts throb. A yawn he attempts to stifle almost tears his jaw from his face. — So, what's up then, Doogie? Lennox finds himself adjusting the dimmer switch on the lamp next to him, as if it will somehow illuminate Gillman more clearly in his mind's eye.

Perversely, it seems to work, as Gillman again finds focus. — I got the information you need.

— What? You mean Mathew Cardingworth, like the stuff I asked Ally Notman to get?

— Mare than that: ah got the fuckin lot, Lenny, and it's a shitshow, pal, he declares in a stunned awe. — And it was nowt tae dae with Notty, cause ah goat it by accident, he insists, before stridently contending, — Nae cunt else could have goat it!

Exhaustion and anxiety battle for control of Ray Lennox's beaten frame and psyche. In this seemingly two-horse race, the winner, confusion, suddenly sneaks home on the blind side. Gillman isn't making any sense. — Doogie . . .

— I need you to say tae ma face, and Lennox feels the urgency and pain in his voice, — Doogie Gillman isnae a fuckin nonce!

— I never said you were, Doogie, Lennox breathlessly coos, as if trying to entice a wounded pet out from under the sink for imperative veterinary treatment. Antagonising Gillman isn't an option, as he discerns his old rival may really be onto something. For all Dougie Gillman's legion of flaws, more often than not paraded with provocative gusto, an inclination towards bullshit was never in their ranks. For this reason, it is important not to taint the conciliatory pitch with the same quality. — It was Thailand and we wir aw pished . . . I just thought it was a bit questionable, the lassie looked young and –

— Ah never fuckin knew how auld she was! Ah thought thir wis fucking laws against that thing there! Ah pit my faith in that country's system . . . ah didnae ken! Ah've a daughter, Lenny . . . ah wis a good cop! You ken that! You mind ay Confectioner! Ah beat the fuckin truth oot ay that fuckin noncey bairn-murdering cunt!

It's true. Dougie Gillman did something that you failed to do: he put the fear of God into Mr Confectioner.

— Yes, you did, Dougie . . .

— Problem wi you is . . . the problem wi you, Gillman suddenly sounds slack again, as if another rush of alcohol has just sloshed over his brain, — is that you think you're the only cunt in the world that can feel pain . . . when they've made a wrong move . . . aye . . . aye . . . Gillman sucks in a long breath. It's a strange sound, like someone coming to the end of a milkshake. — Ah got past the encryption, got Scott McCorkel, wee laptop boy, on the case, Lenny, but that's the least ay it . . . that's fuck all . . .

Besieged by a sense of collapsing into a black hole inside him, Lennox feels that both he and Gillman will simultaneously burst into tears from five hundred miles apart. Propelled by desperation, he begs, — Dougie, please! What the fuck is it you've got for me, mate?

— I'm no like them, Lenny, Gillman roars defiantly. — Ah spent ma fuckin life huntin they bastards doon and lockin them up! Me! You n me never got oan, but we were on the same fuckin side, he says, almost like this constitutes a revelation. — If you were diggin aboot on this Cardingworth cunt, ah kent he wouldnae be a fuckin choirboy. Well, he isnae! And

305

that's the least ay it, Gillman repeats, sounding awestruck at what he's found, before he roars, — But ah'm no like him, Lenny! Ah need you to look me in the eye and tell me that!

You become what you hate . . . — Dougie . . . what's he done? Lennox begs.

— Ah sais ah need you tae look me in the eye and tell me that!

— Of course you're no fuckin like him! Lennox shouts back. — And I will look you in the eye and tell ye that! If you need me to do that I'll get a flight up first thing in the morning, mate! But just tell me first: what is gaun on wi him!

You can't do it . . . you can't get on another plane . . . you're fucked, Raymond.

— I'm pished. Ah cannae dae this now . . . Gillman slurs, — speak the morn . . .

— But, Dougie, fuck sake . . . ye cannae leave me like this!

— The morn, Lennox, Gillman snaps cruelly, and hangs up.

Devastated, Lennox rings back without any confidence his old colleague will pick up.

He doesn't.

Day Sixteen

40

THE SPLASH

Anaemic light seeps apologetically through the expensive Hunter Douglas Pirouette blinds he'd imported from America as Lennox blinks awake. Another Saturday, like where it all began. A week ago? Two? Perhaps a month? He can no longer tell; but fancies he can catch the faint scent of Carmel, her smoky, perfumed aura perhaps lingering on bedclothes he needs to change. Or is it Mona?

What the fuck are you doing, Raymond?

He needs to find her, to ask her about Darren Knowles, and about Mathew Cardingworth. Are they connected? What is she to him? Is Knowles the second tunnel man?

They are here, maybe all of the bastards. Right where I fucking well want them . . . Cardingworth . . . Knowles . . .

You're going to drive yourself crazy with those speculations, Raymond!

Sitting up slowly, mindful of his compromised frame, he hoists his legs out of bed. The digital clock display informs him he's slept in.

Letting out a groan, he reaches for the phone on his bedside table. The notifications blaze in accusation that his life is happening elsewhere and he is lagging behind it.

George:

> Call me. The big contract at that horrible shopping centre, you know it, just came up to tender. I've been strongly advised that we should put in a bid ASAP. Happy days. Or they would be but for this fucking flu.

Aye, strongly advised by whom and for what, you cunt . . . ?
Carmel:

> We really need to talk. It's urgent.

Talk tae fucking Cardingworth, ya hoor!
Now, now, Raymond, no way to treat a lady!
Tom Tracy:

> How are you mate?

You'll never be well enough to spar with him again, that's for sure. Not that it did you much good, Ray!

He goes into one of the albums in the photos section of his phone, and a bank of faces he should have been able to erase. Why did he keep them, if he never looked at them? They were all women he had loved. Glancing through them makes him recount their sacrifices and his own shortcomings, drilling a jagged narrative into his head. From Penny to Catriona to Trudi to Carmel . . . but to his sudden horror, Cardingworth's face appears in the scroll . . .

What the fuck . . .

Then others: nonces from the Sex Offenders Register, all grinning at him in their squalid, goading smiles. He blinks and he can see two faces that jump out . . .

It's them . . .

. . . a fleeting image of the two puses of Hades, distorted and demonic, showing him something, but not enough. Taps go on under his skin, sending brooks of sweat to bubble to its surface . . .

. . . he scrolls back, his heart thrashing, but it's Penny-Catriona-Trudi-Carmel again . . .

. . . then, just as he thinks his senses are normalising, the pictures cruelly change once more: becoming Britney Hamil, then Hazel Lloyd, Valentina Rossi, Craig Connor, Tianna Hinton, some of the children he rescued, other ones he failed . . . and then the lowest of them all, that sneering child murderer, as the vile Mr Confectioner grins back at him.

Poor little mites.

We have to stop this.

You have to stop this.

The phone slips from his hand, hits the edge of the bed before bouncing to the wooden floor. A big crack on the screen and Ray Lennox wants to cry. Instead he watches the device as it starts to ring, vibrating on its back, like a dying insect. He slowly, painfully, gets onto his knees to look at it, the hangover blinding his view of the screen. The act has caused the wounds in his legs to throb, and he rises slowly with the help of the bed, picking up the phone as it rings off.

It was Carmel. No message. What did she want? To tell you to drop this, probably from Cardingworth's bed?

Can't trust 'em Ray. Can't trust any of 'em.

A long, loud creak as he walks to the window, Lennox unsure whether it's in his bones or the floorboards. Ignoring it, he rolls up the blind, hand shaking on the cord. The sun peeks out timidly from behind bloated black clouds swirling in from the Channel with such truculent menace that they almost push him back into bed.

It had been a punishing night. The alcohol and coke had possessed enough staying power to compel a fevered mind to rotisserie his mangled, scarred body. Three times he'd sprung bolt upright in the darkness, trying first Gillman's number, then Notman's, both to no reply. Finally, he crashed into a coma just before light.

His fuzzy brain resistant to even rudimentary attempts to strategise as he picks up his phone. It's imperative to get to Edinburgh, to see Gillman, but George has left another text which he can't decipher through the ruined screen. Unable to face making breakfast, a cursory exploration of the flat telling him Stuart is out, probably shagging one of the regulars of his artsy local, Lennox gingerly peels off one of his bandages. The skin graft donor region on the thigh looks like an angry portal to hell. He gloomily heads to the bathroom to change the dressing.

It takes an age and when he returns to the front room, he sees Stuart, his feet stocking-soled, changing from his wet shoes into a pair of boots. — Fucking rain . . .

— Stu, I'm so glad to see you –

— Not a good time, Raymie, he says, slipping into the dry footwear, kicking the discarded shoes under the coffee table. — Big piss-up yesterday, well, had to after a call from the director, going on about the first readthrough next week. He's shaping up to be a right cunt . . .

— Too bad, Stu . . .

— . . . but fuck them all and the horse they rode in on, I'm straight back on it today. Just heard a local drama club stalwart has passed away. I thought it was strange he wasn't around yesterday. A bit of a bumptious cunt if the truth be told, but I kind ay liked him, and he looks gloomily at Lennox. — RIP, Ralphie!

A bolt smashes Lennox's heart. — Ralphie?

— Yes, Ralph Trench. Did you know him?

— No, Lennox immediately says, telling another false-hood, gambling Stuart is way too wrapped up in himself to notice. — What . . . what happened to him?

You could have stopped this.

— Not sure, just going to find out from the mob at the pub. Probably topped himself; lonely, mentally depressed, you know the playbook. *I* know the playbook. Stuart grips him by the shoulder, his eyes wet. — Family, Ray. Sometimes it's all we have when the going gets rough, and his fingers squeeze like hooks, before he breaks off and heads out.

Lennox looks to his dining-room table. Removes a speck of dust. Is there a stain on the cocktail cabinet? He rubs at it with his sleeve. No. Then he's looking out his window, the sea a strip of gunmetal. Realises he's touring his flat in zombification.

Lennox breaks his own rules going in on a Saturday. He's glad of the distraction and thinks he'll look into the shop-ping centre gig. By the time he manages to wash, clothe and transport himself to Seven Dials and Horsham Security Solutions offices, it's almost 1 p.m. and the best of the day has evaporated. He'd called Ria, asking her if she was free to come in too, suggesting they could get some urgent work done, but really he wants to ask her about Chris. No sign of her so far.

Goes back into his office. Calls Gillman's number. Noth-ing. A hollow, burning spasm in his stomach reminds Lennox that, barring Stuart's champagne-and-charlie combo, he has consumed zero since yesterday morning. He heads outside to the Good Companions for a sandwich. The pub shares the name of the old Edinburgh local in his scheme at Oxgangs, and he thinks of him and Les, riding past on their bikes, watching local characters going in and out on a Saturday. Ordering a BLT, he slips a hair-of-the-dog lager into the mix to keep it company. It offers only gaseous pep, but that's enough to deter him from returning to his workplace.

Instead, he opts to hit the pub on Ditchling Road, by the Level, thinking of Trench and what he knew, hoping to run into Mona. He needs to talk Cardingworth and Knowles with her.

A bumptious cunt if the truth be told, but I kind of liked him . . .

Perhaps it's time to go back to Edinburgh, Ray. Maybe the walls are closing in here . . .

There is no evidence of her, other than the despotic glances of wary men. Are they defining him through that association? He shuffles up to the bar, orders another pint of lager. As he raises it to his lips, a call comes in from Notman, who sounds like he has been crying. — Ken what I did, Lenny, ken what I did back in the day . . .

— Notty . . . how goes? Seen Gillman? He telt me –

— Ken what ah did, he repeats in a long gasp.

His snivelling nasal tones grate on Lennox, who moves to the door of the pub, his gaze falling harshly on anyone who meets his eyes. — Not a good time, Ally, he says, wincing as he finds himself paraphrasing his brother.

— Well, too bad, cause it's a good time for me! It's been eating me up, Lenny, been fucking killing me, Notman bleats.

— What has? What are you talking about for fuck sakes!

— I found out that you and Ginger Rogers had beaten that nonce tae a pulp. The Lollipop Man. Notman's voice goes higher, as the old case sears into Lennox's consciousness. — I found CCTV footage of youse dragging him out his flat and I told Bob Toal, Lenny, Notman spits it out. Then, after a silence, as if he can't believe it himself, gasps, — I grassed you up tae the fuckin boss!

That fucking nonce deserved it . . . Ginger Rogers . . . there was a cop . . . who was it stomping the face of the decked short-eyes? Did you pull Ginger away, or did he? Notman –

— What? What the fuck, Ally, why would you even do that? The device shakes in his hand before he blurts out, — We'll sort this out later!

— I dunno . . . fuck knows what I expected. I was new and daft and I thought it was wrong . . . I went to Toal but he just said, 'Never drop a fellow officer in it again. Now fuck off, I'll deal with it.' He buried it, Lenny. Toal buried the footage.

Lennox finds himself hyperventilating. A drunkard slumps into the pub, sees his full pint lying on the bar, unattended. Swivels round to witness the blazing eyes of Ray Lennox inviting him: *go on, you cunt, gies it . . . gie us a fuckin excuse . . .*

The drunk hesitates.

— Fuck you, Notman, if I see ye again I'm gaunny fuckin smash yir fuckin pus, ya useless cowardly, grassing cunt, Lennox snarls into the phone as the doglike whines of his tormented ex-colleague howl softly in the background.

The drunk moves away from the pint as if it's an explosive device.

— So, keep the fuck oot ay ma sight, Ray Lennox switches off the phone and puts it on silent. Rage eats at him. It scours his insides.

You are going to die carrying all this anger. You become what you hate.

When he gets back to the office about an hour later, after unsuccessfully trying to call Gillman, and then Carmel, who isn't picking up, Ria appears, biting her nails. He notices two large spots on her normally clear skin. He's about to ask Chris's surname, before cop snide takes over and he reasons it's best if he can manoeuvre her into disclosing it. Then Ria thrusts two old C45 cassette tapes at him, of the sort Lennox hasn't seen in years. — Those were left in here for you. With this, and she points to a Post-it note on one of the boxes that simply says: RL.

— How long ago?

— It must have been about half an hour. I had just –

— So you didn't see who left them?

— No, I was in the toilet, I –

Another exasperated fountain of rage explodes from Ray Lennox. — You fuckin dippit wee . . . how useless do you need tae be? One fucking thing –

Ria looks at him in horror. Her bottom lip trembles and she bursts into tears.

Oh my God, what have you done? That poor lassie . . . that lovely young woman . . . you're losing your fucking mind . . . fuck . . . Elaine Rodman . . . what's happening to you?

— I'm so sorry, pal, I was totally out of order there. Lennox gasps, unnerved by his own reaction as he puts a shaky arm round Ria. — I apologise for that . . . you're brilliant, totally sound, I'm just having a really bad time, but I shouldn't be taking it out on you, honey, and he holds the sobbing girl lightly, feeling his own tears condense.

Ria stiffens upright. They step away from each other. — It's not you, it's him! That Chris. The terror leaks out of her eyes. — He says if I don't get stuff for him he'll splash me!

— Splash you? What?

— Throw acid in my face.

Acid . . . what the fuck . . .

— Acid? Lennox immediately thinks of Mona, looks down at Ria's smooth cheek and feels his blood freeze. The muscles and tendons in his own face brace and tighten, as if in anticipation of a devastating assault. — What stuff?

316

Ria crumbles like a burst dam, massive convulsions shake her as she sobs in uncontrollable liberation.

Lennox holds her shoulders lightly. Wants this not to be occurring. Reasons it is. Steels himself to deal with it. — It's okay . . . nothing bad is going to happen.

He fundamentally doubts his own utterances, but Ria seems to access something inside that galvanises her, as her gaze locks on to his. — He wanted to know where you were going, what you were doing. I wouldn't tell him anything. I think . . . I think . . . A sabotaging choke halts her.

— It's okay, pal. Take your time.

Clicking her teeth together, Ria says warily, — I let slip that you were going to do something. I heard George talk about a concrete factory to someone on the phone.

Fucking George . . . two-faced cunt . . . I knew it!

— Who was he speaking to?

— I don't know, but I told Chris. I told him you were going there, and she bites her knuckle, — and then he was gone. I'm so sorry, Ray . . . I know something bad happened out there . . . the state you came back in . . .

A liberating spasm of rage shudders through Lennox, transmuting into an almost luxurious relief.

Chris. You know his surname. It has to be.

Here is somebody he can legitimately vent his anger on. Lennox takes Ria's hands in his, looks searchingly at her. His tones are clipped and precise cop speak: the authority of a man who has the state behind him. But he no longer does. — Any problems you ever had with this little cunt are now over. His, on the other hand, are only just beginning. Believe me when I say that.

She nods at him through her tears.

— Now you have to tell me about this acid stuff. What is this?

317

— Chris's dad . . . he once threw acid in a woman's face . . . and her lips tremble on the words, — Darren Knowles.

But they hammer into Lennox.

Chris's dad. The eyes. The same ferrety eyes.

He has to find Darren Knowles, and before it's Knowles who does the finding. He must be the second man in the tunnel, the one who fits the rapist nonce bill more than Mathew Cardingworth. Yes, he has to confront Cardingworth, wherever he's gone . . . but Knowles, he was at least one of the orchestrators of Lennox's misery. — Who is he?

— He's a real thug. Everybody is scared of him. Chris likes to put it about that he's a big gangster, cause of his dad.

Mona . . . for fuck sakes . . .

Lennox feels a sickness rise in him. — What's this Darren's story?

— He comes and goes. The Knowles family was connected to a group of travellers, ages ago, before they threw Darren out. Ria shakes her head, her lips pressed tightly together, — They want nothing to do with the Knowleses. Nobody likes them! And now Chris says he'll do the same to me with the acid!

— Nae fucker's touching you with any acid, pal. I'm calling you a taxi right now. You're going home and you sit tight, till I give you a wee shout that the coast is clear. I don't want you getting caught up in any more of this nonsense.

— Chris wouldn't stop pestering me, she says, as Lennox hands her a Kleenex. — He was nice at first . . . then . . .

— Then the acid, if you wouldn't go along with his shit. Lennox nods at her. — There was absolutely nothing else you could have done.

— I'm really sorry, Ray.

— No need for you to be sorry, Ria. I'm the one who's sorry; some bad bastards targeted you, purely because you

318

work with me. Let's get you right out of this mess, and Lennox hits the cab app on his phone.

— What are you going to do?

— I'm going to sort this out, he declares, fronting a certainty he doesn't feel. He pulls out his notepad from his pocket. — Write down Chris's address here.

— But you can't, Ray. Ria shakes her head, refusing to comply. — They know everyone in this town!

— They can be stopped and they can be hurt. He squints at the app through the cracked glass. The cab is approaching. He feels ludicrous, a mass of pain, sees the doubt in her eyes. *Who* can he hurt? Who has he ever hurt, except the people he gets close to? — Write it down.

Ria frowns deeply, but complies. — This is Chris's mum's place. But he moves around.

The car is approaching. It looks like a Ford Sierra. He silently curses the cracked glass. — Here's your lift. Go!

— Okay. But please be careful.

— Of course, and Ray Lennox has to fight back a sardonic laugh at his own absurdity, as Ria turns to head outside.

41

ESTATES OF MIND

The Whitehawk estate had looked positively pastoral when Lennox had driven through there, out of curiosity, on a hot day last summer. A community on a hill, it seemed like a little wonderland in the sun. Kids played in the street, people sat in gardens and outside the pub with beers. The smells of freshly cut grass and barbecue filled the air. So far from many of the viciously dull, bleak and unforgiving Edinburgh schemes he'd experienced. Now a late Saturday afternoon winter drabness prevails, but the area retains a hopeful vibe.

Not so Ray Lennox.

He parks a little down the hill. Pulls the old school cassette recorder from the pocket of his big coat, the one he picked up from Cash Converters in London Road. Puts in the first of Ria's tapes.

Raymond had found out about me and Avril and sherricked us badly at his dad's funeral. He was barmy, of course, no right in the head. He'd had some kind of a breakdown, and was taking aw that cocaine, and bevvying away. I mean real bevvying; I ken about all that, and he never had the head for it, and it's no surprising, the poor wee bugger . . .

Aye, that was my fault n all . . . I did something far worse to him than I did to his dad . . .

— You really don't need to continue.

You couldn't continue, could you?

Listening to the first cassette moves Lennox from vengeful to confused and despondent. His hand trembles as it holds the second.

No.

He can't bring himself to insert it. Not yet.

He puts the cassette player and tapes into his coat pocket, and gets out the car. Despite George's brogues being history, his trainered feet still pinch as he walks up through the scheme, as he thinks of it (he never got on with the English term 'estate'), to better take it in. What did he plan to do? Storm the Knowles dwelling as a beat-up wreck? But he's here. In front of him is the low-rise on an orange-bricked terrace of neat, well-kept homes. All he can do is face Darren, or Chris or Julie.

He knocks.

On his third bang, the door opens only wide enough to reveal the chisel-face of a chunky woman with inky hair, undermined by greying at the roots. Her open mouth hangs in slack-jawed dumbness. Lennox instinctively knows the pose of Julie Wilkins or Knowles is daft-lassie affectation in the face of a possible visit from authority. It's betrayed by the incongruously blazing savvy in her eyes. His first thought is that he can't see the angel tattoo, as she wears a white, long-sleeved PVC jacket. The second is that she is obviously Chris's mother. His hooked nose and angular face are replicated here, even if his eyes come from the second man in the tunnel.

Lennox tells her he's looking for her son.

— Makes two of us. He ain't been here for . . . Her face scrunches in attempt to calculate, before she turns and shouts, — Jemma, when was your dad here?

321

The door opens wider as a girl of around eight appears at her side. Her striking haunted cobalt eyes replicate those of Chris and Darren, without yet being infected by the accompanying street snide. — Two weeks. He came by on my birthday with Grandad.

— How is Daz?

The woman recalibrates, looking Lennox over in greater suspicion, pulling the door tighter to her, perhaps annoyed she let her guard down. — Who are ya? You ain't from round here. You a friend of Daz?

— Yes, Lennox lies. — We did a little work together, he ventures, watching her consider this, before adding, — He isn't around, is he? Daz?

He was like you. Joanne's words.

— No, he ain't. Her mood darkens. — And if you really are a friend of Darren's you'll know why, and she slams the door in his face.

Lennox knows that nothing he can say or do will get her to open up again. Turns down the path, onto the street. Then, aware of footsteps behind him, tenses up, before turning to see the girl coming after him. — Mister . . . is my dad in bother?

— No, he's okay, pal. Lennox looks around, feeling he's perhaps the one in bother. But the streets remain eerily quiet. — You're Jemma, right?

— Yeah. Do you really know my grandad?

— Darren? Yes, he says with conviction. He now feels as if he does.

Darren Knowles.

The kid looks at him. Her eyes are wide, but bright with a coy, sad acumen as she sucks on strands of her hair. — I saw them . . . but I wish they'd take me out.

— They will, pal, Lennox says, disquieted by the sound of

a car parking behind her, and the foggy woe in the girl's big blue eyes, — they've been pretty busy.

— Do they talk about me?

— Yes . . . I don't really know Chris, but Darren does mention you, quite a lot, he responds. More lies, but maybe of the sort that serves both parties well. This girl reminds him of so many lost children he's encountered from dysfunctional homes, forced to grow up too fast, yet militantly clinging to their childhood.

Jemma's mouth twists into an oval shape, delivering a subverting response undercooked by her brain. — I don't care what they say about them round here, she doubles down on defiance, — my dad has my name tattooed on his chest!

Lennox spots an opening. — I've seen it, pal, it's a cool bit of ink. Does your gran have any tats?

The girl nods. — On her arm. A silly angel. It's really old.

— You were saying they said things about your dad and Daz. What do they say? Lennox hears himself whisper, as he shifts the weight in his stiff legs.

He instantly knows it's an overreach. Jemma looks at him and for the first time sees something she doesn't like. Something Julie saw. Joanne too. Something Cop. She turns and runs away up the hill.

This emphatic retreat imbues Lennox with a gallows notion that as bad as things are, they are somehow going to get worse. Confirmation is issued when he gets to the Alfa Romeo. It's parked beside a bunch of green and black dump bins, lined up like stoic squaddies. Barely registers the two men stepping out urgently from behind them until they are all over him. He's seen them before; one short but chunky, with the busy, minimal lateral motion of a boxer, the other tall with long hair tied in a ponytail. Even though they probably smashed him, and then there was the terrorised Ralph Trench, and he knows they plan to accost him, Lennox perversely wants to laugh at them. — You're with us, mate, the shorter man suddenly grabs his hair.

That burning of the scalp signals up an old tape and Ray Lennox is immobilised.

Do what you want do what you want do what you want . . .

Lennox knows that he can't fight and he can't run. He feels it in his pocket, the small, sturdy old cassette player.

The tapes.

The confession.

The betrayers.

All of them, like him, seeming to belong to another age.

The street is now deserted, no sign of the retreating Jemma. Ponytail twists his arm up his back, and Lennox is unable to resist anything, to even feel the pain of his physical wounds as they bundle him into the back of a car strategically parked behind his own Alfa Romeo. Boxer pushes his wrists together behind his back. Slips plastic ratcheted ties onto them. Whips his phone, wallet, cassette player and the two C45 tapes out of Lennox's pockets. — What the fuck is this?

— It's game over, Lennox muses.

Boxer goes to drop them in a bin, but Ponytail pivots and says, — Nah, pass them here.

The shuffling Boxer nods, handing over the items. Shuts the car door. Comes around the other side and sits next to Lennox. The captive regards the gently vibrating man, looking at his small hands. Then turns to bury his head in the window.

Jock Allardyce . . . he even went on holiday with us, to Lloret de Mar. With his girlfriend, Jeanette her name was. A brassy cow with her hair piled high. A hostile, strained atmosphere with her and Mum. You saw him, by the side of the pool, touching your mother's pregnant belly when she was carrying Stuart. No cunt

*else saw it but you did . . . it was tender, that's what hurt you . . .
it was so wrong compared to the gruff, transactional way your
parents now spoke to each other. You turned and ran to the bar,
ran into Jeanette who was helping your father with the drinks . . .*

As they go through an underpass, Lennox concentrates on
controlling his breathing. His skin graft pulsing almost ten-
derly, in concert with his scalp. Examines his captors. Both
men appear physically formidable but maybe not as seasoned
as he first thought. He's written off Boxer as the shrouded
force displaying the one-punch knockout power in the dark
void of the concrete factory; the constant head movements
and shifting of weight between buttocks now suggests nerves.
He perhaps lacks the true hard man's gift: that of stillness.
Facial skin smooth and soft, no toughening up through gloved
hands making contact. If slick enough to avoid ring punishment, he wouldn't be doing strong-arm work.

The ponytail guy: Lennox can't suppress a chuckle bubbling up thinking of him as a heavy. Maybe it's just ponytail
guys, possibly he will pay for this assumption. Like Trench
did. Maybe this second time will be with his life. Yes, more
likely Ponytail was his cement works assailant. But with his
wounds, the pain and stiffness, he knows this speculation is
irrelevant. Their captive is a physically broken, hollowed-out
shell of a human being. And now he knows why.

*It was all a fucking set-up. No coincidences. Jesus fuck . . .
you were doomed right from the start . . . you were the fucking
target, not poor Les . . .*

Now Lennox feels as old and useless as he did young and
helpless, back in that tunnel forty years ago. The bounds pinch
tightly, but the pain is just another that nags in the distance,
like a crowd in a stadium a mile away: clamouring to be heard
but too far off to threaten. They drive out of town, towards the
industrial estate and Shoreham.

Then it dawns on him, that compensatory thought that makes his soul drunkenly sing in giddy liberation.

You're fucked. You are done. And you don't give a toss what happens to you any more. So now you have absolutely nothing to lose.

42

THE SLIP ROAD

The captors remain silent, but so does Ray Lennox. Feels this quietude offering him a perverse advantage, sensing their nerves and intimidation at his ease. In his frosty sights: the jolty ADHD specimen next to him, disguising his overwrought condition with the incendiary smoulder of the boxer. Then there is the other man. Despite the risible ponytail, paradoxically menacing in his silence. Proven deadly. Starts thinking about their weak points, how to damage them: eyes, teeth, genitals and kneecaps come to mind. Wonders about them, how *they* got here. Nobody gets into a car like this unless they've lost something. What have they lost? How much more was there they feared losing?

Whatever happens, it is imperative to make them address that question.

Puts his head back, lets out a long, cruel laugh. Savours, from his peripheral vision, the way it freezes the men.

— What's he on about? Boxer attempts to make light of it, only underlining that he's spooked.

— Shut it, cunt. Ponytail grins, yet contradicting this controlled nonchalance, his hand on the wheel is white, apart from a dark red rose tattoo.

Lennox's head smashes into the boxer's face. His captor turns away just in time, taking the blow on the cheekbone, rather than the nose, as Lennox's boot flies up towards the back of the head of Ponytail, who blocks the strike with his shoulder, screeching the car to a halt by the side of the road.

Boxer springs into action, firing a series of punches into Lennox, as Ponytail, clutching a black hood, leans across, pulling it over his captive's head. Plunged into a spinning darkness, neck muscles tearing, Lennox ceases his struggle, but not without a phantom satisfaction that the blows received were a distraction rather than devastating. — You fucking twat, Boxer roars, snapping another cleaner, short punch into his face.

Lennox doesn't even have time to loathe his own complacency as stars explode and the planets twirl in cartoon torment. His head throbs in the blackness. Pushes steady breaths into his body. A wired silence falls and the car starts again, moving through the darkness.

You walked side by side with Les Brodie, pushing your bikes. The only sound that of wheels turning. Nothing ahead: no light. Then you looked behind you into the same darkness, you had hit that point in the tunnel. You were scared and you asked Les if he was still there. Then, in front of you, a torch clicked on to show you that uplit demonic face; ghoulish and clownish under that beam. Eyes wide and blazing with lust. Mouth tight in lechery.

How could you ever forget it? It was the man of your dreams . . .

Body literally spasmed by his thoughts. Forces air in through the bottom of the hot hood. Tries not to panic. Attempts to ascertain where they are heading through the twists, bends and lights. Then decides he knows the destination, and relaxes in a peculiarly soothing dread.

This is where you are. You have always been here: right from the start. Long before you saw Cardingworth in that wine bar.

Yes, Raymond. We're coming for each other. We need to finish this. From that tunnel in Edinburgh to . . .

— We're here, Ponytail announces, pulling the car from what feels like the tight turn of a slip road, and through what the double thud of tyres indicates as two sets of sliding, metal security gates, before it halts. — You can make as much noise as you want now!

He feels Boxer getting out, before reaching back in to remove his hood. Even before the light floods in, stinging his eyes, Lennox knows where he is. Again, Boxer, going round the side and opening the door, grabs him by the hair to yank him out the car. This time, as he stands, Lennox leans right into the pain, looking him manically in the eye, smiling, puckering his lips. — C'mon, you fucking noncey lover boy. Give me it. Or do you want it from me, ya fuckin rapist cunt?

— You fucking prick –

— That's whae you're working for, and both men are taken aback by the bare-toothed sneer of Ray Lennox, — a fucking paedo noncing child killer!

Boxer's eyes bulge, now seeming way too large for his tight face. — You dunno what you're farking on about –

— Did they no mention that, your fucking employers?

— Enough, Ponytail says, talking more to his colleague than Lennox, and the smaller man relinquishes the grip on his hair. Ponytail grabs Lennox by the shoulder and pushes him across the deserted car park.

— You were pretty tasty the last time we met here, has to be said. Lennox looks round at him.

Ponytail betrays no response or emotion, tombstone eyes focused ahead. Yes, he is the real deal. How much does it cost to hire this sort of man to do such things? Lennox lets his eyes sweep the car park; no guards present, just the imposing towers of the abandoned factory looming ahead. And one of those big doors, secured the last time by padlocks, is now open.

You are here.

43

SCHOOLBOY ERRORS

In the fading light the building appears like somewhere displaced from post-industrial Teeside to West Sussex. An angry, bruised sky looks like it has come off second best in a fight, with anything below fair game as a target for its displaced vengeance. Boxer's open palms shove Ray Lennox through the door, Ponytail following them. The ground floor is vast and cavernous, and Lennox can see the twisted metal of the collapsed gangway that almost took his life and, he suspects, that of Ponytail behind him. Facing them ahead, like menacing barrels of a giant shotgun, the massive parallel turbines.

They step into the lift. Recalling it from his last visit, Lennox is astonished it's operational, but it creaks in grudged ascent. Through the gloaming and confusion that besets him he struggles to find his bearings but reckons they've come two floors up. As they step out, Boxer chews gum at a furtive speed, as if it might be stolen from his mouth. Lennox notes how this floor is sealed from the open void area by a higher wall, topped with more comprehensive railing. At the other side, surprisingly ornate floor-to-ceiling windows hang defiantly in rotting wooden frames. A generous oak table, weeping for salvage and restoration, dominates the space, four wooden chairs around it. Two huge Belfast sinks run along one wall. Along another, piles of wooden pallets, stacked high and deep, which appear to belong somewhere else. This seems like it was primarily office and boardroom premises.

Pushing him down into one of the chairs, his captors begin securing Lennox by more plastic ratchet grips, feeding them through the others and around the furniture legs. They place his coat on the table, along with the cassette tapes, recorder and his wallet and phone. He can't believe the anxiety he feels about being so far from his mobile. Sees little point in struggling: sensing the final pieces in the cruel puzzle will now be shown to him.

This is confirmed as Mat Cardingworth, eyes dulled, features slack and sagging, walks in. It's like he's drunk heavily but still nowhere near enough. — Phil and Marco looking after you?

Lennox observes both men flinching at Cardingworth's faux pas in naming them. Takes Marco to be the boxer. Phil is the ponytail: the one who beat up Trench, the silent Balaclava Man who smashed him to the ground right here. Cardingworth seems aware of his schoolboy error too, moving on with haste. — You couldn't stop, could you? Couldn't help yourself.

— Correct, Lennox concedes without a shred of restraint, although aware this endorsement is not in his best interests. — It isn't in my power to do so. Never has been.

Ray Lennox knows this isn't his cop voice, or his civilian one. It's his essence crying out, pure and simple. He knows it's over. The panic is present, it manifests in waves surging over him and retreating abruptly; misery rationed on an internal timer. The inevitability of his demise is a bleak certainty, but is evinced as an intellectual consideration only; not a fibre in his body surrenders. It still says no, like it has all his life. To crossing the line when dark desires gnawed at him. To letting the alcohol and drugs grind him down beyond a point of dissolution he couldn't get back from. To self-pitying acquiescence when life's humiliations lashed open old wounds. Principally, though, it said no to closing his eyes.

And through the lens of his defeat, he sees this is no

victory for Cardingworth, whose own stare is heavy with regret. This hunch is confirmed, as an opened bottle of red wine Cardingworth holds is lowered onto the battered wooden table, along with a solitary glass. — So, I have to end it. But before I do, I want you to know that you've got important parts of your story wrong. You see, it's my story too, though sadly for both of us, not in the way you believe.

Lennox feels a force inside crashing through him. It tumbles from his chest to his guts. Then seems to burst out of his skin.

The tapes.

His glance goes from them to the table. He only has half the information he needs.

— But before I do, Cardingworth grabs a chair and slides it opposite Lennox, sitting a few feet away from him, — you need to tell me what you've done with him, he asks in tones of strained reason, adding, — Chris.

— What? Lennox feels his face break into a smile, this petty compensation igniting his battered soul. — The wee cunt that's been hanging round my office?

George? Surely not?

— You have to hand him over.

— I don't have him. Lennox knows for certain that someone else, probably Darren Knowles, is pulling Cardingworth's strings. But now that someone might have opposition too.

— Well, that's really unfortunate. Cardingworth's face warps in ulcerated distress. — His dad will be here soon. Darren has means of getting people to comply with his wishes.

The maddeningly loud buzz of a text as it pops into Lennox's phone on the desk.

Cardingworth picks it up. Reads it through the cracked screen. Holds it up in front of Lennox's face. It's from Stuart, but the phone is locked, so only the opening of the text is visible:

> They are saying it wasn't suicide with poor old Ralph Trench. They

— Give me the code to open the phone, please, Ray.

— This time, Lennox smiles, — youse cunts actually do have my blessing, his face crumples in a leer, — tae *suck ma fuckin cock*!

— Open it, Cardingworth hisses through a capped gate of ivory, — or I'll have them hunt down this Stuart, and every other person on your contacts list, so help me!

Lennox remains silent.

Cardingworth picks up the wallet. Takes out the Hearts season ticket. Looks at the 1874 on the club crest. Then at Lennox. — Surely not . . . Punches it in, as Lennox feels his heart sink. Cardingworth gapes at him, shaking his head, his shoulders rippling with laughter, as the phone opens up. — Security expert, fuck sake . . .

Lennox is crushed.

Not so much schoolboy error as retarded error.

But there is no gloat from Cardingworth as he reads the full text. He physically wilts, his shoulders buckling inwards. Struggling for breath, he glances at Phil and Marco. Then he shows Lennox the text, concealing it from the two men, as he regards his captive in wide-eyed horror.

> They are saying it wasn't suicide with poor old Ralph Trench. They found him chopped up by his own sword. Is this Brighton or Niddrie?

333

Cardingworth again looks to the hired hands. Lowers his voice, whispering in urgent fear at Lennox. — Give me the lad, Ray, they're not fucking around . . . Darren . . . well, he's one of you lot, a Scot, from travellers who traditionally headed up and down the east coast . . . and he's evolved his signature move from the crude origins Mona experienced!

Darren Knowles. Young Chris, a chip off the old block . . .

Lennox's brain is sprinkled with hot pepper, but he sucks down some air. — I'm getting old and ugly, just like you. A drop of acid isn't going to make much difference now, he laughs, his tone light and conversational, as Marco and Phil, tongue brushing his top lip, look over. — If Chris is in the hands of who I think he is, then that silly wee twat is the one to be concerned about. He's a lot of life left to navigate with the crippling disabilities he'll inevitably suffer, or maybe not. Perhaps I'm not the only one heading for a painful demise, Lennox mocks, his voice rising, looking directly at Cardingworth.

— It'll be more fucking painful than you think, he hisses at Lennox, nodding back to indicate the silent henchmen.

Lennox looks over to Phil, who regards them both with an imperious stare. Then he swivels his gaze to Cardingworth. — Darren will not be pleased with the utter fanny that delivered his son into this evil bastard's hands.

Cardingworth's eyes widen. He looks at Lennox, rolling his gaze to the henchmen. — Who! Who has him?

— Like I'm gaunny tell you a fucking thing, ya paedo rapist cunt, Lennox scoffs. — You ruined my fucking life. So go ahead: take the last of it, ya fuckin useless prick, and he looks over at Marco who whispers something to Phil. — Or maybe first you tell me about those cunts in the tunnel. Darren Knowles was obviously one of youse! Him, you and who was the other fucker?

— You *need* to tell me where Chris is, Ray, Cardingworth hisses through his teeth.

— Way and fuck yirsel, ya noncey short-eyes cunt!

— I'm sorry, Ray, Mat Cardingworth says, sweating as he sweeps a hand through his thinning quiff, — you did have the chance to cooperate.

— These are your associates, Lennox shouts over to Marco and Phil, who look awkwardly at each other and then to Cardingworth, — a bunch of paedos who get their kicks from terrorising wee bairns in a tunnel, he sneers. Then he smiles coldly at Cardingworth. — You fucking hypocrite: you fucking fraud.

— No, Mathew Cardingworth shouts at his two hired guns, then at Lennox, — I made some awful mistakes and got into a fucking mess cleaning them up, he rises and pours some wine into the glass. — But the older one gets, the messier one's life becomes. That's unavoidable, if you have any life at all, he suddenly appeals to the two henchmen who can't seem to meet his eyes. Phil looks off into the distance, out of the thick-with-dirt floor-to-ceiling windows. The trembling Marco's eyes are on the uppers of his shoes.

— It became messy at an early age for me, thanks to you noncing cunts!

— You've got me wrong, Lennox, Cardingworth almost begs.

— No fuckin way, Lennox shouts, desperation breaking out of his voice.

You keep backing him into a corner . . . not very sensible, are you, Ray? Still, passion of the moment, I suppose.

Noice boike . . .

— I did what I could.

— For Ralph? For Gavin?

— Ralph Trench and his sneaky little foster friend Gavin

335

were inseparable. They wanted to get Ralph . . . I couldn't have that.

— So you served them up his wee mate. You fucking evil cunt!

— To save my foster brother!

— And then they chopped the poor cunt to pieces. He looks over at Phil. — Couldn't stop that, or did you set that up too?

— Ralph's death was . . . Cardingworth begins, *suicide* hanging on his lips as he steals a glance at Phil.

— Aye, he hacked himself to bits using his own swords, read the fucking text, Lennox nods to the phone, then looks to Phil, — or ask the swordsman.

Cardingworth turns to his accomplices. Marco gives the game away; his fidgety shuffles have grown more pronounced, and he spits out his gum. Phil remains calm, but a slight smile plays across his face. — Get the fuck out of here, Cardingworth barks at them. — Wait at the van. Go!

Phil rolls his eyes and moves off slowly towards the stairs, followed by Marco, who bites his bottom lip and shrugs half apologetically at Cardingworth.

— Can't get staff, eh? Such reduced circumstances. Like that white van, the one you ditched the Jag for when I made my wee house call. Where were you going in the noncemobile?

Mathew Cardingworth looks glumly at him. — To White-hawk, to drop off some stuff I didn't need, old pots and pans and gardening equipment mainly, to my ex-neighbours, Bill and Lily Warburton. They're getting on and I like to check in on them. The last time I went, I took the Jag, and some envious bastard keyed it. Any other questions?

Lennox can detect no duplicity, but the arrogance rankles. — Tell me about this fucking Bim.

Cardingworth looks at Lennox for a few eternal seconds. —

Knowles had met Bim in prison. I think it was the first time Darren had come across someone who terrorised him, the same way he did with others. Bim . . . Cardingworth's sardonic grin stings Lennox again, — inducted him in a whole new way of life. They were released at the same time, all but destitute on the outside. Darren's family was our neighbours; he knew I was a student and had received money from an injury insurance claim. So, they put the bite on me. They were very menacing, especially Bim. Dragged me up to Scotland with them. You know what happened next.

— Where is the cunt?

— He's around . . . Cardingworth flinches, tries to recover his composure, — just a little preoccupied these days . . . Afterwards Bim vanished, went to sea as he always did. Darren headed to London, was embraced by a bohemian crowd, who celebrated criminality until it got too close to them. There were parties. I went to some. I confess it was an exciting life, compared to my studies at Imperial. Then I met Mona. I fell for her. I wanted us to go away together. I would have packed in everything for her. I saw how Darren treated her, how he made her do all sorts of things.

Lennox feels his oesophagus blister as rising bile chokes him into silence.

— Then she ended it with him. He was, well . . . and Cardingworth looks to the lift and stairs, dropping his voice, — an obvious psychopath. I thought I could protect her. He unleashes a sigh of deep anguish. — That was a joke. He went crazy. Got her with the acid.

— Yeah, I saw your paedo mate's work.

— I was in love with Mona, Cardingworth punches his own chest, — I looked after her as best I could!

— Aye, you did a stellar job there, and with Ralph. You really reined those boys in.

Get him, Bim . . .

Cardingworth looks stricken. Takes a drink of wine. — I thought they'd have a fallout, destroy each other. His head whips to Lennox in appeal. — That was the game I was playing. That would have been the best result for me, you, Les Brodie, the UK taxpayer, not to mention children everywhere! Mathew Cardingworth rises and takes a step towards Lennox. Again, he hushes his tones. — That was my fervent hope, Ray. You know what those sorts are like. They always turn on each other!

Lennox imitates his low, soft tone. — They didn't, though, did they?

— No . . . Cardingworth begins waveringly, glancing to the silent lift and stairs, before recovering his focus, — but I was coerced into the project, caught between two very violent men. They'd formed a partnership to indulge their passions, kicking it off in Edinburgh, where Bim had a friend who owed him a favour . . .

Allardyce . . . Jock Allardyce . . . shagging my ma . . . and kept at it for years . . . Stu's real faither . . . what a fucking mess . . .

— I had no interest in boys, or men. He lets his gaze fall to meet Lennox. — You know my tastes, Ray: as I said, they're embarrassingly conventional.

— Fuck you, you lying cunt. Everything you say is bullshit, Lennox contends, as a thought seizes him. — When did you know I was one of the kids from the tunnel?

Cardingworth takes another sip of wine. — I took an interest when you got together with Carmel, in case you were some sort of nosy journo. He crosses then uncrosses his legs. — I like to know the associates of my associates. My alarm bells were set off when I learned you were an ex-cop, he twists in his seat to steal another glance at the lift and stairs, — with no prior connections to this town. I suspected there was something about you at dinner. But then Brodie . . . he sealed the deal. Cardingworth touches the angry scars on his face. — Before that, I would never in a million years have made you as one of the kids from the tunnel.

— But you were stalking me *before* Les's assault!

Cardingworth's face screws up, slowly expanding as he permits the concept. — Doing surveillance. Fortunately, Brighton is a small pond, and young Chris was already very infatuated by your secretary. He smiles at Lennox. — He was encouraged to up his game.

A chip off the old block.

— And he terrorised a young woman. You enabled that shit, like you did everything else. You're a smarmy fucking nonce, and you're trying to weasel out of your part in this, but I'm not having it. Neither was Les!

— No! Cardingworth pants at him. — I was the one who let you go!

Lennox glowers at Mat Cardingworth. — I saw your face on top of Les. Looking at me. Saying I was next!

— That's fucking nonsense. Cardingworth tosses his head back in authoritative contempt. — That damage was done by Bim and Darren. He moves closer to Lennox and crouches down in front of him, wine glass in his hand. — Somewhere along the line you've got us mixed up. Who was it that was on your bike, riding around that uneven ground, taunting you? Me? Really?

Nice bike.

Cardingworth locks his gaze on Lennox. — I think you know it was Bim.

Noice boike . . .

Lennox writhes, he can't stop it. He wants to put his fingers in his ears, but he can't move his hands. He looks at the floor, shakes his head slowly. — No!

Cardingworth stands up, walks around him, like a matador tormenting a wounded bull. — You don't know Bim and what he's capable of. Bim went for Les Brodie, then Daz had a shot at him. Yes, I'd helped restrain you both, so I'm not blameless, Ray, and Cardingworth wrenches Lennox's head up to meet his eyes. — But I didn't do anything more, and he yanks his fingers away with an enraged flourish, — I was as terrified as you were! I FUCKING SAVED YOU!

Confused images pile into Ray Lennox's head. Faces surge through his mind, nothing gaining traction, like the fleeting considerations of a Tinder game player.

— What did the man in the tunnel say to you, Ray? Cardingworth softly insists.

Lennox raises his head defiantly. — *You* said: nice bike!

Mathew Cardingworth looks disappointed in Ray Lennox. — Oh really? And *how* did he say this? What sort of accent did this psychopath have?

— It *was* you, it was *you* . . . Lennox feels hot tears streaming down his face.

You could never cry back then, not in front of your mum and dad. You could sense they were having problems. Feel their tension. Wanted to protect them, to keep it all from them.

Poor little moite.

— It wasn't my voice, Ray, Cardingworth says sadly, as if informing a dreamy but older child they should know about the non-existence of Santa Claus. — He was from Birmingham. He said, *noice boike.* Cardingworth's bad West Midlands mimicry sears Lennox. — It's true, isn't it, Ray? I know because I was standing there, in the dark, just a few feet away from him!

Nice bike . . . the face . . . coming back . . .

Oh no . . . fuck me . . . how could I have blotted that out?

— Who were the abusers, Ray? Again, Cardingworth looks

to the lift. — A fucking Scottish gypo with twinkling eyes and a sly smile. Oh, the ladies, usually to their great misfortune, like Mona, like Julie, how they adored him at first! And then a big, unshaven Brummie geezer. Those dirty huge hands. Cardingworth moves forward, waving one of his own mitts in front of Lennox's face. Takes a sip of his wine. — I winced when he hit you, Ray. Do you remember that? How he hit your face?

He wanted you to open your mouth. You said please, mister, dinnae, but his heavy hand smashed the side of your face and you saw stars. Then he put a broken beer bottle against it . . .

— And then he held that jagged glass to your cheek, didn't he, Ray?

— Aye . . . Lennox rasps, as some sabotaging part of him acknowledges that horrible truth, — he did . . .

Open yawr fooking mouth!

Cardingworth coughs, a sudden confusion flashing in his eyes as he rubs at his throat. — The other guy . . . Darren, a Scottish accent, he caws, — his family moved around a lot. They did the damage, him and Bim . . . the Brummie sailor.

It *was* Cardingworth who let him go. And it was Bim who was sneering at him in the darkness of the tunnel.

Noice boike!

Yes, those rapists were Bim and Darren Knowles, who initially struggled to subdue Les. But Cardingworth was there. He was younger. Scared. And he held on to the young Ray Lennox, but his eyes were fearful and hesitant. But he was there. — You were there! You were there!

— Yes, but I wasn't the rapist! I let you go, Ray! It was as much as I could do!

He did let you go. You looked into his terror-stricken eyes and begged . . .

Please let me go, mister. I'll no say nowt tae naebody. Please.

And you looked over and saw Les. Couldn't help him though.
Nobody could help poor Les.

And now nobody can help you.

Noice boike!

— NAW, YOU CUNT, YA NONCING CUH-
HHNNNT!! You attacked Les, after I ran away! You all did
him, you bastard!

— Did he tell you that? Cardingworth sneers.

— He told the world it when he glassed you! Why else
would he do that?

— Because he's been as fucked up by those monsters,
those vile jailhouse paedophiles, as you. Did he *fucking tell*
you that, Lennox?

No . . .

Ray Lennox doesn't know. The constant turmoil of bewilderment felt like the ultimate loss. We lived in a world where
those in power reduced the truth to a quiet whisper in our
consciousness, all but blazed out by the jagged, searing, false
narratives they screamed in our ears, in order to meet their
controlling objectives. Their images and messages bombarded
us, scrambling our brains. We were lost. Our doubts and con-
fusions were seen as weaknesses in a volatile world where we
craved certainty. We were easy meat for the fascist, racist and
class supremacist sound bites of our masters and their
lackeys.

Lennox sees his own crippling vacillation in Cardingworth's almost plaintive expression. — Is it coming back to
you now, Ray?

It would be easy for you to say yes. Yes, you perhaps got it
wrong. Yes, you are sorry. To try to deceive him: to attempt to talk
your way out of this.

Not you though, Raymond, is it, mate?

But another brutal truth insinuates; whatever really

happened, Lennox knows this was his life, and Les's too. This belief – and the crusade it spawned – had to be sustained to the end, as nothing else was left. The world is binary. We can no longer function in the realms of nuance and scepticism, once regarded as the cornerstones of intellect and civilisation. Now shoehorned into our entrenched positions, we are compelled to battle on, until some mystic synthesis intimates itself to pull us into the next vague consensus. It is all he can do. Prevail. — Trench. You had him taken out. He knew everything and he wanted more from you!

— You don't know how many fucking chances . . . the bastard had a death wish –

— At first you bought him off, then tried to implicate him by coopting him into whatever's going on here. I'm guessing when they pull this place apart, he looks around the cavernous space, banging his feet hard on the floor, — they are going to find some deranged, abominable shit.

Cardingworth rubs his eyes. Issues a long, weary gasp. — I tried to protect Ralph, to look after him. But he was bipolar, unstable and sucked the fucking life out of me. So stubborn, in all the wrong ways. Why be like that when there's no gain for you? Makes no sense, he says in exasperation.

— You weren't a nonce but you helped them, Lennox jibes. — You weren't a killer but you let them slay *your own brother*. His mouth twists. — You're a weak fool who believes your money makes you strong –

— And you're the strong –

Lennox raises his voice to cut him off. — You're only indulged by an idiocy conditioned to worship the wealthy like they're gods. Look at you: even *I* wouldn't swap places with you. Think about what's buried here, he bangs his foot again, — the bodies of orphan children kidnapped and tortured by beasts!

— Anything here is their shit, not mine, Cardingworth screeches, — I let you go, Lennox! I did the right thing!

— Do it now, Mat, Lennox, through clenched teeth, suddenly beseeches. — Come to the cops with me. Tell them everything!

Mathew Cardingworth's face runs through an emotional obstacle course from pain to horror, before settling on a resigned contempt. — Do you know what I have, and how long it took me get it? Do you honestly think I'd swap that for a prison cell at my age? Seriously?

— It's over. You must know that. It's all closing in on you.

— I'll take my chances. Money is good at shifting blame and making people look the other way. But you were wrong, Lennox. You don't know me. I let you go, and you fled.

— Yes, I fucking fled, too fucking right, I was eleven years old!

— And I would have *fucking fled* too, but they knew where I lived! They always knew, always kept coming back, Cardingworth barks.

Another whir from Lennox's iPhone, and Cardingworth picks it up. He dials in the *1874*, closing his eyes as a caustic laugh escapes him. Opens them to study the screen. — Another woman . . . Jackie . . . she seems to love you . . . there's an attachment.

Jackie . . .

Lennox feels self-loathing cripple him. *1874 . . . what sort of a moron even does that?*

Security expertise, Ray! We all love the beautiful game, though, don't we?

Cardingworth opens the document and his eyes ignite as he scrolls. — Eureka! The smoking gun! Out of the crayons of babes! Look, Ray. He thrusts the phone in front of his face.

Lennox lowers his gaze.

344

— LOOK! 'Raymond L. 11 years' – LOOK!

Lennox looks up to be confronted with his own picture. The one he painted as a kid.

And the attachment, with a note on the email that says I LOVE YOU, comes not from his sister, Jackie, but his mother, Avril.

44

A TALENTED ARTIST

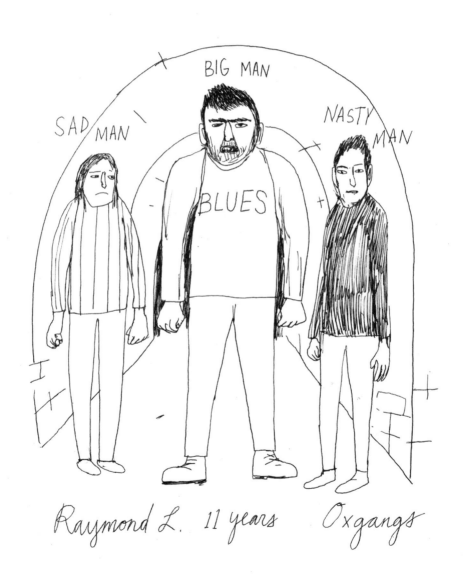

— A security expert *and* a talented artist, Cardingworth mocks. — You really are impressing the fuck out of me today, Ray. He waves the phone in Lennox's face. — So, what does that picture say to you?

Sad Man. Nasty Man. The striped top. And the Big Man: that white top with BLUES in blue letters on it.

Forgot all about that top!

Lennox can say nothing. It's them. The old gang. As rudimentary as those drawings are, they shockingly and starkly confirm to him who the Big Man is. But he'll probably never meet him again, as the Nasty Man is on his way.

— Sad Man. You said it, Cardingworth wretchedly laments, then raises his glass and thoughfully strokes his chin. — You and I come from similar backgrounds, I'm betting, Ray.

Ray Lennox looks at the concrete floor. The thin, asthmatic breathing of his childhood reasserts in wispy pulls. Bound wrists throb in slicing pain. Lacerations pulse and sear.

— We were a tough little mob growing up, Cardingworth waxes, — from the Whitehawk estate. Working-class kids at the bottom of the pile in a snooty town. We were regarded as –

Lennox suddenly raises his head and looks right at Cardingworth. — Fuck off, he says, cold, emphatic, derisive.

This dagger of contempt ruins the self-affirmative party piece of a powerful, indulged man. Violated deeply, Cardingworth's eyes pop.

— I've heard that bullshit come out of every cunt's mouth, including my own, since I was fucking knee-high. Lennox is cold, offhand. — In school, the streets, football grounds, and at work as a copper. Heard it fae polis, fae cons. The nostalgic shite ay daft old guys giein it the big one about how mental, crazy, but essentially *good*, those lovable rogues all were in their youth. He shakes his head brutally. — Fucking tedious pish, mate. Spare me the pathetic bollocks. Did any others

347

become fucking nonces? You were in a tunnel with psychos, terrorising and abusing little kids. Tell me about Bim!

For the first time Lennox sees real hatred in Cardingworth's glare. Realises that he's gained some sort of victory: has shamed him for his sponsorship of the tyrants. Called him out, in the process forcing him to confront what he really is.

Mathew Cardingworth steps back, partly concealing his tight face from Lennox by the glass he lifts in a defiant toast. — It's a pity you can't join me in this red wine, Ray, he wheezes, imbibing a mouthful.

Lennox senses something is badly amiss, beyond Cardingworth's exasperation at the situation they are in. His adversary seems to spasm internally from a wave of nausea. Sucking down his vexation, Cardingworth contends, — I know you'd like it, and he takes another sip, shakily holding the glass up to the light. — It's full-bodied, but there's an incredible smoothness here. He enjoys a more substantial gulp.

Cardingworth's face twitches. Lennox sees he's fighting to regain his composure; tight breaths hauled in with effort, perspiration beads glistening on his forehead. He looks accusingly at his glass of wine.

— Struggling, are we? an arid voice suddenly rasps. It belongs to a figure stepping out from behind the stacks of wooden industrial pallets. As the presence lingers for a moment in the shadows, Lennox anticipates more torment.

Carmel, wearing a dark green hooded top, strides into the light. A serrated knife in her hand. However, it's not him but Cardingworth she's taunting. — You must be experiencing gut convulsions now. — And your gullet should be drying out.

— Whaa . . . ? Cardingworth looks at the treacherous glass he shakily holds.

— Waves of nausea?

Cardingworth gapes at her, then Lennox.

— I didn't believe a word of it at first, not Mat Carding-worth, Carmel scorns, before turning to Lennox. — I thought you were mistaken, Ray. I thought you had somehow primed Les or it was some kind of *folie à deux*. I'm sorry.

About to speak, Lennox sees Cardingworth at pains to do the same, but his efforts are curtailed by another sabotaging croak in his throat. Then his hand goes to his neck, like he's trying to tear a hole in it. Face reddens in an explosive flush. Eyes bulge as if he's trying to force air in between the eyeballs and eyelids.

— People will thank you for at least doing the honourable thing. Carmel's cherry-red lips seem not to open as she speaks to Cardingworth, who drops the glass, grips the edge of the table with both hands. — Falling on your own sword.

Cardingworth hacks out a distorting plea for clemency.

Carmel moves behind Lennox, chopping at his bonds with the blade. Lennox twists to her. — Phil and Marco down-stairs . . . how did ye get past them?

Carmel whispers softly, while sawing frantically, — You just have to pay them enough. Sorry for doubting you.

He turns from his kidnapper, now on his knees coughing, to his girlfriend. — I doubted you, myself, everybody. I'm still trying to piece this mess together. But . . . you . . .

— It's over now, Carmel announces as his left arm springs free. As she works on his right, Cardingworth, ailing badly, reminds Lennox of how he himself was on encountering him in that wine bar. Then bloody vomit explodes from the busi-nessman, splattering onto the concrete floor. He falls forward, strangely coming to rest with his chin nesting in his own puke.

As Lennox's second hand is freed, Carmel hands him the knife. He hacks off the ties on his ankles. Rubs at the wrist indentations. Gapes unflinchingly at the exhibition of her would-be benefactor's disintegration, as Carmel assists his shaky rise to his feet. — Thank you, he says, then nods to the table, — Those tapes . . . And they watch Mathew Cardingworth kick out, and Ray Lennox bears witness to one of the men from the tunnel, who haunted him for decades, take his last breath on the cold floor of the factory.

Carmel's elbow digs into him, and she nods to the goods lift, now creaking and clanking upwards. It grinds to a halt, as Lennox feels his body stiffen. His grip on the knife tightens, anticipating the arrival of Darren Knowles.

But Mona emerges with Marco and Phil by her side. Her vacant, single-eyed stare moves in horror to Cardingworth's lifeless body, before she shouts to the henchmen, — Get him out of here!

45

THE RIGHT THING

Mona leans against the table, scarf-swathed face in her hands. — Why? she bubbles in a sob at Carmel, pointing at the body being reluctantly picked up by Marco and Phil. — Why did you do that? The deal was we'd give him a sedative!

— You don't know what he did, and you didn't hear what he said! Carmel rasps. Moves a step closer to Mona. — He was in with Knowles and the other monster. Her trembling finger points accusingly at the corpse Marco and Phil drag across the floor. — He killed Ra—

Carmel responds to Lennox frantically waving her to silence, nodding urgently towards the henchmen pulling the remains of Cardingworth into the lift.

Did they hear?

They don't cease their activity: Phil slides open the gate while Marco, his face tightly screwed to avoid looking at Cardingworth, hauls the body from under the armpits. Both arrogant businessman and engaged philanthropist seem to have already departed Cardingworth's form. Features spill south on the shapeless mannequin's remains, skin waxy under the overhead light. The gate slams shut. The lift descends.

Mona straightens up. Looks at Carmel and Lennox in deep violation. Hurries out after the hired hands, taking the stairs down. As her steps recede on the creaking metal, Carmel pulls on Lennox's arm. — She'll come round. She and Mat had a complicated relationship. It was Mona who hooked me up with him. She's a technician at the university. We've known each other a while. Brighton, as transient as it can be, isn't a big pond.

— That's what Cardingworth said, Lennox urgently squeezes her shoulder. — Did you need him dead? Like for this deal to go through? When did you decide this?

Carmel brushes him off, takes a step back. — I saved your fucking life!

— I know, but –

— Look . . . Carmel gasps, steps forward, buries her head under Lennox's chin.

Her body vibrations pulse through him. Yet his hovering hands can't settle into a full embrace. One pats her back insipidly while the other arm falls awkwardly by his side.

Her voice growls into his chest, — . . . I poisoned a man. I took his life. I said I would, if he was a beast. He wasn't the worst, but he still planned and took part in the kidnap and abuse of kids. She looks up at him. — At the very least he was complicit in the murder of Ralph Trench.

— He's not the executioner, that Phil –

Carmel won't be detracted. — But there was more to Mat. He wanted to do the right thing, Ray. This way he gets to!

— And your research benefits.

— Mat was on a journey with me, Carmel coughs out. — It was something he was doing that was good. I won't take that away from him, or from me. He wasn't a paedophile or a murderer, but yes, he was weak, and complicit.

— How long were you listening to us?

— Long enough.

From outside: a clanking sound.

Then a muffled shout, and they pull apart.

The slamming of a car boot.

They fall silent for a few beats.

Carmel lowers her voice to whisper. — I thought it through. Better Mathew Cardingworth being seen to do the honourable thing. I doubt he'd have made that choice, so I made it for him!

Lennox pushes his fingers against eyeballs that burn behind their lids. The wine was doctored *before* Cardingworth's revelations to him. What did she find out prior to this? And what did he really know about this woman? Entertains the possibility he's dating a psychopath. — Well, I owe you big time . . . he concedes, — but we need to get the fuck out of here and work out our next move. Those boys downstairs . . . they killed Trench!

— Are you sure of that? Carmel asks emphatically, her eyes bulging as she looks to the table. — What were you saying about tapes?

Lennox lunges over to the foot of the big desk, where his stuff lies. Sticks the phone and wallet in the pocket of his coat. Hesitates with the cassette player and tapes. Then looks at her.

His finger hovers over the play button as Carmel looks pensively at him.

46

EVERY DREAM MUST HAVE A MAN

You know, Raymond, there are three steps you can take here; one of them leads to relative safety, another one leads to my little friend Darren – as I shall always think of him – and the final one takes you straight to me . . .

But I know what you're going to do . . .

You're going to listen to that tape right now, aren't you?

47

REMINISCENCE AND RECALL 5

It's easy to hate somebody without really knowing them. In fact, maybe that's exactly what it takes. You see only the action, the tip of the iceberg, not what's driving their behaviour. We've all got shit to bear. My old man battered the fucking crap out of me for years. It stopped when I got to sixteen. I had started the boxing at Sparta in McDonald Road. As I prepared to head there every night, sports bag slung over my shoulder, he'd observe me slyly from his armchair. He didn't know I was watching *him*. Every month he grew weaker, more thin-shouldered, his voice less brash, increasingly tainted with the sooky lisp of the sweetie-wife. But I kept my powder dry. Silly cunt thought I'd forgotten all about those beatings. When I left the house, two days after my eighteenth birthday, I broke his jaw. Tanned it with a right-hander and watched the old fucker crumple to the deck. My mother crying, 'What was that for?' I didnae say 'He kens', or anything in that self-justifying manner. Gave a wee shrug: 'Just felt like it, ay.' Went round there to see her a week later. He sat there in silence, his jaw wired, sipping watery soup through a straw. Looking at me in the same pathetic way I'd looked at him for years as a kid. He sickened me, his victim mode even more pitiful than his bullying one. If he'd had a second set ay jaws, I'd have cracked it there and then.

I vowed I'd never pass that shite on to my own kids. And I was as good as my word: I never lifted a finger to them.

Everybody else was fair game though, especially all the criminal scum like him who came into my orbit. Fuck knows if it was right or wrong. Only certainty is that I never lost a night's sleep because of it.

But Lenny: poor bastard. Fuck knows what happened in that tunnel, certainly not the old cunt in his reminiscence therapy group gone badly wrong. And that spineless ponce who let him rabbit on: that cunt should lose his job. My daughter shouldn't have to hear that shite: care staff are human beings. They can be as vulnerable as anybody. But listen she did, and so am I.

Raymond and his friend Les had been on their bikes, unaware that Bim and his associates were waiting in the tunnel. He was ten or eleven years old. He came back early that morning, much earlier than usual. I saw him going in through the back door, as I was coming down the stairs. I had been up in the bedroom with the kid's mother. She had already gone down to make a sandwich. I was following and he came in and caught me on the stairs. When he looked at me I knew from the laddie's face that something terrible had happened. Christ, that fuckin look. At me, then through me, like he saw something in me and he connected it up.

I was eaten up with remorse and I still am to this day.

I didnae feel inclined to stick around after what I'd done. Told Avril that I couldn't settle on land, which was bollocks. I could barely look her in the eye, or that damaged wee Raymond and his mate. That other wee guy became a right wee fucking tearaway, by all accounts. Poor wee bastard, but was probably always gaunny turn oot like that. Most of all, I needed to avoid Bim, who was now finished in the maritime trade after almost killing a man in a bar fight in Barcelona. He had beaten him into a vegetative state. But then he was travelling around Britain and the continent, getting into all this evil stuff with his wee gang. When it got too heavy, he would find a boat on a short-term contract and vanish out to sea. He really was like a ghost.

I should have blown the whistle on them but I was too scared.

So, I went back to sea.

It was six years later when I returned to Edinburgh. I had never heard from Bim, nor the other two, Darren, the gangster boy's name was, and the young lad, Mat, I think they called him. I reckoned the coast was clear. John was hanging on, with poor Avril still stuck in this void. And then there was Stuart. He was only a kid. I loved them both, but I realised that I was no good for them. I couldn't keep away though. I contacted Avril again.

Raymond had just finished at school, and became a police cadet. He was doing his IT training part-time at the uni. I was 'Uncle Jock' to him, Jackie and wee Stuart. It was painful. Avril and I tried to leave it, but we just couldn't. We were soon right back into our affair. It went on for years. Stuart grew up. Raymond got promoted. Jackie became very successful in the legal sphere. John Lennox, curse him, he just held on. And on and on and on. My fascination for this family drained everything from me. Estranged me from my own daughter.

It was almost three decades later that John finally had a third heart attack and passed. I was relieved but unnerved at the same time. We'd grown so used to the deception, my Avril and me – and I suppose probably John too, with his denial – that it had become our lives.

Now there was no need. Maybe my body language gave it away, or perhaps John Lennox had told his son. Whatever the reason, Raymond was a detective, and a pretty decent one: he'd worked a few high-profile cases, usually putting away sex offenders. I wondered what part I'd played setting him on that path. Anyway, he found out about us. And at the funeral he turned on us both. Called us out in front of everybody, before tearing off.

Avril was destroyed. My son hates me, she said. Why?

Cause of what went on in that tunnel, ya radge cow. Poor Lenny boy, I never knew. Nae cunt knew.

48

THE LIGHTS GO OUT

With Carmel Devereaux squeezing his hand, Ray Lennox listened to Jock Allardyce's full confessions in excruciating pain and torturous confusion. For forty years he'd believed his assailants to be opportunistic predators: a bunch of rootless, semi-destitute jailbirds hanging out by grim chance in that tunnel. But their presence in the dark underpass was no accident. All those years, in Serious Crimes, he'd hunted serial sex offenders, busted up nonce gangs in Britain, and even once in Florida, without any idea that he himself could be a victim of one. All caused by his father's impotence, his mother's straying and a horrific tragedy that Jock Allardyce had gotten involved in at sea, compounding it by his succumbing to a despicable malefactor.

Now Lennox feels he's very slowly catching up with his own life story. It makes sense that the main players are strangers. They always were. Looks at Carmel, thinks of past lovers, feels as if he has pulled them all into his shipwreck.

Why couldn't you be like Les? Act out, then move on, get past it? Every woman you've loved, Penny-Catriona-Trudi et cetera, they all asked you the same question. And you've never been able to answer it. So, they walked. Carmel will too. They all will until you can resolve this story and move on.

George. The encounter at Harrogate, *of course you are. That staging of my whole life. Surely it's not him that's been doing this to me! I don't know but I'll find out everything one way*

359

or another. Types up a long text, requests a favour of his friend. Aware Carmel is devouring him with her eyes, urging him to share what he's doing. Deflectively says, — You saved me, and I thank you, but you took the vengeance on Cardingworth that was mine.

— But he wasn't your real enemy, Carmel declares, as Lennox fires off his missive. — This Darren and Bim, who scarcely figured on your radar, caused infinitely more hurt.

The blow he felt almost shatter his young jaw had been delivered when his eyes were shut, but he'd seen plenty before that. How could he let those assailants fade through time? How could he not? How could Ray Lennox resist letting memory's sharpness erode, easing its grim image, until Cardingworth's sighting gave him false dominion in his consciousness? It had seemed so real, but the Allardyce tapes supported Cardingworth's contention of his (relatively) marginal role. Yet in Lennox's tricking mind, the Brighton businessman had become the lightning rod, imbuing a pain more savagely dispensed by his cohorts.

Carmel is about to continue. Halts in the face of the clanking sound. The lift: it's rising towards them. They look at each other, the unspoken word *Knowles* on their lips. Lennox grabs the broken wine glass. Indicates to Carmel, who takes the serrated knife from her back pocket.

But it heralds the return of Mona, flanked by an edgy Marco and an inscrutable Phil.

— So, you two were in this together? Lennox asks Carmel, as they approach.

— We *were*, Mona says.

— Mona told me that Mat was involved with a couple of lowlifes, one of whom did the acid attack, Carmel explains. — He had everything, what was he doing in with that sort of company? Putting the knife in her back pocket, she goes over to Mona. Places a consoling arm around her stiff shoulders. — I'm sorry, honey . . .

Lennox moves over to the table, sets the glass down on it. — So, what are we going to do now? he muses. A sudden sense somebody is up close behind him. Before awareness can become reaction, a chunky fist tattooed with a blood-red rose flashes past his gaze, as an arm locks around his windpipe. He can't breathe . . . reaches for the wine glass but it's inches from his grasp. When he feels his feet leave the ground, knows Phil has lodged his hip into his back. The air his vocal cords require to reverberate has been shoved out of him. All he can do is be the silent deponent of the horror in Carmel's eyes as Mona slaps her hard across the face, before Marco grabs her in an armlock. Mona screams at her, — You fucking murdering whore!

Then Ray Lennox is no longer feeling anything, just the oxygen that departed his lungs vacating his brain as coloured rumbling shapes spin around in his head. A sweet-sickness curdles in his gut. The lights go out.

49

DREAMING FORCES

Our friends in China, they really really really did try, in their own way, to make me feel at home there, but sometimes you just need to be with your own lot, don't you, Ray?

I do admire your spirit, Raymond . . . as your most famous country-man said, keep right on to the end of the road . . . but, well, you've done it now, haven't you?

Once again, you are guilty of some bad decision-making, Raymond Lennox. Sometimes the panic button is there for a reason . . . I like to think of myself as a cool-under-fire sort — oops, perhaps not the best metaphor in my case given Mr Baxter's relentless use of that dreadful element, but even I know when that switch needs to be flipped!

Alas, it now looks like your fate is not mine to decide . . . I wash my hands, Raymond Lennox, I really do!

Takes all sorts, I suppose.

So unfortunately, it appears we won't get to meet again after all.

Well, all I can say is: boo-hoo-hoo.

50

THE CONCRETE EVIDENCE

The cold. Seeping through his clothes. Holding him with a shivering tenderness, like a flower in a nervous, gently enclosing palm. Drops of moisture brushing his face. In his ear, the gently shimmering sounds of a cascading waterfall. Then a soft crying, begging, — Please, no, Mona . . .

But it's being drowned out by a grating, truculent roar; harsh and fearsome.

You can't move.

You know how that feels.

It's pushing on you.

Get up.

Get on your feet.

— RAY!

Lennox opens his eyes, and sinks back into a comforting pillow. Then a thick, tainted broth spills into his mouth . . . he splutters it out, instinctively wrenching his head back up. Even as his blurred vision slowly clears, he can't begin to conceive of what's happening to him. Tries to move, but his arms and legs won't cooperate. This quicksand, but like neither water nor earth; it wants him, pulling his head and shoulders back. But he's not falling into it; it is rising around him and he has to fight to keep his mouth out of it. Blinks through the constant splashes on his face and eyes. And the noise. Though held fast, he sees torchlight ahead, cutting through the darkness, where a motor clamours in anger, seemingly bypassing his ears to drill its roar into his skull.

Holding the light is Mona. She stands elevated, looking down on his prostrate figure. But the voice trying to fight over the engine's rumpus is not hers. — Mona, please . . . please don't do this . . . don't . . .

Struggles to hear over the long, growling furore of the machinery, but identifies it as Carmel. Then a splash on his genitals: heavy, freezing, encroaching. Senses burn into operation, as he realises this is from a thick, grey sludge. It flies down a chute, splashing between his legs.

Lennox is lying in what looks and feels like cold porridge. Twists his neck left. Carmel lies next to him, a foot away, her own head and shoulders arched up, smaller body almost covered in what he now computes to be wet cement. A struggle evidences that his wrists are once again locked behind his back. Eyes itch and water, as he further strains his head upwards to witness the sludge massing around him.

They are lying in a two-foot-deep trench chiselled out of the concrete floor. The depth indicates they have to be on the ground level. This cavity is being filled in by cement aggregate from the chute, pouring in around them, the cacophonous mixer rattling behind it.

— Please, Mona, Lennox hears Carmel's muffled squeal, — we were in this together . . . Ray, tell her who Mat was . . . he's not what you think he is, Mona . . . Mat helps paedophiles. He tried to kill Ray . . . they killed Ralph . . . dismembered him . . . she fades into a croaky gasp.

— Fuck you, Carmel, Mona sneers, — you would say *anything* to save your miserable fucking two-faced arse!

For the first time Carmel sees that Lennox is conscious. — RAY! Tell her!

Ray Lennox can only keep forcing his head up, struggling

to fill his lungs with sweet air. — IT'S TRUE, MONA, he screams out over the engine's implacable snarl. — Why else am I here, for fuck sake? Phil fucked me up and cut Ralph Trench into pieces with his own sword, the one he also attacked me with!

— Phil and Marco are with us, and she points in scorn at Carmel: — They aren't the cheating liars!

— They played Cardingworth, Lennox snaps, fighting to prevent desperation from overwhelming his tones as the concrete keeps splashing into their pen. He can see only his toes protrude out. — They'll be playing you! They can serve more than one master!

Mona again points at Carmel: — She fucking killed Mat!

— This is not you, Carmel pleads.

Lennox decides to go for broke. Shouts across at Carmel, — Aye it is. It's *exactly* who she is!

Mona's head rocks back as if from a physical blow, but she looks at Lennox as if now actually seeing him. — What do you know?!

— They've beaten us, Lennox says to her, fusing resignation into his voice as his neck muscles strain to keep out of the concrete pouring up over his bound body. — They've won. They've put their poison into us. Controlling us. Those murdering, acid-throwing, noncing cunts! We're all exactly what they want us to be, and he twists his head at Carmel. — All of us!

Mona's solitary eye glowers, first at Lennox, then at the liquid cement sluicing onto him. She stands up, hauls in a breath and pushes a red button. The roar of the engine cuts, rapidly slowing the sludge to a merciful trickle.

A ringing silence in his ears is broken by Carmel. — Thank God! Now please, help us out of here, Mona!

— Fuck you, you murdering psycho bitch, work it out for

yourself, Lennox watches Mona snarl at Carmel. — Darren is on his way here! He can't touch me as I've paid Marco and Phil to take his son hostage. But when he finds you two, it'll be a sickos' convention. Unlike you, I'm no killer, she whips to Lennox, — thanks for reminding me, Ray, but Darren Knowles certainly fucking well is, and she turns and departs.

— Carmel . . . Lennox twists his head to her.

Only her face in profile sticks out of the aggregate around her. — Ray! This is . . . I can't . . .

— Listen, try and keep your head up. Lennox steers for serenity, all the time thinking of how futile the situation is. They are about to be encased in concrete. If they somehow didn't suffocate they would be prisoners of a psychopath who would exact terrible punishment. But again, there was his body, detached from his cerebral musings, screaming: NEVER SURRENDER. — Don't let it fall back into the cement!

— I'm trying, but it's *fucking sore*, Ray, Carmel hisses in anger, — my neck . . . Listen, the knife's still in my back pocket, and I've managed to get it out . . . I'm trying to saw through the ties on my hands . . .

— Fucking hell, yes, Carmel! That's it, baby, he hears himself coo. — Keep your head up, but try and move it side to side, he says, making the motion himself. But the cement is beginning to set, slapping coldly against his ears. The good thing is that it is stiffening behind his head, making it less easy to completely sink back into it.

— Can't get any traction on this as all my fucking weight is on it, Carmel gasps. Then she coughs and spits out a mouthful of wet aggregate. — Fuck . . .

Lennox feels himself urinate through his underpants and trousers. Wonders if it'll marginally hinder the progress of the setting concrete. — Keep filing, he offers, while believing Knowles is their only alternative to suffocation. With just their faces and toes exposed in a binding amalgam, he cannot dwell on the grim torture that could be exacted.

— I'm trying . . . I'm not sure it's doing any good . . . it's fucking useless, Ray . . . Carmel moans, then instantly, a startled, — *Fuck*, slips from her, — I think something's happened, she squeals, — I think my hand is loose!

— Yes! Can you move it out from under you?

— I think so . . . it's so hard, it's pinned beneath me and this fucking concrete is really setting!

— Keep trying, honey . . . Lennox can barely move his head to the side now. It's as if it's being held in place by a set of jammed airplane headrests. Then he swivels his eyes to the left just as a grey hand and arm springs out. — Yes! Baby, you fucking did it!

— Right . . . now I'm going to free my other hand using this hand, and Carmel takes her left arm across her body and plunges it into the thickening cement. She finds her right arm and assists it out. — Good, she puffs, as both hands rise into Lennox's sightline.

But his neck is giving way. It's as if a hand is pushing firmly, evenly, on his forehead, as he sinks slowly . . .

. . . becoming one with the walls of the tunnel, with the darkness.

His mouth and nose fill with sludge as his breaths bubble to the surface of the thick soup. Body surrendering, its defiant spasms rendered an internal vibration by the thickening mass around it.

Let go, Raymond. It really is for the best . . .

Just step back into the dark, Ray . . .

Yes . . . back in the dark . . .

Then a force, external to him, insinuates itself, resisting on his behalf. It's wrenching him up out of the quagmire . . .

. . . his dripping eyes blink open to see Carmel straddling

him, pulling him by his shoulders, up out of the cement coffin. Her sopping grey figure stands above him, as if emerging like a bizarre statue from the mire. Lennox screams in pain; sludge explodes from his lungs.

— You have to stand, Ray!

Yes, Raymond, stand, we have to meet!

He can only nod like a demented toy dog in the back of a car, trying to force air into his lungs, his tear-gushing eyeballs burning like coal in their sockets as Carmel helps him to his feet. She takes the knife from her belt. Hacks at his bonds, as he wheezily ingests the rancid chemical-stinking air like it was mountain spring water. The cement is solidifying around their shins as they trudge through the thickening gruel, pulling themselves and each other out of the furrow. The thick sludge drips from them, trailing all over the floor. — Thank . . . fuck . . . Lennox gratefully coughs out more mouthfuls of the choking compound.

— Let's get our clothes off, Carmel says, her moon face protruding from a hippo suit, — we have to get this toxic shit off us.

— We need to get the fuck away from here. Lennox hesitates, looking to the stairs. — My phone and those tapes might still be up there in my coat. I need to get them. You go!

— No way, Carmel declares. — We're seeing this out together.

Lennox sees no currency in trying to debate this point. He always suspected that the will of others would seldom dissuade Carmel from her chosen course of action. This has since been underlined. They climb the remaining good staircase, but as its creaks tell them it's going the same way as its neighbour, Lennox wonders about the wisdom of surrendering to his instincts.

Poor decision-making again . . .

— We're taking the fucking lift back down, Carmel whispers. A long groan rips out from under their feet in a stair bend, the platform wobbling.

— Yes.

— Trench told me my research project was just a Trojan Horse for Cardingworth, Carmel hisses as they tentatively advance. — He planned to flip the land to Chinese investment people to build apartment complexes for their students. Four years he strung me along. Bastards like him, entitled rich pricks playing games with people's livelihoods . . .

— So, you killed him for that? Lennox whips round to look at her as they advance upwards into the darkness.

— A fucking pre-emptive strike, Ray! You heard what they did to Trench, she says, her grey figure now looking to him like a petulant sports mascot, — You don't think I wouldn't be on their hit list? And . . . she shakes off her hooded top and throws its silvery weight into the void, exposing her T-shirt with WE'VE GOT THE CHEMISTRY RIGHT emblazoned on it, — I couldn't let him hurt you. I just couldn't!

Struggling in his own heavy cement suit, Lennox is relieved when they step out onto solid flooring. Follows Carmel, ditching his hoodie. — We'll talk about this later.

— Agreed.

— Those fucking tapes . . . if they've taken them . . .

To his delight the coat is there, draped over the table. He pulls it off to reveal the player, tapes and his phone. — Fuck, he gasps an almighty sigh. — I was shiteing it Mona or those two cunts would have taken the cassettes –

— I'm not saying Mat's betrayal on the site didn't influence me, Carmel's eyes blaze in hunger, as she fills a bucket full of water, — we need to get this shit off us, throwing it over Lennox, urging him to reciprocate, — but it's much, much bigger than that. Way bigger than your personal hurt. Trench hinted that there's more kids, buried in the chalk pits behind here. She moves to the rotting-framed window, rubbing a pane of glass to look outside. — This is off-the-charts evil. She turns back to him. — If I'd gone to the cops those bastards would have walked. They always do.

Lennox pulls himself into the coat. — Why the fuck didn't you tell me about this?

— I had to authenticate it first. Trench was unstable: I thought it could all be delusional nonsense. I did call you, left messages . . .

Lennox nods. He didn't check them. — Then poor Ralph was gone.

— Exactly, they fucking well confirmed it for me! Trench told me, 'I'm finished, and it'll be Mathew Cardingworth and Darren Knowles who end it,' Carmel says. She's about to refill the bucket but stops. A burst of sound: creaking and footsteps echo from the stairs.

They look to each other. There's nowhere to hide.

Lennox looks around for potential weapons. Sees the broken wine glass.

The first person to step into the light is Mona.

Any minor relief at this is short-lived, as Lennox and Carmel see it's not their gargoyle presence that scares her. It's the fact that Phil and Marco flank her, the latter with a tight grip on her shoulder. Marco won't meet Lennox's eye. Phil flashes a gallows smile, shakes his head at them. — Fucking mess.

Ray Lennox glances at Carmel Devereaux, sees the fear on her chalky face. Then looks at Mona, calling her name as a question.

Mona turns to him, and then regards the henchmen. Tears run down her cheek from a solitary eye. — You were right, Ray. They betrayed me too.

The duo glance furtively at each other and stand aside, to afford Lennox and Carmel a view of the stair head.

Almost operatic in its ominous build: the creaking on the metal steps like the opening of a coffin lid. Then Raymond Lennox feels everything in him sag and freeze as Darren Knowles, manic stare, clownishly swaggers into the light.

51

DREAMING A DREAM OF YOU

Oh, too bad, Raymond! Looks like somebody's finally going to have to stand in the naughty corner!

52

THE CHEMISTRY

The second spectral force from the tunnel is right in front of him. Clutching a long-necked, thick-bodied Erlenmeyer flask in his hand. Full of a chemical. The man he'd repressed. Not Bim, the chunky-headed demon who had cracked his jaw, with that sneering voice: *Noice boike*.

As it rings out in his head, he now can't conceive of how he ever let himself forget it. And can't understand how he eradicated from his mind this unkempt, wild-eyed creature now facing him.

He was like you.

The unloading began in the unlikely surroundings of Miami Beach: a strange, harrowing business he'd got involved in as an off-duty cop. Then another brutal case, and he had decided that for his ongoing sanity he would unload everything. Not just his then fiancée, but also the police force and his life back in Edinburgh. And he thought he had, until Cardingworth crashed back into his consciousness. Immediately filling the entire trio of nonce berths. Now this man, the second of them, more dangerous than Cardingworth ever was, is facing him.

You must remember Daz now, Raymond . . . must be coming back to you . . .

— Greetings, dafties. Darren Knowles gazes at Ray Lennox, then Carmel. — The state of youse two cunts!

He's like you . . .

373

His Scottish tones have faded, but remain detectable. As everything moves into focus, Lennox feels it so drastically now, warping his insides like hemlock: he's never hated anything so much in his life. This is the man who grabbed Les. His features are still finely carved but further hardened, iron filings sprinkled on his dome, and those devious, unyieldingly crazy eyes. A pretty boy turned rough through age and jail, but still in good shape for a man of his years.

— What's up? Knowles grins. — Looks like a wee science experiment with the ex-cop and the chemistry bird got out of hand. He looks to Mona. — Happens though, toots, ay, and he waves the beaker. She shrinks back, horrified eyes not leaving the vessel he holds.

— Welcome to the acid house. Knowles smiles at Lennox. — The boys were never working for those dozy hoors, and his gaze whips to Phil. — Poor Ralphie should have been joining us. He's in bits that he couldnae make it!

Marco laughs nervously, looking grimly at a broken Mona, confirming his double treachery. — Sorry, sweetheart, but this is more than business. Don't give a shit about Cardingworth, but Daz and I go back a long way.

This is sensed by Lennox as a declaration to Knowles as much as to them, and that Marco is terrified of him. Perhaps even silent Balaclava Phil is. Then Chris Knowles walks in and Mona wraps her arms around herself. Tries to speak but no words will come out.

Lennox assesses the odds. Doesn't fancy them.

Darren Knowles catches the evaluating glance. Reading his mind, he advances a few steps, as Phil swaggers towards Lennox, confident manner indicative he expects no opposition. Lennox backs away, towards the window. — Two dozy hoors and a semi-cripple against four, Knowles's east coast

Caledonian tones are now more pronounced, — I think ye might just have –

Silenced.

Lennox, insect speed belying broken frame, lunges towards the advancing Phil. In one blinding motion, grapples him by testicles and throat, charges and hurls him screaming through the rotten-framed glass window. A banshee shriek, followed by nothing.

All eyes gape in wide shock at the broken space.

Then they turn to Lennox. — Against three, he manages.

It has the desired effect of underscoring the intimidating awe. But even with the adrenaline rushes unleashed by his sudden, decisive act of violence, the effort of transitioning from being perceived as the puniest to the most dangerous person in the room makes Ray Lennox's entire body throb in pain.

A bug-eyed Darren Knowles quickly matches his purpose-fulness, springing forward, his arm's crook choke-locking the still shocked Carmel. The fat-bodied, narrow-necked beaker is extended in his other hand. — Easy, ya cunt . . . he warns the advancing Lennox. — Concentrated sulphuric acid makes a mess of a pretty face, but you know that, ay? He looks to Mona with a cold grin.

— Don't hurt her. Please, Lennox begs.

— FUCK YOU, YOU FUCKING PRICK, Carmel screeches out, twisting in Darren Knowles's grip.

He tips the beaker a little, balancing the muzzle over her cheek.

Lennox is frozen to the spot. Silently prays for Carmel to stop struggling.

She does.

— That's better, Chemistry Bird, Knowles rasps. — Maybe just a wee drip at first, tootsie pie, and to Ray Lennox he now sounds like a snide Scottish grandmother, — see what it does –

— Please don't, Lennox implores again.

Chris, manic grin, cheerleads his father with gusto, — Do it, Dad! Sizzle the farking bitch!

Then Carmel's hand propels upwards in a devastating thrust, shoving the flask back: destructive, corrosive fluid splashes through the air followed by a sizzling sound of sausages frying as man and woman seem to fuse in an extended primordial shriek, with the beaker smashing on the floor.

It defies processing by Lennox's long-ravaged senses. Is he observing this atrocity with eyes gaping open, or imagining it with them slammed shut? What he thinks he sees is Darren Knowles, his grip broken, jumping on the spot, holding his face as Carmel runs for the sink, frantically turning on the tap, thrusting a stinging hand under the running water to a snake-like hiss, as tendrils of vapour stream up and she wails in agony.

— OH MY GOD!

What he knows he hears is Mona screaming out.

It's Marco who convinces Lennox he's been observing this in clarity. It's his stare, not at the unfolding scene, but at Lennox himself, before he turns to a chalky-faced Chris in apology. — Ain't getting paid enough for this shit, mate. Sorry, and he heads swiftly to the stair.

Chris doesn't acknowledge this, moving to assist his father, whose face is literally dissolving in his hands as he stamps on the ground, emanating a long howl. Carmel is crying out: — FUCKING DON'T BELIEVE THIS . . . her hand thrashing in the large Belfast sink that fills with water. Lennox still cannot react. It's as if his feet are once again stuck to the concrete floor. He half expects to see Carmel's hand skeletal as it rises out, but it's still fleshy though a blazing red.

The concrete . . . it protected her . . .

Chris bundles Carmel to the side as he pushes his father

376

to the sink, dunking Darren's head into the water. Carmel jabs a finger from her good hand into Chris's eye, then picks up the wine bottle. Only flying glass and a squeal inform Lennox – who attempts to move forward but can't – she's smashed it over his skull. As the blood cascades, she forces Chris's head under the water with both hands, roaring in rage and pain. Lennox realises his coat pocket has snagged on the table corner. Tugs it violently, feels a rip, but it agonisingly holds. Synchronised with his son's baptism, the father whips up, his eyeless countenance a ravaged mass of raw flesh. Mona, stealing across the room, looks straight at him, her mangled lip trembling.

— Ray! Carmel screams. — Help me!

Lennox realises that brute force won't prevail. Steps back to disentangle himself, then springs forward. A strange gurgling sound seems to be coming from the chest of the blindly flailing Darren Knowles. Mona intently scrutinises, scarf now down from her face, fascinated by Knowles's pain as he lurches zombie-like across the floor. He's on a collision course with the advancing Lennox, who stems an instinct to punch his dissolving face. Instead tries to weave to the side, but the blinded man's withered hand grabs his coat sleeve. Lennox fights to break the grip without touching the corrosive fluid that fizzes all over his adversary. As he attempts to hold off the flailing father, Mona moves over to the sink, kicks the back of the son's legs. This assault paradoxically revives Chris; he breaks Carmel's grip and shoves her, stumbling, onto her back. Then he turns and lashes out at Mona, her head snapping back under his hook as a tooth flies like a bullet from the sweeping mop of hair.

Lennox shakes off Darren, who staggers into a concrete pillar. Chris turns and charges at Lennox in blind rage. All this does is to impale the young man's diaphragm onto a twisting,

377

pivoting straight right, which stops his heart for a beat. Chris stands immobilised, regarding Lennox in a cheated gape, before a solid left hook to the temple and another big right to the jaw sends him crashing prone to the floor. Carmel falls onto the stunned man's back, elbow of her good arm smashing the back of his head repeatedly, pounding his face into the concrete.

— KILL HIM! SMASH THE LITTLE BASTARD'S SKULL, Mona screams in demented encouragement, blood spitting from her withered mouth as she kicks Chris. The smell of burning flesh catches in Lennox's throat, as he moves to restrain Carmel, screams of misery hitting a resonant pitch, tearing his eardrums.

Unleashing deranged punches, Darren Knowles pounds the concrete pillar. He can't see anything, as his head lolls round, his face almost dissolved. Lennox's fevered mind resassembles it as the sneering visage from the tunnel, looking at him from on top of Les Brodie, demented with threat and lust. The dance is obscene, weird and dumb, now conducted in an odd silence; Lennox considers that acid must have gone into Knowles's mouth, working down his throat, burning vocal cords. Steps forward and boots Knowles full force in the balls, but the flailing man is in too much agony to even register it. Lennox moves back out of range of his blind swipes.

All the noise is coming from behind him.

Despite the concrete protection, Carmel's fingers and palm are burned, and Lennox removes his irksome coat then his shirt, wrapping her hand in it. — Let's go. He looks to Mona, who lurches towards the lift. Lennox and Carmel follow, her wincing in pain, leaving Darren, now curled up on the floor in a ball, several feet from his bloody-faced, spread-eagled son.

Chris crawls over to comfort his father, but Darren grabs out clenching him in a vice-like grip. — GET OFF . . .

YOU'RE BURNING ME ... Chris squeals, but Darren Knowles can't hear his son, he's just squeezing this body to him, as Chris roars out in agony, the acidic burning flesh from the senseless father scouring the face of the desperate son.

As the lift clunks up towards them, Lennox squeezes Carmel tight. — It's so fucking sore, Ray, she winces, — but the concrete, it saved me ...

— Fuck your concrete, Mona stands behind her, one eye aflame with rage.

53

THE GROUND FLOOR

In a warped, kinetic dance of descent, Mona and Carmel bicker. An edgy Lennox joins in. The insanity is ended as Mona throws her head up and screams: — OKAY! LATER!

The trio look at each other in guilty silence as the lift hits the ground floor. Lennox checks his phone, an implausibly long-winded email from George. He can't read it all, but it seems he's going to comply with Lennox's request to meet.

Or so he claims.

When they get out into the car park, Phil has astonishingly survived the fall. Lennox tenses, then realises no rematch is on the cards: Balaclava Man's hips appear to be smashed as Marco, furtive gaze flickering over everything, drags him to the back of their van. Also broken is his right arm, which trails by his side. Lennox assumes he'll be accompanying Cardingworth's stiff body in transit. Their desertion will be futile: fancies he already hears emergency services sirens, insinuating themselves through the swirl of sounds in his head. Mona or Carmel will have called them. He is about to get into Carmel's vehicle with them both when a car suddenly turns into the compound.

Stops a few feet from them.

The headlights blaze in their eyes. Lennox moves towards the vehicle.

And straight away he knows the terrifying nemesis of old in the baseball-capped shades-wearing figure behind the wheel. — Get in.

380

He knows that he has to comply. It is the only way to end this.

Carmel cannot see past the shadow that shrouds the driver, but the menace leaks out of his figure. Stepping forward, she shouts after Lennox: — Ray!

Ray Lennox can't even hear her. He knows what he has to do. Slides into the passenger seat and the car speeds off, almost running over Marco and Phil, who huddle for cover on the grass verge at the side of the van, Marco clutching the fence of the factory.

Carmel and Mona watch the car containing Ray Lennox turn outside the gates and vanish, as the sounds of the sirens intensify.

54

DREAM #7

. . . so, you're here with me now, Ray Lennox . . . I knew you couldn't resist keeping right on to the end of the road . . . but what are you going to do now . . . ? how are you going to stop me from tearing you apart . . . ?

55

EMAIL

To: Ray Lennox rayoflight@gmail.com
From: George Marsden inquisitor@horshamsecuritysolutions.co.uk
Re: The Shitshow: How I see it.

Well, Raymond,

Thank you for keeping me in loop, he said dripping sarcasm across his keyboard like phlegm and snot. This flu is adding insult to the injury of you casting me as Mr Mushroom or Toxic Nonce. Well, I accept that my often clandestine behaviour around the fair sex might lead to suspicions of other duplicity, especially in a mind as overheated as your own!

However, this shouldn't need saying, but from day one I've always been a fully paid up member of Team Lennox. So, here's what I've been able to deduce from the scraps you fed me, and my own ferreting around.

Cardingworth's family fostered children in Brighton from 1975 onwards. The first child in their care was Ralph Trench: a surly, overweight boy who had been mistreated by his last foster parents. The lives of the young Mathew and Ralph would change when they came into contact with an older teenage neighbour on the Whitehawk estate, named Darren Knowles.

Knowles had a tougher upbringing than Cardingworth, his family moving through travellers' camps up and down the east coast of the UK, from Aberdeen to Hull. After he was found, as a teenager, sexually abusing a ten-year-old girl, he was expelled from and ostracised by the travelling community. At the age of 15, he was hustling on the London streets.

Relatives from the settled community took Darren into their home in Brighton. At 19, he befriended the swotty kid who lived next door. Mathew Cardingworth, then 15, was being picked on at school, and believed that the association with his hapless 'foster brother' Ralph Trench, a few years younger than him, was the root of this. Knowles was fascinated that Trench was an orphan, and how total strangers could become responsible for a child's welfare. He taught Cardingworth to disdain and bully the boy.

But Knowles was jail-bound: arrested for the abduction and rape of a 16-year-old girl.

If anyone so intrinsically vile and with such a horrendous background can actually be transformed for the worse by their experience in prison, it was Knowles. In the nick he met the shadowy 'Bim', a mountainous merchant seaman with a penchant for violence and cruelty that exceeded even Knowles's own. A multiple offender, Bim was something of an urban myth. Not much on this near throwback to the era of pirates, so all my conjecture: he hung around the ports of Europe and the Americas, picking up ships, often on forged papers. When he met Knowles in prison, Bim saw more than just fresh meat; the two men recognised they were kindred spirits. I'm guessing Bim inducted Knowles in the darker sexual arts, instilling in him a liking for the young men thoughtfully served up by the prison system. Bim shaped and refined Knowles's warped instincts of sex as an instrument of power and control, encouraging the sadist's gratification of abuse.

While poor Ralph Trench was socially inhibited, Cardingworth was a prodigy, going on to university in London at 17. This ought to have ended his association with Knowles, but Darren and Bim sought him out on their release from prison. I'm guessing they strong-armed Cardingworth into accompanying them and giving them a veneer of legitimacy. This was the formation of the noncing gang, Ray, of which you and Les were the first victims.

But this assault on you was too public, which made Bim and Knowles reassess their strategy. I'd guess Cardingworth proved an unreliable ally. So, they found out, probably unwittingly through young Trench, that a neighbour, Julie Wilkins, and her husband Clive, also fostered kids. They looked after a young boy, Gavin Carter, who was a friend of Ralph Trench's. It's probable Gavin became their first murder victim. When he was fostered out to Julie and Clive Wilkins, Trench was concerned. Clive was a chronic alcoholic who was easily manipulated by Julie, who in turn was obsessed with Knowles. When Gavin went missing, Ralph shared his fears with Mat Cardingworth. His old foster brother warned him they were dangerous people and that he should keep his nose out. I'm guessing Bim and Darren Knowles abducted, abused and murdered Gavin, before dumping him at sea.

But like their first rape, their debut slaying was sloppy. Gavin's body washed up on the beach and made the papers. Although he was seen as a runaway orphan, and few questions were asked, Trench was convinced Bim and Darren had something

385

to do with Gavin's vanishing. He grew obsessed with investigating them.

Mathew couldn't get shot of Darren, who had now also moved to London with his girlfriend, Mona Moston, 17. Mona was becoming a fashion model, and from a flat in Islington, Knowles inducted her into a party lifestyle of swinging and cocaine. The marginal, hedonistic life they led probably excited the younger Cardingworth. But Mona was less impressed, and she left Knowles due to his cruelty. Knowles took horrendous revenge on her for this rebuff, disfiguring her by throwing acid in her face.

On prison release Knowles married Julie Wilkins, who had divorced her husband Clive. She had started visiting Darren in jail, had fallen under his spell, and helped him and Bim come up with the fostering scam. They would foster children and designate them as 'problem self-harmers' or 'runaways' and first abuse them, then remove them, claiming they had absconded of their own volition.

Knowles expanded the operation, he, Bim and Julie identifying like-minded twisted men, often hooking them up with weak, pliant women, to register them as foster carers and extend the network. Social workers, often those who had drink or drug issues, and who could be easily bribed and intimidated, were bought off. The ring worked semi-successfully for years, though both Bim and Knowles had low impulse control and often succumbed to the lure of violence, particularly after their own drink and drug intake. Bim was jailed in China, spending time in a Shanghai prison for another incident at sea. He remained the group's nominal figurehead, Knowles being his 'operations manager' in England. But Trench didn't let his covert investigations slide.

Cardingworth, meanwhile, had distanced himself from both those dubious associates. He got wealthier, and made connections with powerful people, including chiefs of police. This deterred Bim and Knowles from putting the squeeze on him and they basically had a relationship of peaceful coexistence for several years.

Trench was busy seeking out information, but Knowles was hard to pin down and Bim did his vanishing act at sea. So in lieu of them, he investigated Cardingworth. He discovered financial irregularities in the campaign to buy the hospital property, and the bribing of opposition groups spokespersons and council officials, evidencing compromising payments made. Knowles in turn discovered Trench had been snooping around and demanded what he had on Cardingworth. A terrorised Trench gave up the details.

It became obvious that Cardingworth could go to prison if the bribery scandal came out and Knowles and Bim played this to their advantage. They advised him to buy the disused concrete factory, which they would manage. Thus, Cardingworth was driven back into association with two dangerous men. The stakes upped further when Cardingworth grew suspicious that they were burying bodies in the basement of the factory. He decided to appoint Trench security guard, thus implicating him in any crime.

Trench began to crack under the strain. He was effectively riding two horses at once: an outward critic of Cardingworth's hospital development, but reduced and compromised to effectively covering up the more heinous crimes in the concrete factory he was now associated with. Drinking heavily and perennially on the verge of a breakdown, he went maverick, and was soon back on the radar of Knowles, who took the decision to have him eliminated.

Bim was released by the Chinese authorities from his Shanghai prison and came back to England.

And no, it's not me! The *merchant* navy, Ray?! Come on! One more thing: you say that I 'seemed to know you previously' when we first met at Harrogate. You cite 'the knowing way' I said 'indeed you are', when you introduced yourself. For pity's sake, Ray, if you remember (and you obviously don't!) you were wearing a sodding nameplate, as was I!

Have I been doing okay, Ray? I'm hoping that you are reading this and thinking that if you had properly let me in, this thing would have been put to bed by now. You were too close to it all. I'm not berating you, here, Raymond (well, perhaps a touch), as I said, I appreciate that you had your reasons for behaving as secretively as you did. Just crowing a little, as is my right in the circumstances. In fact, I'll have you know that I'm typing this from my deathbed; Polly and I really have succumbed to this vile flu bug. I daresay we shall nurse each other back to health until we're fit enough to fuck the remnants of it out of our systems!

BUT I'm informing you that I've also complied with your strange and slightly worrying request. I hardly need to remind you how dangerous the potential ramifications are. So please don't do anything *too* silly. (As I look at that last sentence, I feel futility

and stupidity seep into my consciousness in equal measures.)
Just exercise care, Raymond. I'm feeling that something terrible is going to happen.

Yours in desperate hope,

George

I'll get to this shit later . . .
Moving through those old bodies, I see your temples throb . . .
Finally . . .
I see you, you cunt.
I was always coming for you.
There was never any doubt.

56

THE DREAM SHIP

You're here . . . you made it . . . you can't hurt me, Ray . . . but I can hurt you . . .

57

THE CLEANSING FLAME

A frosty coldness hangs in the Eastbourne air. Across the street from the Rose Garden home, cranes hoist megalithic cladding panels, fleshing the exoskeleton of a construction, shielding more precious natural light from the weak December sun. Inside the centre, a few of the usual suspects sit at their tables in the lounge area. Staff and residents seem on the verge of another humdrum Saturday, preparing to play out their routine, low-pressure dramas under migraine-inducing fluorescent tubes. Later, the neon strips above will click off. Only the huge TV, burning through the darkness, will flickeringly illuminate the faces of the inmates.

Centre manager, Polly Ives, has taken a rare couple of days off sick. Greta and Sally discuss how ill she looked. Agree that Polly and her boyfriend are sensible in opting to stay home. Greta observes in a chuckle, — Yeah, she got a terrible chest infection; this flu bug's certainly doing the rounds!

— Big handsome fella like that, Sally's lips pucker, — could play with my chest any time, if he wanted to. Mind you, he'd have to start at me bleeding knees these days. She gestures to her saggy bosom and guffaws.

— Lucky Polly, Greta agrees. — I wouldn't say no!

The women cackle loudly in accord. This attracts looks from the men, playing a hand of dominoes.

Brian, the large, old paralysed man, is about to partake in one of his much-loved footbaths. He's noticed that this orderly is new. *Where is Gary?* And there's a strange scent to the water that the new man pours into the bowl. Then he splashes some of it on Brian's robe. *Why is he doing this?*

It is cold.

Brian shivers as it seeps through to his back and shoulders. Permanently wheelchair-bound since a second stroke several years back, he can barely move. Gary knows. Gary can always tell. *Where is Gary?*

There's the familiar sensation of his feet being lifted up and placed in the basin, but it doesn't feel right: so cold. Brian wants to get out, but can't move his legs.

In one prompt motion, the new orderly produces a Bic lighter from his pocket, sparks it up and drops it in the basin. The other residents watch in mounting disbelief and horror as flames ignite, burning the big man's feet, licking at his shins. Through his dotage, Brian's screams sear out. Within seconds flames are rising up his gown.

The residents notice the orderly is wearing a surgical mask. Holds a canister; throws more petrol on their blazing friend. The warping flames surge around the big man, mercilessly consuming him as acrid smoke belches out, tripping ear-splitting alarms. People find their voices, screaming out as the blaze threatens to climb to inferno levels.

The orderly of death slips out through the conservatory. He moves jaggedly, but with animal speed; like a dog or cat running from the scene of an accident in which they suffered injury. The panicking inmates barely register him steal across the grounds into a waiting car, which quickly tears off.

The driver is an older, craggy-faced man. There's an omnipresent cruelty in his eyes. He knows he's only here because the other man who called him has nobody else left. The two men exchange nods as the car pulls onto a main road and the orderly removes his mask. They are obviously colleagues but it would be hard to mistake them for friends.

Back at the home, one of the most able-bodied inmates, a short and bespectacled man, Mainwaring, thrashes at the rousing inferno with a blanket. — IT'S BRIAN, he roars, – WE HAVE TO HELP HIM!

As the smoke alarms blare, Brian Ian Manderson burns alive, his screams tearing out across the home, horrifying residents and staff alike. Faces flash through his head. There are many of them. But only two stick. One is a young boy from the tunnel, the very first one; the other, the new orderly who has just gone –

58

LOVER OF DREAMS

. . . but you were here, would know you anywhere . . . why can't I crush you like I used to do with the others before they locked me away in here? . . . I'm trapped but they can't take my spirit . . . the lucid dreaming in my mind . . . Wang they called him . . . I'm free in here, to fuck their wives and boyfriends and children but I'm feeling it . . . oh God I'm feeling this awful pain . . . please stop . . . no more . . . no more please, Mummy . . .

he's hurting me . . .

please stop . . .

hurting meeeee.

59

LET BYGONES BE BYGONES

Gary rushes to the scene, all but driven back by the pungent stink. Grabs a fire extinguisher, blasts foam at the blazing body. All this exercise in futility does is reveal that Brian Ian Manderson has succumbed. What is left is a charred mess in a wheelchair. Black flesh flakes off in layers under the pressure from the jet, revealing wooden-looking white-ash legs. Then he falls through the burned-threadbare seat, jackknifing forward into a vague, steaming form on the tiled floor.

In the heinous aftermath that follows, the residents, glad to be saved from the eardrum-stabbing alarms as much as the acrid belches of smoke, are escorted out to the garden at the back. They are allowed to stop at their rooms on the way for coats. A troubled Gary thinks about how inconsolable Polly will be. In the small control room, the camera's eye is cold and its tapes blank. This expensive security system just installed, yet the intruder had the ability to disable the CCTV cameras and ghost in, leaving this carnage in his wake.

The car now takes a more leisurely pace along a winding coastal road. Its destination is a remote, rented South Downs cottage. The younger man looks to the craggy-faced driver, a decade or so his senior. Stares him in the eye. — You're no like them. No way.

The older man cracks a taut smile.

— One thing . . . how did you know he was in that rest home?

— It's called detective work, he smugly replies. — Once I learned about the rest, I hunted him down.

He sees the younger man is now distracted with a text on his phone.

— My sister, says the younger man. — Reminding me it's my mum's eightieth this weekend.

— You gaunny go?

— Why not, Ray Lennox shrugs, — maybe take the girl-friend up, let her meet them all. See a bit of Auld Reekie. Let bygones be bygones. He cranes his head outside to the waves, which lap the smooth sand. Looks up at the sky. A tempestuous bruising of murky cloud seems to be tracking them. — Anyway, looks like rain coming in. What do you think?

— Fuck knows. Dae ah look like the fuckin weather app?

With his red square face, Dougie Gillman actually does remind Lennox of some app he'd downloaded, though not necessarily for the weather. He thinks about having a sneak-peak at his phone. Decides against it. — No.

Cops and villains: two different strains of the same shit. Feeding on weakness and frailty. Rickety structures bridging the hanging gap between the people we believed ourselves to be, and the ones we actually were. Both best kept out of your life. But if you avoid the death-by-a-thousand-cuts boring fuckers, they're bound to come into your orbit sometime.

Lennox lights a cigarette. Inhales pointlessness.

Thinks about kissing Carmel Devereaux, slowly and deli-ciously, from this position of outlaw equality. *Her sweet, complex, corrupt and devious soul* . . . a shuddering bolt of ennui follows a satisfying tremor in his trousers. But he'll go on, and things will get easier. Or perhaps not: a lot needs sorting out with Carmel and the law. *We only pretended there* was resolution in life. Maybe that only happens, he reflects, *when you finally run out of excuses.*

He was done with saving others. Now he had saved his own skin, but you only saved your own life by living it. That was what he now intended to do.

ACKNOWLEDGEMENTS

One of the best things about writing a book, apart from getting it done, is you get to thank a ton of terrific people. Dean Cavanagh, Dougray Scott, Tony Wood, Katie Barrett, Kathleen Isaac, James Strong, David Hare and Trygve Diesen heightened my continually developing sense of the central character, from *Crime* and *The Long Knives* to here. Emer Martin lent me her eagle eye, big heart and literary soul. Shino Allen and Kim Wedderburn proffered invaluable help on the city of Brighton and English legal processes respectively. My main men on the south coast, Carl Loben and Steve Mac, along with those beauties Wendy Law, Joanne Parker and Jayne Winstanley, Samantha Wools (who paved my Sussex way), Billy Mauseth, Steve Mason, Lisa Gower, Mick Robinson, Billy Nasty and Scott Booth as well as many others (including Chad Jackson and Danny Rampling, who were invariably around to join in the fun), made sure that no corners of the fabulous and hospitable towns of Brighton and Hove were unavailable to me.

Life has its horror as well as its beauty. A big one that I'm gutted to record is that Martin Duffy is now absent from that aforementioned group. I'm not alone in missing this unique, one-off, beautiful soul. You ignited all our lives, Duff.

Because of the above, I've grown to love Brighton. As always though, I need to doff my cap to my home cities of Edinburgh, London and Miami, and my friends and family there. Especially my wife Emma, who indulges – even encourages – me when these multiple voices in my head get vocalised.

Joanne Rowling, Tom Tracy and Ria Thomson were all successful in various auctions to be named as characters in this book. I've tried to represent the respective monikers of those good people with as much dignity as possible.

ABOUT THE AUTHOR

Irvine Welsh was born and raised in Edinburgh. His first novel, *Trainspotting*, has sold over one million copies in the UK and was adapted into an era-defining film. He has written thirteen further novels, including the number one bestseller *Dead Men's Trousers*, four books of shorter fiction and numerous plays and screenplays. *Crime* and *The Long Knives* have been adapted into a television series starring Dougray Scott as Ray Lennox. Welsh currently lives between London, Edinburgh and Miami.

 facebook.com/irvinewelshauthor
 x.com/irvinewelsh